TEMPEST BLADES
The Cursed Titans

ISBN: 978-1-951122-20-1 (paperback)
ISBN: 978-1-951122-24-9 (ebook)
LCCN: 2021930579
Copyright © 2021 by Ricardo Victoria

Cover Illustration: Salvador Velázquez
Logo Design: Cecilia Manzanares & Salvador Velázquez
Cover Design: Alexz Uría, Ricardo Victoria & Salvador Velázquez
Map illustration: Marco Antonio García Albarrán.

Shadow Dragon Press
9 Mockingbird Hill Rd
Tijeras, New Mexico 87059
www.shadowdragonpress.com
info@shadowdragonpress.com

Follow Ricardo at: https://ricardovictoriau.com/

TEMPEST BLADES
THE CURSED TITANS

By

Ricardo Victoria

Acknowledgments

To my wife Alexz.

You are my reason to smile, to work hard, and to improve as a person. You are my muse and my biggest fan.

To my friends Martha, Victor, Kyoko, and Assaph, whose insight, comments, and suggestions helped me a lot during the development of this story.

To Geoff, for always believing in me, my ideas, and in the world of Fionn and friends.

To Marco for once more helping me to give shape to my world in the form of a second super map.

To Monste, for the inspiration of Kasumi's outfit.

To Salvador, for creating amazing covers and giving shape and color to my words.

To the good people of Artemisia Publishing for believing in this project.

To the readers whose support with the first book made possible the existence of a second one.

To Fernando, who suddenly left us, we will miss you.

And to Issac, the best friend one could have asked for. We miss you.

Yumenomori
(Forest)

The World's Scar

The We

Meteora

Kuni E

Sacred Fire
Temple

Quiet Wate
Temple

The Wastelands

Carpadocci

Crimson Sea

Kyôkatô

Concordia
Pass

Lion's Pass

The Straits

Kuni Empire

Angel Rive

Xelahú

Azure Turtle Sea / Slender Sea

Albarran
Point

Sotz'na

Samoharo Hegemony

- The Ouslis Continent -

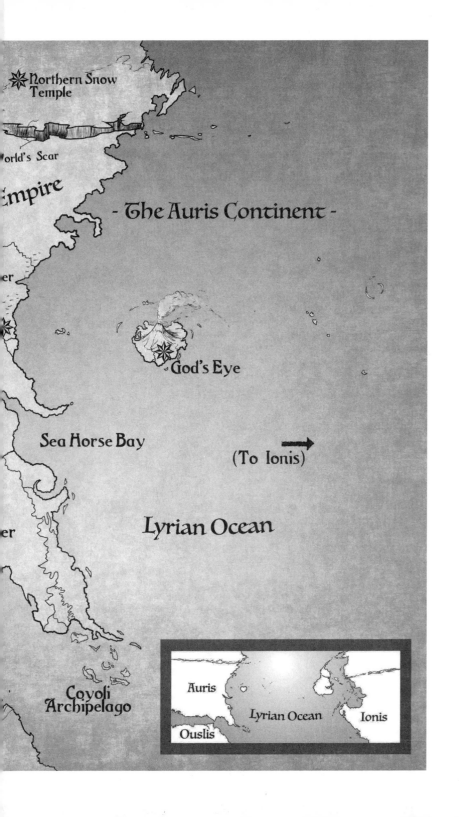

Chapter 1
Unwell

You are not alone.

Sixteen years ago. Albarran Point, on the western edge of the Straits. A few days after the first incursion registered in more than a century.

† † †

"How long has he been awake and running?" Sid asked himself under his breath. His grip tight around the handle of his small axe. He was surprised by the struggle to keep pace with his current target. Sid was fast, but this kid was surprisingly speedy for someone on the chubby side. "At this pace he is gonna collapse."

The rainforest was thick with vegetation, allowing Sid's samoharo features to blend in. As an Áak samoharo Sid more closely resembled an iguana mixed with a turtle. Between his physical features and the olive green cargo pants and old canvas jacket he easily blended in.

He paused, peering through the foliage, watching the kid, only his mohawk sticking above the leaves. The humidity of the jungle was at the limits of what was tolerable for a "hooman". For Sid, it felt like home.

Sid's mind strayed, thinking of his home. He shook his head. *I'm not home, I'm here in the Straits on this boring mission. Alone.* "Fraking punishment," he whispered. "It was still the wrong order. It deserved to be disobeyed." However, his punishment had given him time to work on his secret personal project away from prying eyes: rebuilding a pile of junk that used to be an ancient samoharo mining spaceship. He still had to name it, but that would have to wait. Sid was busy tracking the hooman kid.

Sid had been following the kid for days, watching over him until Sid could find a way to get him and the others out of the deadly, beast-infested place. This whole situation was messed up. Sid had been working at his camp when the Stalkers, the cloaking beasts of prey from the Infinity Pits, had mysteriously shown up. By the time Sid had noticed what was happening, the Stalkers had killed all the adults and most of the kids. The samoharo had then taken it upon himself to hunt down the incursions. While doing that, he'd found the small group of survivors that had taken refuge in a warehouse and befriended them. They were barely in their teens—by hooman standards at least, for a samoharo they were babies—and probably would be dead if it weren't for the kid and the girl with the unsettling blue eyes. Her name was Gaby and he could tell that she had combat training by the way she had coordinated the group's meager defenses. But her cold demeanor made Sid uncomfortable. It was that of a trained assassin, and he was all too familiar with that kind of behaviour. That was a life Sid was trying to leave behind.

However, unlike others in the business, the girl seemed to be a decent person, only concerned with keeping everyone alive. Exceptionally strong and fast and armed with twin blades that glowed red and blue, she had killed two Stalkers on her own. With her, the survivors would have a decent chance. And she had a hidden bone die up her sleeve, one that was proving to be unstoppable when taking down the Stalkers: the kid.

The kid was different. And it wasn't only for the way the irises of his eyes glowed with a golden hued light. He was about fifteen or sixteen hooman years old. According to Gaby his name was Alex, and he shouldn't be alive. From what the girl had told him, Alex would have been the first victim of the Stalkers. He still had the fresh, pink scars from one of their barbed limbs. That sort of wound should have mauled the kid's liver and right lung. An injury that would leave an adult hooman bleeding to death in minutes. Yet Alex was not only uninjured, he was running around the rainforest, taking down the elusive eldritch abominations with relative ease despite lacking combat training. And not any creature, but ones that had the ability to cloak themselves. Samoharo underwent special training to gain the experience necessary to attack such cloaked creatures with any hope of success. But this kid already displayed the experience of a combat veteran as he took on the Stalkers. And then there was the sword. The kid was wielding a strange sword, with a hand guard that resembled three pairs of open wings. Sid had heard about a sword with that description, but right now, with everything going on, he wasn't in the right frame of mind to recall what he'd heard about it.

The truth was that by any other standard, Alex should have been dead. Sid could relate to that. He had been left for dead once, and had survived, after a fashion. The kid needed to know he was not alone, that he had friends to watch his back, even if he could now break a boulder barehanded.

Then there was the other issue, the one that concerned Sid the most: the voices. It was clear that Alex was hearing voices. He talked to himself, but the conversation wasn't a collection of random lines like you might hear from a person when the lost mind sickness struck them. At first Sid thought Alex had fallen prey to that ailment. But after a couple of days of listening to him, Sid had determined that Alex was talking with someone... or something. The other kids found that odd, even scary, but they kept Alex with them when they moved from one shelter to another. When Sid had brought up the issue with Gaby, the only one of the hoomans unfazed by the chatter, she had dismissed it, saying, "That's normal for someone who's gone through what Alex has. He'll be okay in a few weeks."

"How do you know that for sure?" Sid had asked.

"I know. Not my first tournament with that," Gaby had replied cryptically, her eyes glowing with a faint blue hue.

Now that he thought about it, the girl had a similar demeanor as Alex, but in a more nuanced way. She had more control on whatever was happening to them. Sid had a hunch.

Sid had heard rumors and folktales about people like Gaby and Alex. Mortals who had been at death's door but had miraculously survived, waking up with unnatural abilities: the Gift. The last sighting of one of them had been about a century ago. Sid was sure that Alex and Gaby had the Gift.

And that was a problem. Because if the Hegemony leadership found out that he hadn't eliminated them to 'keep the balance' as the insidious rules said, the chances of Sid being able to appeal his banishment became worse than zero. The only way home was killing this kid now, Gaby later. But he had promised himself that he was done with those rules, with that life. They were kids for the Prophet's sake! They could be taught to use their skills, become allies. However, the Hegemony was fearful that leaving them alone would cause new Titans to rise.

I can't blame them, Sid thought. *The Titans wrecked the planet and our lands once in the past. Although from what I've heard, Gifted are nothing like the Titans. They deserve a chance to prove that.* Sid had to make a decision.

I guess this is my proverbial 'crossing the Slender Sea' moment, Sid thought. He would not go back on his word, the possibility for him to return home be damned. If he put them under his protection, it would take every remaining favor he could ask, or dueling his own cousin, to get away with this decision.

"You're wrong, the tracks are to the left," Alex muttered cryptically as he suddenly stopped. He shook his head. "The energy flow goes and comes through that direction. But we can't go that far, the others need our help."

There it was again. Alex was debating with himself. Or the voice. Sid had to do something.

"Hey kid. You have done enough for today and the sun is setting. Let's go back to your friends. You need to sleep. Let me take care of keeping you safe for a few hours, okay?"

Alex turned to look at Sid perched in a tree. The irises of the hooman were glowing with a golden hue and if he squinted, Sid could see faint electric currents running across Alex's arms. Whatever had happened to him, Sid wondered if he could still be called "hooman".

"You are half right," Alex replied. "Rest would be good."

"But?" Sid asked. At least it seemed that the kid was still capable of coherent speech with someone not inside his head.

"I'm alone. I don't have friends anymore. I'm different."

Sid's hearts broke with sadness. He sighed as he knew that what he was about to do would change his life irreversibly. He jumped off the tree and landed in front of Alex. He offered his hand.

"I don't care if you are different. You have me. Let's go."

† † †

Thunder shook the air. Another night of taking refuge for most of the group meant another night of silent torture for Alex.

He was sitting in the corner, his arms around the sword, rocking himself, trying to sleep, to no avail. When his eyes were open, he could see faint auras around everyone and everything. When he closed them, he saw the thin threads of energy lines connecting it all together. The sound of thunder scared him. Every time an electric discharge took place, he could feel the energy expanding in every cell in his body as the lightning displaced the air on its way to the ground. For a moment, as the lightning travelled across the air, he could even sense the flux of electrons. It was weird. The world felt more real now, more detailed, more complex. He was having a hard time trying to make sense of the new and intense sensory inputs. It made him jumpy, twitchy even, always looking over his shoulder.

And then there was the voice. Correction, voices, inside his head. One, a dark one always whispering his failings, his fears, his doubts. The other only appeared to advise him what to do during critical moments. Their presence made Alex's ability to focus difficult at best.

He was well aware that all these new quirks made the others nervous. Under other circumstances, he would be a liability to the group's survival opportunities. And yet they kept him updated on how Elijah, who had been injured by the creatures, was doing. They made sure Alex ate—food now tasted weird—and checked up on him, taking turns during their watches to see how he was doing, but keeping their distance too, not knowing what was going on with him. Given the circumstances, Alex was thankful for that. That's why he made a point of killing as many creatures as he could, to keep them protected. Under his watch, he would try to keep Andrea, Birm, Quentin and Elijah alive. No matter what. Protecting them felt like his mission, something that he was meant to do, even though he had no idea why. And although he was barely aware of it, he had help: he had the other girl and the samoharo.

The girl and the samoharo treated him differently. The girl, Gaby, had kept to herself during the student tournament, but when all hell broke loose, she took charge of the survivors. At nights, she whispered to him when everyone else was sleeping. She told him how she knew what was going on with him, embracing him to keep him focused amidst all the sensory overload and the voices. Her aura was tinged with a blue light and felt warm to him. If his brain was working correctly—and he couldn't be sure because he could feel his synapsis firing at increased speed—he suspected that whatever happened to him, had happened to her, and not that long ago. How she managed to remain so composed was something Alex envied, but at least she was trying to show him how to do it.

The samoharo, Sid, was weird. There was a feeling of sadness around him, but he tried to mask it under a reassuring smile and the occasional joke to break the tension. Alex was thankful he had taken samoharo as an elective at school, as he could understand the basics of what Sid was telling him. Like Gaby, he was trying to help Alex rein in his senses, but most importantly, on filtering what the voices were saying. But what Alex was most thankful for was that when the voices told him to go and hunt the creatures, Sid always went with him, and made a point of telling Alex that he wasn't alone. Sid taught him how to use the bow they'd found to hunt the creatures and the right way to kill them.

Those creatures are all around you. You really think you can beat them? You are a useless kid. You have no

business trying to be the hero, the dark voice whispered.

The creatures dominated his world at the moment. Even when he was asleep, he could see them, *sense* them outside in the rainforest, prowling. The first time he had encountered them, it had been only for a second or two, as he and two of his classmates were exploring a cave with ancient paintings from the akeleth. The creature came from nowhere, killing his companions and stabbing Alex with its barbed extremities. How he had survived, Alex had no idea. He had woken up hours later, his injuries already healing. Beneath him had been a pool of blood: his blood. The strangest thing— that is until he started hearing the voices— was that the family sword was lying next to him. He hadn't brought it on the trip, and he was positive he hadn't carried a sword while they explored the cave. Last time he had seen it was at his grandparent's old cabin outside Xelahú, firmly secured against the wall. No one had paid much attention to the sword, its peculiar hilt suggested it was an ornamental weapon rather than an actual, useful blade. He had been shocked to see it in the cave, but with the chaotic state his mind was in, he couldn't come up with an explanation. But now that it was in his hands, he used it to provide the group with safety as his mind devolved into further chaos.

Alex continued to rock himself as he sat in his corner, the strange, guttural noise that the creatures made echoing in his head.

Kakkakkakkak.

The noise was the only way to find them, given that they were invisible to the naked eye most of time. The only other sure method to detect them was by the foul odor they emitted, but by the time you smelled them, they were too close and the only thing you could do was die.

Kakkakkakkak.

The noise echoed in Alex's head, its obnoxious rhythm upsetting his heart.

Kakkakkakkak.

It made it difficult for him to breath. The noise, mixed with the thunder, with the odd sensations reaching his skin, the lines of energy...

Kakkakkakkak...

Alex rocked himself faster, banging his head against the wall, until he felt a warm trickle of blood from his scalp. The only thing he wanted was to finally sleep and never wake up.

"Are you okay kiddo?" Sid whispered, taking a seat next to him, pouring some weird paste from a flask tucked in his belt pouch into his hand. "That must hurt." He reached for Alex, and Alex recoiled as the pungent smell of medicine hit him. "Relax, it smells bad for your nose, but it will heal your head."

Alex barely opened his eyes as Sid applied the paste over the wound with gentle pressure. His head stopped throbbing, as the coolness of the menthol in the paste seeped over his scalp. He picked out other smells of course, the peculiar odor that samoharo had, similar to wet soil mixed with seawater. He couldn't make out an aura for the samoharo, but that was not his biggest concern right now. The voice was back, whispering things in a language he didn't know. But the meaning was clear: danger.

"What's wrong with me?" Alex asked. "Why can't I make it stop."

"I wish I could answer that kiddo," Sid replied, patting Alex on the arm. "But if we can't stop it, why don't you try to use it?"

"I'm scared."

"Of what?"

"Of being crazy," Alex replied, his eyes welling up, his lower lip quivering. His head was a cacophony of voices from inside, noises from the exterior and blurred images.

"Let me tell you a secret," Sid said, smiling. "In my experience, we are all crazy. The only difference is that there are those that accept it and those that delude themselves into thinking they are sane."

Gaby approached them slowly, trying to keep quiet as some of the other kids were already sleep, exhaustion hitting them hard. And yet she appeared perfectly normal. If she was like him, then why was she fine? Why wasn't she the mess he was? Alex didn't understand and that only increased the sensation of freefalling into a void.

"How is he doing?" Gaby asked.

"Can't tell for sure. But he could use some of your expertise on the topic."

"How do you..."

"You said it wasn't your first tournament. I'm not dumb. Look, you can tell me your story later if you want. Or not. But right now that's not important. He needs help. He needs to know that he is not alone."

"Why are you helping us?" Gaby interrupted him.

Sid's shoulders slumped. "I have seen my share of death. I want to make sure that for once, someone lives on my watch." Sid's voice had a forlorn tone. "I'm going to the roof. The kid says that he can hear a few of those things prowling outside. Can you take care of him, please?"

Alex resented the implication that he was something to be taken care of, like a child, while his friend Elijah was the one who was injured. He saw Sid climbing the wall of the building with alacrity. Gaby smelled nice and fresh, like scented sea flowers. How was it possible when they had been on the run for days?

"Is this seat taken?"

"Only by my imaginary friend," Alex replied, pointing to his head.

"Well, tell them to move aside," Gaby said, sitting next to him. "Sid tells me you are not feeling too well. Is the voice annoying you?"

"Always."

"I know the feeling. Mine tends to be chatty as well in moments like this."

"How do you make it stop?"

"I haven't found out. But what I do is focus on things that make me happy. Do you have one? Something back home?"

"Not really," Alex replied. He couldn't recall a happy memory. He knew he must have one, but they weren't coming to him. His brain was scrambled. A tear rolled down his cheek. "You?"

"I like to sing." Gaby looked off into space with a crooked smile. She then turned to him and caressed his head, avoiding the injury. "Do you want me to sing you something? Maybe it could help you catch some sleep. How long have you been awake?"

"If the dark circles under my eyes is not enough of a hint, I think since the archery semifinal." Alex pointed to his face.

"That was several days ago!" Gaby said. The she looked around to make sure he hadn't woken up anyone. "That's quite a long time. You need to rest."

"I can't protect them if I rest," Alex replied, as he tried to get up. For him, it made perfect sense. But maybe not for Gaby, as she pushed him down with force. Alex didn't argue with her.

"Let Sid take care of that for a couple of hours. You can't push yourself this hard all the time. If you do, you won't be able to protect anyone. Let me share with you the song that my nana used to sing me when I couldn't sleep."

And while Gaby sang to him softly, Alex finally fell asleep, amidst a cacophony of her beautiful voice, thunder, annoying *Kakkakkakkak* noises, and the voice inside his head telling him in a subdued tone that danger was close and not only from the creatures, but from someone else, active deep in the rainforest.

† † †

Sid was knackered. The night had been long, with heavy rain and constant attacks by Stalkers. At some point he was overwhelmed and thought he would die, but Alex and Gaby had come to his rescue, killing several of the creatures. Alex, who looked rested, had come on like a storm, using brute force for his kills. Gaby had been more surgical with her strikes, as she wielded her twin blades with the faint red and blue glow. Together they had managed to keep the creatures a bay. He had to admit that those two hooman kids, acting in concert, were both amazing and terrifying. The level of destruction they brought to the Stalkers was something he had only seen in veteran samoharo hunting units with far more members. His train of thought sent a shiver down his spine. By the time the sun started to rise, the place was full of Stalker bodies turning to dust.

Luckily, we didn't lose anyone else tonight, Sid thought.

Although the hooman called Elijah wasn't improving. Sid had kept his thought about Elijah's injuries to himself, but the kid would be lucky to survive with that kind of spinal injury. He had seen many with that kind of injury. Heck, he had inflicted that kind of injury. And that made him feel even more remorse.

Shake it, you need to keep focus, Sid berated himself. He had sent the hoomans to get something to eat so he could be alone for what he was going to do. He hadn't practiced this particular kind of wayfinding in years, so he wasn't sure it would work now. But at this point he was willing to try anything.

He unsheathed the obsidian dagger he carried and took a deep breath. He looked at the stars that remained in the sky, one shinning brighter that the rest. It was the star that the samoharo called 'The Heartstone' and formed part of a constellation they knew as 'The Flying Rattlesnake', the guide towards a safe haven. Right now, he was mentally aiming to reach his hiding place, the location where he had stashed the rusty ship. It wasn't completed yet, but it would be functional enough to fly and take all of them out of this place. He would need to time things just right to send the distress call and get the hoomans away before the samoharo 'cleaning' squad arrived to deal with the incursion.

If everything goes according to plan, he thought. Sid didn't have any illusion about that. Things rarely went according to plan, especially when said plan had many movable parts like hoomans that are scared and one that was undergoing... something. Sid didn't know if Alex was crazy, or he was transforming into something else. Whatever the folktales said, none of them explained in detail what he was witnessing with Alex, and the mental and physical changes he was suffering. He hated not knowing all the variables.

"Sigh," Sid said to himself. "Here goes nothing."

He mumbled a halfhearted prayer in his native tongue and pricked himself in the thumb of his left hand, spilling blood in the air. The blood fell but it didn't hit the ground, instead it separated into six individual drops, each floating in the air, in a formation that imitated the stars of the Flying

11

Rattlesnake constellation. Sid whispered a second prayer in hushed voice.

"Blood of the ancestors that runs through my veins, lead me to the correct path, keep me from going astray."

Sid blew the droplets away. Each droplet floated in a different direction, tracing through the air an image of the six different paths across the rainforest that he could take. The second to the center left glowed with a green-blue hue, while the one to the right took a sinister red-purple hue.

Great! Go left into the thick of the forest, because the baddies are to the right where the path seems clearer. Of course, it had to be that way, me and my luck, Sid thought. He was trying to plot how to move the injured across the more difficult, but safer path, when he felt a presence behind him. Instinctively, Sid reached for his small axe, while in his other hand he was still holding the dagger.

"What are you doing? Or better said, how are you doing it?" a sweet, female voice came from behind. Sid turned around and saw Gaby staring at the blood paths. For the first time Sid noticed how tall she was, probably three or four heads taller than him. He wasn't a tall samoharo by any means, but she was tall by hooman standards. Her crooked smile made her look friendlier than usual. In the glow of the morning, she looked like an akeleth.

"Ah!" Sid said, and relaxed. "It's you, for a second I thought..."

"That I was a monster or one of the cultists Alex was mumbling about hours ago?"

"Yes, can't blame me."

"No, I can't. But what were you doing?"

"That?" Sid pointed to the blood trails that were evaporating. "It's an ancient wayfinding technique we use to find safe routes for our missions."

"Wayfinding?"

"It's... how do I explain it? In hooman terms it would be our religious beliefs, probably you have heard of them as 'Paths of the Stargazers' combined with magic. It helps us to find our way home, to find a safe spot. It's used a lot by explorers. Wayfinding, or if you like, Pathfinding."

"And does wayfinding imply using blood magic?" Gaby pointed at the nearly evaporated blood trails, and then to Sid's injured hand.

"Not really," Sid replied. He really didn't want to elaborate any further. Hoomans were not keen on blood magic. It wasn't as if he was using the Smoking Mirror Path, only one of their techniques. And the least bloody one. "I usually use the Windstar or the Ghoststar Paths to trace a way to move around. But since we are time pressed and the only stars in the sky are the Flying Rattlesnake, I had to use a bit of blood-letting to get a faster result. It's pretty common."

Gaby gave him a look that told him she was onto him and his peculiar version of the truth.

"So, where are you going?" she asked.

"Not me. We. All of us."

"So, where are we going?"

"You don't want to know why I'm suggesting leaving our place of safety?"

"After last night I doubt anyone thinks this place will be safe anymore. I was about to suggest we leave."

"You are weird. No offense."

"None taken."

"What I'm going to tell you is a secret, one you and your friends must keep. I'm counting on you because they seem to follow your lead and I will be busy keeping Alex in check. You need to know the plan in full: beyond the rainforest, there is an ancient samoharo machine, an airship."

"Airship? You mean a dirigible?"

"No, a proper airship..." Sid was thinking on an appropriate parallel. It was frustrating that hoomans had decided that hyper speed trains were better than actual flight. Maybe if they had developed more of those flying dreadnoughts, they would have put more pressure into the samoharo to recover the old tech. Then he realized what he had just thought. "Remember those dreadnoughts from your history books about the Great War in Ionis? Just like those, but smaller and prettier."

"Oh!" Gaby opened her eyes wide. "That sounds awesome! Does it work?"

"Let's just say that it will work well enough to get us out of here. I haven't had time to finish it, but it should work for now. My plan is to take you to the ship, launch a distress signal to the closest samoharo or hooman outpost and while they get here, we fly away."

"I get the first part of the plan, but why fly away if help will be coming here?" Gaby asked, confusion clear in her face.

"C'mon kiddo, you know why," Sid replied, with an edge in his voice. Time was running and besides, he didn't want to say something offensive about the hoomans of the Straits. "How are you gonna explain to the government of the Straits what happened here? We are their neighbors; they are famous for covering the truth and for midlevel corruption. If anything, they will put the blame on you and Alex, because of what you can do. Plus, they must be on their way here anyways. I'm more worried about the other ones."

"The samoharo? Aren't they noble warriors?" Gaby asked, with a certain innocence in her voice.

"As if..." Sid avoided her gaze and looked back to the paths. "Let's just say that there is a samoharo policy of taking down anyone that develops power above titanfighters or demonhunters, especially without armor or any other kind of aid. You and Alex fit that description. From what I've seen, your powers will only increase. I would hate to see you targeted by the person I'm pretty sure they will send to clean up this incursion mess."

"You sound like you know for a certainty what will happen." Gaby stared at him. Sid felt as if the girl was examining his very soul. When she grows up, she would be downright scary. Sid let out a sigh.

"I know because I used to do that job. I hunted people with powers, like you and Alex. Until one day I refused to do it anymore and got punished."

"Why?"

"I was too good at my job, and it sickened me. And I don't hurt children." Sid said with conviction. He wanted to change topics back to the matter at hand. There was a lump in his throat, and he coughed. He didn't want to bring back those memories. "So that's the plan. What do you think?"

"Let's move everyone," Gaby replied. She seemed to understand. Which made Sid wonder what the Pits had happened to her to make her so understanding of the implications of what he hinted at.

It takes one to know another, he thought. He knew he had blood on his hands. Sid wasn't sure he wanted to find out what had happened to her.

They returned to the ground floor where Birm and Quentin were helping Elijah move, while Andrea grabbed arrows and a bow.

"We need to move," Andrea said. "Elijah is not getting any better."

"We know," Gaby replied. "We have a plan."

"That's great, can't wait to leave this place," Birm added.

Sid looked around. Someone was missing. He cursed the stars that were failing him now.

"Where is Alex?" Sid asked.

"He was here a minute ago. Then he went that way," Quentin replied.

Great, into the wrong path, Sid thought. Time was running out. He needed to take these hoomans to safety, but he couldn't leave Alex on his own. He would never forgive himself if something happened to the kid. He looked at Gaby, who was unsheathing her swords. She was planning to do the same thing he was considering doing. But unlike him, Gaby hadn't seen all the paths. He had to trust her.

"Gaby, follow the plan, take them to the ship," Sid said. He gave her a long, bronze key. "Use this to turn the engines, should work similar to one of your hooman cars, and launch the distress signal. I will meet you there. Keep them safe."

"What about you?"

"I will go after Alex."

"But... I don't know how to fly a ship."

"I'm not asking you to fly it, just keep it warm and ready to take off, till I get there with Alex. Right now, we need to work as a team, and you are the only one that can keep the others safe."

"How do I know you will return to find us?"

"How do I know you won't take off without me and Alex?

After all we have been through these days, these doubts are counterproductive. There is one option."

"Which one."

"Trust each other," Sid replied with a smile, as Gaby stared at him. Both shared a moment of silence, sizing each other up. He knew he was asking a lot of her, but then again, the current situation demanded it. Gaby returned the smile.

"Time to go, kiddo," Sid said. Gaby nodded and both went in opposite directions.

Sid ran towards the right path. He jumped into the trees and moved by leaping between branches. With the thickness of the rainforest, it would be faster for him, not unlike the races back in the Hegemony. He was focused on reaching Alex as soon as possible. He didn't know if it was out of fear for what would happen to the hooman, or fear of what a hooman undergoing that kind of change could do. Sid tried to keep those memories from resurfacing, which left him blindsided. Something tackled him and he fell to the ground, several meters below. The hit had taken most of the air out of his lungs. The only reason he wasn't suffering from a broken back or a punctured lung was the hard plates covering his back.

These are the moments when I love being a samoharo.

The creature was atop of him, one of the Stalkers. It was injured and one of its limbs had been cut, damaging its cloaking ability.

It seems that it wasn't hunting but running away. Focus Sid, focus.

The weight of the creature was making it hard for him to breathe. The bared fangs were too close for comfort, the gaping maw drooling its stinking saliva.

"Have you considered using mouthwash?" Sid asked the creature. He reached for his dagger with his right hand and the small ax with his left. As the creature's maw opened wide to take a bite out of Sid's head, he thrust the dagger deep into what would be the heart of the creature. As the Stalker moved back, reeling from the lethal attack, Sid traced an arc with the ax, cutting its head off in one swing. The creature's head hit the ground as its body twitched. Sid pushed it away from him and took several deep breaths, trying to regain his calm. The moss from the ground felt nice on the back of his head and for a second, he considered taking a couple of minutes to rest.

But the sound of thunder breaking the otherwise clear sky brought him out of his reverie.

"Right, the kid."

† † †

Alex was perched on a thick branch of a kapok tree. He didn't recall how he got there. Weeks ago, he wouldn't have been able to climb a regular tree, let alone one as massive as the kapok. The tree was at the edge of the rainforest, where a man-made clearing was located. From his vantage point, Alex could see a few of the creatures that had been hounding him. He also saw the cultists, the people that had summoned the creatures through some unknown means. The cultists were working on a giant metallic ring that stood in the center of the clearing. It was five meters in diameter, covered in weird symbols. The ring glowed with a purple energy and the light pulsated slowly like a beating heart. Each pulse let out a faint buzzing sound.

A part of him wondered who could be capable of unleashing such horrors upon innocent people. It made him burn with anger. He saw one of the creatures eating human remains and he hoped that it wasn't one of his classmates. As much as he didn't get along with them, he didn't wish them anything bad.

You are going to end like him, and no one will notice, the dark voice said inside his head.

"Shut up," Alex mumbled. The dark voice had become an insistent presence, one that appeared when he was feeling at his lowest.

The crunching noises of the bones being broken and the slurping sound of the marrow being sucked by that maw churned his stomach and brought forth the memories of what happened to him in the cave. Exploring the cave, finding faded engravings on its walls, depicting a familiar sword. Then, the pain. The last memory he'd had was a piercing pain on his right side, blood filled his mouth and, as he started to black out, a bright light filled the cave. The next clear memory he had after he woke up was of wandering through the rainforest, feeling weird, hearing voices in his head and holding the sword. It was then that Gaby had found him and took him to the other survivors. Then Sid arrived to help them.

He shook his head to clear it. And yet the memories seemed a better place to be right now, instead of witnessing the spectacle in front of him.

"I'm afraid," Alex said in a whisper, hoping to not be heard as he tightened his grip on the sword's handle.

"*I know, I'm here with you remember?*" the other voice replied. Not the dark one. Rather, it was the same voice that he'd heard after waking up in the cave. The same voice that told him where the danger was and how to fight the creatures. The one that told him how to use his new abilities. And now it was telling him that to keep the others safe, he had to face the creatures in their spawning site, regardless of how scary the prospect was. Alex felt like he was in one of those horror videogames, a character helplessly controlled by a mysterious player.

"Who are you?" Alex asked in low voice. It was silly to have a conversation with himself in his head this way, but it was the only way he could make sense of it without going crazier than he already was.

"*I don't recall anymore. We are already becoming one,*" the voice replied, with a hint of sadness. Alex knew it was sadness because he felt the same heavy weight in his heart.

"But what if I don't want to?"

"*I'm sorry. It can't be stopped, this is permanent.*" Now there was regret.

"I'm gonna stop being me?" Alex felt a knot in his stomach. What the voice was saying sounded like his mind was going to disappear, his body controlled by someone else. His hyperactive imagination conjured dreadful images of his soul dissipating. It made him feel even worse.

"*No, you, what makes you, will reassert itself in a few weeks,*" the voice reassured him. "*I will become part of that. A voice and a power deep inside you.*"

"Why me?"

"*Happenstance? Coincidence? Destiny? Many options we will have time to ponder when we get out of this.*"

Get out of this? We will die because we are losers. The dark voice joined the conversation. It sounded like Alex, but with an edge, a tinge of sadness and defeat. Perhaps even anger.

"Go away!" Alex replied. He felt his eyes watering. "Stop saying bad things."

It's the truth. You know it. I'm you after all.

"Enough!" Alex replied, defiant. His head was throbbing, as if it were about to explode.

"*I will deal with it, but right now we need to deal with those creatures. The others are in danger,*" the other voice said.

"I don't know how. And I'm alone. I can't do it on my own."

"*I'm here with you. We are one, we are a team. If you give me the control this time, I swear I will get us out of this one.*"

No, he won't.

"*And I promise, I will keep that other guy in check.*" The other voice said, clearly feeling annoyed, as Alex felt that way too. "*But we need to do this.*"

"Okay, but don't get us killed," Alex replied, wiping the tears from his cheeks with his arm.

"*I won't. Now, let's use all those emotions inside you to power this,*" the voice replied. Alex could feel the energy running through his body, a sequence of electric shocks. His fingertips released sparks and his eyes hurt. The irises glowed with a soft golden hue. His heart thumped hard inside his chest. The world changed around him, it felt less physical, but with more vivid colors. The smells were stronger, both from the rainforest and from the creatures, a stark contrast between the sweet smell of land after it rained and the pungent smell of the rotten flesh of the creatures. Alex could now see the ebbs and flows of energy around him and his heart thumped even harder. To his ears, it sounded like thunder.

"What is that?"

"*A storm.*"

Alex's irises glowed more intensely than the previous occasions. He jumped from the branch with such strength that he broke it. He felt bad for the tree, but even the tree seemed to be cheering him on. Apprently even nature didn't like what was going on in the clearing. The strongest flow of energy came from the ring, as well as the worst of the odors. The jump launched him far into the clearing, in the middle of the creatures. Alex landed with force, the impact to the ground making a booming sound like that of thunder breaking the air. The cultists turned around, astonished by what was happening. Alex looked at his left hand; electrical currents were running along his fingers and across his palm. In his right, the ancestral family sword felt lighter than before and the electrical currents ran through the blade. Alex smiled, a feeling of anticipation and excitement surging through him like the electricity running over his body. This would be fun.

The Stalkers jumped at Alex, trying to overwhelm him. He replied in kind, punching, kicking, and slashing them. One punch hit a Stalker directly in the head, making it explode. With a slash of the sword, he caught another Stalker in the mouth, cutting the jaw and the top of the head with it. The battle became a constant sequence of attacks and defensive moves. Alex wasn't fighting like Gaby, who fought with the precision of a ballerina executing a complicated dance. Nor was he fighting like Sid, the samoharo, who attacked with a force and a precision that betrayed his small frame. No, Alex fought like a beast, unleashing all of his accumulated anger in his attacks, ripping limbs, cutting heads, punching hearts out, breaking necks. It was a violent, visceral affair.

"AHHHHHHHHH," Alex yelled with rage.

It was a thunderstorm.

A cultist tried to stab him in the back, but Alex stopped him with a well-placed elbow strike. The cracking noise let him know that he had broken the nose of the cultist. Without a pause, Alex grabbed him by the robe and threw him towards the ring. The man seemed to hit an invisible wall inside the ring, and his body disintegrated in a purple fire.

"That's a portal!" Alex muttered. "The creatures must come from it."

"*Yes, we need to destroy it to stop the arrival of more creatures. Your sword can do the trick. Its edge will be able to cut that thing into pieces.*"

"Let's go for it!"

You will fail, the dark voice said out of the blue.

"*Shut up,*" said the other voice.

"Shut up!" Alex yelled as he cut his way through creatures and cultists alike. He leaped towards the ring; sword held over his head. Putting all his weight and force into the slashing movement, Alex struck the ring and cut it in half. He landed in front of the portal as both halves started to fall apart. Then he noticed the change in the flow of energy.

"Aww crap, that thing is going to explode," Alex said, covering his eyes with his free arm.

Alex had to plant his feet and lean forward to prevent himself from being blown back, as the explosion swept over him, and this gave the Stalkers time to regroup and surge toward him. For a second Alex thought he would die, as the sad voice had told him. But at the last second, he rolled to his right, avoiding the attacks. With a somersault he got to his feet and punched the air, unleashing an explosion of electromagnetic energy that pushed the creatures back and electrocuted the cultists.

"*I know that you will forget all of these moves, all of these techniques,*" the voice said defiantly. "*I know that I will soon disappear and be a part of you. But I'm happy it is you whom I was destined to join. You are a good person. I will always be with you and in time, you will rediscover all of this. I want you to always remember this, the feeling you are having right now, the one that will keep you going against all odds, remember how good it feels to discover what you are meant to do: to protect others. To be a hero.*"

You know it won't last. The dark voice added.

"*No!*" the other voice yelled to the dark voice. "*I'm taking you with me. Alex, you will be in charge soon, take care of us. Of you.*"

We will die! Hehehehe! Sooner or later we will! The sad voice said as it faded away.

Alex's head was filled with a cacophony of voices. His

head was throbbing with pain and his chest filled with anger. The only thing Alex wanted to do was to inflict the pain he was feeling, and unleash the anger boiling inside him. And he was surrounded by the perfect targets for that.

He smiled. He might be a good person, but that didn't mean he had to be nice.

† † †

By the time Sid reached the clearing, the sound of thunder had subsided, replaced only by the sound of birds flapping frantically to fly away. The image would haunt Sid for years to come.

Alex knelt in the center of the clearing, surrounded by the remains of Stalkers and cultists. There was no one left alive. The ground was littered with metallic debris. Alex was bleeding from his right shoulder. He was clutching his sword, and he was crying. Sid approached him, dagger and ax out, waiting to strike, but it wasn't needed. When he reached the teenager, Sid touched Alex on his good shoulder. He felt an electric discharge that numbed his fingers. Alex turned to him. His eyes were red from crying.

"I just wanted all of this to end," Alex said with a creaking voice. His breathing was labored, as if he had run a marathon. His irises slowly returned to their normal hazel coloration, the glow fading away. Sid felt as if a heavy bag of rocks were hanging from his body. Watching the kid like this made him feel emotionally drained. Sid would have to deal with those feelings later, right now, he needed to get Alex out of here. Sid offered a hand to help Alex get up, despite the clear height difference. For the first time he noticed that Alex was also taller than him.

Great, I'm the short one, Sid thought. He looked into Alex's eyes and smiled at him, sharp teeth and all.

"I know Alex. I think it's over now."

"I... " Alex looked around. He seemed to be in shock. "I don't know what I did. Is everyone safe?"

"Yes, you saved them all. You stopped the bad guys. Help is on the way. Now I need to take you with me. You will be safe, too," Sid reassured Alex. In a way it was good that the kid couldn't remember all the details. Doing so brought forth nightmares and regret. Maybe it was for the best.

"You think?"

"I know."

"How?"

"Because." Sid took a deep breath. He offered his hand to Alex, who awkwardly shook it with his left hand. "I swear by my ancestral blood that I will always have your back. And a samoharo never breaks a promise sworn by his ancestral blood."

"Why are you doing this?"

"Because we are friends," Sid winked at Alex, who smiled. "You are not alone."

An eerie silence had fallen over the land and was broken by the roar of an engine. Gaby had done as he'd asked her. Help of one kind or another would be coming. But time was running out and Sid needed to keep Alex safe and find a way to help him He knew the Samoharo would be coming, soon. His people had their 'cleaning' policy for this very reason. Someone with Alex's power and out of control was a danger for all. But Sid knew this kid was different. He could feel it. Like Gaby, he wasn't acting out of malice. Alex needed help to learn to control his new power. Not be punished for it.

Sid had left his old life behind because he believed there was a better way to do things. He would prove wrong those who hadn't listened to him. Sid was sure it would cost him dearly, probably everything he had. But Sid kept his word. No matter how much he complained, he always did.

"Everything will be okay," Sid said aloud, more to himself than to Alex. "I promise."

Sid recalled all what he had heard of the people who obtained the Gift, and looked around once more to see the destruction surrounding them. The scene sent shivers down his spine.

Folktales, he thought, *even they have their share of horror.*

Chapter 2
The Past Catches Up

Harland was starting to develop an aversion to taking any calls that his assistant said was "an important matter of utmost urgency." The last time he had ended up in a crazy adventure, which had begun as a search for a missing researcher from the Foundation and had then evolved into a race to stop a madman and a flying monster that wanted to destroy the Alliance. Harland had manned the guns of a jury-rigged airship, his small contribution—in his opinion— to the brave deeds of his best friend Fionn and his daughter Sam, aided by the newest members to their eclectic 'family': Gaby, Alex and Sid the samoharo. It had been a stressful, dangerous and hectic week. And yet, given the choice, he would have preferred to repeat that adventure and deal with a madman or a monster, then being here.

Here was the private conference room of the First Thane of the Emerald Island. It was a grand and pompous title since the First Thane was the main councilor to the Crown, the right-hand man. He was the person responsible for advising on policy, economy, intelligence and the myriad businesses that the Queen couldn't oversee on her own all the time. The First Thane was not only the ruler of the Emerald Island but also managed the broader interests of the Free Alliance. He oversaw the finer, and sometimes shadier, sides of the political wheeling and dealing that was always necessary. And while the current holder of the office had been a faithful servant for the Queen in particular, and to the Alliance in general, Harland was not fond of the man, for myriad reasons.

Harland sat alone in the large room, fidgeting in his seat, adjusting the table header he'd taken off the long, red oak table, so he could see better. He felt as if he was back in the principal's office when he'd been a young student.

And considering who would join him in this meeting, that wouldn't be too far off.

The first person to enter, walking decisively and cradling a cup of warm tea was Lady Sarah—tall, slender, with delicate features and shoulder-length dark brown hair. Her long-sleeved, floor-length dress reflected the orange hues of autumn, with gold embroidery in the shape of leaves and vines completing the design. She gave Harland a friendly smile as she walked across the room. As a member of the royal house, Lady Sarah was the permanent ambassador before the Council for the Queen. She was also Harland's friend from school.

Lady Sarah placed her cup on the table, kissed Harland on the cheek and took a seat.

"Sometimes your smile frightens me," Harland said. "I don't know if the cat just ate the canary or is nervous about having been found out." He smiled. "You look well, Sarah."

"'You look well'? That's all? You have an adventure worthy of a fiction book and a movie deal and that's all you have to say to one of your oldest friends? How rude of you to hide things from me."

"I have the feeling that this meeting is related to said event," Harland replied with a smile. "So, I'm keeping this spoiler free for the time being. Besides, I wasn't planning to bring up hidden things... like the new tattoo you just got on one of your wrists. I assume it was the left one."

"How did you..." Lady Sarah opened her mouth, only to then cover it with her left hand. She was trying to stifle a laugh.

"You rarely wear long-sleeved dresses, even at formal events. That means that you are hiding something. And you often mentioned you wanted a tattoo on your wrists. Now, knowing who we will be meeting here, and his opinion on tattoos, or any kind of self-expression, really, no wonder you want to hide it from him," Harland explained with a shrug.

"The man does hate anything fun. If he were any stiffer, he would break in two from breathing."

"Always the smart ass in the room," Lady Sarah replied. The door opened, startling them both.

"I hope you are not talking about me. I'm not that stiff. Only a bit sore," said the tall man with close-cut, dirty blonde hair who was entering the room. He was wearing a casual suit that still showed off his fit physique. He had the square chin—with a tiny scar on it—the vivacious eyes, and the dashing presence one would associate with the knights from folktales. One could even argue that this man had all the looks befitting of a king. Which was appropriate because this man, who it was said was the spitting image of his great-grandfather, was Crown Prince Arthur. And his ancestor had been King Castlemartell himself.

Harland recalled what Fionn had once told him about Arthur, *he takes after the King in many aspects, that's true, sans the scars or the beard, of course. And I hope he in time takes after him in character. I already have had enough with the other members of his family.*

From that conversation years ago, Harland had learned that Fionn had a complicated view on the royal family that he had been a comrade in arms with once. Fionn had held only the King and Queen Brenda Sophia in esteem. On the other hand, Fionn wasn't a fan of the Queen's other siblings... and after fighting the Bestial last year and defeating Byron, the less they talked about him the better. But Fionn had never explained why his relationship with Prince Arthur was so complicated. As far as Harland knew, Fionn—after being 're-vived'—had met with the Prince a few times, at the request of the Queen herself, but never elaborated on those meetings.

And after what happened a year ago, he couldn't blame him.

"Don't tell me you spent yesterday at a party," Lady Sarah said to the Prince, who was pouring himself a glass of water, of all things.

"I would love to say that, but no. I'm taking my responsibilities seriously."

"That would be a first," Harland said.

"Believe it or not. I have been training with THE armor for the past few months."

The emphasis on the word 'the' made Harland realize to which armor Arthur was referring. It also hinted at what this meeting might be about.

"So, you are finally dusting off the original armor of the Castlemartells instead of the exhibition piece from the museum," Harland said, as his mind pondered on the only possibility behind the Prince's interest in training with the armor. He decided to change topics as he knew that talking about the Queen's health would be a delicate issue. "Am I the only one wondering why I feel like we are back at school, waiting in the principal's office to get scolded?"

"No, I feel the same," Lady Sarah replied, fidgeting in her seat, clearly uncomfortable.

"Usually because we enacted one of your complicated pranks," Arthur said. "Who thought of the stink bomb in the headmaster's quarters?"

"Yeah, yeah, always blaming me, Arthur. As if you and Sarah weren't willing participants," Harland replied. With the hindsight that comes from years of growing up and facing some harsh truths, Harland thought that as amusing as that prank would have been as a kid, in reality it had been a sign of disrespect for the person who worked hard to give a good education to young pupils.

"Arthur? What happened to 'His Majesty'? Or Lady Sarah?" Arthur smiled. But the smile made Harland feel uncomfortable.

That's when it dawned on Harland. What Alex had been telling him about 'privilege'. The fact that he had studied with members of the royal household and was on a first name basis with powerful people had made Harland forget sometimes what powerful people could do on a bad day. Fionn had experienced that before. And Harland had seen it in real time last year. He grew more uncomfortable, as if his seat was made of thousands of pins.

As he pondered leaving the meeting under a false pretense, the door swung open, making Harland jump. A tall man in a business suit, with neatly cropped black hair and moustache, entered the room, holding a leather binder in his left hand. Harland noticed the tightness of the man's grip around the binder. The knuckles were white.

And now Harland wished he had actually left earlier.

Peter Doncelles, Lord of Severnford and the current holder of the office of First Thain of the Emerald Island. If the Queen was the heart, the Thain was the brain. And what a powerful brain had been Lord Doncelles in the past decades. Always a step or two ahead his rivals, his diplomacy skills were unrivalled as he always knew what the opposite side wanted and lacked. And he wasn't above the shadowy aspects of ruling, especially when it came to protecting the status and reputation of the Queen in particular, and the Castlemartell family in general. Harland had to give it to the man, even if he wasn't a fan of him—due to a long-standing feud over the independent status of the Foundation, a status that Harland's father had fought long and hard to obtain— as his loyalty to the Queen was undisputed. Harland knew Doncelles well, as he had been Harland's mentor once upon a time, but now the Thain was not happy with recent developments. And when Lord Doncelles wasn't happy, he demanded answers.

Which was why Harland guessed he was there, to give answers. He braced for what was sure to be a tense reunion.

The Thain took a seat and looked to everyone around the table, holding their gaze. Arthur's smile faded and Sarah tried to straighten up in her seat, fidgeting with her sleeves to cover her tattoo. Harland found that amusing. Because after facing the mind-numbing horror that was the underbelly of the floating monstrosity that was the Bestial, even the anger of the Thain was daunting. Harland smiled. Doncelles frowned.

"I will cut to the point," the Thain said. His tone was firm, measured, and cold. "After the events of the past year and the revelation of Prince Byron's true form, the city state members of the Alliance feel cheated and are asking for diplomatic talks to reevaluate the status and future of the Alliance. Robbet Dewart is proving to be particularly difficult to deal with in regard to this, even more since he has found an ally in Girolamo Bardi from Portis."

"The southern regions want to separate, again," Sarah added. It seemed that whatever was happening, Sarah and probably Arthur, were already informed. Which meant that the meeting was more about what he and the Foundation could offer than to inform the royal household. He felt cheated. But Harland gathered his bearings.

"They have always been looking for an excuse to ask for a restructure of the Alliance in their favor," Harland said, feigning to have bitten the bait. "What's new?"

He knew what was new.

"Now they have a perfect excuse, thanks to the escapades of the Greywolf and his other friends, and the mayhem resulting from that *adventure*." The Thain raised his voice. "Decades of hard work, collapsing because of the ill-thought shenanigans of a few entitled."

"Ill-thought? Shenanigans?" Harland replied, letting his annoyance show. "If it weren't for those *entitled*, you wouldn't be here speaking in that way. In fact, I could guess your head would be far removed from your body and decorating the top of a spike. So, you might wish to measure your next words if you want my help. Because that's the only reason you sent for me."

The Thain tightened his lips and only let out a hiss. His eyes betrayed the seething fury inside him. A part of Harland understood the anger Doncelles was holding back for the sake of appearances. The Thain was right in the sense that the delicate balance of the Alliance had always been at risk, more noticeable in recent years with the NLP party, the tensions with the Freefolk, and the quest to get the Kuni to join. The Samoharo had declined emphatically after the Great War, and the Straits were... a peculiar case. What Byron had done was to throw a wrench into the machinery the Queen and the Thain had been working so hard to create. It had been almost as effective had Byron succeeded in his plan. But to put the blame on Fionn, Gaby, Alex, Sam, Sid and even himself, who basically had cleaned up a mess hidden under the rug for a century, was unfair.

"Moving on to the next item of this reunion," the Thain said closing his binder. "The Kuni have graciously offered to host the Triannual Diplomatic Talks of the Free Alliance and friendly powers in their capital, on the condition they get to also host the Chivalry Games and enter a team of champions to the competition. While they will remain a neutral party to offer advice, this might be an opportunity for them to finally join the Alliance. Which would help to reestablish the balance. However..."

"I sense that something went wrong with your carefully laid plans," Harland said. The Thain stared daggers at him. Harland's smile grew.

"The Kuni and the Samoharo..."

"The Samoharo are attending too?" Arthur interrupted. It seemed that this was news to him as well.

"Yes," the Thain replied curtly. The way his lips twitched and his nostrils flared, let Harland know that he was trying to contain his anger under a façade of politeness. Doncelles had never liked having conditions imposed on him by anyone but the Queen. "The Samoharo will attend and participate in the Games too. And along with the Kuni, they demand for the Freefolk to attend as an independent nation."

Harland was delighted at the news, even if he couldn't show it. While the Freefolk were nominally members of the Alliance, there were issues that were a sore point for them, such as their ancestral lands being under the control of other city states, or their lack of an actual voice on the decisions of the Alliance. Fionn—not exactly the most orthodox freefolk—had been pushing for solving those issues to give his people a voice and reclaim their lands. But even a legendary hero faced an uphill battle when it came to politicians. So, the fact that the Kuni and the Samoharo were asking for the Freefolk to be granted independent status to negotiate at the table was excellent news. Fionn would be delighted.

"They also asked that the Foundation participate, as an independent, neutral entity with voice and vote," the Thain said with frustration in his voice. The declaration took Harland by surprise. "I assume you knew nothing of this."

"I'm as surprised as you," Harland replied. That was an

unexpected development. One for which Harland didn't feel prepared for.

"I would give you the benefit of the doubt," the Thain said. "But the purpose of this meeting was not to inform you of this, but rather to ask you for insight on your friend the Greywolf."

"Technically," Sarah interjected, "he is Lord Estel."

"Or Lord Greywolf if you like," Arthur added with a grin. Harland recalled that like Alex, Arthur had been somewhat of a fan of Fionn while growing up. It seemed that he hadn't changed much.

"Be that as it may," the Thain continued, the frown in his forehead growing by the minute. "The fact remains that he is a freefolk. And not just any freefolk, but their representative in their talks. I have tried to reach him to talk, but it seems he has been traveling around, having his *little adventures.*"

Harland wasn't sure which delighted him more: the fact that Fionn would be representing his people—which meant that after the Gathering they attended a few months ago, he rose in the ranks—or the way Lord Doncelles had enunciated 'little adventures', with a mixture of annoyance and jealousy. Maybe he wasn't as stiff as Harland had thought. Or maybe it was because he couldn't be sure what Fionn would do.

And thus, the reason for my presence here is revealed, Harland thought.

"So, you want insight on Lord Greywolf's thoughts, huh?" Harland asked, knowing the answer. And he also knew what Fionn would ask for. So many years of being close friends had given him that insight. "Well, knowing Fionn, he will support the Alliance, he bled for it. And for its founder. But don't confuse that with total cooperation with your agenda. And the Queen must know that. He will have requests."

"What requests?" Sarah asked. She seemed confused. For her and her family, Fionn had always been a staunch, loyal friend. To the point that the King Castlemartell had given him a Lordship back in the day and the Queen had reinstated it after he returned to the land of the living. That he might have an agenda that was different from that of the Alliance or the Queen was unthinkable to her.

"Requests? Or demands?" the Thain asked. He wasn't confused, rather, he was annoyed.

"You know?" Harland replied, relishing what he was going to say, even if it wasn't the smartest thing to do, "for someone as savvy for politics as you all are, you are also clueless on what your potential allies might want. Or you are feigning to be clueless. Either way, my answer will be the same."

"I don't appreciate you talking to me that way," the Thain said. "You are a citizen of this island, and if I recall correctly, a couple of those new 'friends' of yours are not. Their visas can expire any day. The visa of one of them is actually up for review this year if I recall correctly."

"I don't like you asking me to sell out my friend, nor threating me or them," Harland replied. "I find it insulting, really. After all this time, you should know me better than that."

Harland stood up and walked towards the entrance. If it wouldn't worsen the situation, he would have punched the man in the face. He stopped, turned around and faced them. "But I will give you this for free. Fionn might be a founder of the Alliance. A lord too, even if he doesn't use the title nor rank. But before that, he is freefolk and for his support he will ask for what his people have always wanted since the Great War: their territories and sacred lands. Or at least a buffer zone around the Scar. And that includes Sandtown."

"That island?" Sarah asked.

"That island is where the Freefolk Nation was founded," Harland explained with a smile. "That they allowed the Alliance Charter to be signed there was because they wanted to cooperate. It doesn't mean that it belongs to you. It's sacred land for them."

"I don't think that neither the Crown nor the Alliance will accept those terms," Sarah replied, unsure of what else to say.

"Then let me give you some advice," Harland said. He wasn't planning on relenting on the issue. He owed Fionn that much and more. If they wanted the Foundation to be a neutral party to help negotiations, he should start now. "You better think about how to convince them of this. Because otherwise you will lose the Freefolk, especially after how the politicians have smeared them in the media. And without them, the Alliance is dead. Don't forget that they are way more powerful than any of us. And if they go, I doubt that the Samoharo and the Kuni will join us. So, if you will excuse me, I have to go back to work. Some of us actually have jobs."

The room felt silent. The Thain's face was red with anger. Sarah was taken aback by Harland's directness. If any of them thought for a second that they could manipulate him or count on him as an extension of their own interests, they were wrong.

Harland was aware of the consequences of his actions. But this was one of the reasons his father had started the Foundation, not just for research, but to become a major player to help the Alliance avoid the destiny of the Old Kingdoms from before the Great War.

"Any other advice, old friend?" Arthur asked, with a calm voice. He was the only one trying to conciliate. In that regard, he was following the guidelines of his family. Most of them in any case. Harland had to give him points for trying to ease the tension of the room.

"You better practice more, because if for some reason you decide to challenge Fionn or the guy that will represent the Foundation, you are in for a world of pain," Harland said. Arthur might be his friend, a fine fighter trained by the leader of the Solarian Knights, the Queen's personal guard and some of the best titanfighters of the Core regions of Theia. But even then, that couldn't compare to the full power of a trained Gifted.

"Is that a threat?" Sarah asked in disbelief.

"Not at all. I swear," Harland explained, "I'm telling you the truth so you can be prepared. I will see you at the conference."

Harland left the room and walked as fast as possible to get out of the castle. Outside, as he recovered his breath, he hailed a cab and gave the driver an address. He couldn't decide if he was hungry, thirsty, or worried. Probably a mix of all three. Aside from the fact that he had to prepare himself for a diplomatic conference, he had to solve a peculiar problem: he had to find three champions to represent the Foundation. And he had a feeling of who would be his only available option.

I hope he doesn't narrate the fights aloud, Harland thought.

Chapter 3
Life is Not a Movie

And thus, the mutant hero is close to beating the foulest villain and..., Alex thought, as he smashed the buttons of the arcade with furious energy. But a small mistake cost him the remainder of his energy, his final life, and his last coin to keep playing,

"So close," Alex muttered under his breath. The words 'game over' appeared on the screen of the arcade videogame. He turned around to see if Sam, Andrea, Birm, or Quentin would lend him a coin to try once more to finish the game that had become the bane of his existence. But he found himself alone in the almost empty arcade. He stared at the cabinet and sighed.

"Maybe next time," Alex muttered. He picked up his duffel bag and left the place. He walked around the Starling shopping mall towards the only place where the others might be: the food court.

Alex mused about the peculiar spatial arrangement of the mall, as he walked across the top floor corridor of the open plan, star shaped mall. The Starling shopping mall was partly built underground, to connect it with the rest of the pedestrian walkways built below the streets of Saint Lucy that accommodate walkers during the winter season. And during its heyday, it had been the place to be. Now, after the 'incident', it only had a few visitors and shops. Alex loved the place, its small indoor amusement park, homage to Korbyworld, the comic book shop owned by his friend Tyler, from where he bought his comics every month. And the north wing he always wanted to explore.

I mean, the food court is the best place to be, unless they went there… but Sam wouldn't risk it, would she?

A freak accident had occurred in the north wing, leaving the location connected to the Tempest and the weird warping qualities of that realm. Alex had wanted to explore it, but that required preparation as it would be akin to visiting a small portion of the Maze. And doing it alone would be stupid, but so far, he didn't have anyone willing to go along with him.

As always, I'm alone, Alex thought. *Then again, I'm used to that.*

Since the day of the battle against Byron and the Bestial, Alex had been feeling unwell. As time went by, the frequency of his anxiety attacks, the sleepless nights and the overall sense of sadness had increased. It had made it difficult to focus on his research project and complicated his interactions with others. Usually, when he got like this, he could go to Gaby or Sid, the only ones who had seen him at his worst and helped him to get back. But Gaby had been traveling with Fionn and Sid has been busy with Harland and the Foundation, rebuilding the Figaro. Heck, even Birm had gotten a job there. And Sam… when he and she got along, it was awesome. But when they didn't, it was difficult. And so, the feeling of loneliness had been growing inside his heart, making him wonder if anyone would miss him if he finally went alone into the darkened north wing.

As expected, he found his friends sitting at a table outside one of the coffee shops still open. If they weren't one of the few people sitting there Alex would have found them anyways, thanks to Sam. She was wearing her purple knitted cap, which let a little bit of lilac light shine through, a sign that her 'allergy' to places imbued with magick was acting up. And given that the incident took place a few meters beyond the food court, that was to be expected.

"Nice of you to leave me there alone," Alex said, taking a seat.

"We did tell you," Sam replied. "But as usual, you didn't listen."

"No offense," Quentin added. "But when you get to playing that game, you become very obsessive."

"Well," Alex said, "I have always wanted to finish that game, you see…"

"You have told us that story countless times," Sam replied.

"Sorry," Alex said, smiling faintly. It was better if he remained quiet. Everyone remained quiet at the table for a second, until an alarm chimed. Andrea took her phone from her purse and checked the time.

"We need to go, our train leaves soon and we really need to get back to Mercia," Andrea explained.

"You have to?" Alex asked, sad. Spending time with his friends helped to keep him distracted from the thoughts running amok inside his head.

"Our holidays are shorter," Andrea replied. "I need to take advantage of the lab to finish the prototype for the new project and Birm has to return to the Foundation and help Sid."

"Sorry man, I would have wanted to stay longer," Birm said. "But duty calls."

"And I need to return as well," Quentin added. "I need to take the final course for the teaching assistant position."

"We'll walk you to the station," Sam offered. "We have a few more days of holiday. Then we go back to real life."

"Which for you guys might involve saving the world… again." Quentin quipped between sips from his coffee tumbler as they walked across the shopping mall towards the escalators that would take them to street level and to the train station.

"Yeah, I hope not," Sam said. "Once is more than enough."

"Don't look at me," Alex added. "I still have nightmares."

As they left the plaza, Alex waved goodbye to Tyler, the owner of the comic book shop. He noticed a trio of guys, across the hallway, drinking sodas and staring at the shop. Alex had a bad feeling about that and what might happen later that night.

And a part of him was glad. He was looking for a fight.

†††

After walking his friends back to the train station, Alex and Sam returned to the downtown building where Gaby had her apartment. While she was out, traveling with Fionn since their last adventure, Gaby had offered the apartment to Alex and Sam to use whenever they wanted when visiting the capital.

As they entered the two-floor apartment, Sam turned on the lights and hung up her jacket behind the door. The living room was spacious, with long, grey couches flanking a glass table in the center of the room. Beyond the couches, large windows gave way to a balcony that showcased the best of Saint Lucy's skyline and the bay. In the right corner, there was a large plant and a piano, and above it, a TV screen. To the left, a kitchen island bar separated the open space of the kitchen from the living room and the corridor that led to the stairs and the bedrooms above.

"So, the nightmares are back?" Sam asked, as she stretched and walked towards the fridge, to pour some milk into a glass.

"Yup," Alex replied as he went straight to the windows and opened them, then stepped out onto the balcony. He looked on the city until Sam joined him.

"Wanna talk about it?" Sam asked.

"Not really. But thanks." Alex wasn't in the mood to talk about the latest, lousy dream he'd had. In fact, he hadn't been in the mood to talk for several weeks. And he knew Sam suspected something was wrong, because she stared at him, as if trying to pierce his soul with her gaze.

"I'm going to bed to read a bit," Sam said, not pressing the issue. "Are you gonna stay up?"

"Maybe. I'm wondering if I should take a walk later on and enjoy the city lights, clear my mind and get tired enough to allow me to sleep. Besides, I don't visit Saint Lucy very often. I wish I could live here full time," Alex said, spinning on his feet enjoying the views that the main streets could offer from the balcony. "But first I need to solve that pesky issue of my visa renewal..."

"You are making no sense, but ok," Sam replied. "And

please, don't stay up the whole night."

"Can't promise anything," Alex said with a smirk.

† † †

After Sam went upstairs, Alex left the apartment, with a duffle bag and Yaha, his Tempest Blade, sheathed on the back of the vest he was wearing. He ran back to the shopping mall, hoping to make it in time. If it was empty before, this time it felt like a graveyard. Which fit Alex's plans perfectly. He entered one of the bathrooms near the multi-story parking lot. Alex put the goggles and the bracers on and folded the duffle bag into a pocket hanging from his belt. Finally, he tied the holster that contained his collapsible bow and its arrow cartridges to his left calf. Just in case, he put the comms bean into his right ear. He looked at himself into the mirror and smiled, as the glow of his irises increased, signaling that the Gift was being activated. What better way to test his proto-type combat gear than beating up a group of criminals?

He ran toward the shopping mall and from the upper floor of the parking lot, looked down, and saw a van parked outside the back door access to the shops. The men he had seen casing the comic shop were removing boxes and bags from several stores.

Seems that I arrived a bit late. I hope they haven't injured anyone, Alex thought.

His phone vibrated with a call and connected automatically to the comm in his ear. He didn't bother to see who it was. He knew exactly who it was.

"Where are you?" Sam asked, annoyed.

"Taking a stroll," Alex replied, trying to sound nonchalant as he observed the men below.

"If that's true, why did you take Yaha and your bow with you?"

"In case of an incursion?" Alex shrugged, as if she could see him.

"I see you," Sam replied. "You left your laptop plugged into the city's security video feed. The Justicar license is not for you to abuse."

"Says the person that is currently in my bedroom," Alex

waved at the camera watching him.

"Please tell me you are not planning to keep competing with that guy from Kyôkatô to see who is the better vigilante?" Sam asked, her tone of voice betraying her exasperation.

"Hero," Alex corrected her. "We are competing to see who does more heroic things."

"I really want to have a word with the friend of yours that put you up to this."

Alex barely paid attention to Sam, his focus on the men below, who seemed to be almost finished packing the van with the stolen goods. Alex's blood boiled. He hated criminals that preyed on hard working people. And it wasn't as if the tenants of that shopping mall were having great sales lately. Between the incident and Byron's attack, Saint Lucy was still recovering. Alex calculated the distance of the jump, as his heart beat like a drum. To calm his nerves, he started narrating.

"In a city riddled with crime," Alex said, with a gruff voice.

"Please tell me you are not narrating out loud as if you were in one of those old movies," Sam said through the comms. "Alex, this is not a movie, you can get hurt."

"Sorry, I have to go," Alex replied. "Enjoy the show. Save the video."

Alex pressed the button on the comms and hung up. He looked down. Heights still gave him pause. But jumping down would be faster than running down three floors. By the time he arrived there, the robbers would be long gone. In hindsight, having a vantage point to keep an eye on those guys hadn't been the best idea. Alex drew air to calm himself. Something he had learned last year was that he could survive these falls if he focused enough. He had the Gift on his side. A second deep breath, and he cleared his mind to allow the Gift to grow inside him from a small ball of energy into a storm that powered his body.

Alex jumped from the third floor of the parking lot, using the Gift to slow the fall, and landed on top of the van, leaving a large dent. The noise startled the robbers, who stopped what they were doing, dropping the stolen boxes from the comic book shop.

"Who are you?" one of the robbers asked, startled.

"A hero who rises to beat the crap out of criminals like you," Alex stood up, pointing at the man.

"Is this guy for real?" a second robber asked the first.

"A movie by Silver Harvest," Alex continued narrating. "Soon in theatres."

"Where did you came from?" a third robber asked.

"I can tell you, it wasn't from that sewer," Alex looked at his opponents, four grown, burly men in ski masks. One was carrying a bat. He smiled. There was no need for him to draw Yaha or even his bow. He wanted to win, but in a fair fight. And he didn't want to kill them, just hurt them some.

"Since you don't seem to be carrying heat, I will go easy on you."

Alex jumped from the van's rooftop with a double kick, hitting the two closest robbers in the face. He landed with ease, standing in a combat guard position, left hand and leg in front, leading, right hand and leg back. Both hands in a fist. A third robber ran towards Alex, trying to hit him with the bat. Alex pivoted slightly and caught the bat with his left hand. He took a moment to see the brand and the signature on the bat.

"A Pepe Cansino bat? Tell me you didn't pay money for this," Alex broke the bat with ease and punched the robber in the face with his right hand. "No, I'm pretty sure you stole it because no one would pay money for this shit."

Alex then threw the broken half of the bat he was holding into the head of one of the robbers he had kicked, knocking him down once more. The three remaining robbers attacked all at once. Alex blocked the attacks to his left and right with both forearms, and then jumped to kick the one in the middle in the face, breaking his nose. The robber to his right charged once more at Alex, who received him with a strong kick to the stomach. The impact made the man throw up. Alex then proceeded to punch the robber to his left with a right hook straight into the union between the jaw and the skull. A crunching noise was heard.

"Sorry 'bout that. I guess you will have to eat through a

straw the next few months," Alex said as he stood in the middle of four large adults knocked out cold, lying on the ground. A few whimpers echoed in the parking lot.

He heard a click and he sensed a small explosion of energy.

Alex barely had time to dodge the bullet, leaning to his right. The projectile impacted on the van behind him. A fifth robber, who had come out from the back door of the shop looked startled, and his shaking hand pressed the trigger three more times.

Alex tried something very, very stupid and risky. Focusing the Gift, he reached with his mind to the electromagnetic field that emanated from his body when he was 'on'. The same energy that fed his vest. Extending his hands, he directed the electromagnetic field to make it stronger in front of him. It felt like trying to push water. The more he pushed, the more resistance the field offered. But the small amount Alex managed to nudge it was more than enough, as it deflected the bullets away from him.

Alex let go of the electromagnetic field, causing a faint crackle in the air.

"That was awesome," Alex stared at his hands in disbelief. "To be honest I never expected for that to work."

"You're a monster!" The man said, throwing the gun towards Alex, who deflected it with his left hand. He barely registered the impact. It seemed that his use of the Gift was improving after Fionn's training sessions at Ravenhall last year.

"Hey! That's not nice," Alex complained, as he saw the man running away. "I guess no more Mister Nice Guy with him."

Alex drew his collapsible bow and extended it. Electric currents ran across the string. As he drew the string, an arrow, made from the same material as the bow, formed between his hands. The arrow was electrically charged as well. Alex let the man run a few meters and then released the arrow, hitting him in the left buttock. Between the electric discharge and the shock of having an arrow in his body, the man fell into the ground, face first.

"My aim is off. I was aiming for the right leg," Alex muttered, and he collapsed his bow and put it in the holster strapped to his left leg. "Right, Ty."

Alex went inside the shop and found Tyler alive, but with a gash on his forehead, tied and gagged. Alex cut the ties and went to the first aid kit below the counter. He pulled out a cotton ball and poured alcohol on it, then gave the cotton ball to Tyler. Tyler applied it on his gash and winced. Alex knelt next down to help him clean the wound.

"I'm glad that you are alive," Alex said. "You were lucky."

"They robbed me, that's not lucky," Tyler replied ruefully.

"But you are alive. That's why I say that you are lucky," Alex said. "And your merchandise and money are in their van, parked in the back, surrounded by the unconscious bodies of those idiots. I do suggest you call the cops."

"I triggered the silent alarm as soon as they entered. The police must be on their way."

"That's my cue to leave," Alex stood up, and then helped Tyler to get up as well.

"Come by next week, there will be a 'thank you' present in your pull box."

"I don't know what you mean, good citizen," Alex looked the other way.

"I'm not blind nor stupid," Tyler replied with a smile. "The mask and goggles don't fool anybody. If you are planning to keep doing this, you need a voice modulator."

"Fine," Alex said, leaving through the back door to ensure the robbers remained unconscious. The moans continued and that gave Alex quite the satisfaction. At least this time he had an opportunity to take out his anger issues with deserving targets. And that ameliorated his depression somewhat.

He ran towards the other end of the parking lot and left the mall through one of the few open stairs taking him to the street level. As he went up the stairs, he pulled back his hood and took off his goggles. The streets were almost empty, but Alex preferred to not risk being seen and took alleys and side streets in order to reach Gaby's apartment. After taking a last back alley behind the School of Media and Communications—with its transmission towers lit in red every night—Alex would reach River Salmon Road Street and the Steam Clock, which meant he was a five minute walk from the apartment.

But the alley's exit was blocked by a guy standing there, looking at him.

"I would appreciate it if you let me pass," Alex said in a calm voice. No point in picking a fight with a drunkard.

"I can't do that," the man replied, as he kicked the trashcans. "I was expecting you."

"Me?" Alex asked, confused. He had never seen the man before. "I'm sorry, but I have no idea what you are talking about. And I'm late for an appointment."

"But not late enough to punch the lights out of those guys, Alejandro León," the man replied.

The fact that the man knew what Alex had done earlier, put him on the defensive. The fact that the man knew Alex's name, put him on edge.

"Who are you?" Alex asked, as he clenched his fists. This didn't bode well.

"My name is Xavier Roché, of the Roché School of fencing, you might have heard of me," the man beamed when he said that. Alex would have found that endearing, if it wasn't for the unsettling vibe the whole encounter was giving him.

"No. Not really," Alex replied, confused.

"Peasant. Your gifts may allow you to ignore those that can oppose you. But I assure you, after tonight, you won't be able to forget me."

"Look, no offense but I don't know you and I'm sure I haven't done anything to you. So why don't you leave the way you came and call it even."

"I'm afraid that's not possible," Xavier said. "See, I have a problem with your kind. So, either you face me now, or I will force you... by having my fun with those passers-by."

Xavier beamed when he said that and flourished a sword with a few swings to the people walking at the end of the alley. Alex turned around and saw a group of college kids loudly yelling and celebrating something. He turned back to face Xavier. The man's face didn't indicate he was joking. As much as he hated it, Alex knew what he had to do.

"Sigh, fine. But let's take it somewhere else, with more space and less civilians. Like the beach a few blocks from here."

"Lead the way," Xavier shrugged. "But don't think to escape."

"Didn't cross my mind," Alex replied as he walked towards the beach.

They reached the sidewalk that oversaw the beach, on the part where the Breen joined the ocean. Alex jumped over the rail that separated the sidewalk from the beach, while Xavier cut the chain blocking the entrance. The air was cold, with a gentle breeze filling it with the salty smell of the sea. The street lamps were in need of a change, as their light was of a sickly orange color that Alex always found depressing. In front of him, behind Xavier, there was a tall building with an attached parking lot. The building seemed to be derelict.

Have to be careful, Alex thought. *A stray hit and that thing could fall on us.*

The sand didn't offer much of a footing, so Alex widened his stance to secure his balance.

Xavier held his sword up, hilt even with his face, and gave Alex a chance to see it better. It was a kind of rapier— one that Alex had only seen in history books—with an intricate crossguard and a thick blade. Seemingly a showman, he jumped and danced on his spot, followed by adopting a posture of classical Ionis fencing: sword on his dominant hand, the right one. Same feet in front and the left one behind. Xavier's left hand was free, acting as a counterweight. His armor emitted faint specs of light with each little jump. The armor looked old, downright ancient, but from a flexible metal and designed for maximum speed, rather than full body coverage, protecting only certain parts of the body, such as forearms, shin guards, shoulders, chest and crotch. Alex had seen one of those before in action. It was titanarmor. Alex wasn't impressed and not amused. Nothing of this impromptu duel was amusing. But the fact that this guy was wearing titanarmor meant that Alex couldn't take him lightly. Learning to wear and use titanarmor with proficiency took years of training and a patron that could afford both armor and training.

Alex drew Yaha from the scabbard attached to the back of his vest. He held it with both hands. While he was not as good as Fionn or Gaby in the sword wielding department, he hoped that his skills would be good enough to get him out of this. He wasn't sure why he'd agreed to this silly duel: out of concern that this maniac might hurt someone innocent, or because a part of him wanted the fight. He knew deep down this was irresponsible, but lately, Alex didn't care much about that. As long as whatever he was doing kept him distracted from the rush of thoughts in his head, he would be in. His reaction to those times when his depression got the best of him, was to push forward, with his work, or a hobby, or in this case, with a duel against an unknown swordsman decked in titanarmor. Which meant that this guy was able to give him a real fight. The last one he had was on board the Bestial.

Yaha's blade reflected the lights of the LED lamps on the beach. Breathing deeply, he reactivated the Gift and Yaha glowed with a faint golden light. While the intensity of the glow didn't compare to Black Fang's when Fionn was fully concentrated, nonetheless it was quite a sight.

"I see you are wearing titanarmor. It must be really old," Alex said.

"Not as old as that sword of yours," Xavier replied, as the armor began to glow around the edges with white light, as it powered up.

"I would hate to damage it. So last chance to retire. No harm, no foul," Alex offered, still holding Yaha at his side, the tip aiming at the sand.

"I would be worried if you were as good as you think you are," Xavier said with a smile. The kind of smile you would expect from a serial killer. Normally Alex wouldn't be scared, but this guy was in titanarmor, which meant he at least had the power, if not the skill, to back up his words. But Alex wasn't planning to retreat now. He had the Gift and that should suffice, hopefully, to get out of this problem. Alex always said to himself that he would get out of any problem eventually.

"Your choice, your funeral," Alex shrugged.

"No. It will be yours!" Xavier yelled at Alex.

Alex and Xavier ran at each other, swords ready for the clash. The hit sent shockwaves into the water. Alex's arms hurt from blocking the attack.

This guy is not joking around, Alex thought. The strength behind Xavier's slash was enough to rattle Alex's bones. In hindsight, maybe rushing to close the distance hadn't been such a good idea. Xavier's attacks increased in number, speed and strength, forcing Alex to remain in a defensive position, only able to parry, deflect and block the attacks, most aimed to his chest or his neck. The same weak spots an incursion had. If he wasn't so busy trying to remain alive, Alex could have even admired his technique. While not on par to Fionn's, Xavier seemed to be good enough to give Fionn a good fight.

That's it, Alex thought. He changed his approach and using the Gift, jumped back to give himself more space and rethink his strategy, changing his stance. *If this guy is as good and fast as Fionn, then I need to fight him with a similar approach.*

Alex took a defensive stance and waited for his opponent. Xavier smiled once more and ran at Alex, jumping to land with a slashing attack aimed at Alex's head. Alex pivoted on his right leg and parried the attack. He then took a step back. While Fionn hadn't given him a more in-depth training with the sword, he had at least taught Alex the basics back at Ravenhall. The rest would have to be done with clever use of the Gift and his own muscle memory, which for some reason recalled and guided him to make movements he had never tried nor practiced before, but were clear in his head since almost the day he was reborn.

If I get out of this, I will have to ask Fionn for more lessons, Alex thought. *I shouldn't have hung up on Sam, I could use some help now.*

Alex focused the Gift, to allow himself to follow the trail of neuronal electric discharges across Xavier's muscles and that helped him to predict, or at least guess what kind of attack his rival would use. That allowed Alex to control the fight on his own terms, enabling him to deflect all the attacks until an opening presented itself. Xavier's last slash had left him open and Alex used that to hit him in the left side of the chest. Alex had hit with enough force to crack the armor, but not with all his strength, as he wasn't planning to cut the man in half, just damage the armor and break a few ribs to deter him from continuing the fight, like he did with the robbers. But Xavier barely flinched at that, looking more annoyed than worried. As if he was mad at himself rather than with Alex.

"Showing mercy to your rival when he makes a mistake might give you the moral high ground, but it's a stupid thing to do," Xavier said. "You caught me off guard and you could have finished this faster and in your favour. But you wasted the opportunity."

"I don't want to kill you," Alex replied, taking a defensive stance, and trying to see the discharges, but the armor was creating interference, cloaking the neuronal transmissions.

"But you were happy to put those robbers in the hospital. Isn't that being hypocritical?" Xavier mused.

"Those guys were hurting people, probably killing those who resisted them. Getting them off the streets was the idea," Alex replied. "But you? I don't know you or what you have done. Or what I have done to piss you off."

"And that's the problem. You haven't done anything. And yet you have those abilities that make you feel that you are superior to us. Judge, Jury and Executioner. What gives you the right?"

"You don't know me either, so don't assume things. I'm not superior to anyone," Alex replied as he blocked an attack by Xavier. Both blades were locked in a struggle of strength.

"In that, I agree. I admit you are good," Xavier said pushing his blade against Yaha with such strength that the latter's edge made a small cut in Alex's chin. "But you are nowhere as good as you think you are and certainly not as good as the Greywolf."

"So...ughh..." Alex struggled to push back. "You weren't looking for a fight with me, but with Fionn."

"No," Xavier replied. "I wanted a fight with you both. Your kind, the Gifted. I just wanted to see if he was as good a teacher as swordsman. But I'm starting to wonder if you might be a really bad student."

"What?" Alex was taken aback by the comment, failing to stop Xavier from kicking him in the right knee, seriously injuring it and making him lose his balance. Alex gritted his teeth at the pain, trying to regain his footing. But by then it was too late. With a swift move, Xavier disarmed him, sending Yaha flying through the air and cleaving a rock behind Alex. Xavier pushed Alex to the ground and aimed to cut off his head with one strike.

"Aww crap!"

Impotent, Alex could only watch the blade coming at him in slow motion, getting ready to roll to his side and hopefully avoid losing his head. But as he made his move, a green light crossed his line of sight, stopping Xavier's strike with such strength that even the crazy swordsman reeled back in pain.

Xavier, visibly upset turned to see who the interloper was that had blocked his strike. Alex simply smiled in relief for the last second save. If the glowing green fangsword wasn't a dead giveaway, the appearance of the man was: tall, tanned, athletic, with long brown hair and big, piercing green eyes, proper of the Freefolk. Wearing red sneakers and jeans. But the two most unnerving things were the way his irises glowed with an intense green hue, and the smile. It wasn't a friendly one. Nor one born of amusement due a potential fight. It was the kind of smile that a wolf regales you with when it is planning to rip your head off and enjoy it. Alex saw Xavier sweating profusely and his sword trembled slightly. His smile was gone. Alex was glad that he was on good terms with his mentor. And felt pity for his opponent.

"I give you three seconds to leave him alone before you find yourself holding your own head in your hands," Fionn said with a low, grave voice. More like a growl than a sentence.

Xavier lowered his sword and took a few steps back, not muttering a single word, unlike before. Alex sighed in relief.

For such was the fame that preceded the Greywolf. The

living legend, the one-man army, the ageless Greywolf that rides with the wind. Fionn Estel had arrived. And with a smile and a single sentence defused the fight. He was not happy.

"It's an honor to finally meet you, Greywolf," Xavier said. "I would love to fight you as well. But one duel per night is enough. Besides if I hurt you now, I will be in serious troubles with my employer."

Xavier then turned to Alex.

"I hope you improve in the following six months. I could use a proper warm up before I go for the head of the Greywolf."

"I'm here, no need to wait," Fionn said with calm voice. He readied Black Fang.

"I want nothing more than that," Xavier replied, as he sheathed his sword and powered down his armor, the glow on its edges dimmed slowly until it disappeared. "But as I said, I would get into problems with my boss if I did it before the Games. See you there."

Xavier turned his back and walked away into the streets, getting lost between the shadows. Alex saw Fionn tightening his grip around Black Fang, until Gaby approached him and put a hand on his shoulder.

"Let him go," Gaby said. "You will probably see him there and then you can teach him a lesson. But for now, let's be glad that Alex is fine and let's tend to his injuries."

Fionn's grip loosened, his expression relaxed, and he sheathed Black Fang. He turned back and extended a hand to Alex.

"Friend of yours?" Alex asked, smiling as he took Fionn's hand, trying to break the tension. "Because he knew a lot about me and the Gift. And he was wearing titanarmor."

Fionn didn't seem amused. Alex gulped.

"You and I will have a long talk, Alejandro," Fionn said, as he helped Alex to stand up and walk. The knee hurt badly, but it wasn't broken or dislocated. Which meant it would heal faster, thanks to the Gift, although not as fast as it would for Fionn, who probably would have recovered from the injury in a matter of seconds. Alex's knee would heal in a few days. But that was the least of his problems.

Judging by his tone, and Gaby's sour expression, Alex knew he was in serious trouble.

But at least he was alive.

Not like that mattered to him.

† † †

"What the hell were you thinking?" Fionn yelled at Alex, visibly furious. So furious, that he had been pacing the living room from the moment they arrived. It was a good thing that his eyes were his normal green and not his 'glowing green eyes of doom' as Alex had taken to calling them. All of them were sitting in the apartment's living room. Harland had just arrived, as Fionn scolded Alex. This had been going on for fifteen minutes.

"That's the thing, he has been thinking," Sam interjected. Her brow frowned and she bit her lip, her face was a mix of concern and anger. "He has been moonlighting as a vigilante for the past few weeks."

"You say moonlight," Alex replied, annoyed. What he did on his own time was his business, and as long as he didn't put anyone but himself at risk it should not be a problem. It was not like Fionn was his father or his big brother. Sometimes Alex wondered if a part of Fionn confused him with Ywain. And he was tired of being compared to his ancestor. "I say test run for this vest, a prototype armor that is flexible but hardens when it receives an impact. No more need for titanarmors exclusive of a few people. It will save lives in the next incursions."

"And that test run includes beating people up?" Gaby asked, as she pressed her right hand to her right temple.

"Criminals that assaulted an honest merchant," Alex said. "They deserved it. And after it, I went for a nice walk. Not my fault that a crazy guy wanted to challenge me to get to you." He pointed to Fionn, who stopped his pacing. The anger was gone

"What do you mean?" Fionn asked, rapidly blinking and squishing his eyebrows together.

"That psycho said that he wanted to test me and you," Alex replied.

"You could have said no," Harland finally spoke. "You don't have to take every challenge."

"I did! But he threatened a group of innocent college students if I didn't accept. Was I supposed to let him hurt them?" Alex asked Harland, letting some of his frustration out. He turned back to Fionn. "Some challenges have to be answered when innocent people are at risk. It seems that he has a grudge against you, that he wants to settle at the Chivalry Games, but, there are none to be held, right?"

"About that..." Fionn said.

"No way, really?" Alex asked, opening his eyes wide, his heart pounding inside his chest. The Chivalry Games, created after the Great War, were a specialized tournament that took place in the triennial diplomatic talks between members of the Free Alliance and their allies or commercial partners such as the Kuni, and occasionally, the Samoharo. In them the best fighters—usually titanfighters decked out in their mystical armor—competed to prove who was the best, and at the same time, represented the interests of the city states that drafted or hired them. Some, if not all the duels, were used to settle disputes between diplomats by using their proxy champions. It was a better way than declaring war, like the Old Kingdoms used to do. Plus, there was the fact that before each duel, the fighters had to reach the arena by going through a special course designed for each duel—which meant that rarely a course was the same for any two duels—and that added excitement to the spectacle. Alex had dreamt about participating in the Games, or at least attending a live duel. But the Straits rarely participated—leaving their neighbors the Samoharo or the Kuni to represent them—and he wouldn't be hired by any city state of the Alliance, as he didn't own titanarmor.

"Yes, there are upcoming diplomatic talks hosted by the Kuni Empire and the Freefolk are sending a delegation and a team of champions to represent them," Harland added.

Even better, Alex thought, as the Kuni were famous for their insane courses. It would be quite a spectacle. Then it dawned on him. This might be his only chance to participate, if the Freefolk were looking for champions. There were only three available spots per delegation. Maybe the Free-folk would send Fionn, who was the most obvious choice. And maybe Sam, given that she was the most gifted magus of the Freefolk. That meant that there was a spot open, so unless they had another fighter ready—unlikely after what happened last year—they might ask him or Gaby. And Gaby wasn't a fan of the Games.

"I guess that without a Dragonking, you and Sam will represent the Freefolk," Alex said.

"Yes," Fionn replied. "But I won't fight. I'm attending as diplomat."

Alex was taken aback.

"Are they sure they want you as diplomat? I mean, you can be kinda mean as a teacher when you are not in the mood, so..." Alex said.

"I told them the same," Fionn shrugged his shoulders. "But the Gathering of the Elders decided that, according to them, I have more experience dealing with the Alliance and its politics and thus, I would be more useful as diplomat, helping the rest of the delegation, than by bashing heads. So, Sam will fight, alongside Gaby and Sid."

"Gaby?" Alex looked at Gaby. "I thought you didn't like the Games? Although you are the best there is. I know I'd put my money on you getting the crown."

"Thank you," Gaby smiled her crooked smile at him, blushing as well. "And yes, I'm not a fan of the Games. However, the Elders asked me directly as a favor. I'm as shocked as you are, but I couldn't say no. Right now, all of their capable fighters are guarding their settlements from attacks by any possible followers of Byron. And there is no way I will fight for Portis. You know why."

"As I said, I get that. But Sid? Is he even eligible?" Alex asked, dejected. Sid was a good fighter, good enough that he had taught Alex to fight with decent success. But he was also lazy and rarely paid attention to any kind of competition. Unlike Alex, who could get very competitive, even playing a board game. And a dark thought wormed its way into his mind as Alex wondered why he hadn't been asked to be part of the team.

Did I insult the Freefolk in some way with my questions at Ravenstone? Or did Mekiri find out I took the data cube from Ravenhall? Alex thought, as he stared at the palms of his hands. *Or maybe I'm not good enough. I never am.*

"My guess is that he made quite an impression with one of the professors from Ravenhall," Sam replied, taking Alex out of his reverie. She offered a faint smile at him, as if she could guess what was going on in his head. "I suspect she proposed him because of that. After all, she asked me for Sid's contact details."

"The lady with the green hair in a pompadour?" Harland asked.

"Professor Ortiga," Sam corrected him.

"Does she have a crush on him?" Alex asked, surprised.

"Are you surprised because he is a Samoharo and she a freefolk?" Sam's expression changed, with a curling lip.

"What? No, of course not!" Alex replied, waving his hands defensively in front of him. "Who do you think I am? I'm surprised because he's, well... Sid. He is my best friend, but you have to admit he's an acquired taste. And is he eligible?"

"An acquired taste like you," Sam replied, visibly annoyed.

"As he is an outcast of the Samoharo," Fionn explained, "technically he is a free agent. He can fight in representation of anyone he wants. Actually, the rules have changed a bit, so unless you are drafted to represent your region or city state, you are open to fight for anyone. That's how Gaby is able to represent the Freefolk and not Portis."

"I see..." Alex replied, looking down at his feet. If he had any small chance to get into the team, he'd ruined it by angering Sam, probably the only person who could have plead his case. "Sam, it's good you will be participating. It will make things interesting for once, instead of the usual Solarian Knight or someone from Montsegur or the Seven Snakes.

"If you need help training," Alex paused and sighed, offering a half-hearted smile, "or with equipment let me know." He felt a void inside his chest. Like when he was a kid, he never was picked to play with others' teams.

"Ahem..." Harland interjected, walking towards Alex and patting him on the shoulder. "I think you will be too busy with your own training. So, cut it with the sad dog face."

"What?" Alex asked, almost jumping from his seat.

"The Foundation was asked by the Kuni and the Samoharo of all beings to be part of the talks as a neutral party, which means I get to take a team too, to help me beat into the heads of those stubborn politicians that the though of splitting the Alliance right now is a bad idea."

"I didn't know that. I assume the meeting wasn't a pleasant one," Fionn said, shaking his head.

"The Thain is not a fan of yours, of any of us," Harland replied with a smile.

"Tell me something I don't know," Fionn said.

"Anyways," Harland made a long pause, as if he was thinking. Probably he was wondering if it was a good idea to have asked Alex to be his champion after tonight's fiasco. Harland had to admit that Alex lacked some impulse control and the Games were as much a metal affair as a physical contest. "I was hoping that you could get Alex in shape for the Games, because from what I'm gathering, he is still in no shape to take on those guys."

"I resent that, I held my own last year," Alex replied, narrowing his eyes and crossing his arms.

"There is no denying that," Fionn said, stroking his chin. "But you also got pretty badly beaten up and from what you told us, the guy was mostly brute force. Here we are talking professionally trained titanfighters, monster hunters, and in some cases, killers for hire. Like that swordsman you just fought. And while the rules forbid anyone from killing their opponents directly, accidents happen, and you could get seriously injured. I'm not taking any chance that someone gets the best of you, Gift or not. Safety comes first."

"I'm not a child, you know?" Alex replied. He could take care of himself. He had survived an incursion with no training. He had beaten an enhanced behemoth of a man without using much of the Gift. And had helped everyone to escape Ravenstone while keeping Gaby from slipping into the 'Ice State'. The Games, while tough, were something he could cope with. But he had to admit to himself that training wouldn't be a bad idea. It was the way it was being offered that had hurt him. "So, another infamous training session with Fionn? Although this time it won't be in a mystical library. And we actually have time to do it properly. Sounds fun doesn't it, Gaby?"

"Actually, I won't be going with you. I'm training Sam separately for the next few months," Gaby said, standing up and sitting next to Sam, patting her leg.

"Why do you get to train Sam on your own?" Alex asked.

"What do you think I've been doing all these months traveling with Fionn?" Gaby replied, raising her voice.

"Do you really want me to guess?" Alex said, tilting his head to the left and staring directly into Gaby's eyes. Gaby started to blush, and her eyes opened as she caught the meaning of Alex's words. Sam looked first at Alex, then at Gaby and opened her eyes, wide.

"Eww!" Sam exclaimed. "You are talking about my dad and my best friend! That's not something I want to imagine. Ever. No offense new mom... I mean, Gaby!"

"Ha, ha, very funny you two," Gaby said, crossing her arms.

"That still leaves me with a problem. I'm two fighters short," Harland interrupted.

"You could always hire Bev Johnson. He is a former champion and I heard he is a stand-up guy. Or Martina the Moon Hammer," Alex offered. He knew a decent amount of information about titanfighters.

"They were already hired by Manfeld," Harland replied. "Same with Simon Belerofont. That might be the team to beat to be honest."

"Hmmm," Alex stroked his chin.

"Great! He is thinking again," Sam said, shaking her head.

"You know, I might have someone in mind for the team," Alex smiled at Harland.

"Who?"

"A friend of mine, who might know of someone else. They are really good."

"Do we know these friends? Are they trustworthy?" Fionn asked. Always the cautious one. Alex guessed it was the experience talking.

"Hey, I know people outside this little group," Alex replied. "And yes, they are."

"I'm gonna regret this, aren't I?" Harland pinched the bridge of his nose.

But Alex was already walking towards the balcony, as he dialed a number.

"Forget it, he's already making the phone call."

Alex barely listened to the subsequent comments. He was busy calling Kasumi. She didn't pick up, so he did the next best thing, wrote a lengthy message.

"This will be fun," Alex muttered. For the first time in months, he felt happy and excited about something. It was a welcome change.

† † †

After the others went to sleep, Harland went to the kitchen for a glass of milk and found Fionn on the balcony, staring at the skyline of Saint Lucy, with the Crystal Towers on the other side of the bay.

"Nice night," Harland said as he stood next to his friend.

"For once," Fionn replied, and then pointed to the sky. "I mean you can see both the Round and the Long moons. And the rings. When was the last time the rings were that visible from the ground? And in a city?"

"Maybe because half of the city is still under repairs and the power has not been restored everywhere. I thought that north of the Scar it was easier to see the planet's rings," Harland replied.

"Not that much, the northern lights kinda mess with that," Fionn explained, as he leaned on the handrail. "To get the best sight of the rings, you need to go south, around the equator. The best place is on the top of the Courtain mountain range."

"You sound tired," Harland said. He noticed the bags under Fionn's eyes. Healing factor or not, a sleepless night took a toll.

"I'm..." Fionn sighed. He inhaled a deep breath. "I haven't been able to sleep well lately. That's why I'm here, so I can let Gaby sleep without me waking her up."

Harland took a deep breath as well, the sea breeze and cold air filling his lungs as he looked around. There were few people walking on the streets below at that time of the night. One of them, a runner, was making his third or fourth pass below the building. Harland was a tad suspicious. He went inside, took a small metal cylinder from his jacket and returned to Fionn, who looked at him confused. Harland activated the device and a small red light turned on. While Harland didn't notice anything, Fionn frowned. The jamming frequency was supposed to be imperceptible to humans, but it seemed that Freefolk did notice. That, or the Gift really enhanced Fionn's hearing.

"Can't you hear the buzz?" Fionn asked, as he opened and closed his mouth.

"No. But if you do, it means it's working," Harland replied. "We need to talk."

"Is that what I think it is?"

"Yes, one of Alex's friends was kind enough to improve the design. It should block any microphone or long-range listening device."

"Something is wrong isn't it?" Fionn sighed.

"I've been thinking..." Harland paused. "On how the first shot of a war is often the most silent. A low key action."

"And how people stop looking at what's important for all, to focus only on what's important for their particular interests? Yes. I've been there." Fionn replied. "Politics has a peculiar way of getting in the middle of things. And you think the first shot has already been fired?"

"Well, that's the thing, we might not have friends with part of the Alliance, or the Crown anymore," Harland said, cutting to the chase. "While it was unspoken at the 'pleasant' meeting I had, the fact that Arthur is taking an active role in the talks and policy means one thing."

"Succession is on the table," Fionn said.

"I guess last year's events took a bigger toll on the Queen's health than suspected."

"It was to be expected."

"I know you are already used to matters of succession," Harland said. "And for the record, when they asked, I said what I assumed would be your position: the return of the Freefolk ancestral lands if they want your cooperation."

"Thank you," Fionn replied with a half-smile that betrayed his exhaustion. "I thought the crown prince is your friend. Same with Lady Sarah, so why the concern?"

"They are... they were. I can't be sure." Harland stammered, as his mind tried to recall and analyze every detail of the meeting. He looked around, but the streets were empty. The runner had left the area.

"You seem worried," Fionn observed. "Or confused. I don't see you that way that often."

"I guess..." Harland paused. "Uh, I guess a part of me is hoping to change Arthur's mind at the talks, when we are far from Doncelles' influence. I know he will understand what is going on. And Doncelles is not a bad man. I don't like him, but I don't think he is acting on bad faith, he is just being a politician, finding the best way to deal with the fallout of a big secret being exposed. But I did have a tense meeting with them and the Thain is not our fan at the moment. He got a bit threatening with the immigration status of Alex and Sid."

Fionn's expression changed. As mad as he was at Alex, he still worried about him.

"Why am I not surprised. That means..."

"We have to plan accordingly to what we have been discussing," Harland said. "Move up the timetable. I know you prefer running things from secrecy or infighting from a defensive position. And I hope it doesn't come to that but..."

"We have to plan for that scenario, instead of letting things happen to us. Prepare for the actual war to come rather than having to deal first with politics," Fionn said, as he turned to face the inside of the apartment, and let his back and elbows rest on the handrail of the balcony.

"Indeed. I don't think Doncelles is seeing the whole picture here. Nor the Alliance."

"That Byron was the first shot in a new war?" Fionn asked.

"Perhaps," Harland mused, as he stroked his chin. "But I can't shake this feeling that as much as Byron was important, there is something else going on."

Fionn remained silent. Harland guessed that his words might have hurt his friend, as Byron was a touchy subject for Fionn, even if the latter had vanquished that particular demon. But the scars remained. Fionn smiled at him.

"If I'm being honest, I have been thinking the same," Fionn explained, turning again to face the streets. A breeze blew gently over the place. "Byron was a serious threat. And I'm glad that he is finally gone. But there was something he told me before I took his head, which has been rolling inside my head ever since. Something about the Creeping Chaos and the Golden King. That can't be good."

"I assume that's why you have been traveling so much of the past year," Harland said.

"Yeah," Fionn replied. "Gaby knows this too; she noticed the hour we started the trip. We have been looking for clues, for signs, but we haven't found anything and that is bothering me. Too silent. Which is why I concur; we need to move the timetable."

"However, this time the island won't be a safe haven," Harland said.

"Not all of the island," Fionn said. "There are parts of the island under the crown's purview. There is a place..."

"The northern point," Harland replied, knowing to which place Fionn was referring.

"The northern point. Under the treaty, that's technically Freefolk territory, guarded by the Scar."

"I thought you didn't like the idea of going back home," Harland said, surprised at Fionn's suggestion. Returning to his hometown was sort of a sore spot for him. Izia's grave was there, too. Harland had made sure she got buried in a nice plot at the local graveyard, after he found her remains next to Fionn's frozen form. Same with Fionn's mother, grandfather and daughter, as well as Sam's parents. Too many painful memories. He could relate to that. Harland had his own ghosts to deal with.

"I have to go there someday, even if it hurts. Besides,

it's the perfect place to train and set things in motion," Fionn replied with a smile.

"Why are you so sure?"

"Because using it as a base was not my idea and the person behind it had at least half a century to set things in motion."

Harland laughed. "I see now that you got your foresight from your mother."

"Also, the good looks," Fionn added with a smile.

Harland stared at the planetary rings. They, alongside the Moons, were a sight to behold. He was intrigued with visiting Skarabear, Fionn's hometown. Having never been there, Harland wondered what he would find there, in a town where Fionn's mother, Dawnstar, had played an important role to keep it isolated from most of the world.

Maybe a light of hope hidden in a basement, Harland thought.

Chapter 4
The Girl with the Iron Will

"I need a break mom, be right back."

To Kasumi Shimizu, a break was more than due. Or the chaos would threaten to drive her crazy.

The Saikai Shopping Street was bustling as usual. The long, pedestrian road that connected two temples, and their respective distant entrances, was one of the main attractions of Kyôkatô, the capital of the Kuni Empire. Nestled inside one of the oldest districts within the city, Saikai, with its large temples, gardens, and maze of side streets, connected the tourists with the souvenir, the hungry with tasty food, the supplicant with the place of prayer, nature with technology, and the past with the future. Unlike anyplace else in the Kuni Empire, the eclectic mix of the traditional and the new attracted locals and foreigners alike, in a total assault to the senses.

That's why Kasumi took her break in the alley behind her family's shop, turning off her combat-ready hearing aids and closed her eyes, to allow herself a modicum of tranquility. When her hearing aids—two tear-drop shaped, small round beads, one each behind her actual ears, and hidden by her hair—were off, she had a degree of peace and quiet. That helped her to regain focus and keep going during her work shift. It also had the side effect of allowing her to concentrate on an ability taught to demonhunters that few managed to master: perceive the energy trails of people and places. The Kuni believed that objects and places have a soul as much as living beings; everything left a mark in the space. Kasumi preferred to focus on that rather than the bustling of people asking for the nth time how much the Omamoris—good luck amulets—cost. Still, she preferred helping her mother at the temple stall, than working in the curry house with her dad. That was mind numbing hectic during tourist season.

As she slowly breathed in and out, she felt a faint wave hit her. The sensation was like nothing she had felt before. It wasn't coming from the hundreds of tourists, or from the local yôkai—spirits that dwelled around the land, known as fae by the Easterners from Ionis—although there was a degree of familiarity. However, it felt more distressed and aggressive than the local yôkai. They were content to receive whatever treats the tourists or the priests gifted them in exchange for performing in the cultural shows. No, this yôkai was different. Kasumi focused on it, trying to track it, but the gentle hand of her mother rubbing her right shoulder brought her back from her meditation. She lost track of the yôkai.

Kasumi turned around and saw her mom. She turned on her aids. Right after the familiar "booting up" chime, sound came back as a thundering crash. Kasumi had to refocus on her mom.

"I'm sorry, but I need your help. Another bus arrived," Kasumi's mother told her, her cheeks blushing, apologetic.

"It's okay mom," Kasumi said and smiled. She stood up and went back to the front to receive the incoming tourists. *Sorry dad, but yes, this is better than the curry house. Although no better than the job I'm still waiting for,* she thought.

And while working hard, Kasumi waited, both for her dream job and to catch the scent of the yôkai once more.

† † †

As the sun touched the horizon and the artificial lights turned on, the shops at Saikai were already closing. The wind gently played with Kasumi's short hair, styled as an asymmetric bob with bangs with electric blue and grey streaks on the longer side. Kasumi, free from the traditional wardrobe she wore in the shop, now sported sneakers, leggings, a blue t-shirt—with the face of a famous feline Kuni mascot plastered on it—and a large black hoodie vest whose trim ended near her knees. She wandered towards the jobs board near the eastern entrance of the temple. It was where neighbors, priests, and sometimes authorities posted jobs for those that belonged to the select elite known as demonhunters—warrior monks and exorcists that were among the best fighters in the Kuni Empire, on par with the titanfighters of Ionis and the trackers of the Samoharo—an elite to which Kasumi belonged. Even if they weren't so keen to have her within their ranks.

"Don't waste your time, Shimizu!" yelled a young man with broad shoulders in demonhunter garb—black trousers, black uwa-gi, and wooden armor plates over them, all covered by a hoodie not unlike Kasumi's—as he passed by along with two other young men.

"Hey, Kasumi," said Hideaki, another member of that group, thin and with a friendlier smile. "Did you know that there will be Chivalry Games later this year? Due to the summit taking place here. There will be a Kuni team representing us. There will be a casting among younger demonhunters soon, to join the veterans."

"Why did you tell her that? You know the elders won't choose her. They don't think she is fit to represent us. Don't give her false hopes," Fujita said, with a mocking tone.

"Bite me, Fujita," Kasumi replied, ignoring the jeers of the trio that now sat on a bench near the exit of the temple and started to drink. *How disrespectful*, Kasumi thought. And yet they got commissions, while she got barely any calls, and those were usually a personal request from her neighbors who actually saw her potential.

To this day, Kasumi didn't know if the reason the assignment committee had barely given her any tasks since she graduated—top of the class she would like to add—was because of something her family had done in the past, or more hurtful, due to her hearing problems. Regardless, she would have to find a way to prove her worth to those old naysayers, while at the same time making them forget the so-called transgression her family had committed a century ago. Kasumi thought it was dumb for them to condemn her family for doing the right thing, for helping to redeem a powerful yôkai, a foreign one from the Wastelands at that. Especially when the yôkai had proven again and again that he had been worth redeeming.

As lost as she was in her thoughts, Kasumi felt the always reassuring presence of her mom, standing behind her.

"Wouldn't it be easier to check the online message board of the guild, rather than this old thing? You know they take their time to update it."

Kasumi turned to look at her mom. She was wearing comfy street clothes and her hair was pulled back in a ponytail. Behind her gentle smile, Kasumi knew her mother was hiding her sorrow as well. Her parents were good at hiding their worries. But not good enough to fool her.

"I got tired of looking at the online board. And I didn't want to chuck my tablet at the wall in frustration. Not again."

"I would appreciate that. We are still paying for the current one. Anyways, no luck again?" her mother asked.

"I'm afraid not." Kasumi pointed at the three junior demonhunters drinking at the bench. "Then again, those doofuses get commissions."

"I wouldn't consider being part of a show meant to attract tourists a serious commission."

"You know what I mean."

"Don't despair. Life is ripe with opportunities when the time is right. I'm sure you will get yours quite soon. Why don't you go to Electric Town with Joshua after his shift at the restaurant? To let go the frustration at the arcades. Tomorrow might bring new opportunities."

"I sure hope so, because—"

BOOM!

An explosion took down a wall of the temple and several trees. Kasumi's first reaction was to cover her mother with her body. Once the dust settled, she saw an advanced mechanoid—a mechanical body, the size and shape of an adult human, with oily black inserts on its back, a mix between a machine and an organic being—emitting a blue vapor. The design was something new to Kasumi, lithe and athletic, but the glow of the vapor was something she knew: it was a yôkai. To be precise, the one she had felt earlier that day.

"It stole one of the sacred urns! Get him!" one of the priests yelled.

The mechanoid was carrying a metallic cylinder in its left hand, while with the right it deflected the attacks of priests and young demonhunters alike. Its movements were seamless, too fluid to be one of those old, clunky mechanoid designs that Kasumi had once seen at a war museum. It was making short work of the young demonhunters, and once free of their interference, ran towards the other end of the street at an incredible pace.

"Someone needs to stop that," Kasumi said, helping her mother to stand up.

"And that's you?" Fujita asked, reeling in pain.

"Yes," Kasumi replied. Her emphatic reply stunned Fujita into silence. She put a mask over her face. A white cat mask with red details and whiskers. It covered her face from her nose up. She started to run after the possessed mechanical creature.

"Told you that your opportunity would arrive soon!" her mom yelled at Kasumi. "Just don't do something stupid!"

Knowing her mother, Kasumi was sure she was already dialing Joshua, asking him to be sure Kasumi wouldn't do anything stupid.

Spoilsport, Kasumi thought.

† † †

Kasumi ran after the mechanoid. The spirit inside was giving it enough energy to make it run extremely fast. Kasumi pushed hard to reach it. Her lungs burned from the effort, but she was thankful she had brought her running sneakers that day, instead of the high heeled boots she had originally considered.

Running with high heels, who the Pits does that? That movie was totally wrong, Kasumi thought, recalling a movie she had seen last year, on the recommendation from her online friend across the sea. *He really enjoys crappy movies.*

As the mechanoid reached the streets, Kasumi was almost a meter behind it. The thing twisted its head and looked straight at Kasumi. The sight startled her for a second, allowing the mech to regain enough advantage to reach the train station, just when peak time was starting. The mechanoid jumped all over the place, dodging the waves of commuters, while Kasumi had to jump on top of the vending machines to keep pace. She dropped a small silk pouch into the hands of the station supervisor.

"That's for my ticket!" Kasumi yelled at the man as she kept running after her target. Along the way, the creature damaged a capsule toy machine, liberating all its wares over the floor. Kasumi barely evaded the plastic balls—and the commuters that had forgotten about their journey to catch as many of the capsules as they could. Both pursuer and pursued reached the small observation deck on the third floor of the station. Kasumi was almost out of breath but had at least managed to corner the mechanoid. A faint whistle announced the passage of a train on the elevated track a floor below. The mechanoid stood at the edge of the deck. A sense of dread filled Kasumi, giving her a knot in her stomach. This was her last chance to catch it and recover the urn from the temple.

"Don't do it. Don't..." she pleaded to the mechanoid.

A mocking, almost childish sounding laugh was the only reply she got from it, as the thing jumped onto the arriving train's roof.

"Curses!" Kasumi exclaimed, frustrated. She ran towards the edge and jumped onto the rooftop of the train. Falling hard, she struggled to keep her balance and not fall from the train. She managed to grab a rail and pushed up to get her footing back. Kasumi looked below; the street was a long way down from where she was. She could almost hear Joshua's voice, telling her to not do something stupid until he arrived to help. But this was one of the few times she could have the whole action and fun for herself, instead of watching Joshua do all the heavy lifting.

While the train wasn't moving fast, given that the next station—the brand new SkySpire—was close, it was still tricky to keep her balance as it started to brake. Kasumi extended her left leg in front of her, and moved her right leg behind her, slightly bent. Her hips were swaying to the rocking of the train, helping her to keep her footing. Looking around her, she had to admit that the view from her position was beautiful. But focus was needed. Kasumi stared at the mechanoid.

"Look, give me back the cylinder you stole, and I won't banish your ass to beyond the Tempest alright?"

The mechanoid faced her and let out another string of childish laughs. The yôkai inside the machine was mocking her.

"Don't say I didn't warn you," Kasumi replied, as she closed the gap between them with a jump and threw a punch, focusing all of her inner energy into the strike. The mechanoid jumped at the last second, making Kasumi's fist hit the train's roof. The impact left a deep dent in the metal and Kasumi had to roll to one side and then jump backwards, to avoid the fast kicks the mechanoid threw at her.

"You are good. But not good enough," Kasumi said, launching a flurry of kicks of her own. The mechanoid countered and soon they began a rapid exchange of kicks, punches, and blocks, with several blows landing on the train's roof, leaving severe dents.

Every time Kasumi blocked an attack from the mechanoid she could feel the sharp pain of the impact on her bones. For her training as a demonhunter to work she had to remain focused on the inner energy the Kuni believed existed in every living being. She achieved her focus by repeating the mental mantras that asked for help from her ancestors. A demonhunter was a monk, a yogi, a warrior, and a shaman, all rolled up into a body trained to withstand the most extreme physical actions. And that was without their armor. With it on, a demonhunter could best a titanfighter in full regalia. That was why so few finished the arduous training and why even less, just a handful per year, managed to graduate. Kasumi was one of them. She had been called the girl with the iron will, due to her stubbornness. Kasumi came from a long, proud line of demonhunters stretching back for generations, to the founder of the demonhunters, the Storm God, killer of Titans. And as much as she thought Fujita and friends were idiots, she knew they were as good as they came, for they were demonhunters too. That this thing had beaten them, made Kasumi relish the challenge and be wary of its strength.

As she turned to block an incoming attack, the train jumped on the tracks as it stopped in the middle of a bridge, and Kasumi lost her balance. As she struggled to keep her footing, she looked up and found herself facing an incoming kick aimed to her head. A kick that never connected.

The metal leg stopped a few centimeters from Kasumi's face, held in place by a hand. The owner of the hand wasn't happy. The tall, muscular man, with a scar crossing his left cheek, black hair with red streaks and yellow eyes, stared at the mechanoid, and bared his fangs. Dressed in washed out, ripped jeans, combat boots, an orange t-shirt sporting a purple penguin, a black trench coat and leather biker gloves, the man started to crush the metal leg with his hand, filling the air with the crunching noise of crushed polymeric steel. Kasumi saw how the trench coat turned into a living shadow, coming from the man's back, swirling around, and adopting sharp forms that cut the mechanoid's outer layer. From an outsider's perspective, the man, or the thing coming from his back, was acting more like a monster from old legends. A yôkai of yore. But Kasumi had only one question as soon as she regained her composure.

"The penguin t-shirt? Really? It doesn't fit with your heroic badass image."

"Laundry day," Joshua replied.

Kasumi smiled. She didn't need Joshua's help. But she enjoyed working with the man. And he seemingly enjoyed working with her family, a tradition that dated from the Great War and her great grandmother's mission into the buried city of Carpadocci.

They surrounded the mechanoid. It twitched, and its head, arms and legs split in two. Each half of the head stared at Kasumi and Joshua, respectively. It looked like a two headed, four-armed monstrosity.

"Great," Kasumi exclaimed. "Now it looks like a human spider."

"Keep your focus on the hand urn," Joshua said.

"I know what the job is. Thank you," Kasumi replied.

And then the fight resumed.

Both exchanged kicks and blows with the mech at an unnatural speed. Kasumi knew exactly where Joshua was aiming with a punch or an attack from the shroud, and Joshua in turn seemed to know where Kasumi's kicks would land.

The air filled with sounds of metal crunching under the continuous, relentless attacks of the two humans on their mechanical foe.

The mechanoid tried to jump from the roof of the train car, but Joshua's shroud grabbed it by the arm, making it crash back into the roof and ripping off one of the arms. Kasumi spun on her heel to kick its head at the same time that Joshua threw a punch to the other side. Their attack crushed one of the heads between them. From within, a black ichor spewed. Kasumi grabbed the urn.

And yet something was off. Kasumi was feeling uneasy, as Joshua cracked his knuckles, ready to finish the still active mechanoid.

Something told her to jump backwards. And she listened.

Joshua howled in pain, as the shroud sprouted straight from his back like a pair of wings made of pure darkness, shaking without control. His eyes opened wide as his body shook in pain, his arms contorting in unnatural forms. The shroud hit the train car, at the spot where Kasumi had been a second ago, ripping apart the metal with ease.

This was it. The very thing that Kasumi had long dreaded in the bottom of her mind.

The Beast was loose.

The Beast was a shadowy thing that flowed around Joshua like a shroud coming from his back. It was the source of Joshua's inhuman strength, speed, and stamina. As well as his annoying tendency to appear and disappear into the shadows, almost as if he teleported into a dark realm between space to move around. It used to be a nice party trick for the Harvest Festivities. But not now.

Not even Joshua knew what exactly the Beast was. He suspected it was a symbiont of some kind, forcibly grafted into his spine. He only had flashes of memory of how he'd gotten the Beast. A scientific experiment. Fire. It had taken place at the cursed city of Carpadocci, the Wastelands, which had once been part of the Empire of Asuria. But that Empire had disappeared during the War with the Freefolk, millennia ago. And Carpadocci had been lost to the world even before that.

So, add apparent immortality to Joshua's skill set alongside the elongated fangs and the creepy, pale yellow eyes when he let loose his powers. For the most part, the Beast and Joshua got along, as befit a symbiotic relationship. But since around the time when the massive, flying eldritch abomination attacked St. Lucy in the Emerald Island, the Beast had become a problem. It would become unleashed, out of control, during the worst possible moments, endangering everyone as its shadowy tendrils whipped everything in sight.

At first Joshua had been able to regain control of it almost immediately. But the fits and bouts, akin to temper tantrums, had started to become more frequent and violent; requiring Joshua to take extreme measures, like enclosing himself in an industrial fridge on the bad days, or drowning in rum or sake to keep it asleep.

And right now, they were far from a fridge or a bar. Unless... Kasumi looked at the river and an idea formed in her mind.

The Beast shook without control or care, as Joshua screamed and writhed in pain, trying to recover control. Every lash that hit the train ripped a chunk of metal. She had seen what the Beast could do to a living being when it 'fed', and it was the stuff of nightmares. It would suck the ever-loving life out of their body, leaving a stony husk behind. That would be really bad for the poor person and for Joshua himself. Kasumi grabbed the leg of the damaged mechanoid and spun on her feet, gaining momentum and force. Her aim was on the mark and the mech impacted her friend squarely in the chest. Joshua lost his balance and he and the Beast fell into the cold waters of the river. With any luck, the sudden drop of temperature would force the Beast to slumber and

71

allow Joshua to put it back into its cage.

Seconds passed, but Joshua didn't resurface. Worried, Kasumi dove into the river. The water was cloudy, preventing her from finding Joshua. She resurfaced, gasping for air. Kasumi looked around for any sign of her friend.

I hope I didn't kill him, she thought, as she bit her lip. A couple of meters in front of her, bubbles appeared on the surface and Joshua resurfaced at last. He was dazed and was having difficulty staying afloat, but at least there was no sign of the Beast. Kasumi swam towards him, double checking that the Beast was truly contained. She went behind him, grabbed him under his arms and swam to shore. Once there, Joshua coughed until all the water was out. Tired, the two friends lay on the riverbank.

"Another bout? Is this the third one this month?" Kasumi asked, trying to remember when the last time this had happened. Joshua had been taking time off from interacting with others out of concern. This was his first proper heroics in a week.

"Yes, they are becoming more frequent and intense. It's becoming hard for me to control them."

"We will find a way to stop them."

Joshua looked at Kasumi. Behind the eerie pale-yellow eyes that slowly returned to brown, there was pain. She could sense it.

As they sat on the riverbank, drenched in water, and covered by shadows, the lights of the city reflected on the water's surface of the Suzunogawa, forming snakes of color crossing the currents of the river.

"So much for laundry day eh?" Kasumi asked deadpan.

Joshua looked at her for a few seconds in silence, and then laughed. The man rarely did—as opening his mouth wide betrayed the larger fangs he always tried to hide—but when it happened, his laughter was contagious. Kasumi joined him and both laughed for what seemed to be hours, until Joshua stopped. He took a deep breath and stared at Kasumi directly in her eyes. There was no pain now, but neither was there happiness. Something was wrong.

"I want to ask you a favor," Joshua said.

"Anything," Kasumi replied. She had known the man all her life. Everyone in her family had know Joshua since her great-grandmother had returned home from her last mission, followed by the foreign yôkai. The family had made the promise to help him become human once more, to keep control of the beast. And her family always kept their promises. In turn, Joshua had become a beloved part of the family. He fought alongside them when the Great Fire took place; he helped with the curry restaurant as a delivery man, and occasionally as assistant at the temple shop. Joshua helped pay the bills and cook the meals. He had helped her with her combat training and learning sign language, he had taken her to school and taught her how to ride a tricycle. For Kasumi, Joshua was more than a friend. He was her older brother. She would do anything for him as she was sure he would do anything for her and her parents. That's what families did.

Joshua took a long pause before continuing. He then turned his gaze up, towards the sky. He was trying to hide the fact that he was crying, but Kasumi knew him better.

"I... I don't want more innocent blood on my hands." Joshua said. Then he sighed. "If... No. When you see that I'm becoming a danger to others, please kill me."

She remained silent and took the urn out from her robes, to return it later to the temple. Kasumi tried to regain her composure. She knew Joshua wasn't joking. It was the same promise he had extracted from her family four generations ago when he joined them.

To the Pits with that, she thought. For it was the only promise she was intending to break.

† † †

Kasumi decided that she had had enough of Joshua's defeatism. He may be down with the idea of allowing himself and the Beast to be killed—if that was even possible—to be free from his curse and avoid hurting others. But she wasn't. For her, Joshua had redeemed enough of his buried sins through his constant good deeds. It would shame her ancestors if she didn't try to save him. And for that, she would have to visit the ancestors.

Kazumi took a few days off to take an early morning bus to the town where the Temple of the Quiet Water was located. The Shimizu family used to be custodians of the temple before the incident.

Nestled into the mountains, the town felt both familiar and alien to her, after the time she and her family had been away. Not many people lived here anymore, since the incident had made the town a haunted place. But for Kasumi, that was part of the charm. She had always liked haunted houses. That's why she had visited the Straits when she was a kid, as the place was full of spooky locales. And that was where she had met a friend that had shared similar interests. Lately, she had been thinking about him a lot. Ever since the news from the Emerald Island had reached the Kuni Empire's news services. While he wasn't mentioned by name, she knew he had to be involved in that clash with the floating monster. After all, the samoharo ship had been there. He hadn't mentioned much on their latest chat exchanges, but the recent activity on the Island, of a vigilante beating criminals, had his trademark, the always comic book loving geek. In a way, both of her friends were involved in a competition to see who could do the most heroic—sometimes the most stupid—thing.

Their antics made her smile.

As the bus pulled away from the stop, Kasumi looked towards the mountain where the Temple of the Quiet Water was located. The sky still dark, the sun not yet up. The chirping of the cicadas broke the silence in the otherwise deserted place. Kasumi tightened the dark blue cloth belt that kept her demonhunter robe closed. She pulled a pair of sais from her backpack and fastened them to the belt. Kasumi took a long, deep breath and started the walk across the abandoned town.

Passing several ruined houses, she entered the woods that surrounded the temple and trekked up the small mountain, following a hidden path she had found when she was a little child. The path had been erased by time and tree roots and eroded stone steps made it treacherous, but Kasumi followed it with confidence, enjoying the smell of petrichor that filled the air. Soon she was climbing, having to use the sais as climbing picks. The noise of her ascent was subdued by the sound of the waterfall to her right. By the time she reached the ruins of the temple, the sun was already up. The clear air filled her lungs, and she took a moment to admire the view.

The forest below was half burned, the main stairs still showed signs of the fire that had destroyed the place during the incident. Kasumi wasn't sure what had happened as she had been a small child back then and both Joshua and her parents weren't willing to tell her much. She did know it had involved an ancient yôkai. A few elders rumored that a titanspawn of fire had escaped the prison under the temple and its sickening fire had razed the place. They had blamed Joshua—for being a foreigner—and her family—for not fulfilling their duty to keep the yôkai imprisoned. That had caused them to be barred from entering the temple and for her father to be stripped of his demonhunter position.

It took a lot of favors from the few family friends that hadn't shunned her family to allow her to join the Demonhunter School. The incident had been as much a problem as her hearing had been. Even with her aids, her hearing was never the same as before. Changes in volume in sounds, and the tendency of people to whisper or muffle certain words— sometimes on purpose—made it difficult for her to respond to her instructors at first. Kasumi had learned to read facial and body expressions as well as lips to better understand her interlocutors. But she found a way to make that work for her, as the need to pay attention to small physical clues helped with her hand-to-hand combat skills.

While Kasumi trained, her parents found jobs with relatives living in the capital. Her father at the curry house, her mother at the temple shops, to afford changing her regular hearing aids for combat ready ones. The memory made Kasumi feel a pang of guilt. It also increased her resolve to find a way to change her family's fortunes. She had a lingering suspicion, a feeling she hadn't been able to shake for quite some time, that a potential solution might be found in the only place no one had looked before. Not many knew of its existence and even less how to access it: the part of the Temple that lay beneath it, inside the mountain. Or at least, it would be as good a place to start as any.

† † †

Kasumi walked into the dead forest around the Temple of the Quiet Water, an omamori tied to her right wrist. The embroidery on it glowing with pure white light, keeping the ghostlier yôkai at bay. She could deal with them, but she was in a hurry and conducting exorcisms was time consuming. Kasumi wondered if the Paidragh lamps that the easterners used across Ionis worked as well as her charms.

Somehow, I doubt it. Otherwise, they would have run us out of business, Kasumi thought.

Kasumi saw the sides of the temple through the blackened trunks, like bars holding back a dangerous person. One of the original elemental temples, the Temple of the Quiet Water had been founded during the Age of Titans. Its wood and stone walls had stood for millennia, before the incident, and Kasumi expected to find a ruin. But the temple appeared to be in good shape, considering the lack of visitors and maintenance. The only signs of abandonment were from the shrubs and vines that grew in the entrance and around the stone guardian spirits. As Kasumi crossed the threshold, the engravings on the stone guardians glowed with a faint white light.

The temple's interior wasn't big and had a limestone floor smoothed by generations of visitors. Statues of minor deities lined the walls, and in the center of the room a dais rose from the floor. Kasumi approached and looked at the small circular pond, no more than a meter and a half in diameter, in the center of the dais. Around it, on the ring of limestone containing the pond, there were ideograms engraved in silver and gold. The ideograms represented text in an older Kuni dialect. And while Kasumi's training as a demonhunter had required learning the basics of that ancient dialect, it took her a while to understand that it was a poem.

> *Beneath the calm eye*
> *Lies a storm*
> *Stand firm in faith*

Quiet the waters of your mind
As they break to the stone walls of time

Kasumi touched her index finger to the water's surface and ripples formed around it. A hint of a white light sparkled for a second. Her finger felt cold, really cold, almost as if she had touched snow.

It's just water, then again that light wasn't natural. I mean, it can't be that easy, Kasumi thought. *Then again no one would suspect that it was that easy.*

She stood up and took a deep breath. She closed her eyes, trying to clear her head, 'quieting the waters of her mind' like the poem instructed. The worst that could happen would be that she'd be drenched in cold water. Kasumi walked into the center of the dais. She opened her right eye, then the left. To her surprise, the water was holding her weight, as if it were as solid as a crystal-clear mirror. Yet, the water rippled as she shifted her weight from one leg to the other. Instead of ending with water up to her knees, she was walking on it.

"This doesn't make any sense," she muttered. A white light coming from below the water glowed with increasing intensity, engulfing her. "Now it makes sense!"

† † †

Kasumi blinked several times. As her sight became less blurry, she found that she had been transported into a cave dimly lit by small crystals placed randomly about. Cold penetrated her whole body and she rubbed her chest and arms to keep warm. She turned around, trying to get a better idea of where she was and realized the crystals were not random. They marked a path through the cave so Kasumi followed them.

As Kasumi descended through the cave, the air acquired a peculiar smell, similar to the one coming from ionizers. Electric discharges ran across the walls of the cave, increasing the illumination. Shapes made of light appeared on the walls, dancing to the rhythm of drums and concerted yells, similar to those heard at a martial arts practice.

"Ha! Ha!" echoed around the place.

And yet, Kasumi couldn't pinpoint a source for either.

The shapes then evolved, forming human silhouettes that danced around her.

I guess these are the spirits of the ancestors, she thought. *They don't feel threatening.*

In fact, Kasumi found herself walking with languid movements and a slow, steady pulse. She was taking in the experience, feeling connected to the energy emanating from the cave. The only sign of discomfort she could perceive was that it was cold. But for some reason, the cold wasn't bothering her as much as she expected. As she kept following the dancing figures, entranced, she lost all notion of time and space.

It was the female voice singing that broke her out of her trance. Kasumi shook her head and found herself inside a large grotto, well-lit by paper lamps. A small waterfall tumbled down the back wall and flowed to the middle of the chamber, forming a pond similar to the one in the temple. However, the water was not clear but had a greyish appearance and was crisscrossed by lightning. It was like watching a thunder cloud. There was a stone toori signaling the entrance and writing on its pillars.

Kasumi got closer to the writing, but she couldn't recognize the symbols. The writing was in an ancient form of Kuni, even older than the one in the dais. One that hadn't been spoken in millennia.

"It says 'Temple of the Storm,'" the female voice said.

"That name isn't on the list of ancient temples," Kasumi replied calmly. Finding someone down here was the least strange thing. She turned around to see her interlocutor. She could only see a blurry silhouette, moving around with slow intent. As the silhouette became more defined, it took on an ethereal quality. It was as if the person in front of her was a hologram become clearer by the minute.

It was a tall woman, with long, dark hair that covered her eyes, and purple demonhunter armor. The style of the armor betrayed its age, as no one had used shoulder fins in more than a century.

"That's by design, young one," the woman replied.

"And yet, it makes sense, the poem says as much, the

calm before the storm and so on." Kasumi shrugged her shoulders. "Who are you?"

"I see that little startles you," the woman smiled. She took a seat on top of a rock covered with red fabric. In front of her a small fire exploded into existence in a stone pit. But the room didn't warm up.

"I learned to remain calm and take things in stride. Makes this easier," Kasumi replied with a half smile.

With a gesture from her left hand, the woman invited Kasumi to sit. "I am the oracle of the Storm God."

"I didn't know the Storm God had an oracle," Kasumi said as she took a seat.

"Not many do. It's not exactly a coveted job," the Oracle pointed to the bandages covering her eyes. "There is a price attached to the ability to foresee things that not many are willing to pay."

Kasumi rubbed her arms again. The sensation of cold wasn't going away. It didn't make sense to her. Why the Temple of the Storm would be a cold place, especially with a fire pit? That would be more fitting of the Northern Temple of the Snow.

"You are wondering why this place is so cold, if it is not the Temple of the Snow."

"How did you...?"

"Know what you are thinking? The magick of..." the Oracle made a dramatic pause. "Common sense. You keep rubbing your arms. I apologize for the cold. The other guest I have has this tendency to bring the mood down when we have visitors. Now, I'm interested in asking you why you decided to seek your ancestors here and not in another, more active temple."

"Since I was a kid, I could feel a presence underneath the temple, one that was reassuring and calm. My family said that wise spirits once lived here, in a secret chamber. Never gave it much thought... until now. So, I took a leap of faith and decided to start my quest here. That still doesn't answer why this place is so cold."

"Temples are like trees. Their roots are deep and grow interconnected with the passage of time. The Temple of the

Snow is connected to this one, as this one is connected to the Quiet Water above, and that one is connected to the Desert temple to the west and so on. That's how the monks used to travel safely during troubling times. And how our other guest was able to reach this place."

Kasumi looked around but she couldn't see anyone else. She closed her eyes and felt a third presence. One she hadn't felt before. It was new, and felt wary, fearful, and aggressive. Like an animal when someone invades its den. It was a spirit, but one of a kind Kasumi could not identify.

"Don't worry. If this chat goes as I expect, the cold will decrease."

"If you are an oracle, you already know how this talk will end."

"The future is a malleable thing, young lady. Especially when you add the free will of living beings to the mix. You can see something and act in consequence, but five minutes later the timeline will become blurry, like throwing a stone into a calm pond. The surface is never the same. Action changes the state of things, thus making it difficult to see what's going to take place."

"Quantum uncertainty principle," Kasumi muttered.

"What was that?"

"No... Nothing, ma'am." Kasumi replied. "At least I can surmise you know why I'm here."

"You are looking for answers, on how to help your friend deal with the beast inside him. On how to regain honor for your family... and how to prove yourself before the eyes of others."

Kasumi looked down, as blood gave her cheeks a tinted rose shade.

"No need for that. You can have personal goals and goals that help others. No shame in that. As long as you don't blind yourself to other's needs due to a selfish quest, you will find that helping others and helping yourself are not incompatible things, rather, they intersect. As it is in this case. The answers you are looking for can be solved by three actions. Three decisions."

Kasumi looked at the oracle. Her ethereal form made

her feel dizzy. She fixed her sight at a point on the wall, in order to lessen the effect.

"Only three? I expected something more difficult. What are they?"

"There is a storm coming, and you need to be there to solve all of your problems in one swoop. The first decision will be the last one to make. By the time you return to the outside, you will find that you have a message, from an old friend, or acquaintance. I'm not sure how you regard him. He will ask you for a favor. Your answer to that will set the things you want into motion. The second one is easier. Are you familiar with the Nine-Point-Star technique?"

"A finger-based acupressure technique. Yes, I'm familiar, but I haven't used it. It's for therapy, not for combat."

"That's where you are wrong. It started as a combat technique to stop the flow of energies of a being, allowing one to keep someone sedated or even kill them. You need to learn it and teach it to your friend or get someone to teach him before meeting in person, for only then will he be able to survive what will happen."

"Where can I learn it?"

"I can teach you, if you want."

"Okay. That decision is easy. But you mentioned three."

"The third one is not yours to make, but by my other guest. For you will need its help in your quest."

The oracle extended her left hand. Behind her a lime-stone wall crumbled away, leaving behind a shallow recess. Sitting on a pedestal inside was an unusual looking naginata. The blade was approximately 50 centimeters long and the thick, staff-like handle was only a little longer. The handle was a long block of black wood with rounded edges, covered in shark skin or samewaga—tinted in clear blue. The blade was straight except for the last third, which swept upwards. It appeared to be made of ordinary, polished steel, except that common bladed weapons didn't glow with a wavering white light speckled through with tiny turquoise sparkles. Only one kind of weapon had the ability to glow and feel like it had a spirit living inside it. She had experienced this once, a long time ago, when she met her odd friend from the Straits.

"Is that...?"

"Yes. A Tempest Blade. One of the Lost Ones."

"Lost Ones?"

"Most people are familiar with the two more famous ones: Yaha and Black Fang. But there are more. A set of twin blades, Heartguard and Soulkeeper reappeared to the public a year and half ago. They are Lost Ones. This is another: The Breaker."

Kasumi looked back to the Oracle, confused. The woman sighed.

"Icebreaker, Wavebreaker... It has a few names. And yes, originally it was at the Northern Temple. But it decided to try its luck and find a worthy partner here. You may be that partner."

"So, I just take it and that's all?" Kasumi got closer to Breaker, to examine it. The quality of the blade was astonishing. Even more considering that Tempest Blades—rumor had it—were centuries, if not millennia, old. And yet this one seemed to be freshly forged.

"It's not that simple. You will find in a few moments that the Tempest Blades have a mind and a will of their own, very much like this Temple. This place only accepts those that it considers worthy, like you or your great-grandmother. A Tempest Blade can disappear and appear in its quest for a proper wielder, a partner. The Blades are never owned but convinced to work with you. But when they do agree, wonders take place."

"I thought you need to have the Gift to use them." Kasumi looked back to the Oracle. She remembered what her friend had told her once and the events surrounding him getting his hands on one of these mystical weapons. "And I'm not planning to die."

"The Gift helps, that's true. But the Greywolf was using Black Fang years before receiving the Gift. A demonhunter with the right connection with a Blade can use them as easily as a Gifted," the oracle explained.

"Then the decision is for the Blade to accept me," Kasumi turned to look at Breaker. The light patterns were nothing if not hypnotizing. "What do I need to do?"

"Take it and open yourself. If the spirit within the Blade accepts you, then it becomes a matter of practicing and communing with it for the Blade to unlock its secrets to you."

"And if the Blade rejects me?" Kasumi wondered. The temperature was descending at a faster rate than before.

"With this one...," the oracle shrugged her shoulders. "You will be lucky if you only get frostbite in your finger, maybe lose a couple. Worst case scenario... you will find out how it feels to drown under the ice of a frozen lake... and die. If the Blade is in bad mood, of course."

Kasumi gulped. To find a way to save Joshua she had to risk losing a limb or dying. Was she willing to do that? She shook her head. Of course she was willing to do that. That was the whole reason she had come to this place. She had never backed down from a challenge and she wouldn't start now. Kasumi breathed slowly, as moisture from her breath gathered in front of her like a small cloud. She rubbed her hands to warm them up.

"There is only one way to find out then..."

Kasumi extended her left hand and grabbed Breaker's handle. It was cold to the touch, as if it had been left in ice for days. Kasumi tried to remove it from the pedestal, but Breaker wouldn't budge. The cold increased, creeping all over her arm. She grimaced at the pain she was feeling in her bones and her hand was turning blue. Kasumi tried to open her hand to let it go, but a strange force applied pressure on it, keeping it firmly locked in place.

A sudden rush of images came to Kasumi's mind, forcing her to close her eyes. Moments from her past filled her head: when she woke up in a hospital, finding that she had lost most of her hearing, the fire at the temple she had called home, her parents struggles, moving to the capital, the bullying received during her training as demonhunter, the lack of opportunities after she graduated, the hours of hard work. The spirit inside Breaker was trying to break her will. Kasumi had faced challenges before that aimed to do just that, and she had always come out on top. Breathing slowly, she focused on moments of happiness from her past: when she met Joshua, when she trained, when her aids were turned on for the first time, when she met those friends from other countries, when she graduated as a demonhunter, when she saved people. But the more she focused on those memories, the rush of sad ones increased.

Kasumi couldn't feel her arm. If she didn't get the Blade to cooperate with her, she would lose her arm and her chance to fix everything. It was becoming a battle of wills; a battle Breaker was winning. Who could stop the force of waves breaking on a stone shore, methodically, day after day, for centuries? The ceaseless pounding of wave and water. The tireless, relentless, repetition of water pounding stone, wearing it down. From massive boulder to a grain of sand. The rock crumbles under the endless cooperation of waves...

That's it, she thought. *The Blade is not testing my will. It's testing my willingness to work with it. And what does a good partner do with the other? Opens up. It's probing for my deepest desires and secrets.*

Kasumi stopped fighting the Blade. She relaxed her body and smiled, opening her mind and heart to it, allowing the spirit within to see for itself the good and the bad, the ups and downs. Even the deepest secret she held: Joshua's true origin and identity.

One question popped inside her head, by a voice not of her own.

If you have to choose between honor and saving a friend, what would you do?

Kasumi didn't hesitate. Just answered what her heart told her was true.

Saving my friend, every time. There is no contest.

Kasumi waited with bated breath and an increasing feeling of emptiness in the pit of her stomach, for a sign that Breaker had accepted her answer. *Wasn't that the right answer?*

Look, Breaker, I need your help if I'm gonna help my friend and my family. I'm humbly asking for your assistance. Not as tool for combat, but as my partner, if you'll have me. Please.

Breaker's blade glowed brighter and the cold receded until it disappeared. Warmth returned to Kasumi's hand. She tried once more and lifted Breaker from the pedestal with ease. It felt light in her hand. She twirled the strange naginata around her, getting used to the position of the blade. Kasumi felt as if the spirit within was telling her unconsciously where the dangerous part of the weapon was at any moment.

"I'm glad to see that you two are getting along," the Oracle said, grinning. "Breaker has been looking for a suitable partner for… let's says a really long time."

"You knew this was going to be the outcome," Kasumi smiled as well.

"Again, free will, on both sides. This was one of the expected outcomes. My preferred one if I can talk with candor."

"It sounds like being an oracle is not like the myths say," Kasumi replied bemused, tilting her head.

As they talked, Kasumi kept moving, playing, dancing with Breaker, and leaving trails of frozen light, in stark contrast with the partial darkness of the place.

"Myth retelling often skips over the unsavory parts. An oracle is a suggestion of a potential course of action, nothing more. At the end of the day, the only one responsible for a particular outcome is the person who set it in motion. You set in motion many things before coming here, and you'll set in motion many other things after this…"

"And they are my sole responsibility. Like taking good care of Breaker."

"You are getting the hang of this."

Kasumi stopped dancing around with Breaker and returned to her seat. She placed Breaker next to her with care. The blade's glow decreased. The warmth of the fire flowed through the place and Kasumi didn't feel as cold as before.

"The Blades take care of their partner if they are reciprocal. You will find that the cold won't be much of an issue for you from now on."

"I have to be honest. Somehow, I thought getting a Tempest Blade would require a longer, dangerous quest. Battling beasts and so on."

"What for? This is not a videogame. It's not like this place is ripe with visitors. The temple has its own security features. Tempest Blades are known for being picky about who they accept as a partner. You would be surprised what the Greywolf had to do to get Black Fang. Besides, getting good at using one and unlocking its true potential takes time. If you can wield it and it hasn't rejected you, you have passed its most important test."

"You seem to be well versed on them."

"I have had my fair share of encounters with the two famous ones." The oracle smiled. "And it's my job as an oracle to keep myself updated."

"I still have a question. If I have the Blade and learn the technique you mention, why do I have to wait? Why can't I go now and help cure my friend?"

"His illness is not an easy thing to handle. You will need a lot of practice and wait until the right moment, when his inner beast is at its strongest and yet, more vulnerable."

"Why?"

"Because the being that did this to your friend is someone of pure, efficient evil. There are safeguards upon safeguards. What is happening to your friend is a desired outcome by the Dark Father."

"It can put a lot of people at risk if I wait that long."

"That's why you are going to use the technique I will teach you, to subdue the Beast once and for all."

"Again, why can't I heal him on my own?" Kasumi kept pressing. The Oracle sighed in clear frustration.

"Have you seen when he unleashes the beast at full power?" The Oracle's voice raised a whole octave.

"Joshua covers everything in darkness and when it's done, all life inside it is drained, leaving only dry husks," Kasumi replied in a low voice. She was coming to terms with the actual danger she faced. The danger Joshua really was. No matter how close they were, Joshua remained a yôkai. And yôkai were dangerous. They were one of the reasons for the existence of demonhunters in first place.

"Exactly. Because the Beast grafted to his spine was designed as a weapon. And for this job, you need the help of someone that can generate enough light to beat this darkness, to allow you to survive the ordeal until you seal the Beast for good."

"So, it's not a one-person job."

"I'm afraid not. The only person that could do it on his own is not in the right mind set to do so, and might choose to kill Joshua rather than help him," the oracle looked downward, as if she was trying to hide great, personal pain.

"Why?"

"Because Joshua is a tovainar, and a tovainar took everything from the person I'm talking about. No matter how good his heart, there are wounds that take time to heal."

Kasumi sat in silence for a long time, digesting all the information. The only sound echoing through the walls was that of the crackling fire between them. Finally, Kasumi broke the silence, her eyes and voice filled with determination

"I will take care of getting the external help I need. Now teach me the technique that will heal Joshua."

† † †

By the time Kasumi returned to the surface, the sun was setting on the horizon. The air was warm. There was no point in returning to the bus stop now, as the trek back was dangerous, even in daylight. She might as well return to the cave and spend the night there. At least the Oracle would be a good conversationalist.

She felt her phone vibrating and took it out.

Right on schedule, she thought.

There was a long message from her friend, Alex, waiting for her.

"Hey! How are you? I was wondering if you would be willing to do me and a friend of mine a favor. See, this friend is the head of the Foundation, which will, for the first time, be invited as an independent entity to the triannual talks. Thus he needs a team to represent him at the Chivalry Games that will take place later this year in your hometown. I know you might want to represent your country, but we could really use your help, and this means a direct invitation so you won't need to waste time beating the crap out of other demonhunters to get a spot. I checked the rules and it is allowed as long as you haven't declared for a team yet. The rest of my friends can't help because they will be representing the Freefolk and I'm alone. So I would really appreciate you agreeing.

Another message followed the first one.

PS: Do you think your friend with the shadowy thing would be willing to join us? Could you ask him too please? Thank you, you are awesome!"

"He does take quite a long detour to get to the point," Kasumi muttered. She smiled and started to type back her reply and all the details she needed to convey. As the Oracle had predicted, things were being set in motion. She was eager to meet her friend after all these years of only talking through chats. Kasumi wondered what he would think of Breaker.

This could be interesting.

Chapter 5
Training in the Mountains

What you did last year was astonishing, considering how little formal training you have had. It's time to fix that. You have the basics. It's time to build upon them. Last time, you learned to control the Gift, Fionn's voice echoed inside Alex's head.

As the sun set, tiny lights appeared on some of the trees, forming a makeshift path. Alex ran through the wilderness, which felt oddly familiar even if he couldn't recall the full details. His irises glowing with a golden hue, bow in his left hand, Yaha sheathed on his back, he reached a boulder on the face of the mountain. A large, crystal clear lake could be seen from there, and at the other side of the lake, in the middle of a heavily forested area, a small town, Skarabear. Fionn's hometown.

Alex couldn't admire the view though, as tantalizing as it was, for he was in a race against time. He jumped over the boulder, landing on a thin path a few meters below.

This time we will focus on learning to use your body to maximize the Gift's effects. We will focus on a few key aspects. First, your stamina. Second, increasing your reaction speed and physical strength.

Alex rolled, stood up and continued running as he pulled the bow's string and shot arrows into three targets tied to tree trunks. Two hit in the center, the third barely hit the target. Angered with himself for not hitting his mark, he kept running downhill, jumped onto a rock and leaped at a metal bar held horizontally between two trees at the edge of a chasm. He grabbed the bar with his right hand and pulled himself up, while with his left, he sent a small electric charge, collapsing the bow and tucking it inside the holster tied to his calf. Clutching the bar now with both hands, he swung until he gained enough momentum to launch himself across the chasm to land on the other side. On impact, he flexed his knees to soften the land. With his hands he pushed to get up faster and kept running.

You have good reflexes, but they can be better. And in a fight, those seconds can make a lifetime of difference.

He reached an old, rickety suspension bridge. It was missing a few boards and swayed from side to side with every step, forcing him to focus on his balance. A ringing in his ears alerted him of an attack, and he drew Yaha from his back, as he dodged arrows fired at him from unseen assailants. With Yaha, Alex deflected the rest of the arrows until he crossed the bridge. He crossed another forested area, on his way back to the shore of the lake. Tree trunks sprung out at him over the path, forcing him to cut them down with his sword.

We need to make your body stronger so you can endure channeling it and you become less dependent on emergency binge eating to get more energy.

He pushed the limits of his body, his lungs burning in pain, in order to reach the shore. Alex reached a spot where the Figaro sat near an old stone and wood house. As he slowed, Fionn pushed a button on the screen of his phone, pausing the stopwatch. Alex was breathing heavily, so he sunk Yaha into the ground and put his hands on his knees as he panted to catch his breath.

"How... I... did?"

"You hit all the targets, but one," Fionn replied, checking all the sensors from the targets. "And you were almost a minute and half slower."

"Aiming correctly is not easy, even less when moving," Alex said, putting his hands on his waist and looking at Fionn. He could feel his face was red and covered in sweat.

"You won't always have all the time you want to hit the target."

"I want to go again," Alex looked at the path, as he picked up Yaha.

"I think for today this is enough," Fionn replied, patting him in the back. "Resting is also part of the training. Pushing yourself endlessly will take you to the breaking point. Besides, I need to reset the course. Tomorrow, we will practice swordfighting together."

"Fine," Alex said, dejected at first. "I still can't believe this is the very same training you underwent with Hikaru a century ago!"

"Are you disappointed?"

"On the contrary, I feel honored," Alex smiled. He had read many books on Fionn, and when younger, he had looked for books describing his training, with the hope he could undergo a similar regime. Never in his life until last year, would he have expected to actually be doing the same training. Long gone was the confrontational relationship they had had at Ravenhall. This time, Alex was grateful for Fionn's more constructive, if exhausting training. As much as his muscles were sore, at least the flabby belly was getting smaller.

"You keep forgetting that despite how much he talks backs to you, he is still your number one fan," Sid added, sitting on the steps of the cabin's entrance, not taking his eyes from the laptop.

"It's... it's not like that," Alex stammered. "And how are you doing with the coding?"

"Slow progress so far. I'm still wondering why don't you or Birm do it?" Sid retorted.

"Because Birm is busy with his dissertation and I suck at math and programming. Plus, samoharos are naturals."

"Ah, that. It's true."

"Dinner is ready!" Harland yelled from inside. Alex grimaced. Harland was not a bad cook, but his repertoire was limited and two months of the same menu was starting to wear them down. Yet no one had the heart to tell him.

"I still don't know why we can't stay at Skarabear. I mean, it is your hometown," Alex said.

"One, the old family house is a museum now," Fionn replied. Alex gave him a quizzical look. "Yeah I know. So, we are using the cabin my grandfather used for his experiments to avoid blowing the town to smithereens. Two, too many prying eyes and I need to keep clear of that as Harland has to do something."

"Ah yes, your secret plan," Alex whispered.

"And I would attract too much attention."

"The result of having a statue in your likeness in the middle of the town square?" Sid added, finally looking up from the screen.

"That too. And it might sound silly but..." Fionn paused. "I'm not ready to be in a place where my family is buried. Let's eat something. I bet you are starving."

† † †

They took a seat at the table, staring at Harland's meatloaf—in his words a balanced meal as it had protein, grains, and vegetables—and as Alex was mustering the strength to take the first bite, he turned to Fionn.

"How long did it take you to train Ywain?" Alex asked.

"Hmm..." Fionn looked at the ceiling. "Around a year and half, for the basics. But back then we were in a hurry and he was a natural. We spent the rest of the war polishing his technique."

"And how long did you train under your master?"

"Ten years.

"And you expect me to become that good in a few months? Is that realistic?"

"No, but unlike me when I was a kid, or Ywain, you already know how to fight for your life and you are a fast learner. So, with any luck, we will make this work," Fionn paused, then continued. "Look, you once asked me who was a better fighter, Ywain or you. Here is the thing: When I met Ywain, he already had the Gift. For all I knew, he was either born with it or acquired it as a baby shortly before the King found him in that burned town. So, he was a natural using it because it was not even second nature for him. That *was* his nature. He used the Gift to enhance his combat skills and achieve feats none of the rest could. He was a lightning storm. Pure raw power. But he never stopped to understand what other things he could do with it, beyond using it to power up engines. You are more like a light bulb."

"So, he was better," Alex said, dejected. His appetite evaporated and now the meatloaf was mocking him.

"No," Fionn smiled at him. "By light bulb I mean that someone took this raw power of nature that is electricity and honed it into something subtle and useful like a light bulb. What you might lack in raw power, you more than compensate with your intelligence and your science knowledge. You might not understand one hundred percent how this force of nature you can command works, but you have a better understanding than Ywain. That's why you have been able to apply it to your bow, or that new body armor that you are working on. That's why when Ywain faced Byron, he played straight into his hands and fed him so much power that he made Byron unbeatable. On the contrary, you found and helped us exploit a weakness and that gave us the edge. So, to answer your question, no, you are not better than Ywain… yet. But you can be. Fighting normal humans or monsters is different from fighting against powered humans that also use every dirty trick in the book to win. And that's what tournament titanfighters do."

"You want me to be better than any of them."

"No. I'm not training you to be better than anyone else," Fionn said. "That's not feasible. I want you to be the best possible version of yourself. Then you will be able to beat any challenge in front of you. Always."

"I need some tools to cut this thing," Sid said, standing up.

"My meatloaf is not that bad," Harland looked at them. "Is it?"

Crickets were the only sound heard in the otherwise silent cabin.

"Fine, tomorrow after your morning training I will go to town and bring back food," Harland mumbled, annoyed.

† † †

Alex and Fionn were standing on the lakeside, their swords in their hands, separated by at least a meter, wearing their regular clothes—jeans, t-shirts and sneakers. Alex followed Fionn's motions, opening his legs and bending his knees, similar to a combat position. Fionn brought Black Fang up to a ready position, a tight grip with both hands on the hilt, the tip aiming towards the sky. Fionn was facing towards the lake, his left leg in front of his right. Alex followed suit.

"First: finish a fight as fast as you can, to avoid potential risks. The thing is, titanfighters know that advice as well. And they will play dirty. So, use all your power in as few hits as possible."

Fionn raised Black Fang over his head, the point now aiming to the forest behind. He took a step forward with his right foot, at the same time he brought down the blade to the height of his waist with such force that a small groove formed on the sandy shore from the air's impact. Fionn then raised his fangsword into a parrying position, with his hands above his head and the tip of the blade aiming to the ground, while the length of the blade protected his neck and back. From there, Fionn made another cut, which left a second groove on the ground. Alex imitated the moves, imparting all his weight and force into the slashes, leaving similar grooves in its wake. Alex had slightly more difficulty making the moves, as Yaha's blade was straight and shorter, compared to Black Fang's longer curve.

"I know Yaha's blade is different from Black Fang. With time, you will adapt these techniques to your own style and blade. What I wanted to show you is that a good stance can help you to impart your attacks with more force and precision. So, with a single, small cut, you can defeat an enemy, without killing him."

Fionn turned to Alex, repeated the same sequence of movements once more, but at higher speed, aiming at Alex's left shoulder. Alex had just enough time and reflexes to block the attack.

"Good! Second: learn to think on your feet and under pressure. Many a fight is decided not by sheer power, but by presence of mind. By the ability to come up with a plan. If you learn to keep your mind focused under pressure, you will be able to find a solution to a problem. We will work also in meditation, so you can keep that presence of mind and remain calm."

Fionn traded several blows with Alex, increasing the strength and speed with each attack. Alex's breathing grew heavy, and he was sweating profusely as the pressure of Fionn's attacks increased. He was having trouble keeping track of all the blows in order to parry or deflect them. Alex put all his strength into the last parry, to force Fionn off balance. In reply, Fionn spun on his heels and brought Black Fang in a wide slash aimed at Alex's head. Alex rolled to the ground and kicked Fionn in the leg, trying to make him fall. Instead, Fionn rolled, got up with a jump, and with a well-placed roundabout kick, hit Alex in the hands, forcing him to drop Yaha. Fionn kept attacking, but Alex, unencumbered by the sword, evaded the attacks and punched Fionn with all his strength in the stomach, knocking the air from him.

"I'm sorry," Alex apologized. "I didn't mean to hit you so hard during practice."

"No..." Fionn said as he raised his hand. The force of the punch had caught him by surprise. That made him smile. It meant that the conditioning was working and from now on he could increase the level of difficulty. "It's okay. I got cocky. I admit that while your hand-to-hand combat technique can use some polishing, Gaby and Sid taught you well in that part. Your swordsmanship on the other hand..."

"I know, leaves a lot to be desired," Alex replied, looking to the ground as he picked up Yaha.

"I wouldn't say that. You have the natural instincts to be a great swordsman, but you still need a lot of practice to make it work against people that know how to fight. As it stands now, you're a better shooter than swordsman, exactly the opposite of Ywain. That can work to your advantage in the Games, as any weapon, except firearms, are allowed. But few use ranged attacks, unless their armors allow for it."

"I took after great grandma," Alex replied smiling.

Fionn sat on the ground, cleaving Black Fang into the sand. Alex sat next to Fionn and held Yaha in his hands.

"Look," Fionn explained, pointing to Yaha, "in that

95

sword, you have one of the finest, oldest swords in existence. You only need to learn to use it properly."

"Did you know that it's around ten thousand years old? Which is weird considering that it's not rusty."

"How do you know that?" Fionn looked at Alex, intrigued. He knew Yaha was old, older than any other Tempest Blade in existence, but he never gave that much thought, until now.

"My friends and I carbon dated it and compared the results to the recorded legends about it. I could only find mention of three known previous users in that entire time span: the first human that used it, the Storm God, and Ywain. That's odd, considering its age. One would assume more documented users, at least from Year One After the Death of Dragons onward."

"Not everyone can use a Tempest Blade. Not with proficiency at least. When you reach the highest level of proficiency, the more in tune you are with a Tempest Blade, the more things you will be able to do with it, including..." Fionn said.

"Increasing it sharpness and resistance..." Alex replied.

"And shape and size," Fionn added to the list. Alex looked surprised.

"Have you done that? I mean, change Black Fang's shape and size?"

"Once," Fionn looked at the lake, wistfully. "It took a lot of mental effort. And it was only for a moment of desperation. Now, as I was saying. The Blades are 'alive' or at least sentient. As sentient as a sword can be anyway. Which allows them one thing that no other weapon can: they get to choose who can wield them."

"What do you mean?"

Fionn unstuck Black Fang, spun it, leaving its blade resting on his forearm and offered the hilt to Alex.

"Here, lift Black Fang."

Alex did as asked, but he had trouble lifting it. The blade fell from his hand.

"It's really, really heavy," Alex said. "How come you can twirl it around as if it was made of plastic?"

"Because we are in synchrony. Black Fang has accepted

me as its wielder. The Tempest Blades are our partners, not our slaves. If they don't like you... Yaha gives electric shocks. Black Fang becomes heavier and harder to wield or even lift. I have seen that firsthand. I shudder to think what Gaby's blades can do to unwanted people. But when they accept you, they are our greatest allies."

"Can they have more than one wielder?" Alex asked. "Emergency cases and so on."

Fionn saw Harland coming down to the shore.

"I'm off to the town, any particular request?"

Fionn winked at Alex, lifted Black Fang and offered the hilt to Harland.

"Hey Harland, wanna try?"

Harland rolled his eyes and picked up the sword with no effort.

"I mean food requests," Harland replied. Then he turned to Alex. "I guess if I were taller, I would be able to use Black Fang effectively."

"How was that possible?"

"Because I trust Harland with my life. And Black Fang knows what's in his heart."

"And on that cheesy note," Harland replied as he returned Black Fang to Fionn. "I better leave now. Sid is a good pilot, but a lousy driver."

"Have fun!" Fionn said to his friend, then he turned to Alex. "Enough rest, let's go practice.

† † †

Harland walked down the narrow, cobblestone road. The three storey brick houses on both sides hid the humble origins of the town. If he recalled correctly, from what little Fionn had told him about his adoptive hometown, Skarabear had started as nothing more but a collection of huts, stone houses, a couple of blacksmiths and a central well near the lake. It had been a place for outcasts, people looking to keep a low profile, and those running away from something... or someone. It became a melting pot for humans and freefolk who lived above the border that was the Scar. And yet, a century and a half later, the quaint town had grown. Not like a city, Skarabear was still small, Mercia was larger. But the town was now full of shops, houses, pubs, gardens and serpentine roads. And yet, something was off.

It was intriguing, like one of those 'ancient conspiracy' thriller novels found at warptrain stations. Harland felt young again and recalled why he had agreed to take over the Foundation in the first place: for the sense of adventure and excitement. To solve the mysteries of the world. And right now, Skarabear was an intriguing one. A passerby or a tourist wouldn't have noticed it, but those chaotic roads were perfectly planned. One could still get lost through the twists and turns of the narrow streets and the similar houses that mixed freefolk and human architectural influences. If you took a wrong turn, you would always end up at the outskirts of the town. Take the right turn and you would end at the main garden, where the black metal statue of a rampant dragonwolf pointed to an old, abandoned shop of medicinal remedies and 'alchemic potions', not far from the town hall. A tourist or a passerby would get confused and ask the silent, always observant but polite residents for instructions.

But if you knew of Freefolk history and lore, as Harland did, you would notice that the streets followed certain patterns, not unlike the ones he had noticed in the maps hanging from the walls at Ravenstone. It was as if an unseen hand had guided the growth and planning of the town with a single purpose in mind. And if he really studied the pattern, and the design styles of the houses and shops, in particular that of the old medicinal shop, he would see where his friend Fionn got his obsession with design from... it was a family thing.

Harland had to give it to Dawnstar, Fionn's mother. She had been busy until her last day, as her touch was in every stone of the town.

Since he had been navigating the town with relative ease, compared to the outsiders that came through from time to time, Harland had attracted the discreet attention of the residents. A glance here, a whisper there, always a polite smile and the offer to sell a handicraft, a well-forged metallic trinket with the shape of a dragonwolf or any other freefolk totem. But he knew he intrigued them, both for his short stature and for not getting lost.

He stopped at a small bistro, bought a couple of pastries filled with ham and melted cheese and a cup of coffee. He walked to a small garden, secluded from most of the town. Beautifully tended, the green grass served as background for the white chrysanthemums and small clovers. In the middle of the garden there was a bronze statue of Fionn and Izia. Harland looked at them, examining their flaws. Fionn's statue got the nose wrong and was slightly shorter in comparison with Izia's. While Izia's might not have been an accurate representation, the resemblance was there. Harland was surprised at how much Sam resembled her ancestors.

I guess the bloodline is strong in them.

"The statue is nice, although with some inaccuracies, from what I've been told," a deep, baritone voice broke Harland's reverie. "The plate with the engraving is better, I believe."

Harland looked up and saw a tall man with thinning, greying reddish hair, covered by a beige beret. He was wearing a casual suit and stubble caressed his face. The piercing, violet eyes told Harland that while human, the man had Free-folk ancestry. Harland got closer to read the plate.

"For a beautiful dream to believe in, I hope to wake up and see you at my side once more."

"We are not sure if it is a quote by the Greywolf's mother, wishing to see her son and daughter-in-law once more after they disappeared. Or words from the Greywolf to his wife," the man added. "Yet I find them bittersweet and touching."

Harland remained silent, as his heart sank, remembering how he and his research team found Fionn years ago, frozen into a magickal sleep and buried in that cave, stretching his hand to reach the remains of another person that, later studies determined, belonged to Izia. The image would remain forever engraved in Harland's mind. But he spoke to no one about it. Not even to Fionn.

"This is a good hour to take a seat on the benches of the garden, eat something and admire this quiet place," The man said, leading Harland with his extended arm to one of the metal benches.

"I beg your pardon," Harland said, "but I didn't catch your name."

"Apologies," the man said while taking a seat alongside Harland. "I'm Walter."

"Harland." He extended his hand to the man he'd come looking for.

Walter must have known, as he gave Harland a knowing smile. "You seem to be quite knowledgeable of Skarabear."

"Everyone living here knows where we came from, as it is our duty to preserve the history. My duty is even bigger as the mayor. Did you know that Skarabear used to be part of the realm of the Kings of the Mist, founded by the Wanderer's Guild and outcasts from freefolk and human lands?" Walter asked, gazing to the statue with yearning.

"The kings of the mist, the kings who are gone, wandering with their ghosts?" Harland replied. It seemed that the conversation would remain somewhat cryptic. He had to give it to the man, he was being as careful as Fionn or Harland himself. He was enjoying the exchange as it allowed him to drink from his reservoirs of historical and folklore knowledge.

"Oh, so you are familiar with the poem," Walter looked at Harland, amused.

"Of course," Harland said. Then recited,
"The Kings of the Mist
The Kings and Queens of yore
The Kings who are gone, wandering with their ghosts
In the ample valleys of the frozen north.
They can't remember their name
They wander through the storm.
Lightning around
From dawn to dusk
Searching for their ancestral land,
The one they never wanted to leave.
The one in the shadow of the Life Tree.
High in the top of the world
The Kings and Queens of the Mist
Wander with their ghosts
Searching for that they loved the most."

"Oh, so you are a scholar?" Walter asked. "I wonder if you know the one about the Montoc Dragons as well? It's a rather obscure poem, barely heard since the days when the last dragon crossed the skies."

"I wouldn't call myself a scholar," Harland replied. "Just someone with a hobbyist's interest in history and folklore. And of course, I know the dragon poem. I learned it when I was six. Harland recited it:

"The Statues of the Montoc Dragons.

"In ages before, dragons were common, as diverse as the species of toads and frogs or as different as human, freefolk and samoharo. There were the smaller ones from ponds, of course. There were those too that gnaw at the innards of the world, in search of treasures to use as nests. They roamed fields and forests alike, dragons of lesser size, but no less impressive when they unfolded their wings and took to the skies from where their forefathers came. Or so they say, the Statues of the Montoc Dragons.

"But the most impressive ones were those born out of a star's heart, in the vast expanses of the Montoc region beyond our constellations, creatures that descended upon our world to watch over the younger races as older brothers. Or so they say, the Statues of the Montoc Dragons.

"Blessed were those in foreign lands that managed to bear witness of those majestic dragons, crossing the oceans and dancing feverish amidst magickal chants of the Great Will inspiration, around storms or mountains; as the members of such a prodigious race were scarce remnants of wisdom that choose to stay on the fertile land of Theia, waiting for more of them to be born out of the dying stars where the Akeleth tended them, or leaving towards the realms beyond imagination that they now rule. Or so they say, the Statues of the Montoc Dragons.

"No, dragons have not gone extinct, they just moved out into a realm of the mind where their mythic figure can surge the skies, leaving us with a few portentous memories. Or so they say, the Statues of the Montoc Dragons."

"Very good, for someone that claims to not be a scholar," Walter laughed.

"I have my moments," Harland said, sheepishly. "It always fascinated me that in the few texts where that poem appears, it is always in reference to an ancient dragon, the so called 'First and Last', but using its real name."

"Why is that?

Walter was being coy. Harland decided that the only way to know was to reveal his hand.

"Because that name has only being used one other time and in reference to a sword: Black Fang."

"So, you know how the story of Black Fang, the sword, starts?"

"Right where the story of Black Fang, the first dragon to guide the Freefolk ends: dying in battle to stop the Bestial. His reward, being reborn as a Tempest Blade, lying in the bottom of a clear lake, till the day a worthy soul claims it to serve a new purpose."

"I see that you are acquainted with our local legend."

"Funny," Harland said, although he didn't find it that amusing. The charade was lasting longer than it needed.

"What's funny?"

"That you call it a local legend when you and I both know very well that it's a true story. I know it firsthand."

"Then you are one of the lucky ones. I can't even say that. Where is he? And how is he?" Walter asked. And by 'he', Harland knew he was referring to Fionn. Even if no one from the Thain's secret service had followed them, Harland had been careful to keep a low profile. But it seemed that Walter wasn't taking any risks either. If what Fionn had told him was true—and it seemed that way—Skarabear was a tight knit community even before he and Izia left on that fateful last trip. One that by virtue of not being human or freefolk, but a combination of both, remained fiercely independent, secretive and united. Such was the nature of these remote towns north of the Scar.

"He's fine, at the outskirts of the forest in an old shack, training one of his students for an upcoming competition," Harland replied.

"I know he is using Greywulch's shack. But why doesn't he come to town? While his old house is now a museum, I'm sure we would have found him, you, his student, and the samoharo that drove you here suitable, private accommodations among our neighbors," Walter said. "Unless it is not a matter of privacy."

"It is, but not for him. He is keeping yours intact. That and like in the poem, he is still wandering with a few ghosts from his past."

"That's why you are here. He must trust you."

"Enough to let me handle Black Fang, I guess. I'm surprised that Dawnstar's shop is still standing. I guess Izia's father's forge is nearby. I always wanted to see some of the gadgets he designed. Fionn told me he was the only man capable of repairing a Tempest Blade."

"I assumed that's what you wanted to see. But the forge is no more as the history recalls. It got moved around the time he and Izia went missing. Its current location is unknown to most."

Harland looked at the man and smiled.

"No," Harland replied, trying to contain his laughter, "I suppose no one knows. Do you think it would be possible to enter the shop? I was told that there must be many interesting things there, especially in the basement."

"Yes," Walter laughed. "The basement is really interesting. I could give you a tour of the place. Currently it is closed to visitors, but as mayor I have the keys to it." Walter stood up, patting the left pocket of his jacket.

Harland followed Walter through the streets. This time it was even easier to navigate, with the help of a local. The few people outside looked now to Harland with a smile, seeing that he was with the mayor.

Dawnstar's shop smelled of herbs and unction's. Now a museum, it was filled with drawings, old sepia photos and signs that explained the history. Fionn's mother had arrive in Skarebear with her only child and elderly father in tow and accompanied by the Kuni demonhunter, Hikaru. They had fled here after a renegade freefolk tribe, the Silverblade, had razed their home and killed Fionn's father, Fraog. The Silverblade had looked down on interspecies marriage and had directed their fear and anger at Dawnstar and Fraog.

Back then, Skarabear had been nothing more but a collection of shacks, huts and tents, inhabited by refugees from the endless cycles of war from the Old Kingdoms. Here, it didn't matter who you were, your past, or your species. If you helped the community, the community would help you and in turn, you became one of them. Dawnstar then did what she knew best: became the healer and trapper of the town, using both her magick and knowledge of medicine and herbs to offer the town a physician in exchange for a place to raise her child.

An old photo caught Harland's eye. Sepia in color, probably the only one of its kind, it showed Fionn as a seven-year-old kid with ragged clothes and a missing tooth, standing next to a smaller girl with freckles and a devilish smile—Izia. Behind them were Ben Shezar, Izia's father, Greywulch, Fionn's grandfather, and Dawnstar. Hikaru was nowhere to be seen.

Harland reflected on how with time, they became a family and from there, the heart of the town. Izia and Fionn became in turn heroes of the Great War and later, when Fionn and Izia were raised to the status of lords, returned with enough funds and helped rebuild the town. Sadly, none of them saw their work finished, as they would have to depart on that journey that set them into a clash with Byron. But Dawnstar had continued with her son's idea, developing a plan on her own, hoping that her son would return someday to put it to use.

Seems that the time is near, Harland thought. Walter led him to the basement, where after three locked doors, they entered a room with a model of the town's layout, split in two sections, North and South. Harland noticed that the northern half wasn't like anything he had seen while walking around the town. Actually, nothing of that layout existed. Currently there was as small forest in the land where northern half of the town should have been. And it was where the forge should have been. At the back of the room, there was another door, from which a faint light came through the edges, and a faint current of air could be felt.

"I see you have followed her instructions to the letter," Harland said.

"Dawnstar was if nothing, a visionary," Walter replied. "No one really knows what was said at the last talk she had with her son before he went on that fateful journey, but after that, she, Greywulch and Izia's family recruited the whole town and set in motion a plan. Even the profile of who should be the next mayor in the following decades as chosen by the town council was developed by her. In a way, me being the mayor was part of the plan. Sometimes I wonder if she could foresee the future."

"Where is the other half of the town, with the forge?"

"An island further north. Almost close to the Frostlands. We usually don't go there, only to check that the forge is in order. The creatures chosen by Dawnstar to guard it are not fond of humans, or freefolk for that matter. They accept us because she asked it of them. But they will only follow orders from her bloodline or the Shezar's."

"That's why no one has seen the forge. Can it be reached from here? Maybe through that door. Some kind of magick portal?"

"You are a clever man."

"I could say the same about you. I did my homework, Walter. Before being the mayor of this town, you were a general of renown. An apt strategist from freefolk and human heritage, just like him. You were chosen by Fionn's daughter to lead the town before her passing, following Dawnstar's plan. You met with Fionn at that haunted mountain of his, a decade ago, around the time he adopted Sam, to talk about some secret. He told me, that's why he sent me to meet you."

"I would like to think I was chosen for this role for more than just that."

"I believe so. You are also trustworthy, if Fionn shared his secrets with you. But I'm afraid there is need to share once more."

"I might be retired, but I'm not isolated. I have friends down south that keep me informed," Walter said, grabbing a lead figure representing a squadron of warriors. "The events of the past year have stirred more than controversy. Old ambitions and even older grudges are resurfacing. The Alliance is a nice dream, but a fragile reality."

"As much as I would like to disagree," Harland replied, grabbing a figurine of a dragonwolf, "you are right. And to protect that fragile dream, we might have to prepare for something worse than old grudges. Enemies so old that defy time and memory."

"Is that so? The legends are real then?"

"More than I would like. Before beheading Byron, Fionn was warned about the ancient foes, the Crawling Chaos and the Golden King. Byron being back, beholden to them was our first clue. For the past year we have been collecting clues, but there are not many. We only know one thing for sure; the upcoming diplomatic talks might be the first shot for an upcoming conflict, currently brewing in secret."

"One for which neither the Alliance nor the other nations might be prepared," Walter added, stroking his chin. "As no one has fought these threats in centuries, if not in millennia, not since the cursed titans or the Asurian-Freefolk war. I see now. We need to plan for an underground army, as things will get worse from now on. Good thing Dawnstar planned for that."

"Can you get your people ready?"

"We have been ready for a century."

"Good."

† † †

Harland found Fionn sitting on the shore, staring at the lake, lost in his thoughts and meditations. He had Black Fang at his side.

"After all these years, I can't believe I've never asked you this," Harland said, breaking Fionn's meditation. "Is the legend true? That you dove into a lake to get your sword and used it to defend Skarabear from those marauders?"

"More or less yes. What the legend glosses over is that," Fionn turned to look at Harland, smiling. He pointed at a cliff on the side of a hill a hundred meters from where he sat. "I had to jump from that cliff, in order to gain enough momentum to reach the bottom of the lake."

"It doesn't seem to be that deep." Harland looked at the lake.

"It's an optical illusion due to its clear water," Fionn threw a rock into it. The rock skipped on the surface several times and then sank, taking a long time to reach the bottom. "In reality the lake is around fifty meters deep. Which for a kid of fifteen is quite a challenge, holding your breath for that long. If Black Fang hadn't accepted me, I would have never been able to get it out of the lake."

"I thought you were sixteen when you got Black Fang."

"No, that's when I joined the King's army. I was fifteen when I got Black Fang."

"So young and you started training Ywain right away?"

"Not right away, but yes. Bear in mind that back then, and especially during a war, at fifteen, you were old enough to be a man and fight. Now you reach adulthood into your twenties. Which is both good and bad. That makes this training a tad different from what I'm used to."

"How's he doing?" Harland asked, staring at the crystal-clear lake. He saw the rock finally touch the bottom.

"Right now, practicing his archery. By the end of the semester, so to speak, he will be in top form and will be a decent swordsman. He even asked me to teach him an old pressure point technique. In case he needs it."

"I'm glad I have more good news then. The mayor showed me what your mother was up to. He concurs with you and the town is ready. They only need one thing. For you to finally come back home."

"I—"

An explosion came from the trees behind them. Fionn saw a tall tree falling into the forest, with a loud crash.

"What was that?" Harland asked.

Fionn got up, grabbed Black Fang and unsheathed it. With Harland next to him, they walked into the forest, reaching a nearby clearing. Several trees were burned, with holes in them. Alex was on the ground, dazed, his bow at his side, sparks coming from it.

"Are you okay? What happened?" Harland asked as he went to help Alex.

"A silly experiment," Alex replied, rubbing the back of his neck.

"What experiment?" Fionn examined the trees with smoke still rising from the holes. They were the size of a fist and lined up as if what had pierced them had gone in a straight line. The burn marks had the signs common on trees struck by lightning. A knot formed in his stomach, as he had a suspicion of what had happened.

"I was trying to concentrate all my energy to create a lightning arrow. Maybe a laser one. It got... out of control. Nothing serious," Alex replied, with a smile. But Fionn would have none of it.

"Nothing serious? I know what you were doing. Where did you hear of that technique? And don't bullshit me." Fionn's irises were glowing as he stared at Alex. To his credit, Alex held his stare, his own irises glowing gold. But Alex's stubbornness caused anger and concern in Fionn.

"Fine," Alex sighed. "I read about it in one of Ywain's diaries. Something about a blurry memory of him holding lightning in his hands. I thought that I could achieve something similar. How did you...?"

"Know?" Fionn raised an eyebrow. "I worked with Ywain on that for years, after I got the Gift, to see if we could project our energies through the swords. And he was the only one to achieve it. But it is too exhausting as it burns all your energy, leaving you weak, powerless. And I'm pretty sure he tried that against Byron, which is why he never recovered and suffered from ill health."

"I think I can make it work better. Light bulb, remember?"

"No. Promise me that you won't do that again."

"I'm not Ywain," Alex stood up to Fionn. However, unlike previous occasions, Alex posture wasn't aggressive. On the contrary, he was slouching and his eyes seemed filled with sadness.

"I know you are not him. I apologize for my reaction. I still don't think it is a good idea to do that," Fionn put his left hand on Alex's shoulder, trying to reassure him. "The important thing is that you didn't get hurt."

"It's okay. Happens. Let's go back to the cabin. I'm really hungry," Alex gave Fionn a halfhearted smile.

Fionn exchanged a concerned look with Harland. Yes, Alex wasn't Ywain. But they shared one personality trait: both could be reckless. Perhaps for that reason, Fionn couldn't shake the sensation at the back of his head that the Games would prove more eventful than he wanted them to be.

Chapter 6
Banding Together

CLACK!

Gaby thrust Heartguard, trying to hit Sam. Sam brought up her weapon and the Blade deflected off the white wood and crystal quarterstaff. Sam spun, her red hair flowing freely in the air, using the momentum to aim for Gaby's legs, forcing her to somersault to avoid the attack. They were practicing on a hill outside Manfeld, far from prying eyes but close enough to the industrial city. While Gaby was taking the fight seriously, having even tied her hair with a black hair tie, she had to be careful with controlling the edge of Heartguard and Soulkeeper, or risk an injury. Or worse, damaging *that* particular quarterstaff.

CLACK

Sam gave a little jump and tried to hit Gaby in the head. Both their irises were glowing, Gaby's icy blue and Sam's lilac. The hits increased in speed, as Gaby changed to a reverse grip and Sam spun the quarterstaff to hit her with force. The exchange continued, a series of jumps, parries and hits. Sam had managed to land a few painful hits on Gaby's arms, trying to get her to drop her blades. As much as Sam was forthcoming on her day to day dealing with people, when it came to fighting, she tried to go for the disarm rather than the knockout. The only exception were monsters and the guards for Byron. Sam did sometimes crack skulls with singular joy.

Gaby reeled back from the latest hit. She was used to harsher blows, but that didn't mean they didn't hurt.

Taking advantage of the space, Sam extended her hand to cast a spell, but the energy coming from her fingers fizzled and she shook it off. Gaby took advantage of the distraction to attack, with Sam barely reacting in time to spin her staff. A loud sound echoed through the valley as Heartguard flew across the field, cleaving a rock. Gaby had Soulkeeper aimed at Sam's neck, stopping two centimeters away. But Sam had her staff a few millimeters from Gaby's head and her leg ready to sweep Gaby to the floor.

"So whattdaya think?" Sam asked, with a smile, as she breathed heavily.

"I think at this point," Gaby replied, lowering her blade and walking to recover the other one, "you could even beat Fionn. I'm not worried about your combat skills. What I'm concerned about is that you haven't been able to cast a spell without injuring yourself."

"I know," Sam looked down to her hands. They still hurt from the failed spell. "I'm glad to be alive with a new heart, but the Gift did mess with my ability to cast magick. I don't feel freefolk anymore. I feel like... I lost what made me, me."

"I feel you."

"Your training?"

"Part of it yes," Gaby said. "You know I'm still looking for that missing part. Don't get me wrong the past year has been amazing, but..."

"You still feel like you haven't found who you are?"

"Yes. I guess it's a constant search. So, I know how you feel right now."

"What can we do then?"

"Well, we have to return to Saint Lucy in a few days, so maybe a quick trip to the Maze to search for Mekiri and Ravenhall?" Gaby suggested, eliciting a laugh from Sam.

"You don't find Mekiri, she finds you. And that could take more time than we have left."

"We could ask Fionn," Gaby shrugged.

"I..." Sam paused. "I would prefer to leave him out of this for a while. You know he will get all anxious and overprotective and weird."

Gaby had to agree. Fionn was overprotective. Not that

she could blame him. He was finally moving on with his life and a new family of sorts. Of course, anything that threatened any of its members would send Fionn into papa wolf territory. Which, come to think about it, would be fitting given that he was known as The Greywolf. However, Sam was deluded if she thought that her father hadn't noticed her inability to use magick by now. Fionn might be a tad scatterbrained at times, but he was also very observant.

I need to teach these two to communicate better... damn I'm sounding like a mom, Gaby thought, shaking her head. This talk about family members having trouble communicating led Gaby to think about her own father and how broken her relationship was with him. *I hope I don't have to meet him at the talks. That's the last thing I want.*

Gaby shook her head, trying to erase that train of thought. The memory of her father was unpleasant to say the least. The less she thought about him, the better.

She said, "Then we will have to think of something else. The bright side is that with your current level of skill, you will be able to deal with any of those titanfighters, magick or not."

"You think?" Sam asked incredulous.

"For one, you have actual combat experience, unlike many of those toy soldiers. Should I remind you of your jump without a parachute? And now you have the Gift. I think you will be fine. And you are in a team with me and Sid, so we will represent the freefolk with dignity."

"I've never seen Sid fight," Sam admitted. Sam and Sid didn't spend much time alone, they usually had Gaby or Alex as a buffer. It was funny, as Sid had told Gaby that he was fond of Sam.

"He's good, but boring."

"How come?"

"Like that. He tends to end his fights too fast because he knows where to hit people to make them yield," Gaby didn't want to elaborate further. She looked at the horizon, a few stars were appearing in the sky and the sun was getting lower. "It's getting late and it's never good to be in an open field outside a city. Let's get some drinks and rest."

††††

After each had taken a bath and changed into fresh clothes—jeans, low-heeled boots, t-shirt, and a blue jacket for Gaby, and a black leather jacket, ripped jeans, ankle boots, and a knitted beanie for Sam—Gaby convinced Sam to visit a pub in one of the less touristy parts of Manfeld, near the factories. As Gaby saw it, anyone looking to give them problems was in for a rude awakening. She had visited that particular pub with Fionn before and had taken a liking to it. As they walked towards the bar, they could see the signs of gentrification reaching the area. While Manfeld wasn't as elitist as Portis, it suffered from the same malaise of the other city-states of the Alliance. They reached the door of the pub, illuminated by a neon sign that said 'Okubo'. Gaby pushed open the door to let Sam enter first. Sam took a seat at the bar. Gaby sat next to her.

"Two large clamato beers and an ultimate dipper tower, please," Gaby said to the waitress tending the bar.

"I still can't get used at how hungry the Gift makes you," Sam complained. "I need to eat several times per day. Even casting magick was less exhausting."

"It has to draw energy from somewhere," Gaby explained. "At least our abilities are not as energy demanding as Alex's."

"He uses that as an excuse to eat all the sweets at home," Sam remarked.

While they waited for their order, both turned to listen to the band currently on stage. It was an oddity and not just for the music—an eclectic mix of rock and screams—but for its members. First, there was the vocalist-slash-guitarist, a guy trying too hard to look cool and edgy and failing miserably with his fake blond hair. Behind him there was a petite woman with long, black hair, olive skin and glasses, playing the bass, with metronomic precision. In front of her, there was a skinny guy with a t-shirt from a monster movie, some marks on his face—leftovers of smallpox—and messy black hair, playing the keyboards. The drummer was the strangest sight of them all: a samoharo. Specifically, a Meemech samoharo, the ones that resembled an iguana or gecko with

113

long hair. Unlike other Meemech, he was thin and played the drums with enthusiasm, his tongue coming out of his mouth as he concentrated. The way he was into playing reminded Gaby of Sid when he was focused on flying the Figaro, even if Sid was of the shorter, shelled *Áak* samoharo type.

"Girl, the band is good, but that guitarist is always a tempo behind," Gaby whispered to Sam. She knew it was not correct to criticize others, but on this occasion, she couldn't avoid it. Listening to the man was torture.

"And his voice is like a cat's claw on a blackboard," Sam concurred. "Why is he screaming all the time? Good thing they just finished."

As their order arrived, Sam saw the vocalist waving his hands in exasperation.

"Why is he yelling at his band mates?"

"Ego, I guess," Gaby replied. "Maybe he feels they are ruining his style? Nonetheless, that's unprofessional."

The guy walked towards them and faced Gaby.

"If you are not fond of my style, you can get out of here," he said, pointing to the door.

"You don't own the place," Gaby replied, standing up from her stool. She was taller than the guy. "And for that matter, a true professional doesn't berate his band mates in public. Even less when he is the one missing the notes."

"I keep missing the note because those amateurs can't get it right!"

"That was uncalled for. You should apologize," Gaby told him, as she clenched her fist. It was taking all of her composure to not deck the guy with a right hook.

"For what? They owe me what they have, if it weren't for me she would be still teaching yoga in a Straits town, he would be playing on the sidewalks for coins and he would have to return to whatever hole the samoharos live."

That was what took down Gaby's composure. Her irises glowed faintly blue.

"I will say it only one more time. Apologize to them."

"Or what?" he replied as he took a switchblade from his back pocket and played with it in front of Gaby's face, trying to intimidate her. He was in for a rude awakening. From a table across the room, two bald guys stood up. By their looks, they might have belonged to a biker gang, or tried to look like they did. But it was obvious they were the guy's bodyguards. And it dawned on Gaby: he was a rich kid trying to live the movie version of the suffering rockstar in search of a break. While Gaby wanted to roll her eyes, she had to admit that once, she had had the same idea. She looked at the bodyguards.

"You two, I suggest you stay seated like nice little boys or my friend here," Gaby nodded to Sam, who saluted to the men by raising her pint of beer. "Will bang your heads together so hard that you will be able to read each other's thoughts for life. And you. I can see you won't apologize, so you better leave, or I will take that switchblade from you and cut your hand so quick and painlessly that you won't notice anything until you try to play your guitar and find that your tendons won't work anymore."

The guy looked at Gaby straight in the eyes. Gaby just smiled at him.

"Fine, you can keep those losers," the guy said, pocketing the switchblade.

He went to pick up his guitar, kicked the drum kit and left the pub in a huff, followed by the bodyguards, who apologized to the rest of the band. The three musicians walked towards Gaby and Sam.

"Thank you, lady, for defending us," the keyboard player said. "But you kinda ruined our only shot. He was not only our guitarist and vocalist, he was the one with contacts in the industry."

"And he was paying for our hotel," the bass player girl said.

"I apologize for that," Gaby replied. "However, no one should treat you that way. A band is a team, respect is paramount for it to work. Or at least I see it that way. As for the other thing. I have my guitar in my hotel and I can go fetch it and play with you, see what happens. Who knows?"

"She is a really good singer," Sam added.

"And for your hotel and all that about the contacts. I will take care of that as well," Gaby offered. "Given that I messed that up for you."

"Why? You don't know us," the samoharo said.

"I think you are good musicians, and I like to help others. Besides, I've learned that you find friends in the most serendipitous situations. That's how I met my friend Sid, he is a samoharo too."

"Sid? You know Sid?" the young samoharo opened his eyes wide. His reaction reminded her of when Alex met Fionn. "He is my hero, my main inspiration to leave the Hegemony... Wait... that's why you looked familiar. You are that girl from the news!"

"I'm Gaby, and she is Sam," Gaby replied. She was blushing.

"I'm Xcub'ub, but everyone calls me Scud," the samoharo said.

"And I'm Pamela," the bass player added.

"I'm Freddie," the keyboard player said.

"Nice to meet you all," Gaby smiled her signature crooked smile at them. "I'm going for my guitar, be back in a few minutes and we will play some music."

As Gaby grabbed her jacket, Sam leaned close and whispered in her ear.

"I think that your quest for finding who you are is complete. You got yourself a band."

"As I said, life throws me serendipitous situations, that's how I met Alex and Sid. And Fionn, Harland and you. I just enjoy the ride," Gaby winked at Sam.

Gaby ran back to the hotel with a wide grin. She felt as happy as the day she met Fionn at that other pub, and got to travel with him in search of adventures.

Chapter 7
City of Blinding Lights

"Welcome to Kyôkatô, the capital city of the Kuni Empire! Located in the Auris Continent, across the Lyrian Ocean from the Ionis Continent. One of the oldest and most populous cities in the Core regions and Theia in general, with a population of 3 million sentient beings," A chirpy female voice blasted through the Figaro's speaker in Core language, but with a decidedly Kuni accent. The kind of voice you would hear in certain cartoons. "Also known as the 'City of Blinding Lights' due to the nighttime illumination, the city is designed after the shape of the national flower, the sakura blossom. For decades Kyôkatô has been a center for technological innovation. Known as the home of the Warp Trains core technology, of famous animated series, and KorbyWorld theme parks. But not everything is technology; Kyôkatô has the largest number of ancient temples, some dating from the Age of the Titans, so be sure to visit them. And if you plan to visit them all, Kyôkatô has the most extensive network of urban trains of the Core to get you to where you want to go. Be advised, they can get a bit crowded at peak times. But if you prefer comfort and don't mind paying a bit more, the city is also known for its efficient and ultra-fast taxi services that can take you anywhere safely and on time..."

"Where did you get that recording?" Alex asked.

"I got it from tapping into the Warp Train international station feed. Since the last time you all complained about me speaking as your captain, I decided to play it safe by adding these recordings to the AI databanks. It's also one of the many, many modifications and additions designed into the Figaro Mark II," Sid replied, as he maneuvered the Figaro to fly over the city as the sun rose and the clouds parted to make way for the dawn. They had been flying, mostly on autopilot, all night, with Sid taking turns with Harland and Alex to check that everything worked, while the rest were asleep. Not that Harland or Alex were good pilots, but at least they knew how the ship worked.

"Modifications and additions?" Alex asked. "Such as?"

"You will see," Sid replied. "For now, keep listening to the recording."

"Kyôkatô," the voice continued. "The city that never sleeps. Its name can be translated to Core as the 'Capital City of Cooperation', and this year the city honors that name by being the host to the triennial diplomatic talks between the Free Alliance of Ionis, the Samoharo Hegemony, the Freefolk, the Straits, and the Kuni Empire itself, as well as the Chivalry Games, showcasing the finest warriors from the Core Regions. As well, don't forget to visit the art exhibition by the secluded artist..."

"I didn't know the Straits would join the talks. They usually are fine leaving this stuff to their neighbors," Gaby said. She carried a thermos filled with coffee and handed it to Harland. Behind Gaby stood Sam, not bothering to cover her yawn, and Fionn rubbing the sleep from his eyes.

"I guess the Bestial really scared everybody," Fionn replied.

"Can't blame them," Harland said, as he poured himself a cup of the coffee.

"Will they have their own combat team?" Sam asked.

"Nah, not at this level," Alex explained. "They have good rescue teams to deal with the predacors and the other creatures that crawl out every time there is an earthquake, but not much in terms of combat. When that's needed, the government asks the Samoharo for help."

"Predacors?" Sam asked, still half asleep. "Can't recall what they are."

"Nasty creatures," Alex replied. "Similar to the things that live in the Maze. Rumor has it that the Asurian Empire created them as living weapons millennia ago, but they forgot about them when the Freefolk kicked their asses. Now we have to deal with them."

"You sound very acquainted with them," Fionn said. "I've never been at the Straits."

"Every kid in the Straits learns the three rules: hide, evade, and find help. We are used to them," Alex replied.

"I'm surprised that your rescue teams don't participate in the Games. Sounds like they would fit perfectly," Sam said.

"Those teams are designed to rescue victims from earthquakes or predacors, not for combat," Alex continued. "So, we usually cheer on either demonhunters or the samoharo teams."

"Are you telling me that you might be the first person from the Straits to actually compete in a century?" Harland looked at Alex.

"Yeah?" Alex replied coyly, his cheeks turning deep red. "I think Yaya Zyanya went once, but she never talked about that."

"I wonder how the Straits government will take that."

"I don't think they will care. But just in case, I might need my resident visa soon," Alex said, laughing. But it seemed that no one bought the fake laugh he used to hide his anxiety.

"We will land soon," Sid said. "I think they are having problems finding us a spot. I mean, it's not like there are many airships on the world. But they promise it will be close to the accommodations. Probably in Nakano Park, wherever that is. We might have to take either the urban train or if Harland's purse is open, a couple of cabs to take us to the hotel and then to the Odayakana Kyojin Stadium."

"Odayakana Kyojin Stadium," Sam said. "That's where the games will take place."

"Oh, I know," Alex smiled. It was a wide, childish grin.

"Why are you smiling?" Fionn asked him.

"He is smiling because near the stadium, there is an animatronic giant statue of a robot from a cartoon he is not even a fan of, but he thinks it looks cool," Gaby replied, rolling her eyes.

"Please tell me you know where we will meet the other

two recruits for the Foundation Team. Or that they will be on time for the registration," Harland said.

"Yes," Alex replied. "Don't worry about that. Their day job requires them to know the fastest routes to move around the city, either by walking or on motorbikes."

"No trikes? They have better balance," Fionn said. His preference for the power of a trike was well known. 'The closest thing to riding a war horse' he often said.

"Some streets are too narrow for a trike to help them with their job," Alex explained.

"And what's that job?" Sam asked.

"They deliver curry rice dishes."

"So, they are delivery people?" Harland asked, concern showing on his voice.

"Yes. Excellent curry rice by the way," Alex replied. He was drooling just thinking of it.

"I'm a fool for letting him find me two more fighters, aren't I?" Harland looked at Fionn.

"Well..." Fionn shrugged. "At least you might get a good meal out of this."

† † †

"This is your third ice cream cone today," Joshua said to Kasumi, who was licking the remains of the cone.

"Well, that is your fourth bottle of sake in an hour, so you might not want to keep a tally," Kasumi replied. She was resting against the handrail of a pedestrian bridge that took visitors to the entrance of Popsicle Town, the shopping center next to the Odayakana Kyojin Stadium. The bridge overlooked the giant robot that was a photo spot for tourists. Kasumi wiped the sweat from her brow. She wore a t-shirt, shorts and flats. She was keeping Breaker inside a fabric case, used to carry practice weapons. "Besides, it's not my fault that it is a really hot, humid day."

"You know the sake is to keep the Beast asleep," Joshua grumbled. Like Kasumi's, his shirt was drenched in sweat.

"I know, but you should have brought spare cologne to hide the smell," Kasumi said. "Our new employer might think we are hacks. Take this."

"What do you know of this Harland person?"

"Not much, only that he is the head of the Foundation, seems to be friends with the Greywolf, really into archeology and history. And that he has achondroplasia."

"All of that is the opposite of 'not much,'" Joshua observed.

"Well, it's not like I know what kind of movies he likes. I only know what you can find on the Aethernet. But if you are wondering if he is trustworthy, well, my friend Alex wouldn't hang out with him if he weren't."

"And you trust this friend of yours?"

"With yours and my life. Besides, he has the same chronic hero syndrome that you have."

"We have. You included. How will we know they are here?"

"How many groups do you know that will be carrying four glowing Tempest Blades, alongside an Áak samoharo?" Kasumi said, pointing at them.

"Just that one?" Joshua shrugged, looking at Alex's group.

"Let's save them from the fans," Kasumi waved at them.

† † †

"Kasumi, Joshua, this is everyone," Alex introduced them. "Everyone, these are Kasumi and Joshua."

Everyone exchanged greetings and handshakes while passersby stared at the eclectic group.

"There is something familiar about you. Have we met before?" Fionn said, as he tightened his grip around Joshua's hand.

"I doubt it," Joshua returned the grip and the sentiment. Alex and Kasumi separated them, positioning themselves between Fionn and Joshua, while Sam and Gaby looked bemused at the scene.

"We will not disappoint you, Mr. Rickman," Kasumi said to Harland in perfect Core. "Alex told us how important this is for you."

"We appreciate the opportunity," Joshua added.

"I'm the one that should thank you for agreeing," Harland offered his hand to both. "Excuse me for the intrusion, Alex did mention your hearing aids, while we were filling the registration forms a few months ago. I have to ask: are those safe for combat?"

"What, my hearing aids?" Kasumi pulled her hair aside to show one of them. "Yes, they are combat tested and shock proof. I'm a demonhunter, so me and my family saved to get them. A specialist from the Straits designed them for me. Actually, it was during that trip that I met Alex and we have been corresponding friends since then."

"May I ask how it happened, or am I being too nosy?" Harland asked.

"No, it's fine. I caught the maroon fever when I was fourteen years old. Many of my classmates died. I was lucky since I only loss most of my hearing."

"I'm sorry," Harland said.

"Don't, please." Kasumi replied, uncomfortable.

"I understand." Harland said. "If by any chance they get damaged during the event, The Foundation will pay for a new set. That, I can promise."

"Thank you. I don't think it will be necessary though."

"Why?" Harland asked, visibly confused.

"Because I'm not planning to lose, even less, allow someone to get that close," Kasumi smiled, winking at him.

"You are confident," Sam interjected. "Competition will be tough. Titanfighters, demonhunters, Gifted."

"I believe she can become a champion," Joshua added. "Even going against your friends."

"I like that," Harland admitted. "Makes me feel at ease."

"She is quite pretty," Sam whispered to Gaby.

"I know that look," Gaby replied. "Careful."

"What?" Sam shrugged her shoulders. "You know we freefolk don't have the same hang-ups about gender and sex as humans do."

"I'm not talking about that," Gaby said, "I don't care about that. What I care is that she is technically our rival in the competition."

"I thought you didn't care about the competition," Sam laughed.

"I don't care about this particular event. But I like to win. And I would hate to have to fight against her. I like her too."

† † †

"Thank the Fortunes for air conditioning," Kasumi said as she placed Breaker on the empty seat next to her. They were sitting in the nearly empty stadium, far from the other delegations and their champions. None of the teams seemed interested in fraternization. Which, by the way both Alex and Fionn were grinding their teeth at a competitor waving at them, was a good thing. Kasumi recognized him from some magazine articles as Xavier Roche', infamous for crippling his opponents more than once. A thug for hire, basically. He was flanked by two fighters Kasumi didn't recognize.

"What's that?" Sam asked, breaking Kasumi's train of thought.

"This?" Kasumi took Breaker out of the bag and showed it to the group. "This is Breaker-sama. As you can see, you are not the only one with a Tempest Blade."

"Where did you get it?" Fionn asked, putting his hand close to Breaker. "I've never heard of it. But it does look and feel like a Tempest Blade."

"When we were at Ravenhall, the old monolith there mentioned other Tempest Blades, but the monolith was too damaged to make sense of it. Maybe there was some mention of this one there," Gaby said.

"I wouldn't touch it," Joshua said to Fionn. "It will give you frostbite. I should know."

"I got it at a temple, at the start of the year," Kasumi replied. "Around the time I got your message, Alex. Funny that."

"What temple?" Harland asked.

"*Himitsu.*" Kasumi said, bringing her right index finger to her lips. Harland looked at her, confused. Kasumi raised an eyebrow. "It means secret."

"Look," Alex interrupted. "Some of the previous champions are entering now, alongside the Judges. There is Augustus Mu, Bev Johnson and Yokoyawa, the samoharo champion.

Augustus Mu was a Solarian Knight, wearing regular

clothes instead of his standard issue gold and silver armor. Bespectacled, with white skin that contrasted with his long, black hair and purple eyes, he was the image of aloofness and professionalism. Alex recalled that Fionn had mentioned fighting him once during a friendly match and considered the man a tough opponent.

Bev Johnson, on the other hand, was a jovial man, built like a wall, with brown skin, his greying hair styled into a big perm, and a neatly trimmed beard. Alex was a fan of him, as Bev had always acted as the exemplary titanfighter: kind, attentive, always willing to talk with his fans, most of them younger kids. Proof that you could be a consummate professional and still be a nice person.

Yokoyawa, also known as 'Big Y', on the other hand, was intimidating. A Meemech samoharo, he was almost two meters tall and built like a mountain. His long, black hair covered one of his red eyes. His tongue came out from time to time. Like Augustus, he wasn't wearing his legendary purple armor, decorated with bones. Instead, he was wearing casual human clothes. Which must have been hard to get, given his size and the long tail. Alex hated the idea of having to fight him.

"What the hell is he doing here?" Sid asked.

"Who? The Samoharo champion? I thought he retired," Alex replied. "Maybe he is here as part of the delegation."

"That idiot," Sid muttered.

"You know him?" Harland asked.

"Unfortunately. After this I need to go talk with him."

"Shhh the address is about to start," Sam shushed them.

As the champions went to their seats of honor in the stands next to the judges table, the three judges walked towards the center of the sandy arena. All three were human, one wearing traditional Kuni robes, the other wearing a suit and the third, a lady sporting a buzz cut, wore a more casual outfit.

The Kuni judge tapped the floor with his foot and the sand parted as a platform rose. Several gears, towers and constructs arose as well. Alex wasn't sure if they were magickal, hard light, memory material like his bow, or something else. Nonetheless the effect was impressive, as it meant that the arena could simulate any terrain or material the judges wished. On the platform where the judges stood, three microphone stands appeared. The second judge tapped the mic, causing a feedback loop screech.

"Welcome competitors to the thirty-third Chivalry Games!" His voice boomed. "As usual, it is heartening to see old veterans," he pointed to Bev Johnson and Yokoyawa. "Representatives of noble organizations," then he pointed to Augustus, "and newcomers. Whatever your expertise in these games, the rules are the same for all."

The female judge spoke. Her voice was firm but pleasant.

"First, this is not a rule per se, but this year entrance themes and musical tracks during the fights won't be allowed. We don't want a repeat of last time, which we won't mention."

"That's a shame, I wanted to test the battle bard theory," Harland whispered.

"What's that?" Alex asked.

"And old theory of his," Fionn explained. "According to some records, some ancient armies, like the Silver Riders and the Montoc Dragons had bards playing music alongside the battle, to generate this weird magickal effect that increased their battle prowess."

"You don't seem to believe in that," Kasumi replied.

"As much as I would like to hear Gaby singing while we fight, I have never seen that. At least not during the Great War. But hey, a lot of information got lost after the Death of the Dragons," Fionn shrugged.

"Now, the Rules!" the Kuni judge said.

"The Ruuuuuuules," The second judge added, with extreme dramatic effect. The female judge slapped him.

"Rule number one," she said. "As you know, this is an aggregated competition, rather than eliminatory. It means that the more you fight, the more you win, the more points you accumulate. The winner after the two weeks of duels will be the one with the most points. If there is a tie at the end of the tally, a special duel will be organized to determine the winner. If the tie can't be broken, or there are more than two contestants tied, the winner will be chosen by election of their peers, based on who demonstrated better fighting prowess and a chivalric attitude during the event."

"Rule number two," said the second judge, rubbing the back of his head. "The duels are one versus one. It means you can't get help from your teammates, because if you do, you will be disqualified. Only life threatening, emergency situations not derived from the duel, allow for your teammates to enter the arena. And you can't fight your own teammates without permission from your delegation or the judges. Any special circumstances will have to be examined by the panel and the veterans."

"Rule number three," the Kuni judge said. "These games are inspired by the titanfighters of old, who had to fight monsters under uncertain conditions. Thus, in some duels, you will have to complete an obstacle course to reach the arena to fight. In others, the arena is the course. The contestant with more experience can choose the course if they wish. You get points for completing the course and for winning your fights, plus the remaining time on the clock. Points are assigned in relation to your 'ranking differential'. A veteran won't get many points for challenging a newcomer, unless they beat several newcomers. But a newcomer could score many points by accepting and defeating a higher ranked fighter. If you withdraw before completing the course, you will lose points."

"And rule number four," the female judge said, while she looked at Xavier and his comrades. "While accidents happen, and this is a full contact event, crippling for life or killing your opponent is frowned upon and depending on the circumstances, could get you disqualified for life. This is a friendly event after all."

"As for how the duels are set, it's simple," the Kuni judge said. "A veteran seeded higher can challenge anyone. Newcomers can only be challenged, they can't issue. Unless the Unspoken rule is in effect."

"The Unspoken rule," The second judge added, making emphasis on 'unspoken'. This time the Kuni judge gave him a look that suggested that he was ready to throw his over enthusiastic colleague from the platform.

"What's the unspoken rule?" Kasumi asked to Harland.

"The idea of the event is that some 'diplomatic' disputes during the Talks among member states of the Alliance and invited states, can be solved by pitting your champions to decide the outcome in a more peaceful way than a war or a battle. So, the delegation that wants to press a claim or win an argument, agrees to submit the duel with their counter-part. Winners of the duel decide the result of the argument, usually following the lead from their delegation."

"Like the old trials by combat?" Alex asked.

"In a way. That's why some delegations hire veterans and pro fighters," Harland replied.

"That gives a lot of leverage to the delegations with more money over those that are poorer, or new to the scene. That's unfair," Alex said.

"But it has avoided major conflicts. Usually, the Samo-haro or the Kuni tend to side with the weaker sides if their opinions align, so they fight in their stead in exchange of small favors, like preferential commercial trades. Such is the nature of politics," Harland explained.

"And that's why this year you, as representatives of the Foundation and the Freefolk delegation, can expect a lot of challenges," Fionn added.

"You make it sound like the fate of the world is on our shoulders," Alex said.

"The fate of the world is on our shoulders. Great," Sid said ruefully.

† † †

As the delegations left the stadium, Sid waited in an empty corridor near one of the exits. He was resting against the wall, his arms crossed, as he focused on the echo of the heavy steps coming his way. If he had seen Yokoyawa, odds were his cousin had seen him too. No need to send messages for a meeting. Sid knew they would find each other. It was that special bond from being hatched together.

"Since when are you wearing braces?" Sid asked, as

Yokoyawa passed by. The height difference was staggering. Yokoyawa's two meters versus Sid one meter and forty-five centimeters. Yokoyawa kneeled to see Sid eye-to-eye.

"Wello, it's nice to see you, Siddhartha," Yokoyawa replied. His voice was a baritone, with a calm quality to it. "As for your question, my teeth finished regrowing after you punched me, but they kept growing wrong, so a human from the Straits suggested that I could use these to set them."

"You know I hate that name, so I would ask you to refrain from using it again," Sid replied. No one used his full name and he liked it that way. "I see the Ajaw and the council sent you. Are you here to compete or to do some cleaning to keep the status quo?"

"You know it's not like that. And things have changed since you left. That's what I wanted to talk with you about. I actually left the organization and..."

"Left? I was banished! So, save me the niceties."

"You were banished because you refused to follow an omega level order and conclude your mission as stated. And on top of that, you not only hit me, your commanding officer, but also the high priest and the Ajaw. It was being banished or executed. I did what I could to get you a retirement plan instead of a funeral."

"I'm well aware of that, cousin," Sid raised his voice as he uncrossed his arms. "I thank you for that. But I will be clear in one thing: those kids are my friends, not targets 'to clean'. My family. And good, decent beings. So, if you or any of the Hegemony dares to even breathe a slightly menacing comment, I will put you all three meters under the ground. And you know very well I'm fully capable of that. I wasn't the Obsidian Jaguar for nothing."

"I know," Yokoyawa sighed. "For what's worth, after your banishment, I quit. I found the omega orders cruel and counterproductive. I'm here for a special request as the new Tlatoani wants to change our relationship with the Humans and the Freefolk. It was your speech when you left that started the changes. Including inspiring some of us to study to become something you could call battle therapist. Things will be different."

"Good to know you found your conscience. I will believe it when I see it. And trust me. I'm watching."

Sid turned around and left without looking at his cousin. Some wounds remained open even after years. But he did hear something as he stalked away, Yokoyawa sobbing as he whispered, "I'm sorry."

† † †

"Are you okay?" Gaby asked Sid when they saw him coming out of the stadium.

"Yes, just a little *friendly* chat with the family I haven't seen in years," Sid replied. "Well, what now? We still have a couple of days free before we start earning our pay."

"You are getting paid? Harland didn't mention anything about that," Alex said, confused.

"Thank you, Sid, as if paying for all your expenses and accommodations wasn't enough," Harland replied, annoyed.

"You need to be a little less tight with the money," Sid smiled at his friend.

"And you need to learn to keep quiet."

"Do they always act like an old married couple?" Joshua asked Gaby.

"Only when they are sober."

"So, what about me and Joshua," Kasumi exclaimed. "Serve as your tour guides and take you to the most popular spots and the best restaurants?"

"Cool!" Alex replied, almost jumping up and down as if he were an overexcited kid... which wasn't that far from the truth, actually. "There are so many places I want us to visit: Electronic Town, the Eden of the Geek. And the Crossing at the Faithful Companion..."

"I would like to visit some Temples. I find their rituals fascinating," Sam added.

"I heard that there is an interesting interactive digital art exhibition not far from here. Better than the creepy one with those ugly statues. What about you Fionn?" Gaby said.

"Personally, I would like to visit a few design stores. I have always liked the minimalist style of the Kuni. And now that I recall, Professor Ortiga and the rest of the Freefolk delegates wanted to try a karaoke bar," Fionn said.

"I hope we have enough energy left for the tournament after this," Gaby laughed.

"I hope we have enough money left," Harland sighed.

"You worry too much," Fionn said. "What's the worst that could happen?"

"Great!" Sid exclaimed. "Now you jinxed it."

† † †

After listening to the rules, and a long day visiting some of the popular spots in Kyôkatô, everybody went to their hotel to rest. Not Alex though. He waited until he was sure most of them were asleep, or at least distracted. He put on a hoodie and left the room, trying to make as little noise as possible. He had at least seven excuses ready in case someone discovered him, including the not so fake line of him being nervous about his first combat. Truth be told, he enjoyed walking at night, when few people were around, the air was cool and the lights' reflection on the wet sidewalks offered him a sense of calm. For Alex, that was the essence of a true city of blinding lights.

The hotel where they were staying, a concrete five storey building, wasn't far from the temple where Kasumi's family had their stall. Alex walked the streets feeling calm, his hands inside the pockets of his hoodie. Not far from here, like a giant candle, the SkySpire, symbol of the modern age of architecture and communications, oversaw the city. Alex crossed the street and passed several stores and traditional restaurants, until he reached the main gate of Saikai Street that led to the temple. He entered. The otherwise bustling street was now quiet, with a few shops still open. Alex reached the second gate, from which the main red and gold temple could be seen, with its giant paper lanterns. On each side of the gate stood a statue of a deity painted in red. The statues were four meters tall and showed the deities performing an intricate dance. Their faces set in fierce expressions. Alex stared at them, analyzing every detail.

"Impressive isn't it?" a female voice said from behind, making Alex jump. His heart was racing. He turned around and saw Kasumi and Joshua, standing behind him. "Sorry for scaring you."

"I'm not scared," Alex said, smiling.

"Then why are your irises glowing?" Joshua asked nonchalantly.

"Ah that..." Alex looked towards one of the statues, as he tried to calm himself. The sudden adrenaline spike has activated the Gift. It still happened to him from time to time. "Who are they meant to represent?"

"Two of the guardian deities of the Kamisava, the universal consciousness. In a way, the equivalent of Kaan'a for you," Kasumi explained. "Ready to go?"

"Lead the way," Alex said. "By the way, are my eyes back to normal?"

† † †

The inside of the curry house was warm. It was a small place with only two rows of booths close to the kitchen. The strong smell of curry inundated the air. Alex took a sip from his glass of water, as Kasumi served the dishes Joshua was cooking alongside Shirô, the night shift cook, and Kasumi's cousin.

"Quiet night, uh?" Alex asked. There was only one other couple, two guys still wearing their suits, probably coming straight from the office, finishing their meal.

"It's Thursday, close to midnight. It's usually the slowest shift. Tomorrow however, this place will be hectic," Kasumi explained, as she walked to the booth and put a plate in front of him. She sat down across from him. "This is the special you wanted to taste. I'm not sure how you can eat this many calories. Especially this late in the night."

The special in question was a large plate of rice mixed with beef curry and garlic, with a large portion of cheese mixed with the rice, a hamburger patty that was filled with cheese and an egg on top of it all. Alex was drooling just seeing it.

"The Gift is a practical thing to have, but its downside, in particular with my expression of it, is that it needs a high intake of calories every now and then, just to allow me to generate the amounts of energy I can expel."

"Are you sure it's not an excuse to be gluttonous?" Kasumi asked.

"I bhh yhhh pahhmm?" Alex tried to speak with a mouthful of food in his mouth.

"Never mind, enjoy, while I help to close the restaurant."

Kasumi stood up from the table and went to the cash register to receive the payment from the last two customers. Joshua prepared a pair of dishes, while Shirô started to clean the kitchen. All while Alex enjoyed the best curry dish he had tasted in his whole life.

Kasumi closed the door after Shirô left for the night, as Joshua finished cleaning the stove and took the other dishes to the table. Alex was still trying to finish his.

"I'm glad you are enjoying that unholy dish," Joshua said. "There is no better compliment to a chef that seeing someone enjoying his creation."

"You are really good," Alex replied.

"I had a good teacher," Joshua explained. "Noriyuki sensei is not only a good teacher of martial arts, but of cooking as well. And I have a lot of time to practice."

"Truth be told, Joshua has been of great help to the family since he arrived... what? How long?" Kasumi said.

"Leave it at long enough to see your grandfather grow up," Joshua replied, averting his gaze.

"Are you sure your parents can spare you for the next couple of weeks? Won't they need help?" Alex asked.

"They will be fine," Kasumi replied. "Since you told me months ago, we have been getting ready. Besides, it has brought good publicity to both the restaurant and the stall at the temple. This was our last night for a while."

"I'm even more thankful for the dish then," Alex said as he returned to finish it. "And about that problem you asked me to look into. I have good and bad news."

"Start with the bad," Joshua said, putting his utensils down.

"Based on what I could find out, and the results of the test Kasumi made," Alex paused to drink some water. "I don't think it is possible to separate you from the Beast... not without killing you."

"Why?" Joshua asked.

"Look, biotech is not my field of expertise, but what I found is that whatever the Beast is, probably came from the Pits. I saw similar things last year."

"Where?" Kasumi asked.

"Byron and the Bestial." Alex explained matter-of-factly. "That makes you a tovainar."

"So, you don't think we can get rid of it? Or you don't want to do it?" Joshua asked. For a second Alex could have sworn he saw Joshua's fangs grow and his eyes turn yellow.

"If you are implying what I think you are, don't," Alex said with a smile. Truth be told, he resented the remark, but could understand where it came from. He had the same reaction when Harland grilled him about his rap sheet. And Fionn had been acting weird around Joshua. But Alex's guts were telling him to trust the man. "Kasumi trusts you and vouches for you. And that would be enough for me. But you already have a track record of helping others. So, I don't care where or how you got your abilities. I want to help you. That's why I don't think it's viable to separate you."

Alex waited for Joshua's reaction. His face returned to normalcy. Kasumi only muttered something in Kuni-go that Alex translated to be 'men and their fragile egos'.

"See, that being has been grafted into you for decades? Centuries?" Alex continued. "The symbiosis is already too advanced, too linked to split you both with what we have at hand. Which admittedly is not much. But even if we had the proper tools, I'm sure it would be impossible at this point to do it without both of you dying. I'm sorry. As I said, this is not my field, but the information points towards that."

Joshua looked down at his dish. His sorrowful expression broke Alex's heart.

"Don't feel dismayed," Kasumi said to Joshua with a smile. Then she said to Alex. "You said you had good news."

"Ah, yes! The split might not be possible, but we might be able to reset the Beast to factory settings, so to speak."

"I don't get it," Joshua said, confused.

"Kasumi's pressure point technique is used to reset the

energy flow of a body, to induce healing. Or to reverse it to kill... anyways. If it works, the Beast would go into hibernation, at least until it's fed," Alex explained, as he drew some diagrams around a human shape on a napkin.

"And how does that help?" Kasumi asked.

"As it would be reset, rather than forced into you, you would have a better chance to get it under your total control from now on, or at least until the technology is available to separate you."

"It's better than nothing. What are we waiting for?" Kasumi said, jumping from her seat with excitement.

"That's the tricky thing. We need access to the core of the Beast to apply your technique and the only way to get to it, is when the Beast is fully out," Alex drew a circle inside the shape.

"That's too dangerous. No," Joshua replied. His tone of voice was serious and forceful.

"I'm aware of what the Beast does to living beings," Alex continued. "Kasumi told me that it sucks them dry of vital energy. But I have a plan. I generate enough energy to keep her safe. Using Yaha to keep the tendrils away, while she applies the technique. I would do both, but I couldn't learn the technique properly, and I can't defend myself while doing it at the same time."

"I'm in," Kasumi added, with a wide grin in her face.

"It's too dangerous," Joshua observed.

"Not if we do it under proper conditions. So, after the tournament ends, we could go to the Water temple and do it there. Can you keep it under control till then? A few days?" Kasumi asked.

"I think so," Joshua looked upwards, stroking his chin.

"So, we have a plan," Kasumi said. "Thank you, Alex."

For once, it felt nice to have someone that trusted him with his plans. Alex felt more relaxed and happy than he had in the past few months, even if it was for a brief moment.

Maybe I could move here after my visa expires, Alex thought. *I mean, what's the worst that could happen?*

Chapter 8
Freefall

I think I spoke too quickly last night, Alex thought as he examined his current predicament. Harland was standing next to him, as Alex got ready for his course.

The Chivalry games had started with a great bang; a duel between former champions Yokoyawa of the Samoharo and Bev Johnson, representing Manfeld. The former champions had given a spectacular fight that Bev won by a slim margin. Sid said that his cousin's heart wasn't in the fight and Alex had been inclined to believe him. For such an impressive warrior, Yokoyawa seemed to be distracted.

Alex's current predicament was a result of the second duel that had rippled across the whole event. Simon Belerofont and his companion mastiffs had challenged Joshua directly, either because he thought he was a newbie that couldn't afford titanarmor—Joshua fought without protection—or because his patrons had asked him to fight to see how much they could get from the Foundation as Harland was looking for their support. But Joshua flipped the script and demolished Belerofont with such force that some wondered if the experienced titanfighter could continue. That win elevated the number of crazy challenges to the champions of the Foundation that Kasumi and Joshua were all too glad to tackle. It was because of these challenges that Alex found himself in his worst nightmare, staring up at the start of the course which was more than four hundred meters above the ground. The stadium had even opened the roof to make space for this particular course.

"You are aware this is a trap, right?" Harland asked with concern on his voice. "Varekay works for Dewart. And he would love to see the Foundation lose ground in the talks, not to mention he would enjoy seeing you hospitalized, or worse."

"I know it's a trap," Alex replied. "Otherwise why would he have gone first in such an insane course? It would have been better for him to let me go first and hope I break my neck. There is some trick to this. He must have bribed the course designer to get it to his liking." By now, Alex had a suspicion on what his opponent's plan was. He had to admit it was a clever rouse. "But I also have a plan... well, more like an idea for one."

"I hate when you say that," Harland replied with a groan. "I think you should withdraw. This challenge is simply insane."

"Doing so would mean a disqualification and would spell problems for you," Alex replied. "And we don't want that do we? These talks are too important."

"I'm worried about you being able to get out of this. That's all."

Alex smiled at Harland as he went into the elevator that would take him to the platform four hundred meters above. How the course designers had achieved that was something that Alex would have to ask about later.

"I'm gonna do what I always do in the face of a problem," Alex said, adjusting his goggles and checking the power running through his vest. The material seemed to be ready to absorb any shock. He waved to Harland. "Push forward."

† † †

Alex eyed the challenge, the wind blowing his ponytail, his irises glowing in the familiar golden hue. The course challenge per se was easy, travel from one point to another. No major obstacles aside from the occasional curve. The thing was that the course was a vertical fall inside transparent tubes of aluplastic reinforced with rings. Each end of the tube had railings, probably for climbing into the tunnel in case one missed the jump or was afraid to hit the end and wanted to hang up for a while. Assuming the shoulders endured the backlash. It wasn't a continuous fall within the tubes though. On the contrary, every now and then there was a floating pool with a concrete base around it, full of what seemed to be water. There was also a final pool on the ground, the goal. The pools gave a false sense of cushioning the fall. He knew better. At the speed he would be falling, hitting the liquid would be akin to hitting a concrete wall at high speed.

"In other words, this is insane," Alex muttered.

Only a titanfighter with the required armor could endure such punishment. Or a Gifted that could control his fall using electromagnetic fields.

How the hell had Sam managed to do what she did when she jumped from the Bestial? Alex thought.

There was no going back. He jumped head first into the tube.

His heart pounded inside his chest. The adrenalin was running through his body, filling it with the Gift. Everything was a blur, the air hit his face with great force and as he spun on his vertical axis to adjust for the curves, he tried to enjoy the experience of falling at great speed and conquering his fear. Keeping control of the fall within the tubes was trickier than he expected. The speed was neck breaking. If it weren't for the goggles, he wouldn't be able to see anything. Alex kept his arms glued to his body, his legs stretched, trying to offer the least resistance possible. There was no point in doing otherwise, or he would risk a fracture or worse. He idly wondered how Varekay had navigated the tunnels. Alex doubted anyone could do what he was doing now.

FWOOSH

Alex had taken time to study the course as the elevator took him to the starting platform, and noticed the rings. Steel rings. And steel worked well with magnetic fields. That meant he could use his trick of applying the excess electromagnetic field that his Gift emanated from his body to better control his fall. In a way, he was using the tunnel the same way a warp train used the maglev railways to keep floating. As long as he maintained his focus, he could subtly manipulate the field around his body to move around and even to slow his fall enough to not hit the liquid in front of him with enough force to break his skull. That solved the issue for him, but still didn't answer how Varekay was doing it. Knowing that was key to learn how to beat his opponent.

FWOOSH

I should have studied more about what titanarmors can provide beyond protection, Alex thought. *Big oversight.*

FWOOSH

The first pool was approaching fast. Alex took a deep breath and moved his arms forward with some effort, due to the air resistance. He stretched them out in front of his face, his hands together trying to keep a sleek profile. The air was oddly warm and his goggles fogged a bit.

FWOOSH

That's odd.

FWOOSH

The hit hurt. The bones on his hands hurt. Even with him slowing his fall just enough, the impact was painful enough that he let out a breath from the shock. He swam as fast as he could inside the warm liquid. It seemed to be less dense than water and the pool had no container. It was all held together through some kind of spell or a field similar to the one that encased the warp trains. Give the hour of the day and the height, he had expected for the water to be cold. Yet it was warm. Too warm.

Alex reached the surface, swam towards the concrete ledge and climbed out of the pool. Being wet made him feel slightly heavier. That would make navigating the next part of the course slightly difficult as he needed to correct for the extra weight.

He heard the faint splash of Varekay hitting the last pool and a small cloud of steam rose through the air. To win more points, he would have to beat Varekay's course time and then beat him quickly once the stopwatch restarted when both were on the ground. Alex would actually have to proactively use his force field to win speed on the last two segments.

You are gonna die, the dark voice said in his head.

Not right now, Alex thought, *I need to figure out what he is planning.*

You are so blind I'm surprised we are still alive.

Alex ignored the voice. Then he saw the next tunnel and the aluplastics was all fogged, like his goggles. Then he connected the dots...

"Aww crap," Alex said aloud.

Fire. He hadn't accounted for that.

† † †

Alex raced through the second part of the course. The wind hit him in the face at greater speed and the air dried his clothes. His heart pounded inside his chest twice as fast as before.

Steam, warm liquid... his armor can emit heat and is using the warm air around him and temperature difference to control his fall.

FWOOSH

A twist here, a spin there and a course correction avoided a collision with a curved section of the tunnel.

FWOOSH

I can do this; I can totally do this.

This time he didn't even bother to make for a diving position when he was close to the second pool. He needed to test something. Focusing his Gift, he imagined the electromagnetic field around him as something malleable by his hands. He projected the field in front of his head. He would break the surface with the field in front of him as a shield. If he could reduce the impact the same way he did it a year ago at the university, he would avoid a serious injury to his arms, which he'd need. And more important, he wouldn't break his neck or his skull on impact. Or at least he hoped so.

FWOOSH

I never wanted to fly, not this way. I hope I don't die.

FWOOSH

The adrenaline rush surged once more through his body. He could feel the energy of the Gift mixing with his blood as he drew a long breath and closed his eyes.

Those were probably the longest seconds of his life.

Alex hit the water with a big splash that sent liquid over the concrete ledge and into the air. Opening his eyes, he found himself almost floating in the air. The shock lasted for a few seconds then he regained his composure and swam towards the ledge, where he stood up and jumped to the last course, not even stopping to admire the view. If he had, he would have noticed the large steam cloud below.

FWOOSH

But he didn't need it. He was almost sure now what was waiting for him and he had a plan.

FWOOSH

† † †

Harland was observing the duel from the edge of the arena. Most representatives saw the duels from their lofty boxes with comfortable seats. Harland chose not to. He had gotten Alex into this mess, the least he could do was to support him from as close as the rules allowed. Kasumi and Joshua were standing next to him, in silence. He was biting his nails. The course gave an advantage to Varekay. Harland knew how Alex felt about heights. A knot at the bottom of his stomach told him he was close to developing an ulcer from worry and concern. This duel was important for another reason: Harland was hoping for a win, so that it could give the Foundation some clout and leverage against the Dewart representative and stop some, if not all, of his lesser plans and force him to reveal his hand.

Harland saw Varekay hit the last pool, generating a huge steam cloud. The titanfighter got out of the pool and Varekay waited, looking at the tunnel. Despite the vapor steaming the aluplastic, a shape could be seen falling through the last section and the trap the titanfighter had set. Varekay threw punches in the air, aimed towards the pool, sending fireballs generated by his armor. The fireballs soon made the liquid boil. Steam covered the end of the tunnel and the environment feel humid and warm to the point of being uncomfortable for anyone not being a samoharo or from the Straits.

Alex's shape got closer.

"Heh, that fool." Harland heard Varekay say.

Something hit the pool and a splash erupted. Varekay didn't waste a second and sent a second barrage of fireballs powered by his titanarmor towards the pool. Anyone inside there would be either steamed alive or passed out, unable to avoid the attacks. The bribe had worked. The trap had worked.

† † †

Alex saw the pool closing in. He unlatched Yaha and let it fall in front of him, while he focused the Gift in to lessen the fall. He would have only a few seconds to pull off this stunt and needed to be as precise as possible. Thrusting his arms forward, with the palms facing up, he reached the end of the tunnel. In a split second, he grabbed the railing and instead of falling into the water, used the momentum to throw himself towards the outside face of the tunnel. He twisted in the air, just like in gymnastic class and hit the tunnel with the soles of his sneakers, then launched himself to land behind Varekay, who was bombarding Yaha with flames.

I hope Yaha forgives me for that.

The cloud of steam covered the entire place, which gave him the perfect cover to approach Varekay. It wouldn't be hard. The guy was gloating loudly. But first, he needed to get Yaha back. Just in case.

"What a fool. If the fall didn't break his bones, he is now toast," Varekay waved his hands around, dispelling the steam, walking towards the pool. While he walked, he looked towards Harland, Kasumi and Joshua.

"That's why rookies that don't own titanarmor shouldn't participate in these Games. I hope he is barely alive, so I don't get disqualified," Varekay yelled at the audience and the judges, taking advantage of the microphones around the arena, which amplified his voice.

"Ha," Joshua laughed, his arms still crossed in front of him. Kasumi was holding the laughter.

"You have something to say, bum?"

"You are such an idiot," Joshua yelled, his voice amplified by the microphone.

Varekay looked into the pool. It was empty.

"What?"

"Before challenging someone to a duel, finish your current one," Alex said behind him. Varekay turned around but Alex's right hook was already on a collision course with his nose.

Crack.

The strength of the punch sent Varekay reeling backwards, bleeding profusely. Alex didn't give him pause. Closing in, he punched repeatedly at Varekay's sides, where the titan armor was not covering. Then he kicked the titanfighter with all his strength, sending him onto the floor. Varekay stood up, clearly angry. Steam was coming from his armor and it took on a red hue, similar to that of a heater.

"That's cheating," Varekay said, his left hand in front of his face.

"That's rich coming from you. I mean, it was a clever ruse. How much did it cost you to bribe the course designer?" Alex asked, as he extended his collapsible bow and pulled the string, forming an arrow from the smart cartridge. "It mustn't have been cheap for a trick you can use only once."

"Shut up!"

Varekay sent a barrage of fireballs towards Alex. But Alex evaded them by running to the left, letting go a series of electrified arrows. The arrows hit Varekay in the parts not covered by the armor, and the electric shock knocked him out. However, a couple of fireballs had hit Alex in the left arm, leaving a nasty burn.

Harland almost jumped into the arena. But Kasumi extended her arm, stopping him.

"It's already over."

Ventilators around the arena activated, dissipating the steam clouds. On the field, Varekay lay on the ground, the arrows sticking from his body, while a few meters away, Alex was catching his breath. He went to pick up Yaha from the bottom of the pool. Alex could feel that Yaha wasn't happy with him.

I'm sorry. Really sorry.

As he climbed up, the scoreboard showcased the judges' decision. A win for Alex, with an accrued amount of one hundred and fifteen points, putting him in the top five of the ranking.

A cheer exploded into the air. Both the Freefolk delegation and his friends were celebrating, followed by claps from Bev Johnson and the Solarian knights. He even saw Prince Arthur clapping. Soon the rest of the audience joined the cheer. Harland, Kasumi and Joshua entered the arena to congratulate him, as the emergency services arrived to help Varekay.

"Seems that you scored a big hit," Joshua said.

"But that burn needs to be treated," Kasumi added. "My mom has an ointment that will take care of it."

"Thank you, Alex, it means a lot," Harland extended a hand to Alex and smiled.

For the first time in... a year perhaps, Alex was happy with himself. He could almost cry.

Chapter 9
Ready? Fight!

In the following days, the outlook for the Foundation became even better, as the newcomers to the Chivalry Games rose through the rankings. By the second day, they were sitting in the top ten.

The course for Kasumi's second duel was short, which meant that the arena would be all that trickier—and all that more dangerous—to fight on. As important as this fight was for the Foundation, it would be all the harder because of her opponent and the bad blood between them.

Hiroyuki Kuromatsu. A famous demonhunter, he had been a student of one of her father's rivals. After the fire at the Temple of the Quiet Water, Kuromatsu had been one of the most vociferous in demanding the removal of her family as custodians. He had also been very vocal in his disagreement with allowing someone with a disability to be accepted as a demonhunter. Despite his unpleasant personality, he was good. Very good. This was going to be a difficult, and very personal, fight. Kasumi was eager to start.

"Don't let him get into your head, not again," Joshua said as he stood beside Kasumi outside the arena.

"Do they know each other?" Harland asked, with a hint of nervousness in his voice. Kasumi winning this fight could give Harland some leverage on the Kuni delegates due to the Unspoken Rule. And he could use any advantage at the moment.

"Let's just say that there is no love lost between them," Joshua replied.

"I got this," Kasumi replied. Without looking at Joshua, she entered the arena as the course built itself. It resembled a series of icebergs floating in freezing water.

Icebergs? The cold won't be an issue thanks to Breaker, Kasumi thought. *The slippery surfaces on the other hand...*

After jumping across several slabs of ice, Kasumi reached the center of the arena at the same time as Hiroyuki. He stood there, his arms crossed, looking at her with the cold eyes of contempt.

"You should not be here, Shimizu. You bring even greater dishonor upon your family, who have already proven themselves failures! You are a mistake, and I will prove it in front of all of these people," He gestured with his arms to take in the crowd. "I will even fight you unarmed!" Hiroyuki sneered.

"Your actions are a disgrace, Kuromatsu-san. They are unbecoming of a demonhunter." Kasumi replied calmly, as she unlatched Breaker and cleaved it into the icy ground of the arena. "And I will face you unarmed too. That's not an issue for me."

"What do you know? You are here by chance," Hiroyuki said, then he turned to the audience and raised his voice. "Start that stopwatch, Judges, I will beat her in less than a minute. Then we can move onto actual duels between actual champions and not amateurs!"

The audience roared at hearing that, as the stopwatch was set. Kasumi was tempted to turn off her aids, to block the noise. But decided against it. Then, she raised her voice.

"I assure you. You will be the one on the floor before the clock marks a minute!"

"Pathetic," Hiroyuki muttered.

Hiroyuki adopted an aggressive position, while Kasumi adopted a more relaxed one, bouncing on the tips of her feet, balancing her hands. The arena activated and a series of platforms rose, covered by a thick layer of snow and ice, making them slippery. Every movement would have to be precise. The platforms rose and descended, accompanied by huge bronze and wooden gears. Both Kasumi and Hiroyuki were raised on top of one of those platforms. Hiroyuki initiated the attacks, first with a kick aimed to Kasumi's knee, which she evaded with ease, then a series of punches aimed to her face. Kasumi deflected the punches as she walked around to trade places in the limited space. Her left foot was too close to the edge for her taste. Kasumi feinting an attack.

The clock reached the fifteen second mark.

Hiroyuki smiled and attacked again with a series of kicks that Kasumi evaded, hoping to make him fall. However, Hiroyuki used the impulse of the last kick to reach a new platform that was rising, and from there jumped back to hit Kasumi, who barely had time to evade it. A quick exchange of fists ensued. Kasumi managed to block a punch, but Hiroyuki used that to grab her arm and bend it into a painful lock as he kicked her several times in the back. If it weren't for her armor, the damage would have been more severe. However, despite its age, the armor did its job.

Kasumi used her left knee to kick Hiroyuki in the chest. While the attack was unsuccessful, it allowed her to break the lock. Hiroyuki used the opportunity to kick her once more in the back, sending her reeling to the edge of the platform and over it. At the last second, she managed to grab the edge of the platform. Her back hurt like hell. A platform below her was slowly rising. She could hear Hiroyuki bragging how he had beaten an upstart that should not have been allowed to be a demonhunter in first place.

The clock passed the thirty second mark.

Kasumi bit her lip, as she focused on how to get up and not dwell on the pain. The second platform continued up, allowing her to fall and land there in a crouch. She gathered her anger and frustration and clenched her fists. With a scream, she jumped with all her strength, leaping high above Hiroyuki's platform. As she descended, Kasumi put all her weight behind it, landing a punch to Hiroyuki's face, taking him by surprise and breaking his nose. After landing, Kasumi delivered a sequence of jabs aimed to Hiroyuki's jaw, until she felt the bone breaking under the skin.

That should shut him up, Kasumi thought.

Kasumi followed with a left hook and then a roundhouse kick to the left temple, which sent Hiroyuki reeling back, clearly dizzy and with a cut above the left eyebrow. As he tried to stand up, his mouth full of blood, he tried to kick Kasumi, but she countered with a block, grabbing the leg and hitting it with her right elbow above the knee, breaking the femur. Hiroyuki fell to the ground. He stood up once more, hobbling.

I give him that he won't quit, Kasumi thought. *If that's how he wants it.*

She moved around the platform with small jumps, as Hiroyuki got up, trying to scream, moving his hands around. Kasumi jumped over him, landed at his back and hit him hard between the shoulder blades.

The clock was nearing the fifty second mark.

Hiroyuki got up once more and tried to hit Kasumi, but she only evaded the hits. She jumped once more, screamed at the top of her lungs, and hit Hiroyuki square in the chest, sending him off the raised platform, landing on one being elevated—an impact that broke his right arm—and then he bounced off and landed on the floor with his limbs akimbo.

The clock stopped with one second to spare.

Kasumi stood there, looking around the stadium, as the audience sat in silence. She knew that among those seated in the stands there were people that had mocked her during training. They had told her to quit because she would never get any job at the demonhunter guild. They had been rude to her family for what had happened at the Temple, with the yôkai.

They knew now that she was no joke.

A solitary clap broke the silence, followed by another, and a third one. Soon the air filled with applause and the audience erupted in cheers and roaring ovations.

She bowed to the judges, pulled Breaker from the platform and then jumped off. After landing, she saw the emergency services entering the arena with a gurney, to take Hiroyuki to the hospital. A pang of guilt hit her. He looked severely injured. And that meant that the Kuni delegation might have lost one of its champions, putting them in a difficult position for negotiations.

The applause continued as Kasumi left the arena. She had beaten her opponent in less than one minute, without having to use Breaker. She had not only beaten him but left him in such state that he would never, ever disrespect the honor of her family again. She wanted to feel content, yet the only sensation was of a lump of regret in her throat.

† † †

As Kasumi entered the corridor to the locker rooms, she found Sid standing there, his back resting on the wall, arms folded across his chest. His eyes were closed and she decided to pass him. Although Alex had called the samoharo his best friend, Kasumi wasn't sure how to deal with him, in light of the fact that he hadn't go with Alex to the meeting at the curry house.

"Good fight, kiddo," Sid said as she passed by. He barely moved. "You really trounced that guy. Broke him. His self-esteem won't recover as fast as his injuries. If ever."

"Thank you," Kasumi replied, not sure how to react to the comment. "I think the result really helped the Foundation by racking up a hefty amount of points for their current talks. And my own score."

"It wasn't meant as a compliment," Sid said, opening his eyes. His gaze felt heavy. "You really did a number on him. Granted, he deserved to be taken down a peg or two. What he said was a disgrace. Most of these guys and their egos do need some humbling. But that's all he needed. There was no need to put him in the hospital."

"And your point is?" Kasumi was confused.

"That you are on the verge of a very slippery slope. One very similar to theirs: of a mercenary." Sid unfolded his arms and pointed to the other titanfighters in the stands. His gaze changed from determination to sadness. "You are doing this for other reasons than just helping Harland. I know that look you have when you fight. I used to have that look, the need to prove something. I know where it takes you. It's not pretty."

"Are you saying that I shouldn't fight?" Kasumi replied, raising her voice. Anger was starting to bubble inside her chest. "Why do you care? Are you messing with your competition through mental games?"

"Pffft! Mental games? I don't need them. Besides you

are in Harland's team and he is my friend. I wouldn't cheat a friend," Sid said. "I'm only here because people close to me asked me to do it. And I will help them to the best of my abilities. I don't care about a stupid competition. Fight, don't fight. It's your choice. But if you do it only for something like recognition or honor, you might end up losing both, the fight and what you are seeking. However, when you fight for something else, for someone else, for a higher purpose, you might win or lose, but no one will be able to take your honor away."

"What do you know about honor?"

"I come from a culture that puts honor on a pedestal," Sid said. He looked down, his shoulder slouching. His voice became almost a whisper. "And I have seen where that can take a whole nation, too scared of letting go of the status quo, stagnant, even willing to follow a path that hurts others. I won't do that anymore. Don't get me wrong. I enjoy a bit of competition. I like to win. But I've learned that trying to prove something to others only sets you on a path of failure. When you compete, you have only one person to prove something to: yourself. Because at the end of the day, you are the only one you can't run away from. And trust me, that cohabitation is not easy."

The PA system announced the next match.

"And noooooooow! Barry Yosef representing Arajuan, versus Sid, a samoharo in exile, representing the Freefolk! There is a political aspect to be settled with this duel!"

"Seems that I'm next," Sid said ruefully. "They could have skipped the exile part."

"Good luck."

"Thanks kiddo," Sid winked at Kasumi.

Kasumi watched Sid walk towards the arena. She went after him as she was curious to see him fight. Samoharo's usually sent the big ones to this event, not the small ones like Sid. And yet the way he talked was filled with regret and sadness. Kasumi wondered how he would match his words with his actions. Was he going to throw the fight or give it his all? In any case, it might prove to be an education, because Kasumi knew she might face him at some point.

† † †

Sid completed the course track part of his challenge quite fast and was now facing his opponent in the arena. Yosef was a tall man with a beard, and a musculature that barely fit within the titan armor, leaving several body points exposed. Judging by his expression, Yosef seemed to be bored or uninterested. Sid smiled, it was always good when people underestimated him. It made his work easier. The arena initiated the particular scenario for this bout, but Sid didn't pay attention to it. He would not need it.

"I can tell that you don't want to be here," Sid said to Yosef. "You know your boss is wrong on this one."

"It's not a matter of what I want, or think" Yosef said, looking down at Sid. "I'm being paid for this and that's how I support my family."

"Then let me ask you something," Sid replied. "Do you get paid regardless of the result?"

"I was paid in advance."

"That's all I need to know," Sid smiled.

Yosef moved faster than Sid had expected. But given that he was a titanfighter, such speed regardless of size, was to be expected. Yosef landed a right hook straight into Sid's face.

The punch sent Sid flying. Dazed, he stood up. He spit the blood from his mouth. The red mixed with the specks of biliverdin in the samoharo blood. Sid smiled. It would take more than that to knock him out.

"That was a pretty good punch. You got your shining moment," Sid said. "Let's finish this so I can go eat."

Sid ran at his opponent, sliding between his legs at the last possible second as Yosef tried to grab him, using the shell-like structure of his back to slide further. From behind, Sid punched Yosef with both fists above the knees, right on the sciatic nerve with just with enough force to buckle them.

Just the right force to topple him without serious injuries, Sid thought.

As Yosef fell, Sid jumped on his back, and somersaulted over the man's head, in order to reach his shoulders and hit him on the left brachial plexus, to leave the left arm numb and weak, while causing pain. With Yosef kneeling in pain,

Sid kneeled as well, and got closer to his solar plexus.

"I promise I won't hurt you much," Sid said with a smile. "So you can keep fighting. But find a new employer next time."

"Okay," Yosef said, amidst tears.

Sid punched him in the solar plexus with enough strength to knock the air out of Yosef, without causing lasting damage. Yosef fell to the floor, unconscious.

Sid dusted his hands and left the arena, walking towards Kasumi. This time she stood with her arms folded across her chest, her right eyebrow raised. "You ended that fight pretty fast."

"Wello, I did say that I like a bit of competition. That doesn't mean that I can't enjoy a good fight." Sid said, shrugging his shoulders. "But I don't need to humiliate or seriously hurt the guy, just to get him to stop fighting. I have seriously injured enough people in my life, I don't want to add another."

"I think I see you point now," Kasumi mused. "But I would like to talk more about it with you."

"It seems my schedule just cleared up." Sid said, as he watched the score board and the list of challenges, including the sudden withdrawal of all the ones previously paired with Sid. "Do you know a good place to eat? All this activity makes me hungry. And I don't like physical activity. I'm more poet than warrior."

"Sounds more like you are lazy," Kasumi laughed.

"I have a personal philosophy," Sid replied. "Do your work fast and well, so you can have more time to be lazy."

† † †

"What in the Pits am I'm doing here?" Gaby reflected with a certain sadness. It was the third day of the Chivalry Games. She had been wondering for the past few days if this was the path she wanted her life to take. Adventuring alongside Fionn had been awesome on its own, for many personal and sentimental reasons, yet a year after she started her journeys the sensation that her life was missing something was still present.

Gaby was sitting on a bench in the locker room,

adjusting the straps of Heartguard and Soulkeeper that kept them fixed into the protective vest Alex had given her. She could hear the whispers of other fighters, mumbling about how poorly made her 'armor' looked. Most of them had titanarmors that probably were three times as old as Fionn, if not more. Several of those fighters came from families not unlike hers, families with money, power, and political clout. The kind of people she avoided like the plague. Their pretentiousness grated her, while reminding her of her own privilege. Probably what irked her the most, was that barring a few honorable exceptions—such as Bev Johnson or August Mu and his Solarian knights—these guys had never cared or dealt with incursions, leaving the job to local defenses, with the risk that it entailed. They forgot what the titanfighters were meant to be: protectors of those that couldn't defend themselves. These were professional glory hounds.

She examined the vest and the bracers. They were similar to the ones Alex was wearing, meant to be an accessible alternative to titanarmors. She smiled. Alex had been working on these for a decade. And while not entirely refined, what he, Andrea and Birm had managed to create was something to be proud of. Her fingers ran across the grooves between the pads of synthetic leather, filled with impact gel that absorbed the shock of any hit. Coupled with the energy that the Gift expelled naturally from her body—although not in the same amount as Alex's unfortunate case—the vest and the bracers would be protection enough.

"That's crappy protection gear," a male voice said. Gaby looked up. A young man stood there, not much older than her. His titanarmor was composed of several interlocking plates. It resembled Madam Park's armor. So similar, that she wondered if they were the same, or were crafted by the same artisan. "But those blades are nice looking. How much?"

"They are not for sale," Gaby replied, returning to her work. She noticed how the rest of the competitors left the room quickly.

"Everything is for sale," the man insisted, as he tried to touch one of the twin blades. But Gaby slapped his hand away.

"I wouldn't do that. And you are wrong. Not everything in life is for sale."

"Funny, coming from one of the heirs to the Galfano's fortune. How much they cost you?"

"Never in your life would you be able to pay their cost. Leave me alone, okay?"

"No. I want those blades. If you won't sell them, then I will have to take them from your unconscious body after our fight."

"You would do that? Really?" Gaby couldn't believe the words she was hearing. She wondered if that was how this moron had gotten his armor.

"Sometimes you have to tear down a house if you want to rebuild something better. And that includes getting rid of a few pests," the man said with sarcasm dripping from each word.

The words sounded familiar. Very familiar. Gaby had heard them once, from the lips of Madam Park during their fight atop the Bestial. She wasn't planning to unleash all her power during the tournament, but this guy was making a good case for it. She felt the rush of adrenaline that preceded the surge of power from the Gift, as her irises glowed icy blue. Gaby looked up, straight into the man's eyes.

"I hope your insurance is up to date," Gaby said. The man remained silent, taken aback by the comment and left the room, leaving her alone. Gaby sighed. This was going to be a long tournament and she wasn't sure she was up to it. But the Freefolk asked her to help them and she wasn't going to let them down. Even if her heart was only half into it.

But when you have the Gift, even half is enough, as the man that tried to buy her Tempest Blades would find out in a few minutes.

† † †

The course seemed taken straight from one of those videogames Alex once had cajoled her into playing. They were inside a transparent box, where a series of structures that resembled multicolored snakes moved in every direction. Gaby—with Soulkeeper in her right hand and Heartguard in the left, her irises glowing icy blue—had to keep running and jumping from one to another to keep herself from falling into what seemed to be a swamp with nasty crystal spikes peeking out.

Which had been easy for her with her Gift and a change to the Sisters of Mercy 'ice state'. That technique allowed a person to become a one-woman army, but at the cost of one's soul. But by singing a song in her head, Gaby could predict things, even if it was just a few seconds into the future. No need to wait for prophetic dreams, she could either see things a few minutes before they happened or, as it was in this case, everything in slow motion. Which in this fight, came in very handy. The goal was to reach the exits at the top, in order to use the top of the box as a more stable arena. But it seemed that either the judges didn't care, or no one told the guy she was facing off against—the one who'd tried to grab her blades in the locker room—who went by the name of Jean Baptiste, the Knight of Thorns, for the thorn whips he could summon through his armor—that he should be a sportsman and not keep trying to hit her during the race. So instead of reaching the top of the box to fight, they had started to hit each other on the chaotic course, which by the roaring sounds from the crowd, met with their approval.

Thus, Gaby found herself jumping from snake to snake, while at the same time dodging the metallic thorn whip from Jean Baptiste and hitting him hard in the face whenever she had an opportunity. Which had been several. By now the man's face sported several bruises and a broken nose. Gaby, by contrast, sported several gashes and cuts, mostly on her tights and arms. The guy kept aiming his whip to those regions, with a clear objective: get her to drop one or both of her blades.

One hit was successful. The whip went straight to her neck and Gaby barely had an opportunity to block the attack, which hit her square in the biceps, with one particularly sharp thorn sunk in the arm's nerve. A wave of numbness hit her, which in turn made her lost her grip on her blade.

Gaby dropped Heartguard, and it fell, hitting one of the snakes and embedding itself into it.

"Crap," Gaby muttered as she jumped down from one snake to another, trying to reach Heartguard, before Jean Baptiste. The guy was racing her to the bottom to get the sword first. Gaby could swear he was salivating at the idea of getting his hands on it. And while Gaby didn't want to lose her blade to anyone, even less to that moron, she knew there was an ace under the proverbial sleeve. One that was very dangerous.

As she was descending onto one of the snakes closer to Heartguard, Jean Baptiste snared her right ankle, tripping her. She hit her head on a snake that was passing by.

Her sight became blurred for a few seconds, as she tried to keep her grasp on the snake and regain her footing. Dizzy, Gaby managed to get up onto the snake. She shook her head to clear it. By the time her vision returned, Jean Baptiste was about to grab Heartguard.

"I wouldn't do that, for your own sake!" Gaby yelled at Jean Baptiste.

But the man smiled at her as he grabbed Heartguard's handle.

"Big mistake," Gaby murmured.

Heartguard's blade glowed bright red as Jean Baptiste held it aloft. He celebrated for a second, until the glow started to cover him. His expression changed from happiness to concern. He tried to let go of the blade, but as much as he shook his hand, the blade didn't let go. Jean Baptiste started to scream louder and louder every time.

"No! NO! Leave me alone! Stop! Go away ghosts! I did what I had to! Leave me alone, please! I beg you!!"

The screaming continued till his eyes rolled white and he fell into the swamp, hitting the crystal shards, breaking several of them. If it weren't for his armor, he would have been impaled. He seemed to be suffering from a panic attack.

Gaby jumped down from one snake to another until she reached the bottom. She picked up Heartguard and sheathed it in her back sheath. She grabbed Jean Baptiste by the arm and got him out of the swamp. No need to let him drown.

"I told you that you couldn't pay the price. Heartguard constantly judges what's in your heart and sends you feedback about that. Be thankful you didn't grab Soulkeeper. You wouldn't be able to survive what that one does to you."

As she left him on the shore and the course disappeared, she kneeled next to him. His eyes were glassed, staring into the void.

"Just to be clear," Gaby whispered into his ear. "I didn't buy these blades, they chose me. And one more thing: tell your master, Madam Park, that the next time she wants something of mine, she better come in person to take it, instead of sending her pawns."

Gaby stood up and left the arena while Jean Baptiste babbled incoherently. It would take him years to recover from the experience.

The Tempest Blades might be the greatest weapons of them all, but being able to wield them wasn't for the faint of heart or the corrupt of soul, as they judge their partners every second they held them in their hands.

Gaby knew that very well as she judged herself every day.

† † †

Alex, Gaby, and Fionn were in the stands, watching Sam's fourth duel in the fourth day of the events. The course on this occasion was a series of raised platforms, covered in grass, held up by thin pillars. That was the easy part. The interesting bit was that in order to jump from one to another, you would have to evade either the flying crimson bitters—a species of amphibious creature that jumped in the air to catch and kill their prey —or chains covered in oil and set on fire.

Yes, the person who was designing the courses had been playing too many videogames.

A titanfighter or a demonhunter could survive that scenario. After all, that was what they trained for: the craziest scenario possible, as incursions tended to warp reality in odd ways. The titanfighter in questions was a Solarian knight by the name of Cesarion "The Boulder" Chakumuy, who was agreed by pretty much everyone as a nice, jovial fellow in the body of a bull.

Sam—whose eyes glowed with a lilac hue—had the advantage that the Gift enhanced the perception of reality and altered the body to act in consequence. And she had been trained by two of the most effective fighters in the current age. Her training showed as she performed a perfectly timed jump, catching "The Boulder" in the middle of his own leap, her quarterstaff hitting him squarely in the groin. While the armor must have absorbed most of the hit, it was nonetheless uncomfortable to watch, as the collective gasp of the audience indicated. Sam apologized to her rival. So far, the duel had been relatively polite.

"That must hurt," Alex winced at the hit. "You trained Sam well."

"She already had all the elements," Gaby replied, then looked at Fionn with a smile. "I just helped her to put them together."

"There is one thing that seems odd to me, though," Alex continued. "Is it just me or has she not used a single spell in any of her duels? I mean, she is like a combat wizard, but there has been more combat and less wizard of late."

"She has been having some issues with casting spells since she got the Gift," Gaby replied. "It has become a tad... difficult to do it the way she used to do it."

"I was afraid of that," Fionn muttered as he watched every movement Sam performed in her duel, as she barely dodged one of the spinning chains of fire. "At least her reaction time is better now."

"Why?" Alex asked.

"There are few records of freefolk with the Gift, and even less of a Gifted casting magick," Fionn explained, without taking his sight from Sam. "It seems that the freefolk traditional way of magick and the Gift are not one hundred percent compatible."

"How do you know that? Did she tell you?" Alex continued.

"No. Izia," Fionn said, with a tone that indicated that he wouldn't entertain more questions. His fist clenched as Sam took a bad hit on her left ribs.

Neither Alex nor Gaby pressed the issue. When Izia's name came up, Fionn usually stopped talking. Izia remained the open wound for Fionn, ironically, given his enhanced healing. Gaby had managed to get him to open up more during their trips, but a part of her felt like Izia would always cast a shadow on their own relationship. And yet, when she heard stories about her, Gaby couldn't avoid identifying with her, as if those stories had happened to her. There were a few possible explanations, depending on your religious beliefs, but Gaby preferred to not think about them. They made her uneasy, as she felt that they robbed her of her own agency.

Sam blocked an attack with her quarterstaff while a chain hit Chakumuy in the back sending him into Sam and pushing both of them from the platform into a pool below. Both came to the surface and looked at each other. Chakumuy carried Sam to the end of the pool while Sam kept hitting the crimson bitters that got close to them. Both climbed out of the pool, the water dripping from their armor, and Chakumuy raised Sam's fist as he laughed.

"And a first in this Chivalry Games, a tie between Samantha Ambers-Estel, representing the Freefolk delegation, and Cesarion Chakumuy representing the Emerald Island," The announcer said. "Give them thunderous applause for their show of chivalry and sportsmanship!" A loud cheer filled the arena. "That's all for today's competition. Come back for tomorrow's duels, including the main card of the night: Joshua Kovac, representing the Foundation, versus Salvador Drakaralov from the Emerald Island Solarian Knights, both with a record of 4-0 and 435 points, which put them in the competition for the title."

"Well," Fionn said out of the blue. "No offense to your friend Joshua, but that won't be the main fight tomorrow."

"What do you mean?" Alex asked.

"Tomorrow we will discuss the main topic of the conference and it will get ugly."

"Which is?" Gaby was the one asking this time.

"The future of the Alliance," Fionn replied with a somber tone. "Tomorrow it might be decided if it continues or if it breaks apart."

"Please don't kill anyone that wants to break it apart," Alex suggested. "Remember, you are a diplomat."

"Alex is right," Gaby added. "It won't help to make your point."

"I won't make any promises."

Both Gaby and Alex knew that Fionn wasn't joking. And that worried them.

Chapter 10
Diplomacy by Other Means

"No country has endured by being a meek participant in a stagnant alliance," said Robbet Dewart, the representative of Portis. Potbellied, with a grey and black beard, the man wasn't a pleasant person to be around, unless your checkbook represented an advantage to him. He was greed in human shape. "That path leads to collapse and weakness. Put in other words: nations do not survive by setting examples for others. Nations survive by making examples of others."

"What you are asking for is a return to the old days where everyone was at war," Harland objected. "And where did that lead us? Peace requires more courage than picking a fight. Splitting the Alliance would result in a return to the old kingdoms. And we all know how well that worked out: endless conflicts that left them too weak to face the Horde, sending the continent into chaos." Harland was mustering all of his will to not throttle the ambassador.

"And see how much that forced us to progress, technologically and economically. If war is the result from breaking the alliance, so be it. Thus, only the fit will remain to fight that shadowy menace the Freefolk claim are coming for us. If that even exists. The Freefolk are prone to flights of fancy. They believe a goddess walks among them!" The ambassador's laugh was cut off by a loud crack as Fionn's hand slapped the table, cracking it. Everyone fell silent. Maybe seeing the Greywolf angry would give some sense to the gathering, or so Harland hoped.

"Only a coward is eager to send others to fight a war

in their stead," Fionn said calmly, a wolfish smile on his lips. "While they stay safe in their offices, counting their war profits." There was a faint green glow coming from his irises and Harland knew that Fionn was seething with rage. "Only a coward proposes war when innocents will be the ones suffering."

"You fought in the Great War under King Castlemartell. Are you saying he was a coward for sending you to war? What does that make you?" The ambassador raised his voice. "A tool? A glorified weapon? You are no different from us for you enjoy conflict as well."

"That's right. I might have been a tool. And I have made my peace with that. The difference, ambassador," Fionn replied, his tone full of scorn toward the man, and seemed to freeze the whole room, "is that I joined voluntarily to follow a king that till the last day of his life, fought at the front, side-by-side with us, so that your generation didn't have to fight for survival. To stop innocents from being butchered by ambitious, evil beings. You are nothing more than a greedy, spineless, warmonger. You are no different from the Horde. You disgust me. And your presence, your sole existence, insults both the King's memory and the other diplomats here trying to do something useful for others. Shame on you."

Fionn stood up and left the room, leaving the rest of those gathered there speechless. Harland noticed that the ambassador was clutching his fits, enraged. He also noticed that the man had soiled himself.

As the meeting was adjourned, Harland, dejected, was feeling a heavy weight on his shoulders. He didn't blame Fionn. Actually, he had been surprised at how restrained his friend had been, all things considered. And he knew Fionn hadn't meant ill. For the record, most of the diplomats were in agreement. But the delegate from Portis held a great deal of because of the city state's economic power. And thus, reality ensued, and the talks were now at risk.

The ambassador is a bully, nothing more, Harland thought. However, he was a powerful bully who would complicate things. Harland knew Fionn was right on this, and on taking measures for dealing with the real enemy. But he was hoping not to add half of the Alliance to the list of forces to deal with when things got really bad.

Why is it so hard for them to see the big picture?

† † †

"Don't worry. I'm sure things will improve once calmer minds prevail," Vivienne Ortiga said to Harland in the hallway outside the conference room. She was part of the Freefolk delegation, and a teacher at Ravenstone. Her trademark green hair brought some color to a grey afternoon. Harland had met her last year at the Freefolk School for magi through the most unlikely person: Sid.

"I'm sorry it came to this Vivienne."

"We appreciate the support you have given us, even at the risk of the existence of the Foundation. And about Fionn, don't worry, we and the Elders knew exactly what we were getting when we asked him to be part of the delegation. I didn't expect less from him and at least I'm thankful for both of your efforts to keep the Alliance intact. As imperfect as it is, as much as it has failed in certain areas, unity between all of us is the best option to move forward. Take a break. You deserve it."

"I should be the one reassuring you," Harland offered her a halfhearted smile. The Freefolk had been trying to be gracious even in the face of Dewart's constant badgering the whole week. It couldn't have been easy.

"Maybe we are reassuring each other," Vivienne put her hand on his shoulder.

"Harland!" a familiar voice sounded behind him. Harland turned and saw Prince Arthur coming his way.

"I think you two have things to discuss," Vivienne said, then she smiled at him. "But I mean it, take a break. We will do the same. We are planning to go to a karaoke bar."

"Have fun."

Vivienne left as Arthur arrived. Harland wasn't in the mood to talk much. Confusion, hurt, anger, and a migraine had him in foul mood. Vivienne had managed to help him to calm down somewhat. But to what extent, he would find out in a few seconds.

"Where is Sarah?" Harland asked.

"She had to leave, so I'm in charge of our delegation for the time being. Things got ugly back there, huh? I never expected the Greywolf to react that way," Arthur tried to laugh at what had happened.

"Fionn," Harland pinched the bridge of his nose. He was starting to wonder why he had been friends with Arthur all these years. Had they changed so much and drifted apart so far as they grew up? "His name is Fionn. Are you planning to take this seriously or like a joke, like most things?"

"Why are you reacting like this?" Arthur shrugged. "Dewart was just pointing out some obvious things."

"Obvious?" Harland said. If he wasn't short, he would have slapped Arthur on the head, or straight up punched him. "Geez. Economy and politics above wellbeing is obvious? And you wonder why Fionn reacted like he did?"

"I don't get it."

"Of course you don't get it! At first, I didn't understand why Fionn secluded himself on that mountain for so long. Now I do. Fionn is tired. Tired of fighting the fights of others. Tired of working hard to help build something good for everyone, for a jerkass to come and tear it down. Above all, he is tired of sacrificing his life and his family for others' sake and seeing that his efforts are for nothing. And to be honest, I'm tired too of trying to make you see how things are. I can see now that Doncelles has you well under his thumb."

"For the sake of our friendship, take back that," Arthur said, almost as a growl.

"For the sake of our friendship, I take back nothing," Harland looked up, straight at Arthur. Harland was done being intimidated by someone in higher positions. "You need to learn to hear harsh truths. You need to realize one thing, that we are not in our positions as some sort of privilege, but in one of service to the people. Someday you will take the throne, and you will lead. I hope that by then you become the person I know you can be and not the one the others are trying to make you be, for the sake of political convenience."

"And giving back the Freefolk those lands is not political convenience? Better them than the southern regions of the

Alliance? If we are not careful, we will end up being weakened."

"Those lands were theirs from the beginning. And they don't mind sharing them as long as they are treated as equals. A good leader would find a way. And by the way we should consider ourselves lucky."

"Lucky?"

Harland was worse than annoyed. He was disappointed. And as Fionn once said, that was worse. It was a sign that you cared too much for someone that was not worth such attention. "Because the Freefolk, despite what has happened, are not only open to talks with the Alliance, they are willing to continue being a part of it, despite the many broken promises and racial attacks. Why? Because they see the big picture."

"It's easy for them to say that when they used to have one of the greatest powers. They still have advantages due their magicks."

"Yes, and they got destroyed by a human nation and their lands stolen by the Old Kingdoms after they sacrificed their nation to save us from a monster that Fionn and our friends had to take down. Again. So, we are lucky they are only asking for that and not planning to take it back by force, or enact revenge. We wouldn't stand a chance."

Harland turned away and walled toward the door. He was done trying to play diplomat, trying to make people see the bigger picture, of trying to convince them that cooperation was the way forward. He was done. He wanted to walk into the crowd, there in the city and disappear for a while.

"Where are you going?"

"Vivienne is right. I need a break. From everything."

† † †

"That was close," Alex whispered to Kasumi, as they watched Joshua evade one of the air-cutting attacks by Salvador Drakaralov. The man could use his sword and his armor almost as well a Fionn with Black Fang, obliterating most of the obstacles in the arena. Balding and with a neatly trimmed goatee, Salvador was a polite, but relentless opponent. One of the few Solarian Knights that Alex actually liked. It was as if the Queen had sent the nicer members of her personal squad. Although nice wasn't the same as ineffective. Joshua was having trouble evading the attacks. And without a weapon to defend himself, the difficulty increased. To boot, Joshua was avoiding unleashing the Beast. He looked tired, almost as if he was sick. This didn't look right.

Alex and Kasumi were watching the duel from ringside, along with Sid, while Fionn, Sam, and Gaby sat in the bleachers. Fionn had been in a foul mood, with the only explanation offered that something had happened at the conference. Alex had decided to give him some space. Harland was nowhere to be found. And this duel was of particular importance, for while it had already been scheduled, Prince Arthur had invoked the Unspoken rule on it.

Alex was having the same sensation he had in his nightmares, of walking a tight rope without a safety net, and a churning stomach. He was having an anxiety attack, and he didn't know why.

The course had been easy: dodging falling fireballs from a simulated volcanic explosion. But Joshua's usually quick reflexes were failing him. No wonder he was having trouble even getting close to Salvador. In a way, Alex was grateful Harland was not there to see this.

"Is it me or does your friend looks sick?" Sid asked. "And what's that black thing coming from his arms."

Alex and Kasumi looked at each other.

"Do you think—" Alex started.

"That he is barely keeping the Beast contained and that's why he is having troubles with the fight?" Kasumi ended, as Joshua was hit in the abdomen. He grabbed his stomach, bending over in pain.

"If that's the case, why did he accept the duel?"

"Maybe it has to do with the Unspoken rule. Joshua always tries to fulfill his promises, even to the detriment of his own health."

Salvador stopped his attacks and got closer to see if Joshua could continue.

"Sounds familiar," Sid interjected. "What's the Beast?"

Alex looked at Kasumi and she nodded at him.

"The symbiont thing that gives Joshua his abilities," Alex replied.

"It's like this thing made of pure darkness, a shroud if you like, that comes out to kill all the lights and energy around it to feed," Kasumi explained. "He usually keeps it under control, but lately he has been feeling ill. We were hoping to help with a potential cure after the tournament."

"Well, it seems that the Beast does not like to be under his control anymore," Sid pointed out.

"Aww crap," Alex muttered, as his left hand reached for the holster on his leg. Time to remain calm under pressure, as he had practiced with Fionn.

Joshua extended his arm, his hand open, as his eyes turned from their regular color to yellow.

"Stay away... please."

"Should I call the physician?" Salvador offered.

"No..." Joshua replied, as his fangs grew. "Run."

From his back exploded a wave of darkness, which for a second resembled bat wings. It then turned into a tattered shroud so dark, that no light could pierce it. Salvador, dumbfounded stood there, immobile, as a tendril of the shroud moved towards his neck. An electrified arrow crossed the air, hitting the tendril. Three more arrows landed near Joshua, keeping the shroud distracted. The audience screamed in confusion as Alex lowered his bow.

"I think we will have to speed up our plan. Ready?" he looked at Kasumi.

"Yes."

"What's going on?" Sid asked, as Kasumi and Alex jumped into the arena.

"Whatever happens," Alex replied. "I need a favor for our plan to work. Don't let Fionn to get inside the arena."

"Why?"

"Because Joshua is a good guy who happens to be a tovainar. You know how Fionn feels about them."

"Oh boy. He is not going to like it. I don't like it."

"Do you trust me?"

"Yes."

"Then let us do our work," Alex said.

"This is gonna get ugly," Sid whispered, while Alex and Kasumi ran to the center of the arena.

† † †

Salvador was having trouble countering the attacks coming from the shroud. Another set of electrified arrows crossed the air, hitting the ground, attracting the tendrils, as flies to honey. They were looking for energy to feed on.

"What's going on?" Salvador asked Alex and Kasumi as they got closer.

"He is ill, and his illness got out of control. You better leave this before it gets ugly, we will take care of it," Kasumi replied.

"You being here is against the rules," Salvador said.

"We are trying to save your life," Alex replied, getting between Joshua and Salvador. Kasumi stood beside him. "We can argue about this later!"

A tendril from the shroud sliced part of the podium where the judges were sitting. They looked at each other and ran.

"I will say this only once," Kasumi said to Salvador, not taking her eyes from Joshua, "If you want to live you better leave this arena now. And get everyone to evacuate the stadium."

"But..."

Kasumi glared at Salvador. Even Alex was taken aback at the severity of her gaze.

Remind me to never piss her off, he thought.

Salvador ran out of the arena, as he yelled to everyone to evacuate.

"Joshua, calm down," Alex said, extending his right arm, hand open in a conciliatory gesture.

"Joshua is no more. I am Shaliem."

"The Beast has a name?" Alex asked, confused.

"Well, I want my friend back," Kasumi exclaimed.

Joshua growled in response, getting into a combat stance, ready to claw out their faces. The shroud at his back grew larger and waved with frenzy.

"Let me do it. I'm the only one that can get close without

dying. As soon as I get you an opening, you hit him," Alex said to Kasumi.

"Forget that!" Kasumi yelled.

Joshua wasted no more time and charged at them, unleashing a flurry of blows with his hands and from the tendrils made from the shroud. The attacks focused on Alex, who activated the Gift, his irises glowing with a golden hue.

I think I'm the tastiest meal for that leech thingie, Alex thought. The speed of the attacks increased, forcing Alex to drop his bow and draw Yaha in order to use the sword to block the most dangerous attacks. The shroud transformed into sharpened blades made of darkness, cutting the air and light in their wake, attacking from all sides.

Alex and Joshua exchanged blow after blow, kick after kick. Each contact sent shockwaves that rattled Alex's bones. While Joshua, or the symbiont, or Shaliem—whoever was in charge—attacked in a feral manner, with as little technique as possible, Alex opted for a more technical, methodical approach. He focused on his training that had taught him about keeping the calm under pressure, rather than the part where he tried to end the fight with one blow. With Joshua, doing that would leave him open to a devastating attack. Instead, he needed to take his time, waiting for the right window of opportunity to enact his part of the plan. Joshua thrust both arms forward, in an attempt to grab Alex by the neck in a chokehold. Alex ducked and answered with a jab to the jaw, with the hope that the force of the punch would knock, or at least daze, Joshua long enough for Kasumi to attack. Instead, Joshua only reeled back, growling in anger, and the shroud launched an attack aimed to separate Alex's head from his body.

Alex bent backwards as the dark blade passed millimeters from his face, cutting a few hairs from his head as he fell to the ground. As Alex lay on the floor, the shroud morphed into several daggers that tried to stab him. Alex rolled to the left and the right, as Kasumi ran to help him, Breaker in her hand. The blade of Breaker shimmered with white, icy light that sliced the dark daggers. Using Breaker as a pole to gain momentum, Kasumi landed a hit to Joshua's face. The sound of breaking bone filled the air. And yet, Joshua didn't bleed from the nose. Kasumi, determined, faced Joshua while Alex recovered.

Despite the apparent difference in power, Kasumi was more than a match for Joshua, keeping up with his speed and strength. It was obvious they had sparred against each other for years, because Kasumi knew exactly how to counter each of his attacks.

Maybe we should have traded places, Alex thought as he stood and picked up Yaha.

Frustrated, the Beast grew in size, becoming a large sphere—at least five meters in diameter—that encased the area were Alex and Kasumi were standing.

"This is the attack where he absorbs all the energy of the subject, right?" Alex asked her.

"Yes," Kasumi replied, readying Breaker, aiming it at Joshua.

"I'm sorry," Alex said as he pushed her with all his strength out of the way, as the sphere closed over, trapping him into an asphyxiating darkness.

I guess it's too late to think of another plan.

Darkness engulfed him, cutting Alex off from everything. The darkness crept over his legs as Joshua stepped closer, only his yellow eyes and large fangs visible amidst the impenetrable shroud. It was a creepy, terrifying, claustrophobic experience. The kind of event Fionn had trained him for. Alex couldn't see anything, but as he focused his Gift, suddenly all of the Beast's energy currents blossomed before him.

If the shroud absorbs energy to feed the symbiont, there must be traces of the flows to the core.

"I'm sorry for this," Alex said to Joshua.

The key to Alex's plan was to server most of the connections between Joshua and the Beast. If his research was right, that would keep them both alive, but weakened, while Kasumi's pressure point technique would reset—so to speak—the union and the Beast, allowing Joshua to regain control over it. The cost of this would leave Joshua unpowered, like a regular mortal... or close to it.

Thing is, I have never been good with the sword, Alex

thought. But if there was a time to keep calm under pressure, this was it.

The darkness enclosed him in a rapidly shrinking space. He had to hurry and execute his plan or he would be killed. And having his life sucked out by a mass of darkness wasn't in his plans for today.

Alex took the stance that Fionn taught him, holding Yaha with both hands, hilt over his head, the point of the sword aimed at the floor, the blade guarding his left shoulder and flank. Focusing through the Gift, the connections between the symbiont and Joshua became clearer: currents of energy, flowing from seven spots in Joshua's body to corresponding spots in the Beast's corporeal form. Seven of them.

Putting all his strength into the attack, Alex slashed through the shroud. Yaha pierced the darkness as a ray of light casts off the night. With a single movement Alex managed to sever five of the seven connections, leaving intact only the one at the heart, to keep Joshua alive, and the one at the base of the spine, to keep the symbiont alive. Even if common sense screamed that this was the best opportunity to destroy a tovainar, and hopefully free Joshua from his curse, Alex's heart whispered that even the Beast, or Shaliem, deserved a second chance as it had helped to save people in previous occasions. And with any luck, if Kasumi's technique worked, it would help Joshua to reassert control.

The sphere of darkness exploded, freeing both Alex and Joshua from Shaliem's black cage. Reeling in pain, Shaliem let out a primeval scream full of pain and anger. Joshua, still in a savage mood, took a few steps back, growled and ran at Alex, throwing a punch at his face. Alex caught the fist with his right hand, on reflex, owing more to muscle memory than intentional thought, Alex moved his left arm, to attack Joshua with Yaha.

Joshua, in turn, grabbed Alex's forearm, with enough force to make Alex wince in pain and drop Yaha. Locked in the struggle, Alex yelled at Kasumi, "Now!"

He didn't have to wait long. Kasumi moved quickly, sliding under both men, standing up and hitting Joshua's abdomen with a quick succession of blows. Using her index and middle fingers from both hands, Kasumi hit the seven points of energy with enough strength to leave bruises on Joshua's body. The one over the liver left such a wound that Joshua growled in pain and his grip on Alex's arm tightened, snapping the bones as if they were twigs.

"Arghhh!" Alex screamed, as a sharp pain invaded his arm, numbing it. Joshua's grip lost strength and Alex let his arm fall, weakened, as tears welled in his eyes.

Joshua, on the other hand, opened his eyes wide and fell backwards, hitting the ground with a loud thud. He stopped breathing, locked into a catatonic state.

Alex stepped back, to allow Kasumi to have some room to check Joshua. Kasumi put her fingers on his neck, trying to gauge if there was a pulse. Joshua's eyes changed back to his normal color, and then he sucked in a breath in a large gasp, his upper body springing into a vertical position. Confused, he looked around, in search of his previous opponent.

"What happened? Did I kill someone?" Joshua asked, short of breath.

"The only thing you killed was my arm," Alex smiled, cradling his broken arm. "I think it would be better if Kasumi takes you to the locker room to recover and then out of here. I will deal with the rest."

"I'm sorry, "Joshua replied. "Thank you."

"Are you sure?" Kasumi asked, as she helped Joshua to stand up. The arena had been evacuated and it was almost empty now.

"No, but someone has too, and this was my idea," Alex replied as he saw Sid coming towards him, followed by the arena's physician.

The pain in his arm was excruciating.

Note to self, add more protection to the arms, it hurts like hell, Alex thought.

Somehow, Alex suspected, the pain he was feeling right now, wouldn't be the worst of his problems to come.

† † †

"Careful, you are lucky the bone only broke in two. But if you keep moving or using the arm, you risk further complications," the stadium physician told Alex as she finished placing the fiber cast on his arm. Alex winced. "If the pain gets to be too much, then you can take the pills I gave you. Two every eight hours."

Sid watched the whole procedure while resting against a wall. He had his arms crossed, digesting what had happened. Joshua was a tovainar, or so he understood. And Alex had risked not only his life and that of Kasumi, but the Foundation's chances to compete and earn leverage during the talks as well, to save a man he barely knew. With one of his harebrained trademark plans that worked by sheer willpower. On one hand, he didn't expect less from Alex. That was on brand. And Kasumi seemed to be the same as him. Maybe that's why they seemed to get along. But on the other hand... Alex and Kasumi had put lives at risk, and the consequences for that could be far reaching. If the three of them got disqualified, the Foundation and by extension, Harland, would lose any bargaining position, which could have further ramifications for the whole Alliance.

Melodramatic much? Sid thought. *Then again, it's the result of years of experience.*

Whatever the results, Sid knew things would get ugly soon. And unlike Fionn, who was walking with long strides towards them, followed by Gaby and Sam, who looked equally pissed, Alex didn't heal as fast. Faster than a regular human, yes, but it would still take days.

Fionn was drawing slow, steady breaths, as his nostril flared. His eyes were cold and tight, with a small hint of a glow. Sid knew that look. Anger mixed with disappointment. Sid couldn't blame him for feeling that way. A part of him was feeling the same. But getting angry and yelling wouldn't change things. And knowing Alex, it would make things worse. He didn't like to be yelled at. What surprised Sid, to a point, was that Gaby wasn't calming down Fionn. She was angry as well, although in her case, Sid hoped it was more out of worry than from anger. And Sam... he would never fully understand Sam and Alex's relationship.

Why do humans and freefolk have to complicate things so much? Sid thought. It was a good thing Kasumi had taken

Joshua to the locker rooms. The storm was here.

Sid pushed away from the wall and walked over to meet them. He wanted to calm things down before they got worse.

"Don't even try it," Fionn said, as if he knew what Sid was about to say.

"Unlike the rest of the world," Sid replied, looking up at Fionn. "You don't intimidate me. I know you three are angry. I'm angry as well. But what you are thinking of doing won't do much good."

"Sid, not now," Gaby said.

Fionn pushed Sid out of the way. Under other circumstances, Sid would have replied to that by breaking Fionn's leg several times. But it wouldn't do any good either.

"What the hell were you thinking?" Fionn screamed at Alex.

"This was reckless, even for you," Sam added.

"And the worst thing is that you didn't even tell us what you were planning," Gaby said, in a lower tone. "We are supposed to be friends. We tell each other what is happening."

The physician slowly backed away, as Alex looked at the three of them. Sid knew that look. He face-palmed himself in his mind.

"When was the last time we actually *had* a conversation, Gaby? You were off seeing the world with your fancy boyfriend on new adventures. But you forgot that the rest of us existed," Alex said. "And you Sam, no offense, but I'm sick and tired of your constant complaining about every idea I have. I get it, you think I'm an idiot. But reckless? Have you seen yourself in the mirror? What about your dive without a parachute last year?"

"Tone it down, boy." Fionn growled.

"Last time I checked the calendar, I'm not a boy," Alex said, standing up to Fionn. Sid had heard that last year Alex had done something similar at Ravenhall. Unlike the rest, he believed it. "You've taught me a lot of things for which I'm thankful, but stop treating me like a kid, or like your second chance at not screwing up things with Ywain."

"I'm not joking Alejandro," Fionn replied. "That was stupid. You almost let a tovainar kill innocent people. You should have told us what was happening. They are dangerous. You saw it with Byron."

"That," Alex said. "That's why I didn't tell you. You are still so hung up with your past that you couldn't see that Joshua is not your old pal. He is a good man. I've seen what he has done. And Kasumi trusts him."

"You trust her so much," Sam interjected. "But you barely mentioned Kasumi before you told Harland about her."

"Contrary to popular belief, I do have friends outside this circle," Alex replied. "They might not be many, but I do have them. I don't go around poking about your other friendships."

"You still haven't answered why you didn't tell us what was happening," Gaby said.

Alex pinched the bridge of his nose with his good hand. He looked at Fionn. "If I told you Joshua was an alleged tovainar, that he needed help, would you have helped him?"

"They are dangerous," Fionn repeated.

"See? That's why. I can't believe I'm the one saying this. We don't have these powers to just help those we like. If we don't help others, on the assumptions and biases we have, we are no better than those that care only for their own interests. Like you know? The bad guys?"

Sid had to give it to Alex. He was expecting fireworks and instead Alex was holding a heated, yet civilized discussion... Sid opened his eyes in realization.

How many times had he practiced these words in his head before this? He knew this could happen and planned accordingly.

It was time to jump in again and try to stop things before someone said something they would regret.

"Don't even try that lame comparison with me," Fionn said. "Do you realize the position you have left Harland in, the Foundation? It will be a miracle if Kasumi doesn't get disqualified. Because you, with that arm, are out of the competition. And I won't allow Joshua to fight again."

"It's not your call," Kasumi said, returning alone from the locker room.

Smart girl, Sid thought.

174

"This is a mess," Fionn said.

Oh boy, Sid thought. Alex's posture changed in subtle ways. He wasn't standing tall anymore. His shoulders slumped.

"You know what?" Alex replied. "Yes, I'm a friggin' mess. I'm stupid and reckless. Everything I do is a friggin' mistake. Anything else? Because for all I care, I'm done with the lot of you."

Fionn clenched his fist, something that Alex must have noticed. Sid prayed that they wouldn't come to punches. *Not right now.*

When did I become the one with common sense? Sid thought.

"And one last thing. If any of you dare to go after Joshua, Kasumi won't ever have to bother dealing with you. Because this time I won't pull any punches as I have been doing till now. You all can go to the Pits. I don't care anymore," Alex turned to Kasumi. "I'm done. Can you help me find a place to stay?"

"Don't worry, you can stay at my house. I'm sure my folks won't mind," Kasumi said.

Alex turned his back to the rest of them and went to help Kasumi take Joshua home. Sid hoped that after helping Joshua, Alex would stay at Kasumi's house until he figured out what to do next. Sid was pondering doing the same.

Fionn walked after Alex, but Sid got in the way again.

"Push me once more and you will find out why I got expelled," Sid said to Fionn. "I think we are all done here."

"No," Sam said. "We need to work this out. Now."

"Hurtful words have been said," Sid replied. "Angry minds won't help right now."

"He's right," Gaby added, standing next to Sid. "We all need to calm down."

"Gaby, do yourself a favor and check your calendar," Sid said. "You might be able to salvage whatever friendship you had with Alex. As for the rest of you. I will fulfill my contract with the Freefolk, out of respect for Vivienne. But, after that, you better find a way to get back on your own. I'm out."

"What about the Foundation?" Fionn asked.

"That's between me and Harland, Greywolf."

"Where are you going?" Gaby asked.

"To buy a present, kiddo," Sid replied.

And it dawned on Gaby as she opened her eyes wide. "How could I forget?"

† † †

Alex arrived at his hotel room. He turned on the shower, dialing it up to the maximum heat. As the steam filled the bathroom, he popped another couple of analgesics. Gift or not, having broken bones hurt like the Pits. The hot water helped to lessen the pain and relax the overused muscles. The physician had said that with the Gift, there was a chance his broken arm would be mended in a couple of weeks, instead of the usual months. And in the meantime, he would have to deal with the itchiness caused by the cast. It was a shame he didn't share Fionn's enhanced healing, he probably would be good as new in a matter of hours.

"Stupid," he muttered, as he leaned his forehead on the tiled wall, allowing the hot water to run down his back. He didn't know if he was referring to Fionn... or to himself. He didn't want to think about it. He turned off the faucet and left the bathroom, putting on his t-shirt and a clean pair of shorts. He packed the rest of his things in his duffel bag, while leaving the extra hard suitcases he had brought unopened. Alex looked at his laptop, the screen showing the progress of the algorithm he was running. He thought about shutting it down, but against his better judgement, he decided to let it run.

I need to apologize to Harland, he thought. *I hope Kasumi can still remain in the competition.*

Setting the alarm on his phone to wake him up in three hours, he dropped the phone on the small bed. Then he let himself fall onto the mattress. A shiny object on the lamp table caught his attention. He looked at it. It was the data cube he had 'borrowed' from Ravenhall. Alex hadn't finished pouring over its contents, but what was inside had helped him and Sid to finish Elijah's tracking algorithm, to understand how the Beast inside Joshua worked, and how many other ideas might become feasible. A part of him felt bad for having stolen it. Another part told him that it was for a good cause.

I guess I need to apologize to the librarian as well.

Alex sighed. It was getting dark outside. He saw the screen of his phone one last time, focusing on the date. He tried to smile, but doing so pained him more than the broken arm or the injured vertebra. His eyes watered and a sense of solitude invaded him. He wondered if someone would miss him once he was gone. For now, his only wish was that with any luck, it would be a dreamless sleep. With any luck.

Happy birthday to me, Alex thought before falling sleep.

Chapter 11
Restless Voices Carry into the Night

Harland was mentally and physically exhausted after the bad day at the talks. After the abrupt end to the meeting from Fionn's outburst there were calls to resume the talks, once tempers had cooled down. Harland had gone to his hotel room, changed into comfortable clothes and then walked to the nearby subway station. He took the next incoming train with no apparent direction in mind. He rode for a while and finally chose a random station to get off at and walked around until something caught his eye. Trekking uphill, he found himself staring at Kyôkatô Tower. He smiled, as it brought back happy childhood memories.

Built on a deserted hill a few decades ago, the area was now full of buildings and houses. Kyôkatô Tower was built to enhance the communications across the city through the transmission of signals into the Aethernet, above the interference of the power lines. In a single day, Kyôkatô Tower had managed to connect the sprawling city. It was a symbol of technological progress. However, these days it was more of a touristic attraction, as new technologies and a new building—the SkySpire—had replaced the old tower. He entered the building at the base of Kyôkatô Tower and went to the ticket counter where he bought a pass to the observation deck, two hundred and fifty meters above.

As he waited for the elevator, Harland examined the leaflet with the map of all the amenities inside the new base building and the tower itself, which included both an indoor amusement park for children, and restaurants and bars with slot machines for beleaguered parents. For a second, the temptation of going to the bar, drinking all the beer and spending all his money gambling mindlessly at a slot machine grew stronger. But as the elevator door opened with a ding, he cleared his head. Years ago he had gotten into serious gambling debts and Fionn had to intervene to stop Harland from selling his family's heirlooms. Since that day Harland had learned how much that help had cost Fionn. And yet his friend had done it without a second thought, asking only that Harland went clean and attend a support group to deal with his gambling addiction. And he had done that. He had been clean for more than a decade. No matter how bad things were, Harland would not succumb to his worst instinct. He owed Fionn that much.

After a few minutes the elevator doors opened and Harland entered the observation deck. The place was practically empty, probably because most people were more interested in the tournament.

It's a shame, he thought, *the city does have great views.* He had been here as a child. His father had brought him along on one of his trips and he had fallen in love with the views from the observation deck. On a clear day, such as today, it was possible to see the volcano in the God's Eye Island almost fifty kilometers out in the bay. But what Harland liked most was that you could see the city come to life as the sun went down and the lights came on and peppered the city like fireflies. To him, each light represented a life, a person doing something, existing and interacting with others. It reminded him of how tiny a person could be and yet how, when everybody pulled together, you could change a whole region. The massive city, one of the largest in the Core region, was a testament of that.

Harland walked towards the railing and let himself drop into one of the empty seats in front of the window that looked toward the bay. He had to give it to the Kuni, they really cared for making visitors feel welcomed, and the seat was more comfortable that it should be. He turned off his cellphone and allowed his mind to wander as the afternoon went by. Out of nowhere a black and red raven flew over his head, cawing loudly and landing near him, its claws grasping the metal bar used to separate the visitors from the glass.

He looked around to see if someone had noticed that a raven had somehow entered the enclosed space. But there was no one else. He stared at the raven, who returned the look, tilting its head to the right, as if it was studying him.

And then, it spoke.

"There you are."

"What?" Harland reacted, jumping from his seat in surprise. "Did you just talk?"

The raven cawed once more. Harland rubbed his eyes and when he was done, the raven was gone.

"I'm tired, that's it. I mean, it's not like I'm the main character of a poem," Harland murmured to himself.

"Is it really hard to believe that a raven can talk? I mean, look who your friends are, what they can do. What you have seen in recent years. Surely a talking raven would be the least strange thing you might have witnessed," a feminine voice said. It had a sweet quality, but something about it made Harland feel uneasy, a mix between awe and fear. He had experienced something similar just twice: once, when he had met Fionn for the first time, and the second, a little more than a year ago, at the Maze...

It sounded like a voice that was older than time.

Harland turned to his right and saw a tall lady sitting next to him. Long hair with fiery red and jet-black strands framed a face with olive skin and freckles. A friendly smile accompanied big eyes of a deep turquoise color that when you looked into them, pulled you into a timeless pool. She wore tight black leather trousers, red ankle boots, and a zipped up, black leather jacket decorated with feathers, metal spikes, and chain mail bits. The back of the jacket had a pair of silver wings embroidered across it. It was an odd mix of modern biker clothes and combat armor. On her left wrist was a silver bracelet with a jade stone set in it. She looked freefolk, and there was an air of familiarity. She could pass as Sam's cousin. And she resembled as well the freefolk magi and librarian they had met at the Maze... And then it dawned on Harland. His and Fionn's suspicions might be right.

"Is it you, Mekiri? Or should I say your Grace, The Trickster Goddess," Harland said, with a slight tremor in his voice.

"You are faster than Fionn, I give you that, faster than most mortals I ever encountered. Your mind truly is your best weapon," She smiled and gazed towards the skyline.

"We had our suspicions."

"Suspicions are not the same as certainties, which you seem to have," she put a hand on Harland's shoulder and just like that, all the fear and tension pounding inside his chest, evaporated. "You can relax now. I'm not going to cast lighting on you."

"I assume you are taking a form I feel comfortable with?" Harland asked. "And why are you here, your Grace?"

Then he realized what he just said and his eyes opened wide in fear.

She waved her hand, dismissing the comment.

"Not exactly. I did that with Fionn because, let's admit it, he can be a tad guarded when confronting someone he doesn't know. And back then, time was pressing. This is my actual form. Or how Mekiri looks in her true form when not dealing with the Freefolk. This body... this avatar, is inspired by how Asherah looked back in the day. It's my way to honor her."

"If I might say so, it's a really beautiful look," Harland said. "What's wrong with me, my tongue is loose! I apologize for my comment, your Grace."

"You don't need to apologize for speaking your mind. I'm not like my siblings that go around smiting people. Plus, I'm sure Asherah would have liked your compliment."

"You talk of her as if she was your friend."

"She was, my first mortal friend." The Goddess smiled. And the room lit up.

"It's curious the resemblance you have to Sam, and to Izia, judging by the pictures I've seen of her."

"Family inheritance I guess," The Goddess replied, leaving Harland surprised, but she cut him off before he could ask his next question. "But I'm not here to talk about that."

"Then why are you here?" Harland asked, puzzled.

"Seems to me that you needed someone to talk to. And

not someone involved with this whole situation," the Goddess smiled. It was friendly smile, the kind of smile that you would get from a spiritual guide. Which given the circumstances, would be the most accurate thing.

"I'm frustrated," Harland blurted, with a sigh.

"That much is obvious. Why?"

"Because there are people in positions of power that prefer to think about short term gain rather than on long term safety, and they are ruining what should be a discussion on how to move forward, not about reviving old grievances. It should be about finding common ground in light of recent events, to find solutions that help all, not ostracizing the others because they are different. We did that to the Freefolk and what did it get us? Centuries of chaos. The Kuni? They are allies, up to a point. The Samoharo? They barely leave their continent anymore. The Straits are a mess and let's not mention the Wastelands nor the Grasslands nor the Southern Regions, as they barely communicate with the Core. Yes, the Free Alliance is not perfect, and keeping that particular skeleton in the closet about one of its founders hasn't helped. But the idea was good. That putting together our resources and skills can make our differences work for the betterment of all. And now they want to break it all, to go back to a time where everyone was at each other's throats. For fucking profit!"

"I can see how that is infuriating. For the record I feel the same," the Goddess replied, as she stood up and leaned on the handrail. She crossed her hands. "After all this time, I'm surprised and saddened at the shortsightedness of mortal beings. You have a set of precious gifts: life, free will, love, the mere experience of watching the sun rise and set, but you squander them in petty concerns, opening the door to *them*."

"Now you see the reason for my frustration," Harland replied. He put his face in his hands and took a deep breath. It was strange how the air around them had a subtle smell of petrichor and wild berry. It was comforting. Then the smell of hot chocolate hit him in the nose. He looked up at the Goddess offering a cup filled to the brim, the smell telling him it was prepared like the drink from the Straits. Harland turned around; the concession stall was closed. He shouldn't have been surprised. It was magick. The Goddess winked at him as he took the cup.

"Let me tell you a story, since you are a lover of history," the Goddess started. "There was once a species, the first to be born into reality, in a beautiful garden. They were children of the universal conscience, the being some humans call Kaan'a, or the Freefolk call the Spirit Above All and the Samoharo, Itzmana Kub. They were the elder race, older than the Montoc dragons born from stars. And as elder children they rose high. So high, that part of them transcended reality and became gods unto themselves, messengers to teach and guide the younger species. But their pride got the better of them and in their fall, they allowed the Old Nightmares, beings that were in the chaos before Existence, to enter it and destroy and corrupt. Until they were sealed again in the space between spaces…"

"The Infinity Pits?" Harland asked. He took a drink. The faint hint of chili gave it a subtle kick to the taste buds and the brain.

"Indeed. But by then, it was too late, for the only thing remaining of the Akeleth were the ruins of their star-spawning civilization as testament of their prowess, defenseless younger species, legends, and the remaining spirits of those not ascended, roaming in penance through what was left of that idyllic garden, now a lonely planet floating in the cold universe."

"Theia?"

"I'm glad that you can keep up. I miss having someone to chat with in this manner."

"But if they were so powerful, why did they fall?"

"As I said, pride mostly," the Goddess said. Her expression was too human, too pained. Full of regret. Harland wondered if deities could feel mortal emotions. But he let her continue instead of asking that.

"Too proud to learn when to stop. Too proud to present a united front until it was too late. And their pride cost countless lives and planets of the younger species. That's why we… they… tried to do right by saving the three major species from their doomed realms and brought them here. So, with time, they could rise to the challenge their forerunners were not able to meet."

"Are we talking about the Akeleth or the gods?" Harland asked, confused.

"Yes."

"That's not an answer."

"Does it matter?" The Goddess smiled.

"I guess that at this point, it doesn't," Harland said. There was no reason to keep pushing the point. "I have a better question for you: if your kind are so powerful, why are you not doing more? Why don't you act? If you are the Trickster Goddess, patron saint of heroes, magi and Freefolk, why don't you intervene? Why don't your siblings?"

The Goddess remained silent for a minute. The longest of Harland's life, as he could feel his very soul being pierced by the stare that the Goddess was giving him. He looked around, waiting for the smiting lightning. But nothing happened.

"We can't interfere in the physical realm," the Goddess said, "not without breaking it. Last time I did, I scarred the world. Thus, I use avatars, little pieces of me that can interact with you without breaking your minds. To tell you what you need to hear. And who says we don't intervene? Only when things go wrong, do people notice what's going on. A job well done means no one notices. Plus, even now it is hard for us to agree to cooperate. Finally, this is your world now, your existence. If we presume to act on your behalf, our pride will be our collective undoing once more, and we already paid a high price for that. No, it's better if the younger species learn their lessons on their own, so their progress is built by you and for you. Power without understanding is a dangerous proposition."

"And if we fail?" Harland asked. He knew history all too well. And while he tried to keep up with the philosophy his father had when creating the Foundation, of hope in the best parts of mortals, especially humans, Harland had trouble not being cynical.

"You will rise again," The Goddess smiled once more.

"Then why are you helping us?" Harland was more than confused. He felt vertigo. Not for one moment would he have thought of having a debate with a deity. This was too much for him. He drank the chocolate in one go, wishing it packed more punch. "Why are you telling me all of this? Wouldn't be better to tell Fionn? He is the hero. Or Gaby, she is more than capable and smarter than all of us. Even Alex would know what to do when he clears his mind. I'm just a regular, humble human."

"A human that walks tall alongside true titans, unflinchingly. You mortals remind me of what we once were. What we could have been. And because..." the Goddess made another long pause. For a second Harland thought that she was blushing. "I actually like spending time with you."

"I'm not a titan, and I'm not a hero." Harland looked down. For the first time in a long time, he felt self-conscious about his stature and physique. Rage and sadness swirled in his heart, as he clenched his fist around the cup. As a kid, when the only thing he could do was read about the exploits of others, he wondered why he had been born. Being with Fionn and the rest had made him forget about his deepest insecurities, as if he was one of them. But not right now. "I don't risk my life like my friends. I can't, even if I wanted to. I'm useless in that regard."

"I beg to differ," the Goddess said, with a tone that verged on annoyed, almost angry. "Do you know what a hero really is? A person that decides to change the world for the better, with whatever tools they have available. So yes, Fionn and Gaby and Alex and Sam, even Sid, are heroes. But the truth is that you are a hero, too. Because through your choices and actions you are effecting change. You give others an example to follow. Otherwise you wouldn't be able to hold Black Fang. You, more than anyone, are following the legacy of The Founding Parents, of King Castlemartell, trying to steer others into cooperating for a common goal, to have a future."

"I'm not them. I'm just a small man surrounded by powerful beings," Harland could feel his eyes welling up with tears. He felt her hand on his shoulder and he grabbed it. He was dying to ask her to transform him, to give him the tools needed to be a hero.

"Your physical attributes don't define your worth," the Goddess replied. "It's the size of your heart and the strength of your will. What you decide to do with your life is what defines who you are. For even the humblest person can create great change and be the hero we need. And you will know what to do with what you will remember of this chat."

Harland looked at her eyes. They were full of love and compassion. In that moment Harland saw her not as a deity, but as a friend. How odd was it to think like that. Friends. He realized that, aside from Sid's lousy jokes about sharing a similar height, none of his friends had ever looked down on him. Fionn, Gaby, Alex, Sam, and Sid, they all treated him as an equal. As family. Sid had even trusted his most beloved possession, the Figaro, to him. And the Freefolk had requested that he, as head of the Foundation, join the summit, because they knew he would try to do what was best for all. He smiled. Then he realized something, as his eyes opened wide.

"Wait. What do you mean by remember?"

"Daydreaming can play tricks on the mind and memory. And regarding Alex, he could use a friend too now. And a chocolate cake. Remember being the change," the Goddess said, but her voice became faint, as if the wind took her words away.

Harland shook his head. He found himself alone in the observation deck. The distant sound of a vacuum cleaner his only company. His mouth could still taste the chocolate, but there was no sign of a cup ever being in his hands. Had he been daydreaming again? But it felt so real. The sun was setting on the city. It was time to get back to his hotel. And for some reason, he felt that Alex needed help. Harland wasn't sure what he could do to help Alex or what was wrong with him. But he had learned something from all those years having adventures with Fionn. Sometimes the only thing you need is a friend.

I hope there is a bakery on the way back to the hotel, he thought as he walked back to the elevator. *Need to call for a ride then, I better turn on my phone.* Harland pulled out his phone and turned it back on. Almost immediately it started to vibrate and bleep with incoming messages. He opened the messages and saw the attached video of Joshua's fight.

This is not good, Harland thought. *I need to fix this.*

† † †

Alex woke up, so to speak. The landscape that surrounded him was familiar, but not in a good way. This was not the hotel room he'd been in before falling asleep. This was the place his mind tended to drift to when things got bad inside his head, when the voices became louder: a lucid dream. Or in this particular case, an all too familiar nightmare.

He was sitting on a raft made of discarded wood, floating through a flooded city. The dark waters covered most of the features except for the taller buildings, which were brilliantly lit up. A faint mist covered the grey skies and far in the background was an odd, giant mask, seemingly made of white ceramic. The mask whispered from time-to-time words that were lost to the wind. But Alex didn't need to hear them. He knew exactly what they said: the things that he said to himself during the bad days—and sometimes during the good ones—listing all of the reasons why he sucked. He'd learned to mostly ignore them, even if it wasn't possible all the time.

Perhaps that's why he reacted the way he did after Joshua's incident. Because he was already telling himself all the things that Fionn, Gaby and Sam were saying, and worse.

"Why can't I dream about a better place like Korby-World, or a beach?" Alex asked, although he knew no one would reply. "I think even my subconscious hates me. Not that I can't blame it."

"Understatement of the century," a voice next to him said. A female voice with a strange quality. It came from a little girl, with wild red and black hair, and on top of the wild mess of hair, two rabbit ears. She was wearing an old green poncho with raven feathers sewn into it. Her bright, colorful large eyes were full of playfulness. "This is not a good way to live, y'know? Telling yourself all these horrible things all the time."

"I know, Mekiri," Alex replied, recognizing his companion as the freefolk custodian of Ravenhall. He tried to smile but failed. "It's not like I enjoy it."

"How long has it been this way?" Mekiri asked.

"I was diagnosed with chronic depression when I was a teenager," Alex replied and turned to meet Mekiri's gaze. "Before the Gift. Don't feel guilty about it."

"I don't know what you mean," Mekiri replied coyly. "And we are moving."

"Ah yes, at some point the raft always moves and ends up going to that building back there," Alex pointed to a tall concrete building, designed in the heavy utilitarian style typical of the industrial city of Manfeld.

"The barely lit one?" Mekiri asked, curious. She seemed to find the place a true oddity. It made Alex feel uncomfortable, ashamed. He knew his own head was a mess.

"Yes, then I usually enter it and the dream ends."

Mekiri remained silent for a moment and then said, "Have you looked for help?"

"I tried," Alex replied, then sighed. "But it's hard to talk with someone about the unique experience of having another voice in your head, which comes with the Gift, along with the one that keeps telling you that you suck. Not to mention that not all meds work with the altered metabolism that comes with it."

Mekiri turned her head to look at the building. She was oddly subdued from what Alex remembered of their last encounter. The small magus liked dramatic scenes. This was far from it.

"I'm sorry you have to go through this," she said, offering a faint smile.

"Stuff happens," Alex shrugged.

"And that's why you are taking increasingly riskier actions? Pushing yourself to the limit? Having unhealthy habits to activate your powers? Trying to do everything on your own?"

"In hindsight," Alex said, stroking his chin. "That makes a lot of sense."

"Why do you do that?"

Alex took his time to reply. He was having problems, not

only to think, but to breathe. It was as if there was a hole in his chest, where his heart was. And the hole's presence hurt even worse than the broken arm or the injured back.

"I'm broken, so I don't work well with others. I try, but it rarely works out. And I know it's my fault. I'm not an easy person to get along with. The usual: anger issues, mood swings," Alex replied, waving his hands for emphasis. "So, I prefer to do things on my own to avoid making others feel uncomfortable. It's not like anyone is going to miss me when I'm gone."

"Don't say that. First of all, I'm sure plenty of people will miss you if that happens. And second, it's not your fault, so stop saying that. There might be things you can improve as a person, everyone has. But you are not broken. You are not a bad person and it's not your fault you have this shadow inside you. Suffering from mental health issues is not a weakness for which you have to overcompensate by taking increased risks. Unless you want to get yourself killed by being a hero. And that's not an option."

"Says who?" Alex asked.

"Are you challenging me, kid?" Mekiri replied, her tone of voice unlike the childlike one she usually used. This one was pointed, more serious... and had an unearthly quality to it, as if it carried its own echo chamber. It cowed him.

But he wasn't challenging her. It was how he truly felt. This current bout of depression had lasted several months and the only reason he kept dragging himself out of bed was because of his sense of responsibility. He had promised Kasumi to help her with Joshua. He had promised Harland to do his best at the Games. But he was running out of the will to keep pushing, to keep smiling just for appearances. His reply wasn't a challenge, rather a sample of his state of mind.

"I wouldn't dream of it," he said. "I mean, that would be stupid, considering who you really are." Alex said, raising his hands to defend himself.

"I have no idea what you are talking about." Mekiri turned her head, pouting like a small child. Her expression broke the tension between them.

"You don't fool me. And I doubt you have fooled the rest.

We talk to each other..." Alex felt a pang in his heart. He remembered what had happened earlier today, the fight, the heated words. "Used to anyways. And your real identity is not that much of a secret. My guess is that you appeared here in a form I wouldn't perceive as a source of conflict or pain and that means appearing as Mekiri, who I barely know. And probably the form you feel more comfortable with for the past millennia."

"You are smarter than you give yourself credit," Mekiri smiled with a wide grin. Then her expression became all serious. "But not that smart. No offense."

"None taken, albeit I'm curious, why do you say that?"

"Because you have to understand something, no one is a single cloud in the sky. We are interconnected. Which means that you are not alone, nor do you have to do things on your own. It's ok to falter. To admit that you are afraid. To ask for help."

"I... I... You are being very forthcoming. I mean isn't the Trickster Goddess known for playing tricks on her targets?" Alex asked. This was a surreal experience, even for a dream.

"No, not in this case," Mekiri replied in a serious tone, like that of his yaya when she was scolded him. "That's the last thing you need. Your own mind is playing enough tricks with you. What you need now is to be listened to and guided, if you want to."

Both were silent for what seemed to be hours, as the raft moved closer and closer to the building. Mekiri sighed.

"I told this once to someone I cared for, as if she was my own child, and now I tell it to you," Mekiri finally said. "A hero is at their strongest when they have fallen, for when they rise again, they have learned a lesson. A hero is as strong as the friends they have, for when the time comes to ask for help, the love for each other can change the world. The key lies inside their heart."

Mekiri then hit him in the chest, using her right index finger. "Ouch!" For someone so small, she packed quite a punch in a single finger.

"And you have too much heart, that's why things hurt you twice as much. But that also makes you twice as strong as anyone I've seen before. No obstacle will stand in your path when you realize that."

Alex remained silent, so Mekiri took his hand and squished it really hard. This mere act let lose something inside Alex, as tears welled up behind his eyelids. The raft finally arrived at the building. The door of the main entrance was ajar. And yet a strange knocking sound echoed around.

"Seems that we have arrived at your destiny. Think about what we talked about," Mekiri said, jumping out first and entering the building. She turned to face Alex once more, this time smiling. "And about that cube you 'borrowed' from Ravenhall. I will take it back. Or you will risk altering the causality too much if I allow you to keep peeking at future inventions."

"It was fun while it lasted," Alex replied with a smile. He knew that was bound to happen. At least he managed to finish a couple of projects. "Thank you for the pep talk."

"If I am who you say I am, and I'm not saying you are right," Mekiri winked. "I would be a lousy patron saint of heroes if I didn't take care of their minds and health from time to time."

"I'm not a hero," Alex looked down, a sour taste in his mouth.

"Ay Alex," Mekiri said, changing her freefolk accent for that of the Straits. "Alex, Alex, Alex... I hate that you guys keep saying that..."

The knocking sound became so loud that Alex turned around to search for the source, but when he looked again at the doorway, Mekiri was gone. She'd jumped out and entered the building. Alex followed and everything went black.

† † †

The knocking on the door become louder, as Alex stirred from his sleep. He woke up, barely paying attention to the blinking spots on the computer's results of the scan. It was already night. Still groggy, he stood up and went to answer the door, not bothering with turning on the light. The streetlamp outside his room gave enough illumination. He opened the door and looked around until he saw it was Harland.

He was carrying a small box that smelled like chocolate cake.

"Happy birthday." Harland offered the box to Alex, who struggled with his good hand to take it without dropping it.

"How did you..." Alex said.

"A bird told me." Harland smiled.

"I guess it's the same bird that made an unexpected visit to my weird dream."

"Wanna trade stories while we eat this?" Harland asked, taking out a pair of bamboo forks from his pocket.

"Sure, it's not like I can do much with my arm in a cast," Alex showed Harland his arm. "Cake would be good."

Chapter 12
Rude Awakenings

Kasumi was walking around Electronic Town, the place to be if you wanted to buy any possible electronic device, videogame, or action figure under the sun. The place was an eclectic mix of lights, sounds, and colorful products that clashed, as the screens on the stores showcased the newest offers on the products inside. Breaker was safely tucked into its sheath, which hung from her back, held by a strap across her chest. The cacophony around her, the vibrant lights and the amount of people walking in and out from the stores in the old, towering buildings, had a numbing effect on her. And right now, not feeling much was what she wanted.

Part of her felt guilty for having dragged Alex into her and Joshua's problems. Regardless of the oracle's recommendation. Another part of her felt angry at the others for how they had reacted to the whole thing. Plus, she had to wait until the Rules Board judged if she would still be allowed to keep competing after what happened.

I would do it all over again if I had too, she thought. There were no regrets in her heart, even if the personal cost could affect her plans to regain her family's honor.

Kasumi had gone to Electric Town after dropping Joshua at his place and seeing Alex to the hotel. She was going to pick him up later tonight to take him to her house. Meanwhile, she was looking for a present for him. In part to thank him for helping her with Joshua's problem, even when it got him into trouble, in part to thank him for including her on the Foundation's team, and in part for his birthday, which strangely his friends had forgotten.

I better get him three presents then, Kasumi thought.

She entered a popular shop that carried a wide range of action figures and vinyl toys based on popular cartoons, videogames, and old monster movies known as kaiju. While technology was the main export of the Kuni Empire, the second biggest was that of media productions, with the third being merchandise based on those productions. As such, the choices were staggeringly large.

Maybe I should pick these three kat-kaijus, Kasumi thought, *and be done with this.* She grabbed a plump metallic, bipedal cat that resembled a giant robot, a similar one but with black scales and electric blue lines, and a third one in red, but instead of a snout, had sunglasses and a beak. Kasumi looked up, as she mused on which one to buy, and found herself face to face with Sam. She was holding a box that contained a replica of the giant animatronic combat robot known as the 'Griffin Mecha' that was on a square not far from the Stadium.

"He already has the metallic one. He bought it right before his first fight at the games. But I don't recall if he has the black one," Sam said. "Or the red one. Honestly, he has way too many figures to keep track of."

"Let me guess, Alex wanted that one too," Kasumi replied, pointing to the box Sam was carrying. She left the metallic and black toys on the shelf and took the red one.

"No, but I know he likes giant robots and was looking at videos of the animatronic lightshow on our flight here. I'm making an educated guess," Sam replied, holding the box tight. Kasumi gave Sam a close look. She wore ripped jeans, flat-soled ankle boots and a leather jacket. She had a certain charm that Kasumi found attractive, even if she wasn't in the mood to deal with the freefolk girl. What she had seen, Sam had spent equal time arguing and chatting amicably with Alex. Kasumi was confused about some of the easterners' social mores.

"He is so predictable," Kasumi added. "Then again, most guys are. I don't know who's easier to give a present to, my dad and his fishing lure collection, or Joshua and his liking for pet monster figurines."

Both of them walked to the cashier and joined the queue to pay for their selection.

"Joshua seems to be a nice person," Sam said, as she fidgeted with the toy box.

"He is the best not-older brother one could ask for," Kasumi smiled.

"I... I want to apologize for before," Sam blurted. "My family has a complicated relationship with tovainars, even former ones."

"I was told as much," Kasumi replied. "That's why I guess Alex decided to keep it a secret."

"Good point," Sam said. "Look, that's no excuse for what happened. I'm really sorry."

Kasumi looked Sam in the eyes. The latter was blushing, in a shade that matched the color of her hair. It seemed to be an honest apology. And while Kasumi was still angry at how the Greywolf had spoken to her friend, Sam was not her father. There was no point in not accepting the apology. Doing so could lead to a clearing of the air later on.

"Thank you, but I'm not the one you need to apologize to," Kasumi said. She paid for her purchases and Sam did the same.

"Right, Joshua and Alex," Sam stood there, in the middle of the store, blocking the entrance for the other customers. Kasumi rolled her eyes.

"Unless you are planning to become part of their figurine exhibition, you better move, you are blocking the entrance," Kasumi said, dragging her out of the way. "You want to come?"

"Where?"

"I'm planning to get something to eat and then go deliver these to the birthday boy."

Kasumi led the way and Sam followed her in silence. Kasumi was confused about why Sam was acting the way she was, as she struck Kasumi as a pragmatic kind of person. And seeing as how Kasumi considered herself an expert on the human condition, her guts told her that there was something else bothering the freefolk woman. Kasumi led her to a group of food trucks parked outside a building hosting a videogame tournament, left Sam at a table and went to see the offerings. She skipped the curry one. If she wanted curry, she would have taken them to the restaurant. Sushi? She didn't know if Sam was allergic to raw fish. For that matter, do the freefolk have the same allergies as humans?

I don't think it's the moment to find out, Kasumi decided.

Ramen might have been an option, same with the minced meatballs filled with chopped onions. In the end Kasumi decided that the orange flavored pancakes were a safer option. They were tasty, simple and warm. The kind of meal that could cheer up someone down on her luck. And while Kasumi's first instinct was to make snarky remarks, she knew it was not the time nor the place. She bought two orders of the cream bathed orange pancakes, two coffees and took the tray to the table.

Kasumi couldn't avoid noticing how the competitors of the videogame tournament looked at her. Maybe because she was still decked out in her demonhunter attire. Maybe because she looked like a cosplayer, with the big weapon at her back and the blue strands of hair. Or maybe, as she saw in a reflection on the window of the building, that Breaker was glowing faintly. Kasumi still wasn't sure what that meant. Maybe she should ask Alex about it. She put the tray between her and Sam and offered her the food.

"Try them, they are really fluffy and delicious. I should know, I like to study the competition in the food business."

Sam grabbed her plate and started to eat. Kasumi did the same. And while the food was superb, to the point that she was considering getting a second order, Sam's demeanor was too uncomfortable for her.

"Can I ask you a question?" Kasumi asked.

"Sure," Sam replied, in a subdued tone. She was staring at the pancake, although judging by the subtle smile, she was enjoying the meal.

"Someone told me that you were the most promising magus of the Freefolk," Kasumi continued. "But I watched your fights, and you haven't used any spell, aside from the shield one. How did you become such a good fighter?"

"I had good teachers," Sam replied with a smile. "Gaby is an even better fighter."

"Perhaps, but you would challenge most of the demonhunters I know. But I wonder, why don't you cast anything? It's not against the rules. I checked," Kasumi said. And she had checked. Her philosophy was to know everything she could about her opponents and arrive at the battle with a plan already in mind. And if someone was allowed to cast spells, she didn't want to leave that to chance, so she would have a counter for that.

"I can't," Sam replied, lowering her head. The answer took Kasumi by surprise.

"What do you mean?" Kasumi leaned forward.

"Since I got the Gift, I have been unable to do so," Sam explained, looking up to meet Kasumi's gaze. "I can barely cast my True Spell now. The shield one you saw."

"True Spell?"

"Some of us develop a spell defined by our nature, one that we can cast while barely thinking about it. The Bubble Shield is mine. But other than that, it's not working."

"Do you know why?" Kasumi was intrigued. Part of the demonhunter training was learning how different traditions used magick, but human rites—which were diverse as they were—worked different from the Freefolk, by orders of magnitude. Onmyōji, the specialists on magick and divination in the Kuni Empire, like her mother, used a series of rituals and talismans to get things done. Nahuales from the Straits used a whole different approach. And that didn't include the scarce shamans that dwelled with spirits and were dispersed between both continents. The Samoharo... well, aside the rumored use of blood for their spells, they were a mystery. But for Kasumi, the Freefolk were the most intriguing. For they were not users of magick... they were magick. And that one of their famed magus was now unable to use magick was a whole new situation.

"The Gift doesn't mix well with the Freefolk's way to cast magick. We draw magickal energy from the world around us and channel it through our bodies to alter reality. In a way, it's similar to having another sense. The Gift generates its own energy and alters your perception of the world, making that sense useless."

"How?"

"It's hard to explain," Sam looked up, as if she was trying to come up with an explanation. "It's as if the world looks in greyscale and when you awaken the Gift you suddenly see it in high-definition color and your understanding of it changes. And that is not conducive of the freefolk way to cast magick. And because of that I feel like I lost something inside me."

Sam's eyes welled up and Kasumi felt bad for her. It was an all too familiar feeling. One that was painful to the extreme. She offered Sam a napkin.

"It's my turn to ask you a question," Sam said, while drying her cheeks. "Was it hard to get used to the hearing aids?"

"My fashion statement? Some sacrifices have to be made for the sake of originality in a complacent society."

Sam was taken aback by the reply, but Kasumi let out a laugh.

"Relax, I'm joking," Kasumi said. Not everyone was used to her joking about her disability. Then again, if she didn't take it with humor, life would become harder. "Look, at first it was hard when my hearing problems appeared, because I was fourteen and it came during a time when my family was going through some difficulties. But I got used to them after a while. I did struggle at first, understanding what my teachers were saying when I couldn't see their faces, not to mention the ostracism by some of my classmates. But my parents went through a lot to get these combat ready hearing aids, to help me fulfill my goal of being a demonhunter, so I can't let them down. They were so supportive of me, even when everything seemed to be against me because of my disability."

"How come?"

"Let's say the other trainees weren't keen on a hard-of-hearing girl beating them in every test and then laughing about the whole issue."

"Sounds like it was tough," Sam said. "I guess it changed your whole outlook on life."

Kasumi remained silent. She raised her right index finger, asking for a pause, went for a second order of pancakes and then continued.

"Years ago, I accepted that it was part of me," Kasumi said, her tone to the point and serious. This was a topic she had meditated upon a lot over the years. "You say that you feel your connection to magick is different, as if something is missing. Even with my hearing aids, I don't experience sound as before. Everything sounds a tad metallic to me. However, I have learned to ignore that, as well as to practice other things I can do. If doing magick is like a sense, maybe you can hone the Gift to act as sort of a replacement. Maybe your connection to magick is not totally lost. Perhaps the key lies in figuring out how this different perception can be used to your advantage."

"What do you mean?"

"Answer me this first: is it possible to cast two or more spells at the same time?"

"No," Sam explained matter-of-factly. "No one has achieved that. Your brain would fry itself by attempting it, as you need to think on how to focus the energy to alter reality to make a single spell work. You can stack them though, to cast one after the other in sequence. That's super difficult, but can be done with enough experience. Asherah, the first Dragonqueen, was able to do that in a natural way, which I assume would look as if she was casting multiple things at the same time. Why?"

Kasumi finished her second order of pancakes and drank her coffee.

"I'm wondering," Kasumi replied. "You still have some sort of connection to that part you feel is missing, as you can still cast the True Spell, even if it's with difficulty. So, you didn't lose your ability. I think that what changed is the way to focus the energy. In rehabilitation therapy we call that 're-framing'. If the Gift works as you say, maybe you don't need to draw the energy through your body, but instead play with the one surrounding it, like in mizu-do when you redirect the attack of an opponent and use it in your favor."

"Using the Gift's energy as an extension to my mind and hands," Sam's eye opened wide in realization.

"Exactly!" Kasumi exclaimed, startling the other diners. "And if I'm right, you might be able to cast two spells at the same time, because if the Gift tells you how reality works, you don't need to focus your mind on achieving one thing. The Gift will do that for you."

"It could work," Sam said, staring at one of the posters behind Kasumi. "But I would have to practice a lot to get it done without blowing up a building. Magick can have nasty side effects."

"Or you could ask Alex how he does his trick with manipulating electromagnetic energy. It would be the closest thing to what you need. A reference of sorts so you don't have to start from scratch."

"You have a tactical mind," Sam noted. "And for that I need to apologize to him."

"I can't allow myself to get confused or startled," Kasumi replied, pointing to her aids once more. "I don't have that luxury. For me every centimeter of advantage must count."

Kasumi picked up all the trash from the table and took it to the trash cans, separating paper from bamboo from plastic into their respective places. Kasumi walked to a nearby parking lot, full of motorbikes, followed by Sam.

"I'm going to meet Alex now, you are welcome to come," Kasumi said, opening the travel compartment of a black and blue motorbike, placing her purchases inside. She took Sam's and placed it inside as well. Closing the lid, she got on the bike and started it.

"On a motorbike? Why not a trike?"

"I work as delivery girl in a city with narrow streets. A bike is more practical than a trike. Those things are way too large. Maybe they work fine in Ionis, but not here."

Sam got on, behind Kasumi, who handed her a helmet.

"Safety first, have my helmet."

"What about you?"

"I will wear my driving shades," Kasumi said, placing the dark shades with black and blue rims over her eyes. "Beside we are not that far, and I know shortcuts. We will be there in a flash!"

The bike's engine roared loudly, shaking the ground

and the nearby windows. Kasumi turned off the engine. She looked around, confused. Something was off. The vibrations from the engine shouldn't be that strong.

A second roar echoed across the streets, activating the alarms of several cars. Kasumi felt a finger poking her shoulder and she turned to see what Sam was pointing at.

Something that appeared to be a mechanical wyvern flew by the street, roaring and spewing fire on cars and closed stalls alike. The orange of the flames was a stark contrast on the twilight colors of the end of the day. The silhouette seemed familiar to Kasumi, a recent sight she had been seeing during her delivery routes. An image that for her, was an eyesore in the otherwise familiar city.

"What was that?" Sam asked. "It can't be a dragon. They're all gone."

"I would say that it was that horrible wyvern statue belonging to that equally horrible art exhibition across the city. Somehow it came to life. And it seems to be heading to your hotel."

"You don't find that strange?" Sam asked.

"I'm a demonhunter," Kasumi shrugged her shoulders and turned on the engine, revving it. "Strange is part of the job,"

"Y'know? This might be the start of a beautiful friendship."

"Hold tight. I like to drive fast," Kasumi smiled. She wasn't lying. Inside, she could feel the rush of adrenaline surging through her body. The excitement of the mystery flooded her chest as her heart pumped faster. This was it. Her second chance.

"And I like to go fast," Sam replied.

The motorbike darted at high speeds across the streets, following the path of the wyvern a few meters behind it. The wyvern was fast, but not that fast. Kasumi dodged cars and obstacles in a frenetic chase. Behind her, Sam screamed. Judging by the sound, it was a scream of joy.

†††

Alex and Harland sat on the floor, their backs against

the bed. There were crumbs all over the carpet. Between them sat an empty plate.

"That was a good cake," Harland said, leaving his fork on the table.

"That wash greash cake," Alex mumbled, wolfing down the last big slice of cake. He enjoyed every bite till the end. "Thank you. I needed something like this."

"So today is your birthday," Harland stated.

"For a few more hours at least," Alex replied, grabbing his phone to check the time.

"Why didn't you say anything?"

"I didn't think I had to."

"You are right," Harland replied, embarrassed. He pointed to Alex's cast. "Rough day, uh?"

"Please, I know you already know everything that happened," Alex said, a tad annoyed. Given the hour, Harland had to know every single detail of what had transcended. "It's your job to know. And I'm sure that Fionn and Gaby already gave you the rundown."

"I want to hear your version," Harland said, looking Alex straight in the eyes.

"Why?"

"Because," Harland replied with a smile, as if he was remembering something. "When we met for the first time, you taught that what you do, no matter how criminally stupid it may be, has a good cause beneath it. And I like to learn my lessons. I don't want a detailed narration of the fight. I want to know why."

"I had to save him," Alex stared to the wall, his face poorly illuminated by the laptop screen and the streetlamp outside.

"I get that, but why? Why risk your life and that of others, for someone you didn't know before, and who is a tovainar." Harland said.

"Was," Alex replied. "And as far as I know, not by choice. According to Kasumi, he was experimented on. Joshua could have chosen to follow that path, but he didn't, he is working hard to be a good person. If I can't help someone like him to get better, what does that say of me, that I'm broken inside?"

Tears ran down his cheek. Harland offered him the last clean napkin.

"That said," Alex continued. "I want to apologize to you."

"What for?" Harland asked, clearly confused.

"I basically ruined the team's opportunity and put you in a pickle if you need to negotiate something through a challenge."

"Don't worry about that," Harland waved his hand. "I'm just happy that you and the rest are safe."

"So, what now?" Alex looked down. His fingers played with a loose strand from the carpet.

"I managed to keep Kasumi in the competition," Harland explained. "Joshua is banned, no surprise there. And while you don't have a ban exactly, it's clear that you are in no shape to continue."

"Kasumi can do it," Alex offered. He knew it sounded lame. But Kasumi was by far the best non-Gifted fighter he had seen in his life. Pits, she could even be on par with Gaby and she was still a regular human. If life were fair, she would already be the champion of the Games.

"Oh, I have no doubt of that. I'm sure she will end up being the champion," Harland smiled. "I wanted to tell you, that I sorted your visa. I know I should have done it before and that would have reduced your stress."

"Thank you," Alex replied. Then he extended his right arm to grab the analgesic pill bottle. Harland helped him to open it and Alex took out two pills.

"How bad is the fracture?"

"Bad enough to keep me from competing. Not enough to keep me from using the left hand. It hurts, that's all."

"You should avoid using that hand. Gift or not, you need to let it heal."

"I know. And I..."

A loud beeping echoed across the room. At first, Alex couldn't think where it was coming from. Maybe the fire alarm went off? And then he remembered what his laptop had been doing before he fell asleep. He went to the desk, grabbed it and showed the screen to Harland.

"What's that?" Harland asked. "What am I looking at?"

"A program my laptop was running," Alex explained, hitting a few keys. "The one that Sid helped me to finish coding. It was originally created by my friend, Elijah. He also created the Figaro's AI. This program was meant to replace the traditional incursion alerts by one that could forecast them, by tapping into the climate probes floating around cities and alterations on the Aethernet network."

"You talk about him in past tense."

"He passed away a few years ago," Alex said. Despite all the time that had passed, the memories of it, the funeral, the aftermath, still left a sour taste in his mouth. He often wondered if he hadn't been dealing with the other voice at the moment he got the Gift, maybe he would have been able to prevent Elijah from getting badly injured and disabled. "Of all the group—not counting myself—he was the one with the worst injuries, but he wasn't lucky enough to get the Gift. He never recovered fully from his injuries and they passed on a toll."

"I'm sorry to hear that," Harland said. "So, all the tech you have been developing these past years as a group has been a way to honor him and a way to stop others from going through what happened to you."

"Pretty much. And if this is finally working, then I have bad news for you."

"How bad?"

"Five readouts," Alex pointed at five different dots blinking over a map of the city. All at different locations but seemingly all surrounding the SkySpire. That's odd."

"What's odd?"

"Those energy signatures. They don't seem to be from incursions. The readouts make no sense. There hasn't been something living with that energy output in... I don't know."

"How dangerous?" Harland asked.

"I won't know until this is plugged into the Figaro's mainframe, hopefully we will get a better readout. And to make things worse: one is on a course here." Alex hit a couple of keys and the screen changed, showing a feed from a camera in the next neighborhood. "I'm tapping into the security feed of the street cameras to get a better view. Good thing we are in the safest city on the continent."

While the image wasn't entirely clear, what he saw was a machine, with a black structure, illuminated by the reddish glow of a furnace in its innards. Its shape resembled that of a fire breathing dragon, but with only a pair of legs instead of two. An abstract, weird mockery of a dragon fused with metallic elements, more akin to a wyvern than one of the dragons of yore.

"Aww crap." Alex exclaimed. "A biomechanical wyvern?"

Alex passed the laptop to Harland. He stood up, raised his duffel bag and dropped all of its contents on the bed. First, he struggled into his vest, which glowed with a faint blue hue as soon as he finished zipping up. The vest inflated as current passed through it, becoming hard as armor. He hung a pair of goggles from his neck. Then he put a bracer on his good arm. Tying it up really hurt, as he had to use the hand of his broken arm. He grabbed his collapsible bow, checked that there were enough rounds in the arrow cartridge already plugged into the bow. He took the spare cartridges and placed them in pouches around his waist, doing the same with several chocolate bars. Getting prepared for a fight was becoming second nature for him. Broken arm and hurt back notwithstanding. He popped another couple of analgesics.

"What are those for?" Harland asked, pointing to the chocolate bars.

"If I start run low on energy they will give me a sugar rush high enough to keep me working for a few more minutes," Alex replied as he went to the corner and grabbed Yaha.

"You know you risk getting diabetes, right?"

"I know," Alex replied as he sheathed Yaha into the scabbard inserted in the back of his vest. He was well aware of how hard he tended to push his body to keep up with Fionn, Gaby, and now Sam, and his own energy requirements. Of all of them, his version of the Gift was the most taxing in terms of energy consumption. Alex placed a comms bean inside his ear. Then he gave another look at the laptop screen and pressed a key, changed it to a map overview, where a line was tracking the path of the wyvern. Alex dragged the hard suitcase over by the bed and released the locks.

"What's inside?" Harland asked.

"Combat gear tailored for you. I was trying to finish this, but I ran out of time," Alex explained. "But it should be functional. Andrea assured me that the battery should last long enough to get you out of any situation."

"You... you didn't have to do that."

"You are part of the team, logic says that you will require protection if you are going to keep joining us in these crazy events," Alex said, not taking his eyes from the screen. He was trying to calculate how long he had until the wyvern came by the hotel and planning alternate routes of interception in case that didn't happen. "I would love to explain in detail how it works, but once you get the goggles on, you will find how to operate it. I think it would be a good idea to get to the Figaro so you can find what those signals are and also contact Gaby and Fionn. I can't shake this feeling that things will get worse."

"Aren't you being a bit pessimistic?"

"Life has taught me I have to be realistic." Alex stood in the middle of the room, closing his eyes for a moment. He focused on his breath and how it synchronized with the visualization of the Gift's core that lay inside of him, just like Fionn had taught him. He felt a surge of energy as the core fed from his breathing, under his focus, as the Gift awakened inside him. Deep down, Alex felt a thrill every time he awakened the Gift. Even if it was for a brief moment, it made him feel able to achieve anything instead of the constant failure he felt most of the day. "Now if you'll excuse me."

Alex's heart beat like a drum, increasing speed with each pulsation. His irises changed, glowing gold. The world around him took on a different quality, a sense that could only be described as a more solid version of reality. He could feel the surge of adrenalin running through his blood, and with it, the energy surged across his body. The lights of the room flickered as electrical currents ran across his arms and legs. Lines across his combat vest shone blue once more as he put on his goggles. Alex felt his right knee trembling, and nausea inundated his throat.

This is not the moment to have an anxiety attack,

Alex thought. He took a deep breath to calm himself. Concentrating, he saw the energy from the power lines that ran underground, the energy coming and going from the SkySpire, and more importantly, from the incoming enemy. He had to time his jump. He opened the windows of the room's balcony and walked to the back of the room, then turned around to face the open exit.

"Please tell me you are not going to do what I think you are going to do," Harland said.

"I have an idea," Alex smiled at Harland. Truth be told, his plan just went as far as 'getting on top of the wyvern and find a way to disable it'. He would have to work out the finer details as he went. Good thing he had eaten a good chunk of the cake. It would give him enough energy to recover what he'd lost from the fight against Joshua. And if he was lucky, he would take out the wyvern quickly and leave the rest of whatever was happening to the others.

"Are you sure about this?"

"I can't think of a better one right now," Alex shrugged his shoulders. "Wish me luck."

"Good luck," Harland said. His voice was trembling. Alex knew his friend was concerned.

Alex counted, following the increasing number of beats from his heart, which threatened to explode at this pace.

"One... Two... Three!" Alex exclaimed as he started his run with all the speed his body could muster. In a fraction of a second, he had crossed the room, jumped onto the handrail and from it, took a leap towards the street, falling into the void.

† † †

The speed at which Alex had crossed the room left Harland speechless and on the floor. There were scorch marks on the carpet. He turned his head in time to see Alex fall out of sight, but almost right away, the wyvern passed by and attached to it was Alex, hanging from one of its appendages. Harland ran to the balcony and saw Alex holding on for dear life with one hand onto the back of the biomechanical wyvern. Its shape seemed familiar to Harland. As realization dawned on him, Harland's eyes opened wide: it was one of those creepy statues from the city's art exhibition of the work by that secluded artist whose name eluded him.

"Fionn, Gaby, Sarah..." Harland mumbled as he returned to the room. He dialed a number on his phone and put it on speaker, while he closed Alex's laptop and put it in the backpack Alex had left for him. The call was still trying to connect, so Harland opened the case that Alex had labelled with his name. Inside was a comms bean, a combat vest similar to Alex's, but with a fully charged battery attached to it. There was also a pair of goggles and a set of bracers, all made to Harland's measurements. He put on the gauntlets first and then the goggles. The latter activated and showed him a HUD that let him know that the bracers had enough charge for twenty shots each. He wondered what the bracers shot, but he would have to find out later. The call failed.

Curses, Harland thought. He had to hurry to warn Fionn and the rest. He looked again towards the balcony. He could only hope Alex would be careful this time. *I hate it when Alex says he has an idea.*

Chapter 13
Under Pressure

Of all my ideas, this has to be in the top ten of the most stupid ones, Alex thought as he hung by one hand from a spine on the back of a biomechanical wyvern that until an hour ago had been an ugly statue created by a deranged art-ist-slash-scientist. Alex struggled to get a purchase on the wyvern with his feet.

I don't want to use my bad arm, but...

If he didn't, he would soon fall and then he would have more than just a broken arm to be complaining about.

The wyvern violently shook as it turned a corner, and spewed fire over a store. Alex's hand slipped, a combination of the inertia and the sweat in his palm.

Should have created magnetic gloves to help with these eventualities.

Desperately, he tried to regain his hold. He kicked with his legs, trying to find a crevice in which to support himself.

No, no, no, no, no!

Alex lost his grip. He felt the pull of gravity, calling him to meet the ground. It was as if everything moved in slow motion and he could see, moment by moment, the last avail-able hand hold escape from his grasp.

Aww crap, he thought as he braced for hitting the pave-ment, trying to remember Fionn's lessons on how to survive a fall.

Time resumed its usual fast pace as a hand grabbed his right arm, lifting him onto the wyvern, as it toppled a bus with its tail. Alex hit the back of the wyvern with a loud thud, but he was thankful that this wasn't as painful as it would have been hitting the pavement three stores below. He looked up to see who had rescued him and saw the smiling face with bared fangs of Joshua. His eyes were mostly brown, with few yellow specs, a sign that the Beast was still asleep for now.

"So much for resting after having the Beast put to sleep," Alex quipped. "And thank you." He grabbed tightly one of the spines on the wyvern's back, as it continued flying across the city.

"So much for resting your broken arm," Joshua replied. "And you are welcome."

"How did you get here so fast?" Alex asked. Perhaps Harland had warned Joshua as well.

"See that burning building behind us?" Joshua nodded. "That's where my flat is... was."

"Sorry man."

"Don't be. I was alone in it, so thankfully nobody was hurt. But if we don't take this thing down, that won't be the case for long. Any idea?"

"I'm not sure if you can kill a bio machine."

Alex thought long and hard, as the wind hit his face. How do you kill a biomechanical wyvern that spewed fire and was propelled by it at the same time? This wyvern wasn't exactly alive, as it seemed to be made mostly of metal, polymer and a strange organic black material. It shouldn't be able to fly in the first place. It was more machine than being, like the Figaro, when it had a dragon core attached to the main engine...

That's it! Alex thought. He focused the Gift, trying to find the trail of energy left by whatever core was fueling the wyvern. After a few seconds, he detected it from a point near the base of wings. Three separate energy flows met at that point. A bright one that trailed into the large belly, where the furnace that powered the beast lay. A second one, slightly below, went from the core to the mouth, fueling the fires coming from its mouth. The third one was odd as it went from the wyvern to some point in the city. But he didn't have time to study it further as the wyvern made a swift bank to the left and torched a temple nestled between two tall buildings. A curious choice of target to say the least. Alex grabbed one of the spines with his bad hand, as he pulled on one of the wyvern's metal plates with the good one, trying to pry it open. Without a word, Joshua joined in the effort, allowing Alex to unsheathe Yaha in order to widen the gap with a swift cut. He thought about stabbing it, but the core seemed unstable every time it had to power the chamber that kept the wyvern afloat and create the fire breath. Joshua finally tore away the plate and a tongue of fire shot upward, burning a few hairs. Once the flame subdued, Alex looked into the hole and saw a rotating, pulsating ball of black metal. For every complete spin flame erupted.

"The core that keeps this thing functioning is inside that hole," Alex said.

The wyvern shook violently.

"I think this thing is trying to get rid of us," Alex observed as he grabbed a spine to keep from falling.

"It finally noticed us," Joshua said. "Can you deactivate it?"

"Not without burning my good hand."

"Would ripping it out kill this thing?"

"Yes, but..."

Joshua plunged his free hand into the chamber without hesitation. A few seconds later he pulled it out. The skin of his hand was full of blisters as he held aloft the pulsating core covered in flames. It was the size of a small melon. The flames went out as a small shadow, coming from Joshua's fingers covered it briefly. The wyvern shook violently, as it tried to keep afloat. It was in a collision course with the road outside Saikaitsuki station.

"Aww crap," Alex said as he tried to hold onto one of the crevices between the scales.

† † †

Kasumi saw the wyvern losing altitude and pushed her bike's engine to match the creature's speed as it passed by a second level road. Sam held on tightly. As she travelled parallel to the wyvern, Kasumi saw Alex and Joshua holding on with difficulty from the wyvern's back.

"Need any help?" Kasumi yelled.

Alex and Joshua both nodded.

Kasumi took an exit and reached the street below. She raced the wyvern and overtook it. Pulling ahead she slammed on the breaks, the bike skidding sideways on the asphalt, and Sam holding on tightly. She threw out her leg to keep them from falling. Sam got down and ran to the sidewalk, as Kasumi drew Breaker from the sheath on her back and extended her arm. She reeved the engines as the wyvern dived into the street, while Alex and Joshua held on for their lives. Kasumi let go of the brake and drove straight towards the wyvern, Breaker serving as a makeshift lance. The wyvern continued to fall. Kasumi raised her blade and drove under the belly of the wyvern, slicing through its metal hide. At that moment, both Alex and Joshua leaped to the street. Alex landed on a bush, while Joshua, still holding the core, crashed into a vending machine that released several cans of coffee and beer.

Kasumi thought it would be harder to cut open the wyvern, that it would require a lot of strength. But Breaker did most of the job. Honoring its name, Breaker split the wyvern lengthwise in two with a clean cut, its power creating a slash that ran through the wyvern's whole body as if it had been clay. Both halves crashed to the ground, leaving a deep gouge as they skidded along the asphalt. Kasumi drove back to her friends, as Sam helped Alex to stand up, while Joshua, still dazed, rubbed the back of his head.

"Are you okay?" Kasumi asked Joshua.

"Nothing that a good coffee or a beer can't shake off."

"Well, you are in luck," Alex replied, looking at the cans around him. Sirens could be heard in the distance. "We need to find the source of power of that thing."

"Maybe this could help," Joshua replied, showing them the core of the wyvern.

"What's that?" Kasumi asked.

"Some sort of core," Alex explained. "It's different from all the ones I've seen, this one... the energy it releases is different, kinda like that from an incursion."

"Like the one in the Bestial?" Sam asked.

"No, it feels different," Alex explained. "I'm not sure how to describe it. It might sound stupid, but it feels like a seed of some kind. What I can tell you is that it's still active, growing in power and tied into a feedback loop with an emitter coming from that direction." He pointed at the zone from which the SkySpire dominated the skyline.

"How do you know that?" Joshua asked.

"I can see the energy flow with the Gift. That's how I could find a way to reset the Beast. We should be on our way to its source. I'm not sure how long we have before something big and bad happens. And as we saw with that wyvern, big and bad is a not so good combination."

"He is right," Kasumi said.

Alex's phone rang. "Now what?" Alex said as he answered it. "Hello, Sid. What?" he looked around for a sign with the name of the nearby station. "Yes, I'm near that station... what? Okay, I will think of something."

"What's going on?" Sam asked.

"Nothing," Alex said sarcastically. "Just a runaway train on a collision course to that station behind us. And Sid is aboard. I need to figure out a way to stop it and track the source of the loop with that thing."

"That's nothing? Let's go. You will need help for this," Sam said.

"You do that," Joshua said, as he turned in a circle to see from which direction the core got a bigger reaction. "I will find this things source."

"Fine," Alex replied. "Find it and call us back. Sam and I will get there once this crisis is resolved."

"I'm going with you," Kasumi said to Joshua.

"No," Joshua replied. "Let me do this so I don't feel completely useless. Besides, Alex and Sam will need your help to evacuate the station and stop the train. I will be fine. Go!"

† † †

What the Pits I was thinking?

Of all his ideas, this had to be the craziest, or the most stupid. Even worse than trying to ride that wyvern. The jury—mainly Sam—was still out on that. Alex barely had time to come up with an idea to stop the incoming maglev train from crashing into the station and killing Sid and everyone on the train and in the station. The plan was simple: Kasumi would evacuate everyone that might still be in the station, while Sam stood by, ready to cast her protection bubble spell—which she claimed she could still do properly—in case the first part of the plan failed. And said first part was the crazy one. For he would try to stop the train without derailing it, by using his Gift to create a magnetic field strong enough to do so.

"So, run that by me again," Alex said to Sid thought the comm, as he arrived at the platform.

"Some ugly critters crossed the path of the train, and between those that collided with it and the ones that infested the train, they damaged I dunno which system that sent the train onto its collision course," Sid replied. "Where are you?"

"In front of your final destination. What about the conductor? And the critters? And the brakes?"

"The conductor is alive, but injured," Sid explained. "I killed all the critters. Brakes won't hold longer."

"Okay, that's unfortunate," Alex replied. "What I need you to do now is get everyone on the last car and unplug it."

"Already tried that, but the train can only split in half and at our speed, it would topple with the people inside."

"Then get them all in the front car and power down the train when you see the station."

"Are you mad? The inertia will keep it going or topple it!" Sid yelled through his phone.

"Let me take care of that, I have an idea."

"You know I hate when you say that."

"Trust me. I already tested this one. Last year, to save us from smashing into the ground."

"Alex wait..."

Alex hung up, as he already knew what Sid was going to say. But as he saw it, the options were limited and time was running out. And if it had worked to stop the Figaro dropping from the sky, it should work with a train on the ground. Should, being the operative word.

And I thought riding a biomechanical wyvern was my most stupid idea. *This one takes the cake*, Alex thought. He looked around and found a reel of copper wire in the maintenance locker of the platform. He took a segment and wrapped it around his cast, covering almost the entire surface. The extra weight sent waves of pain through his broken arm. But this would be safer than wrapping the wire around his healthy arm, as he didn't want to end up with burns. He hoped that the cast would withstand the heat of his really, really stupid idea. *I hope the Gift comes through.* Then he ate the whole pack of chocolates he had with him. The sugar rush kicked in right away.

Alex opened his compass, one leg on each side of the third rail. Electric arcs leaped from the metal to his legs. The first contact stung badly and the smell of burnt hair filled his nostrils. He could feel the energy running through his body, adding to the one his Gift was generating on its own. Alex knew that for his idea to succeed, he needed more energy than he could generate in his current condition, so it was imperative to get any extra help from whatever source he could.

As the electricity supercharged him, his breathing slowed, to keep the pain at bay and to focus on the difficult part of the task. His phone rang once more, sending the call though to his comms.

"We are—*bzzt*—stations from you—*bzzt*—would become—We are—*bzzt*—minute—*bzzt*—from you."

That was the cue. Alex started to run along the tracks, with the station at his back, as fast as he could. He pushed his legs to the maximum, feeling the fibers of the muscles in his calves stretching. His legs ached from the effort.

Focus, Alex, focus, he thought. As he moved along the tracks, with the help of the Gift, he saw the energy flow around him: the tracks, the surrounding power lines. And he also saw something else, exactly what he needed: magnetic fields.

Alex was planning to use the trick he used in his first duel, but at a larger scale and with some tweaks. When an electric current was in motion, it generated a magnetic field. That was why he was running as fast as he could, faster than he had ever run...

Thank you, training in the mountains.

He had learned through painful experience that with

enough concentration, he could draw and redirect electric charges and magnetic fields in ways that didn't always followed logic or rules. And that gave him ideas. This would be the mother of all tests for those ideas.

This won't work. And you know it.

As he ran, the copper wire around his cast served as a coil, dragging the magnetic field generated in his wake. As he moved further, the field grew in size and strength. The heat generated from this melted the wire, melding it with his cast. Replacing the cast would be a pain in the ass later on.

The further he got from the station, the harder it became for him to move, as if he was dragging a truck with his broken arm. The pain, similar to being pierced by thousands of tiny needles made him grit his teeth...

Don't break the concentration.

He could see the paths of the magnetic field around him. They covered a wide area and were strong enough to start affecting the metallic objects on the zone.

Your plan will fail.

Not now. No room for doubts right now.

You are nothing but doubt.

Each step became torture, to the point he had to stop.

This should be enough, now comes the tricky part.

Now comes the failure.

No, Alex told himself. *This will work.* He began to narrate, using his movie voice over.

"A simple man, trying to do the impossible. It's said that faith moves mountains. It was time to put that theory to the test."

Alex moved his arms to put them in front of him, with his hands extended. It sounded easy, but it was harder than anything he had done, including keeping the Figaro afloat for a couple of minutes. It was as if he was trying to swim through thick treacle, while holding twenty kilo weights in each hand. Compared to that, drawing his bow felt like a breeze. He didn't struggle as much with the right hand, but the left was another tale. Moving a broken arm was a bad idea—even with the aid of the Gift to heal it somewhat. Doing so while dragging a focused magnetic field was really stupid.

Whatever part of the fracture that had healed, broke again. This probably compounded his injury. But Alex was willing to tolerate the pain if that meant saving Sid and all the people on the train coming his way.

Alex bit his lip, drawing blood. Sweat ran down his face, as tears welled in his eyes, which at this point were glowing gold with unusual intensity. He pushed harder.

I can do it. I can do it.

"Argggg!" Alex yelled with the last push, finally arranging the magnetic field as he wanted.

And just in time, the train hit him.

"Aww crap!"

† † †

Alex's back hurt like the Pits. And the less he thought about his broken arm, the better. Tears streams down his face from the pain and the frustration.

That's right, be a crybaby.

What was I thinking, trying to stop a train barehanded? Alex struggled, using the Gift to keep the train from being derailed.

As usual, you weren't thinking.

It was as if the train was the physical manifestation of all of his frustrations, anxieties, and inner turmoil.

You are not cut out for this.

He struggled, trying to ignore the dark voice.

You are useless!

He kept pushing against this unstoppable object to the point that he didn't know what he was pushing against. He only knew the old inner voice was back with vengeance.

You are a failure. You are pathetic.

He pushed to forget his troubles back home. He felt himself buckling under the effort.

You always get yourself into trouble!

He pushed against the guilt for every time he had made a mistake. His left arm felt as if it was on fire.

Another mistake! You are weak!

He pushed against every time he had been told he couldn't do something. His sneakers' soles were starting to melt, only his own force field keeping him from injuring his feet.

Give up, idiot! You can't do it!

He pushed against the impotence he felt to change things. Every one of his muscles felt as if they were tearing.

I don't even know why you bother to wake up every day!

Above all, he pushed because he had no other choice. His lungs burned with every breath.

Just quit.

Because he didn't know any other way. Just keep moving. Find a solution to the problem at hand. His heart was about to explode.

Quit!

He had wanted to quit. Many times. To give up. He grit his teeth, trying to draw in more power. Pushing. Straining.

Just die!

He wouldn't. He couldn't. He didn't know if it was pride, responsibility, or simply stubbornness.

No one will miss you!

Because no matter how many times he had wanted to do it, dying had never been an option.

"Carajo!" Alex yelled at the top of his lungs, letting it all out. That included everything he had inside. All the Gift's power he had stored in reserve. He pushed back. "No. No! NOOOO!"

Sparks and electricity arced all around Alex and the train.

The storm erupted. He hadn't felt this surge of power since that fateful day when he got the Gift and had fought the incursions.

His back spasmed, but he was beyond the point of feeling any pain. He was numb. He was nearing the end of his reserves. Then he noticed the light, bright and casting his shadow against the front of the train. And with the light, the train slowed in a shower of sparks as it hit the concrete rails.

I might still make it, Alex thought, as his strength faltered.

† † †

An explosion of light exploded in front of the train's cockpit. Sid had to cover his eyes to avoid being blinded. As the light faded, he cautiously opened first one, then the other eye.

Sid wasn't sure what he was seeing, and even after spending so much time with people who had the Gift, he was surprised by the sight. As Alex pushed against the train, a pair of incandescent wings on his back, looking like the ones on Yaha's hilt, were spread wide. He looked like an angel. Sid didn't know if they were a manifestation of the electromagnetic energy Alex was manipulating, part of the Gift, or something else. The image was awe inspiring, but Sid only had one thought.

Alex, please don't die.

† † †

Sam extended her hands. If there was a moment to test Kasumi's idea, this was it. She tried to focus her Gift-enhanced senses into detecting the flow of the magick field emanating from the land. Rather than absorb it as she used to do, she tried to grasp it, as if it were a viscous fluid. Her irises glowed lilac as she pushed with every fiber of her being, her mind focused on the only spell she knew that could be cast: her True Spell. As she pushed, Sam felt as if her abdomen was splitting open. Sparks came from her fingertips and ripples appeared in front of her, as if reality was a pond. With a final push, she was thrust back, but she dug in her feet and then, like bubble-gum being blown up, an energy shield popped into existence in front of her. Sam kept her arms extended to maintain the shield as the train, with Alex at the front, arcs of electricity that resembled a pair of wings unfurled from his back, got closer and closer. Sam closed one eye and braced for the impact.

† † †

"Me lleva la...!" Alex yelled.

The train kept moving forward, the station platform sliding by.

Too fast! Too fast! Alex pushed more. Then, the train slowed. It kept slowing, and the end of the platform came into view. Alex saw the shimmer of Sam's bubble shield appear behind him. Then the train stopped, Alex's back mere centimeters from the bubble shield.

Then the pain hit Alex in a massive wave. His legs felt heavy from exhaustion and buckled. He extended his right arm to support himself against the wall of the train track. He could hear the doors on the train open, hear the sound of scared occupants exit the cars. He rolled onto his back and could see the people rushing for the exit, being helped by a pair of station workers. Then he saw the legs of a samoharo appear at the edge of the platform. Sid was the last one off, and he looked pale. He hunched over, one hand resting against the train's hull, and then threw up.

"From now one, I will only travel in the Figaro," Sid exclaimed.

Alex saw Kasumi hurry over, and felt Sam jumping down next to him on the tracks. As she reached down to help him, Alex said, "I guess I can now tell Gaby that I know what it's like to be hit by a warptrain." He tried to smile, but pain shot through his whole body. By Sam's expression he knew that she was getting tired of him constantly pushing himself.

"It's not funny, Alex," Sam replied with a tone Alex knew all too well: she was angry at him.

No surprise there. Alex thought. He extended his hand so Sam could help him to stand up. "Help me to get out of here first and then we can discuss what's funny and what's not."

† † †

Alex was taking a break at a bench, removing his burnt shoes.

"You are lucky the only thing that died back there were your shoes," Sam said.

"I'm lucky I didn't burn my feet or tear my knees," Alex smiled at her. Her annoyed expression didn't change. "My left arm though, I think I messed it up more. I think I set back the Gift enhanced healing a few days. Unless you know some healing magick."

"I told you before. It's not my specialty. And right now, my magick is not working properly."

"Then I will need stronger painkillers."

"Here," Sid gave a bag to Alex. "I was planning to wrap them at the hotel, but I guess you need your birthday present now."

Inside the bag, there were a pair of brand new Artemis electric blue sneakers in his size.

"Thank you," Alex said, holding back the tears. He took off his damaged footwear and donned the new one. "They fit perfectly."

"I'm the one who should thank you," Sid replied. "Now, you need to rest. You can't keep pushing yourself this way. Not again."

"There is no time for that," Alex replied, annoyed. "I will rest when I'm dead. Now? We need to find the source of these attacks. And you need to get to the Figaro. I don't think these have been isolated incidents. And we will need the ship."

"What about Joshua?" Kasumi asked.

"Sam and I will go after him. Can you take Sid to the Figaro? You are the one that knows how to drive a bike and move around the city," Alex replied as he stood up. "Now, let's go. We need to hurry."

Alex tried to smile through the pain in his arm. There was something that was bothering him, beyond the pain. But he couldn't pinpoint what it was. The only thing he knew was that the air was filled with a sense of dread.

Chapter 14
The Insidious Enemy

Kasumi rode at high speed on her bike—with Sid holding on to her waist for dear life—from Sakaizuki Station to Nakano Park where the Figaro had been parked since their arrival. However, instead of being filled with raccoons, as the park's name implied, it was filled with biomechanical creatures surrounding the Figaro. Some looked humanoid, like the two that Kasumi had faced earlier in the year. The others resembled a bipedal scorpion, with long, oblong heads, huge mandibles, humanoid hands and a long, serrated tail. Their bodies seemed to be made of the same material as the body of the wyvern. The wind blew leaves off the trees and they flew around the Figaro. It reminded Kasumi of old movies about dueling warriors that her dad liked to watch.

"What now?" Kasumi asked Sid.

"We cut our way through them to get to *my* ship," Sid replied. The way he said it Kasumi could tell that he was very attached to the Figaro. She found that amusing, but managed to suppress a smile. Kasumi unsheathed Breaker and whispered something to the blade.

"What was that for?" Sid asked.

"A small prayer for the spirit that inhabits Breaker-sama," Kasumi explained. "As I don't have the Gift to properly bond with it, like Alex, I like to ask for its cooperation when I'm going to use it."

"Fair enough," Sid replied, unsheathing his dagger and his small war axe. "And trust me kiddo, count your blessings. I have seen first-hand what obtaining the Gift can do to the mind of a person during the first days, and it's not pretty. On the count of three we do the stupid thing?"

"Run head first into danger?" Kasumi asked, smiling. Her demonhunter armor and Breaker's blade shone.

"Yep."

"Three!" Kasumi yelled, as she ran towards the enemy, holding Breaker with both hands and cleaving the closest biomechanoids in two.

"What happened with one and two?" Sid asked as he ran, jumped on a rock, and leaped on top of one of the scorpion-like creatures, stabbing it in the head with the dagger and fending off the tail with a swift slash from the axe.

For it being their first time together, Kasumi realized how easy it was to fight alongside Sid. The samoharo clearly had experience in this kind of combat, and despite his size, he had proven in the Games that he was able to take down larger rivals. This allowed Kasumi to focus on taking down as many of the creatures as she could without having to worry about her companion. Breaker felt lighter by the second, which allowed her to take advantage of the long handle of the naginata for long reaching attacks, as well as leveraged slashes up close that could split the creatures in half with ease. The body parts were piling up: heads, limbs, and tails. Kasumi attacked with circular movements, clearing the space around her. Sid was jumping from one side to the other, always going for the head, be it with stabbing attacks, decapitations, or crushing skulls with the samoharo's superior strength. Black, oily blood covered the ground. Compared to her first encounter with this kind of creature, this was a walk in the park, fittingly enough. There was a problem however.

The creatures' numbers didn't diminish, no matter how many they destroyed. Instead, their numbers seemed to be increasing. If Kasumi didn't know better, she could swear this had been a trap. A poorly conceived one at that. Because they had no trouble taking down the creatures... unless the aim wasn't to beat them, but to keep them busy.

Now that I think about it, the creatures had only been making the least effort to defend themselves, Kasumi thought. *But why?*

Sid seemed to have noticed this as well.

"Is it me, or is this really odd? They are not even trying," Sid said.

"There are too many of them, not enough of us and we are pressed for time," Kasumi said. "So yes, it seems on purpose."

"I have something for this kind of situation," Sid replied. He raised his left wrist and spoke into the bracelet he wore. "Figaro, activate Fire Blossom Protocol!"

A chirpy sound came from the Figaro. It sounded as if the Figaro was delighted about what was about to happen. From different crevices all over the ship's hull, small cannons appeared, all tracking the creatures' movements. The Figaro emitted a second chirpy sound.

Sid pushed Kasumi into the ground and covered her with his body. Kasumi could barely see what happened next. Red beams shot across the air, a few hit trees and rocks, but most of the beams struck the creatures. The air filled with the pungent smell of ozone. The red flashes lasted for a minute, until a third chirp echoed through the air. Sid stood up and helped Kasumi to her feet. The park looked like a battlefield. All of the biomechanical beings had been cut down, their bodies riddled with small holes. Kasumi looked at a tree to her left and stared through a perfect hole drilled through its trunk, a small flame licking the bark. The small cannons returned to their hiding places in the hull of the Figaro with a mechanical whir.

"What was that?" Kasumi asked, as she walked around, cleaving any creature that still moved.

"After last year's experience with the Bestial, and its multiple tentacles and flying critters that damaged my ship, I decided I wasn't going to let that happen again. So, I designed the Fire Blossom Protocol to help me deal with that kind of situation," Sid smiled. "And it seems to be a good plague killer too. Sadly, I can only use it once. The crystals that focus the beams burn out after one use."

"You sound too enamored with your ship."

"No one messes with my ship."

A scorpion-type creature jumped from behind a tree

and aimed its tail at Kasumi's chest. Sid barely had a second to react and push Kasumi out of the way, but a blast of blue fire roasted the creature mid-air, leaving nothing but ashes. A few meters beyond, stood Vivienne Ortiga. Her hands held aloft as small flames still flickered across her fingertips. Sid smiled at the woman.

"Vivi," Sid said as she came close. Behind her, two more Freefolk magi were putting out the fires with magick spells.

"Sid," Vivienne replied, returning the smile.

"You are a wonderful sight for sore eyes," Sid said as he took her hands. Vivienne cleared a strand of hair from her face. Kasumi wondered if Sid was as interested in the woman as he was in his ship. Once more she had to refrain from laughing.

"Aren't you the Freefolk delegation?" Kasumi asked. "How did you find us? And thank you for the help."

"We were at a karaoke bar across the street and saw the fight. We came to help."

A screeching sound interrupted the talk as a cab stopped in front of the park and Harland, wearing high-tech goggles and bracers and a vest that sparkled with blue energy lines, hopped out and ran towards them.

"What the hell are you wearing?" Sid asked.

"Professors Ortiga, Vertiz, and Bloom." Harland greeted the Freefolk.

"Mr. Rickman," Vivienne returned the greeting.

"As for your question, dunderhead, this is a gift Alex gave me. We have to go."

"What's going on?" Sid asked. "Alex didn't give me any details. Just told me to get the Figaro."

"Multiple incursion-like events are happening around the city," Harland replied. "Including five signals the size of a whole block and growing."

Sid didn't reply, he turned and stalked to the ship. With a voice command, Sid had the Figaro open its cargo bay door and he, Kasumi, Harland and the three Freefolk boarded the ship and went to the cockpit. The Freefolk seemed nervous, but Kasumi was enjoying the sight of the Figaro's cockpit. Two seats in front, five in the back, around different stations.

A clear dome above them and consoles full of tiny lights. Sid took the left seat as Harland took the right one.

"Where to now?" Sid asked, as he started the Figaro's engines. The ship roared and rumbled.

"The museum gala," Harland replied, as the Figaro took off into the skies of Kyôkatô. "We need to pick up Fionn and Gaby on our way to help Alex."

† † †

This exhibition sucks, Gaby thought. She didn't want to be there. But she had promised Vivienne and the rest of the Freefolk delegation that she and Fionn would cover them at the private showing of this *peculiar* art exhibition, so they could have the night free to see the town, after days of tough negotiations. That had been before the whole mess with Alex and Joshua at the stadium. While Gaby would have preferred to be at the hotel, trying to make amends with Alex, she had to keep the promise. Now if only Fionn could keep his promise to be punctual for once.

The museum was exhibiting a collection of paintings and sculptures, and was one part of a larger exhibition that included bigger statues placed in different places around the city, in celebration of the Chivalry Games. The art, if you could call it that, depicted biomechanical beings in gory scenes, with highly detailed anatomical features in inhuman positions and a lot of black, shiny paint. It had been created by the conceptual artist Gilles, who had been a hermit and had lived decades ago, creating his art over a twenty-year career. The art was so peculiar that it had even inspired a horror movie about an alchemist that contacted the very beings that had stormed the gates of Last Heaven, and had sold his soul to create what he called, 'magnificent' art, taking him to the point of madness. The movie had been so disturbing that many viewers reported having suffered from nightmares and night terrors, talking about a 'spiraling, crawling, chaos that engulfed everything'. A few even suffered heart attacks. The movie had been taken out of circulation and became a 'cult classic', which meant that of course Alex had watched it a few times with Gaby and Sid while growing up. Gaby found the movie and the art off-putting; Sid had said that it reminded him of certain things he had seen years ago, but didn't explained further. Alex, oddly enough, said that it was 'interesting', and wasn't any worse than the things he usually dreamt of.

As a result, the atmosphere in the exhibition felt uninviting, oppressive, almost asphyxiating. The exhibition seemed to be endless, corridor after corridor of strange statues and paintings, as if space itself was warped, chaotic. Gaby had been feeling headaches since she'd arrived, waving and waning at times, until she had found the illusionist to focus on until Fionn arrived.

"Rise! Rise!" a human illusionist, dressed in a tight tuxedo, exclaimed as she agitated her hands.

As Gaby watched the illusionist levitating her hypnotized assistant—a beautiful girl in a lavender satin dress that contrasted nicely with her dark brown skin—Gaby wondered why humans enjoyed this type of show.

Maybe because actual magick, reality warping magick, is almost only done by the Freefolk, so at least we can dream of actually doing magick without going through endless rituals, Gaby thought. *Or without getting killed on the process.*

What was killing her now were the heels of the burgundy, knee-high boots she was wearing. After several months traveling or training, she had gotten used to use comfortable footwear and thus going back to heels was hurting. She would have preferred to wear sneakers or at least flat shoes, but they wouldn't have fit with the gala's dress code. And while she wasn't a fan of conforming to dress codes, sometimes one had to take a proverbial bullet for the team, especially when the situation at the talks was still tense and every detail counted.

Her only hope was that the event would finish soon so she could go back to the hotel or the Figaro, whichever was closer.

The rest of her outfit was more comfortable. Black leather leggings and a black jacket over a silk, burgundy halter top. The jacket—it was actually her combat vest that Andrea had designed to double as casual wear—had detachable sleeves and was warm, without causing her to sweat.

"Y'know? You would be a stunning assistant for an illusion trick. Would you like to try it once?" a male voice said behind her. A voice that always caused her heart to flutter. She turned around to meet Fionn in the eyes.

"And you know that your pickup lines are still as bad as when we met the first time?"

"I thought you found them endearing," Fionn rubbed the back of his neck with his free hand. He had Black Fang, sheathed in its scabbard, hanging from his belt.

"I do. They're still awful."

Gaby looked Fionn up and down and shook her head. "And here I thought I was underdressed for this event. You come in here in your black jeans and your red sneakers. And let me guess, you are wearing a t-shirt under that dress shirt?"

"Guilty as charged. I also have my comms in my ear, as I'm sure you have as well. Although to be honest, anyone would look underdressed compared to the guys here flaunting their titanarmors or their expensive suits. Besides, we learned an important lesson when we visited Larabe last year."

"According to you, always wear comfortable clothes because you never know when a fight or an incursion will take place. I recall a different lesson though."

"Which was?" Fionn smiled at her.

"Always carry your weapons with you if you are planning to make a living as an adventurer," Gaby replied as she showed him her own blades, inside a silk sack with an embroidered golden design.

"Nice bag," Fionn said.

"Got it on the way here, as I knew you would be late. As usual. Also, it's less conspicuous than just blithely carrying your weapon through the museum. Now do you actually know how to do illusions? You never told me." Gaby smiled her trademark crooked smile.

"I'm a Freefolk that can't do magick to save his life. I know not all Freefolk do magick, but in my family it was never a big thing, so I picked up a few skills along the way,"

Fionn shrugged. Gaby found him endearing when he acted like that. But she also found his tendency to arrive at the last second annoying.

"Can I ask why you were late, leaving me here alone in this horrid "art" exhibition?" Gaby said, emphasizing the word with air quotes.

"I was looking for something that could be a good birthday present–slash-apology token for Alex, but I don't know where to start."

"He is not that difficult to buy a present for. And you are in Kyôkatô, I'm sure you won't run out of options. You have seen his room?"

"I have. And I guess you already have something for him."

"Not exactly," Gaby smiled as she walked around the exhibition, softly holding Fionn by the arm. "But I do know what to give him. I feel so bad that I forgot his birthday, and even worse that I missed the signs, so I'm planning to take him to KorbyWorld after the Games finish. He has never been there. Maybe Sam and the rest would like to come as well."

"You are a good friend." Fionn replied. The he looked at her, confused. "Wait…signs of what?"

"He's depressed." Gaby sighed. It was painful to her to admit that she and Alex had grown distant over the past year. She also regretted not having finished her psychology studies and dropping out of college. Maybe then she would have noticed the signs earlier and the argument at the arena could have been avoided. "And when he is depressed, he tends to not take care of his health and his bad habits become more pronounced."

"So, he has acted like this before?"

"He has, but not as bad as now. Not with such dangerous decisions."

"I should have noticed during training," Fionn said. Gaby knew that expression on his face, he was mentally kicking himself for making a mistake. She patted him on the arm.

"The thing with Alex is that he's suffered from depression since he was a teenager. So, he is pretty good at hiding the signs until he bounces back, or Sid and I catch him and work with him to get out. But I guess we have been so busy with all that has been going on that he relapsed, and we didn't notice."

"Teenager? So, after he got the Gift?" Fionn tilted his head.

"From what little I've learned from his parents, it was before that."

"I'm worried."

"Me too," Gaby said. "We should leave. We fulfilled our duty to cover Vivienne and the rest of the delegation. We should go to the hotel and check on how Alex is doing."

"Leaving so soon?" another male voice said behind her. The trend was becoming annoying. Especially because she knew his voice too, but this one didn't make her heart flutter. She turned slowly to see her father. He was as tall as her, with the same icy blue eyes. He had graying hair with a well-trimmed moustache, and a suit that had to cost more than what his employees made in a year. Girolamo Bardi represented pretty much all that she hated and what she had lost, including her mother. "Interesting to see you here Gabriella, I thought you hated these types of events?"

"I don't hate the events. I dislike some the of people that attend them," Gaby replied. No smiles, no courtesies.

"Still looking for something to do with your life? So much spent on your education, for you to end up running around with the likes of him. What a waste of potential."

"Hey! Take that back," Fionn said, placing himself between Gaby and Girolamo.

"He is not worth it." Gaby replied, gently pushing Fionn out of the way. She looked her father straight in the eyes. "Are you still mad you lost your personal assassin? I assumed you would be here with Dewart, after all, you and he are the same kind of person: a scumbag."

"You are not my daughter," Girolamo said, biting his lip, trying to hold back his anger. Even after all these years Gaby knew her father, who was a bully with his words, would not risk a public scene, for appearance's sake. He didn't want to scare potential victims, also known as potential investors.

"Good thing I changed my last name then," Gaby replied

with a smile. Not her crooked one, which was reserved for the people she cared for. It was a polite, socialite smile, cold as the Pits. "Because grandpa was a better father than you. I think you should leave. We have nothing to talk about."

Gaby and Girolamo stared at each other, holding their gaze for almost a minute. Girolamo finally puffed out his chest and left. He spotted Robbet Dewart a few meters away and walked over to him. What the two men were talking about, she didn't care, but Gaby was sure it wouldn't be good. She felt Fionn's strong hand between her shoulder blades as he gently led her to the next exhibition room. They spotted Yokoyawa standing alone, studying one of the sculptures. Like them, he was carrying his ancestral sword, which if she recalled correctly from Sid's few comments about his cousin, was called the 'Stellar Ehecatl', or something like that. It was a large scimitar, larger than Sid, whose blade was made of black obsidian. It was funny how it better resembled an actual black fang rather that Fionn's trusty fangsword.

Fionn put his arm around her, and she put her head on his shoulder. Gaby closed her eyes, as a sharp pain hit her inside her head. As if sharp needles were being inserted in her brain, a millimeter at a time. She pinched the bridge of her nose, rubbing it trying to lessen the pain.

"Are you okay? Someday I hope you tell me the whole story," Fionn said, tightening the embrace.

"Someday, not today. And it's just a migraine," Gaby replied, smiling at him with her crooked smile. The only thing she wanted now was to be alone with him and forget about the rest of the world for a second. "Every time I have to deal with the man, I get one. I guess I must have sensed him when I got here because it comes and goes in waves since then." She rested her hand back on his shoulder, determined to forget her father. "Seriously, who calls this art?"

"I grant you that, Miss Galfano," Yokoyawa replied politely with his baritone voice. His demeanor was so different to that of Sid. While her friend was a ball of anxiety, always thinking on the worst-case scenario, Yokoyawa had this aura of peace and calm that seemed at odds with his size. He towered over Fionn by two heads. But his movements and gestures were gentle. "It's quite grotesque and unsettling. I couldn't avoid listening that you might be suffering from a migraine. I could recommend you an herbal remedy that is good to soothe the pain without impairing your cognition. I believe Siddhartha must have some of it in his ship."

"Siddhartha? Is that his full name?" Fionn asked, trying to suppress the laughter.

"He is not fond of it," Yokoyawa shared the laughter. "I would prefer if you don't tell him about my slip. I'm trying to mend things with him and..."

A new wave of pain hit Gaby. A stream of images flashed in her mind, as they downloaded from whatever place she got her visions. She couldn't make sense of it, but the surge of adrenaline in her body, the increased speed in her heartbeat, told her that whatever was going to happen, it would be bad.

"This doesn't seem like a regular migraine. Your eyes," Fionn told her, as he pointed at her. Her irises were glowing icy blue. The Gift had activated.

"Something is about to happen," Gaby replied.

"How can you tell, Miss Galfano?" Yokoyawa asked.

"I have visions from time to time," Gaby replied, then pointed to her eyes. "It comes with the Gift." Yokoyawa only gave her a quizzical look. She would have to ask Siddhartha... Sid at a better time about that.

"Can you fight in those heels?" Fionn asked as he unbuttoned his shirt and drew Black Fang. His irises started to glow green.

"It's times like this when I thank the Sisters of Mercy training, which included fighting in high heels in case of emergency." Gaby said. She pressed a button on her jacket and activated the armor which glowed burgundy. Despite being sheathed, Black Fang, Heartguard and Soulkeeper emitted their familiar, warning glow. Gaby noticed how the Stellar Ehecatl reacted to whatever was happening too. The shiny obsidian blade filled with tiny white specs that swirled, forming an image resembling sidereal space. It would be a beautiful image if it weren't for what was going on: all the statues around them cracked open, releasing biomechanical creatures. They growled, snarled and drooled, as they tensed their visible tendons to leap on the attendees.

"We need to get everyone out of here." Fionn said, then he looked at Girolamo and Dewart. "We can skip a few people though."

"Be nice, Fionn," Gaby scolded him. "Even cockroaches deserve to not be eaten by the artwork."

"Both of you are right," Yokoyawa replied as he readied his scimitar.

† † †

The flaw with whoever's plan of attacking an event that had titanfighters in attendance is that said titanfighters would make quick work of most assailants. Add a former Samoharo *Ek'tangatatoa*—elite warrior—and two Gifted, the result should have been predictable, a total rout that would see the reanimated sculptures being shredded. However, there were two reasons that logic was flawed: the sculptures were very dangerous, as they were fast, had sharp teeth, claws, serrated tails, talons, and every assorted weapon a biomechanical mix between insects and humans could have. The second reason was that no matter how many of the creatures were destroyed, more kept coming.

Fionn split one in half. A second one took a bite from his left shoulder. Through gritted teeth, he reversed the grip on Black Fang and impaled the creature, but it didn't budge. Yokoyawa came to his aid and cut off the head, then with his large hand grabbed the head and crushed it. He smiled at Fionn. Now, samoharo smiles are, by nature, not pretty, but this one unnerved Fionn, although he knew Yokoyawa was being polite. As soon as the samoharo got rid of that creature, three more came at him from the rear. He was saved by Gaby who danced around them, leaving their limbs in pieces.

As Fionn's shoulder regenerated, he noticed that some of the creatures regenerated from the split components. Others kept coming from the other rooms of the exposition, even when there shouldn't be enough statues for them to come from. It was almost as if whoever sent the creatures didn't care much about who got killed, as long as the attendants were busy.

I can't be the only one to have noticed, Fionn thought, as all the fighters were closing ranks around most of the guests and waiters. Someone bumped Fionn's healing shoulder. The bump sent faint waves of pain across his arm and he turned around to see who it was.

"My Lord," Fionn said to Prince Arthur. He was the picture-perfect image of the dashing, debonair swordsman of fairy tales. Fionn noticed that Arthur was using the ancestral family sword, Veritas, which brought memories of Fionn fighting side by side with King Castlemartell and Queen Brenda.

"Lord Estel," Arthur said with a smile as his blade cleaved a creature's head. "I always wanted to fight alongside you as my grandmother did. But I'm not sure these were the circumstances I had in mind."

"One can't always choose the moment for a fight," Fionn replied, Black Fang cutting a creature in half. "And it's not advisable to be looking for them either."

"Forgive me for the callousness," Arthur replied, Veritas skewering two creatures that were leaping toward him. "I kind of prefer this than dealing with politicians. This gives you a better perspective of what's happening rather than being stuck in a meeting room, deciding the lives of others from afar."

"The king used to say," Fionn said, his blade decapitating a snarling scorpion-creature. "'That a man that doesn't fight alongside his soldiers in the trenches, doesn't deserve to lead, and even less to rule'. Even Byron understood that for a while."

Fionn saw the prince digesting the words, as his swordplay crossed the air with the same dexterity of an artist with his brush.

"We have a lot to talk about," Arthur replied as he cut a creature in two. "As I think we have common interests that should not be hindered by politics."

Fionn smiled. Maybe Harland didn't need to be concerned about his old friend. In that moment, as the prince took down two creatures and extended a hand to help a waitress to get behind the defensive line, risking the hand in the process, Fionn saw the old king in his descendant.

"After we survive this, my lord. First, we need to get out of here. Quick. I have a suspicion this is nothing more than a distraction."

"I was wondering if Augustus and I were the only ones that had taken notice." He nodded to the Solarian Knight and former champion of the Chivalry Games, Augustus Mu, wielding his own blade. He was joined by Salvador, another solarian knight that Fionn recognized from the Chivalry Games.

A scream of terror filled the air, calling for their attention. In a corner, Dewart was cowering, as a large creature, this one with a human head and two large horns was drooling as it closed on the delegate.

"Dewart," Prince Arthur said, with scorn in his voice. It was clear there was no love lost with the man.

"I will go for him, you keep helping those waiters. They didn't ask for this," Fionn ordered. Surprisingly, the prince didn't say a word and he went straight to work with Augustus Mu always at his side.

Fionn ran toward Dewart. While a part of him didn't care if he got there on time, he could hear Gaby telling him to be nice. A creature leaped from behind a pedestal on his right, but Yokoyawa tackled it. The samoharo was terrifying with his sword, even more so in hand-to-hand combat. To think that Sid claimed he could beat him made Fionn shudder.

Sliding on the polished floor, Fionn went through the legs of the creature that was menacing Dewart. Rolling to the right, he stood up, and as he did, he pushed Black Fang upwards, splitting the creature in half. Behind him Dewart kept crying and sobbing, mumbling incoherently.

The man has lost it, Fionn thought. Until Dewart said something that caught his attention.

"He promised," he blubbered.

"What?"

"He promised we would be fine, that we wouldn't be attacked. We're supposed to get our earnings."

"Who?" Fionn turned to him and grabbed Dewart by the

collar, growling. "I'm not asking a second time."

"Gilles, the artist of the exhibition," Dewart replied, clearly shaken. "He also goes by Marius the Miracle Maker. He said he could tap into mysterious powers of chaos and occult science to give us what we wanted."

Hearing that made Fionn's blood boil. His grip on Dewart's collar tightened to the point his knuckles turned white. His irises glowed fiercely. He lifted the man with one arm and was ready to throw him to the creatures.

"You sold us so you could get a better financial quarter? Give me a good reason not to feed you to those things."

"Because you are better than him," Harland said through the comms, breaking Fionn out of his rage.

"Fine!"

The museum's massive windows exploded as the Figaro's thrusters blew through them. Blasts of magick energy, cast by Vivienne and the Freefolk delegates, kept the creatures at bay, while Gaby destroyed several of the creatures near the windows, allowing guests—including her father—and employees to board the Figaro. Fionn dragged Dewart by the collar and threw him into the cargo bay.

A runaway creature charged past the Freefolk magick, its sharp claws slashing Fionn across his back. Skin and muscle opened and a strong wave of pain ran through Fionn. It was almost as bad as being impaled. His arms and legs went numb for a moment, making him almost drop Black Fang. Before the creature could finish him off, Gaby sliced and diced it into smithereens. Yokoyawa picked up Fionn and helped him to get inside the Figaro.

"Are you okay? That almost cut your spine," Gaby asked, concern showing on her face.

"Nothing that won't heal in an hour. Let's go." Fionn replied as the injury healed amidst tiny green sparkles of energy, compressing months of healing and rest into seconds.

"We will cover you," Prince Arthur said, nodding to his fellow Solarian Knights, who fell into a semi-circle formation, closing ranks, becoming a human shield protecting those boarding the Figaro.

† † †

Harland watched Fionn, Gaby, and Chakumuy through the Figaro's cameras as they helped the delegates and waiters, enter the cargo bay while Prince Arthur, Yokoyawa, Augustus Mu, and Salvador kept the creatures at bay. Any other time, Harland would have admired the combat prowess of the Solarian Knights and Prince Arthur. Above all, he was astonished at the efficient brutality of Yokoyawa, whose results resembled the devastation left by a giant meat grinder.

"I wouldn't admire him so much," Sid whispered.

"Why not?"

"Aside from the fact that I can beat him, after we survive this, I will tell you about the Konik Policy of the Hegemony." Then, he yelled through the comms. "Time to go kids, get on or lose it!"

Prince Arthur was the first to board, followed by Augustus and Salvador. Yokoyawa was the last one as Kasumi pressed a button on her console and closed the hatch. Harland watched Fionn, Gaby, and Yokoyawa leave the cargo bay and head towards the cockpit, as the Figaro took off.

"We have a problem," Harland told Fionn as the trio entered the cockpit. Harland closed the door, locking the rest of the passengers in the cargo bay. He hoped Vivienne and the Freefolk would keep them in line. And perhaps Arthur would do the same.

"We know," Fionn replied, taking a seat. "Dewart made a deal with whoever created those creatures, as a ploy to derail the talks."

"What?" Harland replied with a somber tone. He shook his head and pointed to one of the screens that showed five blinking spots. "No, not that. You don't know the whole story. There are multiple energy surges in different zones of the city, around the SkySpire, and if the algorithm on Alex's computer is right, the energy signatures are too big for normal incursions. Like nothing seen on this planet for ages."

"Another Bestial?" Gaby asked, as she unzipped her boots and looked for a pair of more comfortable shoes under her seat.

"No. I think someone is trying to recreate the Titans," Harland replied.

"Aww crap!" Gaby and Fionn replied in unison, using Alex's trademark expression.

† † †

Joshua walked across the empty streets, using the core of the biomechanical wyvern as a compass. It glowed with greater intensity when he chose certain paths. The city streets were empty, something which, that early in the morning, was weird. The city was not known for solitude and quiet, even after midnight. People were always coming and going from bars or late-night shops, restaurants, or coffee places, well into the next day. Especially in the zone that surrounded the SkySpire. It was the 'it' place to be. But now there was not even a rat running around.

In his bones, Joshua could sense that something was wrong. The place was full of oppressive malevolence, not unlike the bottom of a turbulent river, where the pressure takes the air out of your lungs and you lose all sense of direction while you sink deeper.

He turned a corner and Joshua found himself surrounded by several biomechanical creatures, like those horrible statues that peppered the city celebrating the art exhibition.

A deep voice, with a quality that couldn't be produced by human, Samoharo or Freefolk vocal organs broke the sepulchral silence.

"I think that titan seed belongs to me."

"Titan seed? Who are you?" Joshua asked the air.

"I have many, many names... but the only one you should care for is Marius, The Dark Father." The voice revealed itself, as a head came from out of the shadows. It was a human head, but it seemed to be attached to a larger body. And judging by the insectoid features, Joshua could guess the shape of the body hiding in the darkness.

Joshua's head hurt, as a ringing in his ear grew. It was as if he had been hit in the head with a bronze bell. He closed his eyes, trying to soothe the migraine, to think clearer. But he couldn't shake off the images that flashed in his head:

he was inside a chamber... a laboratory where bioweapons were developed... he was carrying out the experiments, as a genius that had helped create monstrosities... he was the experiment, the final test subject tied to a metal table while a black fluid came from the cenotaph, ebony tendrils impaling themselves into his spine, filling his body with the 'Beast'. The 'Dark Father' clapped in delight at transforming Joshua's flesh into a monster. A 'tovainar'. He recalled the bindings trying to control his fury, the flames burning down the room, the explosions bringing down the statues consecrated to the Creeping Chaos. The fire and the dust carried sickness from their experiments and reached a city, Carpadocci, burning away any trace of life, cursing the city to become an eldritch abomination of its own.

"You are the avatar of the Creeping Chaos," Joshua staggered back, grabbing his head and dropping the core of the wyvern he'd been holding in his hands, as the ringing became the music of a violin.

"I see it rings a bell. Although holding memories in a regular brain is trickier when you have lived for more than a century," the avatar said as he picked up the core. "And thank you for bringing back this titan seed. As you can understand, these are irreplaceable."

The flood of memories increased: living in the slums of Meteora with his friend Aldai. Returning to Carpadocci to rescue her from tomb raiders. Forcing her to lead them into the laboratory where he was created, to unearth a weapon. That's where he met Kasumi's ancestors, where he failed to save Aldai from the curse bestowed upon her, being forced to kill her to save her soul. The anger he felt bubbled inside him as if it was a magma chamber.

"That you can recall something that ancient means that you were not a total failure as an experiment to revive the titans."

"I would never work for you."

"You almost did, but even doing something as easy as exploding during those silly Games, killing most of the attendees was beyond your capabilities. And to think, I kept sending some of my creations to infect your symbiont and make it explode when the time was ripe… But it's fine. Really. I have a replacement here," the avatar said, and from a side street, Varekay appeared, ushered out by a pair of larger creatures. He was still wearing bandages on the places where Alex's arrows had hit him. "He will have to do without having the modifications you or my pet had. But for progress to be achieved, sometimes improvisation is needed."

"Hey!" Varekay said. "I'm here because I was told that I could get enhancements to win the Games'. But why is that loser here?"

"Ignore the failure there," the avatar said to Varekay. "Dewart was right. I have something here that will give you the power you need to beat those upstarts. After all, there is an order in life, and you are far superior to those inferior fighters. Of course, that's if you want it, because it will come with a price."

"More power?" Varekay seemed to muse over the proposition for a second. Joshua hoped that the man would realize the evident trap. "Of course! I don't care about the price if the crown is mine. I will do it if you can make me as powerful as Xavier."

"Hold this." The avatar pushed the titan seed into Varekay's chest with such force that the man spewed blood from his mouth. Joshua guessed that several of his internal organs might have exploded. He didn't have long to live. The core…. the titan seed… glowed brighter, as it pulsated inside what was left of the man's chest. Varekay fell to his knees, his eyes wide open. He tried to speak, but only gurgles came out. Joshua grimaced, feeling pity for him.

"See? Mortals are foiled by their own inner weaknesses, their own undisclosed desires for more. It doesn't matter the species, they always do. Although humans are more susceptible. Perhaps that's why they lost their original homeworld so fast. At least the samoharo put up a fight. And once I get my own titans, I will be able to find that damned Tree of Life and storm the gates of Last Heaven itself. Chaos and darkness will reign supreme once more in a miasma of dead matter!"

"I have a friend who's smart enough to find a way to stop you."

"Oh, I know," the avatar said with a smile that reeked of sneer and viciousness. "He has been a hindrance to my plans for quite some time, but frankly I want to meet him... before I rip his heart out of his chest with my own hands. But that's something you won't get to see. Trash, such as failed experiments, has to be shredded and disposed of."

The head returned to the shadows and its overbearing presence disappeared from the place. Varekay squirmed on the ground, as the titan seed glowed as red as the fires of a volcano. His skin and his armor melted. The man stood up, screamed in pain, and ran away into the streets as his body was engulfed in flames.

In turn, Joshua found himself surrounded by biomechanical creatures. Unlike the one he fought atop the train, these seemed to be more vicious and dangerous. He tried to call the Beast forward, but it didn't respond. He could only feel a sensation of heat running across his body, but not strong enough to wake up his symbiont.

"Curses," Joshua mumbled as all the creatures jumped at once and started to hit, cut, and maul him. He tried to run away, to escape, or at least to return the attacks. But there were too many and he was still weak.

I need a miracle to get out of this one, Joshua thought.

And a miracle he got as he heard a voice say, "Leave my friend alone, you fugly art pieces!"

Chapter 15
Dying Inside

"Do you think it will work?" Sam asked, as her eyes, glowing with the Gift, half closed and she focused on the energy around her.

"I think so. As we discussed, focus on the energy around and pull it to your hand," Alex replied, sounding tired. "Then release, like a rubberband. That's what I do."

BAM!

A blast of energy shot from Sam's fingertips, forming a small, crystal-like, elongated structure, which glowed with bright, purple light. It hit the black biomechanical creature that was about to bite Joshua's head off. In exchange, Sam's spell blasted the creature's oblong head clean from the neck.

"Told you it would work," Alex said, as he slashed one of the creatures.

A second blast left a hole in another creature's chest just as its serrated tail was getting ready to attack. Kasumi had been right, and while she couldn't cast more complicated spells yet, it felt good to be able to do magick once more. She cast a third blast to get rid of another creature that was closing in on Alex's back. For some reason, the creatures weren't attacking her.

She watched Alex. He seemed tired. And yet, he mowed through the remaining creatures with ease, wielding Yaha in one hand. The uninjured one. His left arm hung at his side, weighed down by the cast covered by melted copper wire. But it didn't keep him from slashing the creatures in quick succession. Whatever her dad had put Alex through during their months of training it had clearly worked, as Alex was a more refined, confident swordsman, even with one good hand. Alex cut the head off one of the creatures, pierced the chest of a second and with a twist, cut a third in two. In no time, the biomechanical creatures that had been attacking Joshua were dealt with. Sam went to help Joshua to stand up. Bruises and lacerations covered his face and his t-shirt was drenched in blood.

Sam wished she knew more healing spells, beyond the very basic one to enhance a body's natural healing. Most people assumed that healing magick was easy. In reality, it was one of the most difficult forms to learn, and it required levels of specialization on par of a physician to even heal anything beyond basic wounds. This was because the caster needed to know the body intimately, like a physician, and then understand how the magick could warp reality to heal the body without causing more damage, like tumors. That was why healers were highly sought after, why most worked in temples, and why magick couldn't be used to heal every single disease in the world. Healing her dad was easy, his Gift did a good deal of the job. But healing others was difficult and even more so in her current condition. Sam wasn't willing to risk further harm to Joshua. He smiled at her, as Alex broke the silence.

"That's odd." Alex mused as he kicked at the carcass of one of the smaller creatures he had just decapitated with Yaha.

"What's odd?" Sam asked.

"When you cast that spell, they stopped noticing you. Like you were invisible," Alex explained, as he went towards Joshua. "Are you okay? They hit you pretty bad."

"I'm fine," Joshua replied.

"Really? You look like a champion used you as their personal punching bag," Alex said.

Sam noticed a hint of sadness in Joshua's eyes as his smile faded. A similar look to the one Alex has been sporting for the past few months. Maybe Joshua didn't get pounded involuntarily. Perhaps he had let himself get punished. But why?

"Maybe it's because the way I cast spells had to change after you know... the Gift. Kasumi thinks..."

"So now you like Kasumi?" Alex remarked with a half-smile.

"That's not the point," Sam replied, annoyed. She didn't appreciate Alex's poor attempts at sarcasm. "The point is that apparently, now instead of drawing the energy through my body like the rest of the Freefolk, I can warp the energy around me to cast the spell."

"If you warp energy," Alex said, stroking his chin, as he took a seat on a concrete bench, "you might be bending reality as well, which means that for a moment, you might become invisible to things that are not native to this one... like the incursions. If we weren't pressed for time, I would like to test that theory."

"That's kinda what Kasumi suggested we could do," Sam replied.

"That will have to wait. Right now, we have to do something about that," Alex pointed to the SkySpire's point, which glowed with a faint blue hue. Then he turned to Joshua. "So, the plan is to recreate the Titans? Good thing we still have that core from the wyvern. It hinders their plan and gives us a bit more time."

"About that..." Joshua replied. He looked down. "I'm sorry. I lost the core. They took it."

"Damn!" Alex said. "Okay, I will figure out how to solve this."

"And I'm afraid that's not all," Joshua continued. "I'm sorry for another thing."

"What?" Sam asked, confused. Judging by Alex's reaction, he was confused as well.

"Apparently, I was the one that came up with the idea. Once, a long time ago. In a previous life, I was part of an ancient weapons program to win a war."

"Where? When?" Alex asked.

"Carpadocci." Joshua replied. "As for when, I couldn't tell you."

"Carpadocci? As in the lost, buried city of the Asurian Empire?" Sam interjected. "I thought it was a fable."

"I can assure you it was very real, until I destroyed it... I think. Since then, I've been there, trying to find clues into who I am, what I am... And the only thing I know for sure is that I got transformed into that thing you call a tovainar... I can't... I can't recall the details, yet it all feels so true. This is my fault. I'm a monster."

"You say you razed it, as in a fire or an earthquake?" Alex looked at Joshua quizzically.

"The first time. Why?"

"Because I saw the Beast creating a shadow from your hand and put out the fire of the core from the wyvern. I'm starting to wonder if the reason the Beast acted the way it has for years is because it was hungry from using all its energy to burn a whole city. Maybe it's hibernating right now."

"Meaning?"

"That there might be a way for you to recover power," Alex smiled.

"What for?" Joshua asked. "I'm a monster. Why would you want that?"

Joshua looked defeated. In other times, Sam would have either joked or yelled at the man. Maybe both. If what he was saying was true, then he would be guilty of helping to create a nightmare. But, as she had to admit, he was a good person. Maybe she needed to give him the benefit of the doubt. As Alex had pointed out, Kasumi vouched for him. And Sam was starting to consider Kasumi a good judge of character.

"For what it's worth," Alex said with a sincere smile. "And coming from a professional screw up, I don't think you are a monster. I doubt you are still that same person, and from what I've seen, and what Kasumi has told me, I know you are a good person. If she vouches for you, that's good enough for me."

Alex held up his uninjured hand to Joshua, who took it into a handshake. Sam wanted to roll her eyes.

"Lovely talk. Hate to interrupt your therapy session, but what we are going to do?" Sam asked.

"Stop that—" Alex replied, but got interrupted by Joshua.

"God," Joshua added, with a somber tone. "And he is expecting you."

"Good. That thing might believe himself to be a god," Alex corrected. "But I will be messing with his plan with one of my own." Alex grinned.

Sam felt a knot in her stomach. She knew that grin all too well. As Gaby and Sid had put it, Alex's plans had an equal chance of working well, or failing catastrophically. And in the past year, and more importantly, in the past few days, as the cast on his arm proved, it meant a toll on his health.

"I'm afraid to ask," Sam replied, reluctantly. "What has that crazy mind of yours come up with?"

"Ignoring that comment on my mental state, I'm glad you asked," Alex said. "You know how I can 'see' the flow and ebb of energy right? Well, I'm seeing that there are five flows coming from, and this is the interesting part, going *to* the SkySpire. So, my guess is that whatever he is doing to feed power to the titans to be, is not all giving. It's more like..."

"A symbiotic relationship?" Joshua added. "I have some experience with those. It makes sense. That would give Marius control over the titans, so he can control their power."

"How do you know that?" Sam asked.

"A hunch, but I think that's what I would do to keep some measure of control. Probably did."

"Exactly," Alex continued. "Or a parasitic relationship. In any case, the plan would be to disrupt that to give time for the others to stop the titans before they grow too powerful and level the whole city. Which means we have to get inside that place to do it."

"There are many variables to make it work," Sam pointed out. This plan seemed riskier than previous ones. Alex had to know that. And while he always pegged her as quirky, this level of risk taking was above what he usually did. After enduring many sessions of playing cards and board games, Sam had learned that Alex wasn't cautious, but neither reckless. He always looked for a Plan B or something else to back his actions, and he had this tell, a childish smile that he always tried to suppress that let her know that he had a plan and was aiming to win. Except this time. Instead of a smile, Sam saw fear and anxiety in Alex's eyes.

"She is right," Joshua said. "I'm going with you."

"No," Alex stopped him with his healthy hand. "I need you to deal with one of the titans. The fire one that you saw being activated. Call it a hunch, but I think you might be the best option to do so. For this to work, I need to trust that someone will take care of the titans while the energy is out."

"You have a broken arm and internal injuries, based on the way you are standing," Joshua said.

"Perhaps, but I'm the only one that can create the EMP needed for it, without having the tech available. And for that to happen, I need to get closer. I'll be fine," Alex said with a smile. Sam knew that smile. It was the fake one.

"Track that fire titan," Sam offered. "I will go with him." Joshua stared at at her with a slightly raised eyebrow.

He is as concerned about this plan as I am.

Sam was getting an inkling of Alex's plan. She didn't like where she thought it was heading.

†††

"You don't need to come with me," Alex said to Sam. They were walking on the bridge that ran parallel to the train tracks that would take them to the SkySpire. The night was cold. Dawn wasn't that far off. "You already stated your opinion on my plan. As usual."

"What does that mean?" Sam asked, annoyed at Alex's tone of voice. In her opinion, he could be such a child at the worst possible moment.

"Maybe that I'm tired of hearing how everything I think of is a bad idea? I mean, I don't see you or any of the others proposing a plan. And if I remember correctly, the last time I was the one that figured out how to take Byron and the Bestial out. I think I deserve a bit more credit." Alex sighed and he slouched his shoulders as they walked.

"I think that we are well aware of that. What do you want? A parade?"

"I don't want a friggin' parade. What about a little more respect? Or at least a tad more faith?"

"I respect you," Sam said.

"Ha!" Alex laughed. But it was clear he didn't find the comment funny, or honest.

"I do respect you," Sam continued. "But I won't support you when what you are doing is risky and puts you in harm's way."

"Like you have supported me otherwise?" Alex replied, turning his head to face her. "That's a bit rich coming from a person that jumped without a parachute from a flying fortress to rescue people in free fall."

"I did what I had to do and I knew I could get myself out of that situation. You on the other hand, come up with half-baked plans that end up hurting you," Sam raised her voice.

"Since when you are averse to risk?" Alex asked her.

"I'm not averse to risk. I'm averse to getting killed by playing the hero."

"Why? Because the last time you almost died and got the Gift? And that messed up your magick? What? Did you really think no one noticed? I'm not blind." Alex said, with a hint of anger in his voice.

"You have no idea what it cost me!" Sam replied, furious. Obtaining the Gift had been a horrible experience, and one that she couldn't forget. Feeling how her heart exploded inside her chest and her mouth filled with blood. How her life left her body only for it to suddenly return in a wave of energy and a cacophony of voices. The worst part had been feeling a new heart growing inside her chest in a matter of seconds. Not to mention the whole issue with her ability to cast magick. Alex's comments had hit a raw nerve.

"Well, you are not the only one that got a raw deal. So, spare me the pep talk. There is work to do." Alex increased speed.

"Why are you so unhappy all the time?" Sam asked, pressing the matter, wanting to win the argument.

Alex sighed and turned to face Sam. His lips were trembling, as he tried to contain his emotions. The street lights around them flickered as his irises started to glow.

"What do you want me to say, Sam?" Alex raised his voice. His face was red and beads of sweat rolled down his forehead. Sam had never seen him this angry or agitated. His voice trembled. "That I feel like a failure? That whatever you tell me I've achieved is meaningless? That unless something changes, I will be forced to return to the Straits, to a place I've never fit in, with a family that I love but can barely get along with for more than five minutes? To a dead-end job with no prospects? That I'm not good at anything else? That every choice I make is wrong or useless? And the only thing I'm good at—you, and Fionn, and Gaby, and *everybody*, always thinks is a bad idea? Is that what you want me to say? That my life hasn't turned out as I hoped? There you go. That's the big confession.

"But there is something else: when I'm out there, doing the stupid things you say I do, when I'm *helping* others, it's the only time when I'm free. That I have worth. So yeah, you're right, I don't care what happens to me during these 'stupid plans' because at least then I actually achieved something with my life. Even though no one will miss me when I'm gone, at least I will go knowing that I helped someone. And that's better than living my whole life hearing the voice in my head telling me that I'm a failure!"

And now she understood why Alex was worried, angry, and... depressed? He had never been good at working with teams. Sam had heard complaints at the University, of how Alex always wanted to do things on his own, even if that meant being overworked. He only asked for help when he admitted that he was in over his head. That's why he developed his projects with Andrea and Birm, because he already knew how to work with them, but even then, he felt anxious for having to depend on someone else. This time, he would have to depend on others for this to work and Sam was sure he was hating every second. Despite what happened last year, and in light of the argument he had with Fionn, Gaby, and herself the previous day, Alex was worried whether he could trust the others to follow a plan, when all of them had made clear what they thought of his ideas. And in his mind, of him.

Sam took a step back, staring at her feet as her lips quivered, trying to find what to say. If she had known he felt this way, if she had been more observant, a better friend... Guilt flooded her.

"I'm just trying to help," Sam said, her voice cracking.

"You want to help? Fine. Take this and be invisible," Alex

exclaimed as he pushed Yaha into Sam's hands. "I have a *stupid* plan to follow, and I won't waste more time on this." He turned and stalked towards the SkySpire.

Sam stood there, holding Yaha as the sword gave her faint electric shocks, while Alex walked away from her. She had been waiting for a bigger shock, but Alex's words had made that a moot point. Sam could only think on those words and wanted to leave. Then again, Alex had given her Yaha. She recalled what she knew of the Tempest Blades and their relationship with their wielders. Yaha wasn't complaining much about being in her hands. Which meant that... Alex's plan became clearer, and it made her angry at the implication. Sam's eyes opened wide and her irises glowed lilac, as she started to walk after him, muttering curses.

† † †

Alex looked at the towering SkySpire as he moved toward it. Despite the darkness the sky had a purple tint. He knew that tint was a warning sign of hurricanes. The Straits paid particular interest to those signs, as it was routinely hit by those powerful storms. People from the Straits—and Xelahú in particular—learned from an early age to identify the signs so as to be ready for any evacuations. Survival depended on that.

At the base of the SkySpire, across from a large promenade, there were a slew of shops, galleries, and coffee houses, a few of them dedicated to specific animated TV series. In any other moment, Alex would have spent a whole day there, browsing and looking for collectables. But not now. Alex went up the external concrete stairs that led to the second floor of the tower. The shops along the road were empty, but open, as people had left in a rush. Or so he hoped, as the black pools of goo that littered spots around the cash registers and the displays made his stomach churn.

Alex paused before entering the building. The bad voice in his head was whispering things he barely registered. He leaned against a wall and closed his eyes, letting it out all. His chin trembled and tears rolled over his cheeks and he let himself slide towards the floor. He clutched his stomach, which was hurting, and whimpered. His heart beat faster and he began to shake from the adrenaline spike.

Fear gripped him, holding him hostage. He knew his plan was a long shot, and for the first time in his life he wasn't sure how he was going to get out of this problem. Until now, every time things got hard, Alex told himself that he would find a way out, to fix the problem. This time, he wasn't sure of that, and he hated the feeling. It was as if he was walking on a tight rope, with no safety net and in a space so dark he couldn't see. He hated the sensation. The anxiety. He wanted to run away, but he also knew that he couldn't do that. If his guess was correct, this was the only option open to him. As he stood up, he got the feeling that something was expecting him. He was sure he was being watched though he couldn't see anyone inside. But the electronic board with the eerily creepy message of "Welcome Mr. León. I'm waiting for you," confirmed his suspicions.

You are gonna fail.

"Not now," Alex muttered under his breath at the dark voice in his head.

You know your idea sucks, like every other idea you have ever had.

"Focus Alex, focus."

Alex hated to be in a position where he had to take the lead. For all his bluster and anger, he was afraid of confrontation, of making a mistake. The Gift had solved that to a point, at least he knew when he could beat the other guy without hassle. But now, he was on the spot and was, as always, afraid of failing. And if what Joshua told him of what he was about to face was right, even a little bit, then the odds of him failing this time were astronomical. He wondered how Fionn had felt that day at Ravenstone when he faced Byron for the first time in a century. Or how he felt on the deck of the Bestial, facing his mortal enemy once more, the one that had beaten him twice. Alex took out his phone and dialed. It was time to make the call he had been postponing.

"Alex? Where are you?" Fionn asked right away.

"I'm afraid," Alex said. He felt relief by saying it. As if a heavy burden had been lifted from his shoulders, even if the fear was still present in his heart.

"You don't have to be. We are on our way, just tell me where you are," Fionn replied. He sounded concerned.

"Don't. I need you to track the signals of the titans and destroy them before they grow to full power. The city depends on that," Alex said. "I will give you a window of five minutes when they won't be at full power. That's when you have to kill them."

"We can think of a better plan," Fionn offered, his voice sounded calm.

"There is no time," Alex countered. He had run the numbers in his head. "I know my plans always suck, but this is the only way."

"Your plans don't suck," Fionn said. No witty remark, as Alex had expected. Maybe he was actually worried.

"I... I...," Alex stuttered. This was hard for him to admit. "I'm sorry. I want to apologize to you, to Gaby, to Harland and Sid, to everyone for always making things worse, for always making mistakes and being an awful person to be around."

"None of that is true," Fionn raised his voice. There was a hint of anger. "You are not an awful person. We all care about you. Let us help."

"You will help me more if you follow the plan."

"We will, but..."

Alex interrupted Fionn, cutting him off mid-sentence.

"Do you think Ywain was afraid when he faced Byron, knowing he could die? Were you?"

There was a pause, and he could hear Fionn breathing deep and mumbling. The Figaro wasn't that far away from his position. Knowing Sid, he would be tracing the call.

"Ywain once told me that he often felt like he was standing on the edge of an abyss. And that was the only moment he felt both afraid and brave. So, I guess he was afraid back then, but he never backed down. As for me, I'm always afraid, but then I remember what I'm fighting for to bring the best out of me."

"Thank you for being my teacher. I need to go. Be ready for the EMP."

"Alex... Alex!"

Alex hung up the phone and turned it off as he wiped away the tears. He needed to stay focused. He checked the battery of his vest and the bow tucked in the holster on his left leg. His back felt light, without the extra weight of Yaha.

The SkySpire's lobby was intermittently lit only by the flickering screens flashing the same message for him, "Welcome, Mr. León. I'm waiting for you." Through the flashes of light Alex could see that the shops had been abandoned quickly, and he could see the forms of biomechanical creatures skulking in the shadows. They didn't attack, just stayed at the edge of his vision.

As Alex went through the hallways, a chill ran across his back. He passed a store that sold traditional handicrafts, including some weapons. As tempted as he was to grab a fangsword to defend himself, he knew they were hard to use with only one healthy hand, unless you were Fionn. He looked at the smaller weapons and saw a sai, resting on a rack. He grabbed it and secured it in his belt, at the small of his back, and covered it with the vest. Alex left a couple of wrinkled banknotes.

He continued walking, following some of the critters across the aquarium. It was colder than the floor below. The only sound echoing through the place was the calls from the penguins. Alex had always found them unsettling, unlike Sam, who thought that they were cute. He hurried through the space thankful that he didn't come across any of the flightless birds. Upon exiting the aquarium he found himself in the promenade, where the elevator would take tourists up to the observation deck. A poster informed visitors that it had been out of operation for the past year. But Alex knew it was bullcrap. That's where he was being invited.

The elevator door opened as Alex approached it. A screen inside the elevator showed a message "I'm looking forward to meeting you."

While common sense said that it was unwise to ride an elevator in a building with power failures, and any sense of preservation would advise against entering one with a screen showing that message, it was too late to turn around.

The screeching creatures closing in behind him seemed

to be a sign that this elevator would take him to his destination. Alex took a deep breath and looked around one last time.

"I feel like I'm walking into a slaughterhouse," he said aloud. "And I'm the cow." He shook his head. "I know, I know. It's my decision. My stupid plan."

The door closed and the elevator started to ascend.

Could be worse, I could be walking into a trap while hearing that horrible Copa song that every elevator seems to have, he thought.

Copa started playing over the tiny speaker.

"Aww, crap."

Chapter 16
Big Damn Heroes

"What now?" Sid asked as Alex cut the call. He maneuvered to keep the Figaro afloat next to Kyôkatô Tower's observation deck, as Harland had suggested to use it as a base to plan a counterattack. As Sid locked the ship into a stable vertical hover everyone in the cockpit looked at Fionn.

"Why are you looking at me?"

"Because you are the closest thing we have to a leader, and if we don't coordinate efforts, Alex is toast," Sid replied, as he pulled the lever to open the cargo bay hatch and allow the diplomats, Arthur and his knights, and the Freefolk to disembark. Only Fionn, Gaby, Kasumi, Harland, Yokoyawa and Sid remained in the cockpit of the Figaro. He was right.

Fionn felt a heavy weight on his shoulders. One that he hadn't felt in a long time. Last year, things had been a coordinated effort, using Alex's discovery, with Gaby's insight and the input of the rest to develop a plan to deal with Byron and his eldritch abomination. Now, the plan seemed straightforward, but no one wanted to offer any input. Probably because the situation was too emotional after that call, for anyone to think with clarity. Thus, all of them, Kasumi included, looked to Fionn for guidance. He was supposed to be the one with the experience of being a cool-headed leader during a crisis. Truth be told, Fionn was as anxious and stressed as any one of them. He couldn't avoid thinking about Ywain's last mission before he disappeared. How his best friend might have felt, alone, against a terrifying enemy. And the thought made his stomach churn.

This time, however, he could make a difference and be there on time. He took a deep breath. Back in the saddle after a century... give or take.

"There is not much of a plan. We will take on one titan each. Harland will coordinate from the Tower and keep us informed. As soon as you finish your fight, the goal is to reach Alex's position at the SkySpire to help him. Harland, I need you to keep trying to contact Sam. She might be in a better position to help. Sid, is there any way to check where the titans are and how they look? I need to see what we are facing."

"What about the Solarian Knights and the other titanfighters? And the demonhunters?" Gaby asked. "They could help."

"I'm not sure the current crop of titanfighters are up to the task," Fionn replied. "And we will need extra hands to evacuate people from the danger zones. Let them take care of that."

"So, you want us to take on the titans on our own?" Kasumi asked, clearly not convinced.

"Alex's life depends on getting this right," Fionn replied. "And I only trust us to do that. And according to Alex, they are not at full power yet. That gives us an edge."

"This is crazy..." Kasumi said.

While the discussion kept going, Sid pushed a couple of buttons on the console and the two screens above the pilot and copilot's chairs turned on, showing the images from the city's security feed. All across the city there were damaged buildings, demonhunters protecting people from the lesser biomechanical creatures unleashed all over the city, evacuation procedures, and the bodies of several titanfighters and a few demonhunters that hadn't survived their encounter with the titans.

"There you go, fearless leader," Sid interrupted with a grim expression. "The targets you are sending us to fight against. They don't look too weak to me."

"We can handle them," Fionn said, trying to sound confident as his own stomach continued to churn.

Harland pointed at the computer's map projection.

"These are the five signals the algorithm detected. Four

of them are around the SkySpire, quite close, no more than two kilometers from there."

"The feedback loop Alex mentioned," Kasumi said. "They can't move further away if they are to keep themselves connected to their power source."

Each screen changed to show a split image. The left side of the screen above Sid showed a human floating above Electric Town.

"Isn't that the asshole that sent several fighters to the hospital and beat the crap out of Alex?"

"Yes, that's Xavier. He's mine," Fionn replied with such ferocity in his voice, lowering it a whole octave, that no one dared to contradict him.

The right side showed a titan almost as tall as the giant robot statue next to him. With leathery, grey skin, sharp claws, a head without eyes and four rows of serrated teeth in four axes, going from the mouth to the back of the head, it was a nightmarish creature. It was outside the stadium, where a few of the titanfighters were gathered and were trying to fight him. Bev Johnson was blasted towards a wall by one of the titan's fists. Three other fighters tried to attack him from the left, but the titan's skull split in four as it slowly turned towards the assailants and emitted a screech that sent them reeling, as their limbs trembled and twisted in a sick mockery of a dance.

"I better turn off the sound on that one," Sid said, as his hand trembled.

"That's mine," Gaby said."

"No," Kasumi countered. "It's mine. I'm the only one here that won't be affected by its sonic attacks."

"Why?" Gaby asked.

"I'm gonna turn these off," Kasumi replied with a smile, as she pointed to her hearing aids. "That way I only have to worry about the physical aspect of the shockwaves, and not the disorienting effects of the sounds."

"She's right," Fionn added. He was well acquainted with a demonhunter's training. And he'd seen Kasumi fight. A part of him felt pity for the titan. But not much.

"Fine, I will take that one," Gaby said with a crooked

smile, pointing to the one on the left split of the screen above the copilot's seat. "The one made of rock that is attacking that temple."

"What about the fire one trying to melt the city?" Sid asked, pointing to the one on the final screen. It was at least as tall as a four-storey building, and while it had a humanoid shape, it appeared to be made of nothing but fire.

"I will deal with it. I'm already there," Joshua's voice broke through the comms of the cockpit.

Everyone looked at Fionn and his reaction. This time, he knew why. He had his doubts about the man. He was a tovainar, a biological weapon like Byron. And yet... he had fought for the Foundation without asking for anything in exchange. Alex risked his life to help him. And Kasumi seemed to trust him with her life, a tall order for a demonhunter. And from what Alex had told him, Joshua had been protecting people and making daring rescues. He had asked Harland to take a leap of faith when Gaby introduced them to Alex and Sid last year. It was time for him to do the same.

"Be careful, Joshua," Fionn said. "And as soon as you deal with him..."

"I know," Joshua replied.

"Where is the fifth?" Yokoyawa asked.

"Not in the city," Harland replied with a somber tone. "That's the only one that has fully hatched and is out of range."

"I know where it is," Sid replied. "That one is mine. I'm the only one that will reach it in time."

"How do you know that?" Gaby asked.

"Purple skies mean only one thing." Sid pointed to the sky outside the cockpit. "A typhoon is closing in on the bay."

"Are you sure you want that one?"

"No," Sid sighed. "But I don't trust any of you to fly the Figaro into a storm. And I made a promise."

"I'm going with you," Yokoyawa said.

"Then you better buckle up, because it will be a wild ride," Sid replied.

"I better leave now. All of you, take care," Harland said, taking the computer with him, as he walked towards the door.

Fionn bumped his fist. "See you on the other side."

"Be careful," Harland replied. "By the way, there is something for you under your seat."

As Harland left the Figaro, Sid pushed the lever to close the cargo bay hatch. He pulled the yoke and the ship rose above the Tower.

"And all of you, I won't be able to drop you slowly or softly, if I'm gonna reach the storm before landfall," Sid said, as he increased the output of the core to the engines and thrusters.

Fionn took his seat and pulled a bag from under it. The Figaro roared and Fionn felt himself being pressed against his seat. Opening the bag, he found a vest, similar to the one Gaby was using, and to the one Alex had designed for himself. On the back, it had the Greywolf clan sigil, a rampant dragonwolf. The crevices between pads glowed with a faint green light. Fionn smiled.

"Let's go help our friend."

† † †

The Figaro passed over a pedestrian bridge in Electric Town that connected two buildings at the fourth floor. Fionn jumped from the Figaro onto the bridge and rolled to absorb the shock of the fall, then stood up. The pain of the landfall eased right away and he unsheathed Black Fang. Five meters away was the one person he was most eager to fight since Byron: Xavier. After all, he had defeated Alex, purposely crippled a titanfighter, and was now threatening the city and its innocent inhabitants. Three out of three. Xavier was decked out in his titanarmor, fused with shiny black protuberances that gave Fionn the impression of a mantis, or one of the incursions he fought after the Great War. There was a foul odor as well, not dissimilar to Byron's. It was revolting. In the center of his chest, where Xavier's sternum should have been, there was a sphere the size of a football that swirled and pulsated. The titan core. Fionn wondered if it was an excess of confidence that made his opponent showcase his target so prominently.

"Y'know?" Fionn yelled, as he looked Xavier up and down. "For a titan, I surely expected something... bigger."

"Mock all you want. Unlike the other idiots, I'm in total control of the titan core. I have all the power, without requiring me to transform into an abomination. Like the titans of yore, I'm in control."

"Says the person that sold his soul to a madman."

"A god. And I gladly sold it to be granted the power to beat cheaters like you, your students, and friends."

"Cheaters?"

"To become a titanfighter you need to undergo grueling training. And I did more than that as I aimed to become the next legend, even better than you. Then I found out that not only had you returned, but you got your skills from some mystical mumbo jumbo given to you by chance. The same with your pet projects. You robbed me of my opportunity to become a legend!"

"Trust me, none of us asked for what happened. You, on the other hand, willingly joined a madman."

"A god. The Crawling Chaos will usher in a new age of madness and conflict where I will thrive as the best warrior..."

"Y'know? I don't have time for your crap." Fionn leaped forward, covering the distance in less than the blink of an eye and punched Xavier in the face with such force that he broke his fingers and sent Xavier falling from the bridge. "I'm on a tight schedule."

Fionn jumped from the bridge to go after Xavier, but the titan was nowhere to be seen. As his hand healed, Fionn walked with both hands gripping Black Fang. Goosebumps covered his back, alerting him of danger. As he turned to his left, a gust of wind sent him crashing through the wall of a shop, landing in the clothes section.

Fionn caught his breath. He was expecting broken ribs, maybe a punctured lung, but the vest had absorbed the worst of the attack, leaving him only sore. He rotated his shoulder, to get rid of the stiffness. Now he was mad.

He stood up from the pile of clothes and accessories and ran. The force from his legs left cracks on the ground and accelerated the crumbling of the wall. Fionn reached Xavier and without losing a second, unleashed a whirlwind of slashes and stabbing thrusts. Xavier replied in kind, exchanging furious attacks with Fionn. They ran and jumped all over the streets of Electric Town. Xavier sent a slash so strong that Fionn found himself landing on top of a taxi. Xavier, not losing a second, tried to cut Fionn in half lengthwise. Fionn managed to roll to the right at the last second as Xavier cut the taxi clean in two.

Damn it! Fionn though. *He is fast. And knows all of Hiraku's techniques.*

In a sense, it was like fighting himself. Xavier matched Fionn in every aspect: technique, skill, speed, and strength. Fionn pressed the attacks, trying to force Xavier to make a mistake, but the man... correction, the titan, was a perfectly tuned killing machine. Fionn managed to force Xavier into locking both blades and tried something else. Fionn let his feet slide a few inches backward and then moved to the right, hoping to make Xavier fall by his own inertia. But the titan floated in the air and with a pirouette landed behind Fionn.

"As you can see, I have studied your school techniques. That might have worked with Byron. I'm not him."

Fionn lost his balance due to the lunge, and Black Fang hit the ground, getting stuck there. Fionn had enough time to pull it and parry a hit by Xavier, aimed at his head. The force of the impact sent Fionn crashing into the ground, bouncing several times on the asphalt and hitting a sidewalk, landing in a stack of boxes left outside a shop.

Fionn, dazed, gathered his bearings. Other, lesser blades, would have been snapped by the attack. But Black Fang was pissed off.

You and me buddy, Fionn thought as he stood up. *You and me.*

Xavier flew away and unleashed an attack with his sword, slashing part of the top of a building and damaging the supporting beams of a statue of a monster from a popular TV show.

"Crap," Fionn murmured as the giant head of a TV monster fell on him.

† † †

The Figaro passed over the trees around Seven Fortunes' Temple and Gaby jumped, landing in the middle of the courtyard. Around her, there were seven wooden buildings with ceramic tiles on their rooftops. On each stood a two-meter-tall statue of one of the Seven Fortunes, representations of beings that were crucial for the creation and development of the Kuni Empire, including the Storm God, who had beaten the original titans millennia ago. That statue caught Gaby's attention, as it was holding a representation of Yaha. Or a very similar sword.

"That's curious," Gaby said.

Gaby pulled her attention away from the Storm God to focus on the inner-city Forest surrounding the temple as the titan approached. Each step boomed, shaking the ground, signaling its approach to the temple. In its wake, trees fell, scaring up dozens of birds. Gaby walked slowly around the courtyard, sizing up the creature. The wind blew orange leaves from the trees.

"Hey you!" Gaby said. "Why don't you mess with someone your own size? Or power level?"

In front of her the towering titan howled as it lumbered towards her. It was at least five meters tall and had a vaguely humanoid form with four massive arms and a body that was composed of rocks. Gaby tied her hair back with a black hair tie. She unsheathed Heartguard and Soulkeeper and got ready. Her irises glowed blue.

For such an awkward creature, it moved fast as one of its hands shapeshifted into a rock ax and tried to cleave Gaby in two. She evaded the attack by somersaulting back, landing on the roof of a small shrine. The titan wasted no time and smashed it with its fist.

Maybe I shouldn't have said that, she thought.

Gaby jumped from rooftop to rooftop of the temple, avoiding the punches and attempts to be grabbed by the titan, while looking at the core.

She ran as fast as her legs allowed, breaking tiles from the rooftops in her wake. Focusing the Gift into her muscles, she leaped from the last rooftop at the titan, Heartguard and

Soulkeeper ready to strike. She had to reach the core and stab it once and for all.

As she landed on the chest of the titan, the creature split into a dozen floating boulders. The core was nowhere to be seen. Gaby fell to the ground and rolled, ending up several meters from the titan's pieces and turned around.

"You've got to be kidding me," Gaby muttered. A blurry image of what would happen in the next seconds came to her mind and she ran. The floating boulders spun on their axis and flew at her with enough speed and force to leave a small crater in the spot that she had just occupied. More boulders followed. Gaby zigzagged to avoid them, but two of them moved around, tracking her movement like bloodhounds. When they got closer, sudden acceleration sent them into a collision course, forcing Gaby to evade them at the last second. Gaby jumped to the side, taking cover behind a fountain. The boulders didn't hit though, transforming again into small golems. They began pummeling the fountain. Overwhelmed, Gaby ran to avoid the golems and a second round of stone missiles until one of them hit her square on the chest and sent her flying into the forested area. She landed in a stream. The jacket absorbed most of the impact, only leaving her winded. Most of the time, Gaby enjoyed combat, as it was similar to playing a new song on her guitar, one chord after another in perfect sequence. But this fight was more like someone playing an out of tune violin. Torture.

I think I enjoyed the Games better. Heck, compared to this I would enjoy a root canal more.

†††

Kasumi's head was filled with silence, as her implants stopped transmitting the sound to her. She jumped out of the Figaro as it slowly flew along nearly at ground level outside of Odayakana Kyojin Stadium. She rolled as she hit the ground, softening her landing and walked towards the sonic titan. Around her, the bodies of several contestants, of people she had fought against during the Games, laid on the ground, unconscious, barely breathing. Many had blood coming from their ears.

A shockwave hit her hard, letting her know why no one else was standing. She could feel the impact from the sound waves on her skin. Kasumi also felt it in the ground as it shook. Even her bones felt the vibration and made her feel queasy. She grit her teeth and unsheathed Breaker. The ice-like crystalline structure of the blade shone like a prism in the early morning light. She breathed. She might not have the Gift, but she was a proud demonhunter and she would be damned if that creature got the best of her.

Kasumi ran towards the creature, pushing against the force of the sound. Jumping up, she hit the shoulder of the titan with Breaker, getting it stuck in its flesh. With a kick, she freed the weapon, the force of the kick sending her reeling a few meters. The titan roared and its skull opened, unleashing the attack that had affected the other titanfighters. The vibrations shook her armor and her body to the core, startling her. Pushing through the pain, she slashed the titan's left arm with her blade, cutting it clean off above the elbow. Black ichor mixed with blue blood came from the injury, and the titan howled. It aimed its head towards Kasumi, sending a shockwave that hit the ground, pulverizing the asphalt. As Kasumi jumped to the side to evade it, the titan hit her with its giant hand, a blow to her left side that shattered her demonhunter armor and sent her sprawling onto the base of the giant robot.

A wave of pain came from her side. She had broken ribs. Her right wrist was sprained, as she was having difficulties holding Breaker. A metallic taste filled her mouth. She looked down and saw one of her molars on the ground. Maybe this fight was over her skill level. Maybe her pride had, as Sid had put it, sent her onto the wrong path, one where her body wouldn't be able to cash the check. She saw the flames coming from a few blocks away, where Joshua surely was fighting a titan in a weakened state. She saw the explosions of light coming from the SkySpire, where Alex was dealing with whoever was controlling the titans. She stood up. She always stood up, even when the odds were against her.

Kasumi felt a vibration on the ground, a percussion. She looked around, searching for the source. The titanfighters that hand't been affected by the sonic attacks were stamping on the ground with their feet and clapping.

Pum. Pum. Clap.
Pum. Pum. Clap.
Pum. Pum. Clap.
Pum. Pum. Clap.

It wasn't just any stomping. It was a percussion rhythm of a popular song used in sports competitions. The injured titanfighters and demonhunters still conscious were cheering her on. Her eyes watered, but she wasn't sure if it was due to her injuries or for the gesture. She wiped her face with her left wrist. She knew time was running out. And she was in pain. But she would end that titan.

She focused all her attention on her rival.

It would be the fight of her life.

† † †

Joshua stood atop a building in the commercial district around the SkySpire. Before him the fire titan was growing by the minute as it consumed everything flammable in the vicinity. The feedback flow to the SkySpire was more noticeable than before. For the first time in his life a sour taste invaded his mouth and he was sweating profusely, and it wasn't due to the heat. He was feeling dread. Before, he would have jumped blindly into the fray, without regard to the consequences because he had nothing to lose. Who would miss someone... something like him? Now, feeling in control of his life and with the Beast subdued, he finally had something to lose.

Screams broke him from his reverie. He glanced down to see people running for their lives from the burning buildings. He heard a PA announcement telling people to evacuate from the area. There were people counting on him to stop that creature. People that didn't see him as a monster. People that he couldn't disappoint. Through the comms in his ear, he heard Harland saying something about not having to hold back as the city was being evacuated. They could give it their all. But what did he have to give?

How do you beat a being made of fire without powers?

Joshua thought. *I'm useless. And this is my fault.*

He remembered Alex's words: *a plan will come to my mind somehow. It always does.*

A bright flash of light came from the SkySpire and the lights in the buildings around Joshua flickered. The feedback flow was interrupted, stunting the creature's growth to merely the size of a three-storey building. Joshua cleared his mind, he needed something to help him beat the creature, or at least get close enough to rip its core out as he did with the wyvern.

Easier said than done, he thought. He looked around the roof and next to the rooftop access he saw a fire hose.

Joshua ran to the hose and broke the glass with a punch. He opened the valve and carried the hose back to the edge of the roof as it filled with water. Once there, he opened the nozzle and aimed it towards the titan.

The kickback of the water stream almost knocked him back, but Joshua stood his ground. As pain gushed through every part of his body from his injuries, the water gushed from the hose and struck the titan. The titan roared and a cloud of steam erupted from its body. It lifted an arm to shield itself, as the water slowly reduce the flames. The titan, angry, launched a punch towards Joshua's position, hitting the wall. Joshua jumped to the right at the last second. The impact hit the hose and the sudden rise in temperature, coupled with the pressure, caused an explosion of steam that burned his arms.

"Frikking Pits!" Joshua said through gritted teeth. The hose was destroyed and as the water evaporated, the heat increased. The titan was recovering its flames. Joshua wasn't sure how long the interruption of the energy flow from the SkySpire would last, so he had to hurry. Joshua could see the parking garage across the street, and he knew that the fire averse Kuni would have placed fire extinguishers throughout the space.

Okay Beast, I need your help. I will let you out, if you follow my lead, Joshua thought. He didn't get a reply, but somehow, he got the feeling that the Beast had agreed.

He ran across the rooftop and jumped, barely reaching

the other side of the street. He landed hard, one deck below the top level, scraping the skin off his forearms as he rolled. Standing up, he hurried towards the closest fire extinguisher, broke the glass and ripped the canister from the case. He then threw the canister towards the titan. When the canister was near the creature, Joshua extended his arm, a tendril of darkness came from his back and sliced the canister in two. The pressure contained in it allowed for an explosive decompression of its contents, hitting the titan right in the chest, putting out some of the flames.

Gotcha! Joshua thought. He threw three canisters, one after the other. Each time the flames subsided, leaving the pulsating core exposed.

I ripped it out once, I will do it again, he thought, as he hurried towards the last canister. As he broke the glass, a wave of heat hit him. He turned to see the titan open its mouth and a column of fire coming towards him. Joshua barely had time to grab the canister as the cars around him exploded.

"Damn!" Joshua yelled as he dove for cover.

† † †

Sid knew this was a bad idea. In the world's history of bad ideas this probably ranked in the Top Ten. Maybe in the Top Three. Funny thing was, this wasn't an Alex idea. Sid had come up with it on his own. The ironic part was that he was doing this to help his friend. Sid pushed the thruster control forward, increasing the speed of the Figaro. The ship shook and rocked, but not because of the speed. It was from the crosswinds it was starting to encounter.

"This is a terrible idea." Yokoyawa said, breaking the silence that until then had reigned between the cousins.

"I know that." Sid replied, glancing at the tridimensional HUD for the location of the storm's core.

"And yet it seems the most advisable course of action." Yokoyawa surmised. "Even if the chance of success is limited."

"I know that, too," Sid sighed. In front of them loomed a hurricane that had to be larger than anything registered in modern history. However, this one moved against the prevailing winds, on its own volition, and it was on a collision course with the islands. The titan creating it was following its orders. And in the middle of its path was the Figaro Mk II. The small samoharo airship was the only hope to try and stop the massive storm.

"Scud would relish the thought of such a crazy plot," Yokoyawa added.

"Well, Scud is barely out of being a hatchling. He knows nothing. I don't relish going storm chasing inside that hurricane," Sid replied, annoyed. He knew what his cousin was trying to do. But it wouldn't work. Having been around humans for so long had left Sid unaccustomed to the way samoharo talked through a situation to solve it. And yet, he had to appreciate the effort his cousin was making. Instead of the intense rivalry and clash between them a few days ago, this time Yokoyawa was trying to be helpful. With no instruction from Sid, he knew exactly what button to push or what lever to pull to help Sid navigate the rough winds. After Harland, he couldn't ask for a better copilot. "I pity the poor captain that has to have Scud as pilot of his ship."

"What makes you think the elders will authorize more ships?"

"After this, and if we pull this off, I don't see them refusing. Who knows? Maybe a joint program with the humans and the Freefolk will help to ease tensions."

"Your time with the humans and Freefolk has made you more hopeful than you were, and less pragmatic."

"What can I say?" Sid shrugged. "They do rub off on you. What's the speed?"

"The wind speed is reaching an average of two hundred and seventy-five kilometers per hour." Yokoyawa picked an image from the floating HUD and expanded it. It was a satellite image of the hurricane. The winds around it were moving very fast, faster than any other hurricane that hit the Hegemony's coasts. Lightning streaked around the top of the hurricane. "Power output is reaching levels of a small tactical nova device."

That's enough to blast the whole city back to the dawn age, Sid thought. The Samoharo had only used a tactical nova device twice since arriving to Theia. The rings around the planet, composed of billions of pieces of ice, dust, and rocks, were the result of one of them.

"However, the eye of the storm is not moving fast," Yokoyawa continued. "I would dare to say it's even moving leisurely. At this pace, the outer wall will reach the tower in fifteen minutes."

"That's because the titan at its core is taking its sweet time to reach the tower. Good, that gives us time to reach it, hunt it, and kill it for good."

"That is a terrible idea."

"You already made that clear a few minutes ago."

"It does make you wonder. If titans were this powerful back in the day, how did the titanfighters and demonhunters manage to hunt them down."

"That, cousin…" Sid replied through shortened breaths, as he pulled the yoke of the ship, steering it upwards. "Is a question for historians, prophets, and bards. I will tell you this though: never underestimate human resolve and free-folk power."

"As the old saying goes, Samoharos are mighty, Freefolk are powerful, Humans are indomitable."

"Exactly."

Sid was hoping that the Figaro had inherited something from the indomitable humans that had helped this not so powerful samoharo to build it. He increased the output of the Figaro's three dragon cores to climb up in parallel to the storm's eye wall.

While the Figaro was capable of speeds far superior to the winds revolving around the storm, that didn't mean it was smart to try to cross the storm wall directly. Too many factors: lightning, crosswinds, debris, and the actual titan inside it, could cause severe damage to the ship. And Sid wasn't planning on losing this one too. This time his steel dragon would come out on top. And for that, it would have to reach the top.

"May I ask you a question?"

"If you are gonna ask me if I stole your Pocchuc conserves, yes I did. I regret nothing."

"I had my suspicions, but that's not what I was gonna ask."

"I really don't think this is the moment for questions. How close are we to reaching maximum ceiling?"

"Two more minutes, according to the hacked samoharo satellite you are linked to. That's what I was going to ask, how did you do it?"

"Samoharo security codes are not that hard to crack by the Figaro's main A.I."

"A.I.? A stable one? I thought those were still a theory."

"For the most part. But a hooman I knew long ago managed to crack how to make it work through quantum neural pathways and a semi-empathic code. It's like talking with a very smart kid."

"Where is this hooman now?"

"Long gone. It's a shame he didn't live long enough to see how his invention worked. But his friends have made good use of his legacy."

"That is how we achieve true immortality."

"Indeed. But right now, I'm not planning to test that. I want for us to make it out alive."

The Figaro reached the upper layers of the atmosphere, at the border of outer space. Sid wasn't planning to stay there long. The Figaro didn't have its radiation shields fitted yet, nor the oxygen generators at full. They could only last here for a few minutes.

Sid allowed himself to admire the view. For all its potential destructive power, the sight was breathtaking. There was a wall of fluffy white clouds around the eye. The sky was clear blue, and the sun shone brightly in the distance. Above them a few stars could be seen, along with the Long Moon and the dust rings that orbited Theia. Sid inhaled deeply. It was about time to start the dangerous part of his bad idea. Sid guided the ship downward, towards the eye of the storm. As the Figaro descended, the winds started to pick up. Around the ship, lightning streaked across the white walls. Those walls were made from tons of water suspended by the strong winds. And something else.

"I don't see a titan at the bottom. So, from where is it

controlling the storm?"

"Wanderer, run a spectrum scan around the ship," Sid said aloud to the AI of the Figaro.

"Do you suspect anything?"

"Maybe the titan is not at the bottom of the storm. Maybe the titan is the storm. Or at least the inner wall."

"Why do you think that?"

"I dunno, the slow-moving nature of the storm perhaps. Just a hunch."

A ping sounded. The AI generated a tridimensional model of the storm, with a red dot—the core of the titan—moving inside the air currents, but close to the eye.

"I was right. The core is close to our side of the storm, probably because the titan's sensors need it to keep control."

"A literal eye of the storm. What now?" Yokoyawa asked.

"We are gonna ride the storm and fish out that core." Sid replied, aiming the Figaro towards the wind wall. "You hear it. We have five minutes or less to find that core, in the middle of the biggest hurricane ever seen."

"There is a way to do it faster." Yokoyawa said, taking a small obsidian blade from his belt.

"Bloodtracking. You know I would do it, but I have to pilot this and the Elders blocked my ability to do it."

"I will do it."

"Please don't stain the ship." Sid replied.

"I won't. Can you open the roof? Do you have titanium cables?"

"What are you planning?"

"What your friends are doing: a very stupid idea."

"Please tell me you are not going to do what I think you are going to do. My ship is not your personal surfboard!"

"You want that titan dead or not?" Yokoyawa yelled from the hallway. "Just get me close to the core. I will do the rest!"

Sid sighed, then yelled back, annoyed, "Fine! I frigging hate surfing."

†††

At the observation deck of the Kyôkatô Tower, Harland was trying to set up the equipment he needed, while having to deal with a more annoying problem: Dewart's constant verbal attacks.

"Seems that your friends are not doing too well. That's what you wanted us to see, Rickman?" Dewart said. Harland couldn't tell if the man was scared or sarcastic. What he did know was that he'd had enough. He walked from the console towards Dewart and looked up straight into his eyes. Harland wasn't a fighter, but he was tired of seeing his friends putting themselves at risk, while people like Dewart and his ilk sat in their comfy chairs, doing nothing but arguing about 'optics', 'policy' and 'earnings'. All the frustrations Harland had been bottling up for the past week at the talks exploded in an unexpected way.

Harland punched Dewart in his groin. He did it with more force than he thought he possessed. The pain in his bones made him shake the hand to get rid of the numbness. What finally subdued the pain was seeing Dewart writhing on the floor. Prince Arthur smiled at him, but Harland wasn't finished. He grabbed Dewart by the beard and forced him to watch the screens, while pointing with his free hand.

"See that? Right now, you have humans, freefolk, and samoharo fighting together. People from Ionis, from the Kuni Empire, from Ravenstone, the Straits, even the Wastelands, risking their lives to protect others from a giant threat. That's what the Alliance is about. That's what we are trying to save from the ambition of the likes of you. Samoharo are mighty, Freefolk are powerful, Humans are indomitable. That's true. But together we are unstoppable. It could be a pandemic, it could be an invading army, or monsters from our past. But if we stand together, we can face them. We have one world, we need to cooperate. I don't want the Alliance to be broken. I want to expand it, to include the freefolk, the samoharo, and the human realms like the Kuni Empire as members on equal standing. Call me naive if you want, but I want to believe in a world where we can stand together, for the good and the bad."

"You are not naive," Dewart said through gritted teeth. "You are an idiot. No one can beat the titans."

"The only idiot here is you. Your ambition caused this,"

Harland replied as he again punched Dewart with a right cross. "I'm gonna make something clear, if any of my friends die today because of your stupid deal with the devil, I swear I will make your life so hard that you will wish to be sent to the Pits instead."

"You and your Foundation will pay for this, Rickman!" Dewart yelled. Arthur helped the diplomat to get on his feet. The he turned to his Solarian Knights.

"No, he won't, if I have something to say about it. Put him and his followers someplace where they won't hinder our efforts," the prince ordered. "And if he becomes a nuisance, I will punch him myself."

"Our pleasure," Salvador replied with glee, dragging Dewart out of the observation deck.

"What else do you need?" Arthur asked, looking at Harland.

"Help protecting the civilians from the collateral damage and whatever creatures are still on the loose," Harland smiled at his old friend. Maybe there was still hope for the crown. "I will coordinate from here."

"Augustus?" Arthur turned towards the leader of the Solarian Knights.

"On our way, my liege," Augustus replied with a formal salute.

Harland returned to the console. On the screens, he saw Fionn and Gaby struggling with their opponents. There was no sign of Sam or Alex. Joshua was also nowhere to be seen, and the cameras on Kasumi's location were too damaged to be able to see what was happening to her. He turned on the comms and spoke to them.

"Fionn? Gaby? Alex? Sam? If you can hear me, I need you to remember that you are not fighting Byron. You are not on the Bestial. The longer the fight lasts, the more casualties there will be. You need to finish it fast. So, if there is a time to let go and unleash your full power, this is it. Kasumi, Joshua, you can do this. I believe in you!"

Harland plugged a cable from his pad into the console and tapped a few keys on the computer. Then, he pushed play on the computer's music player, sending the signal through the city's PA system. A guitar chord blasted through the air, followed by a female voice, Gaby's voice. The same song she sang before they fought Byron, but now with musical arrangements. Harland smiled.

If it worked before... Let's see if that old theory about battle bards works with some modern technology.

Chapter 17
Ride the Storm

The elevator stopped with a ding. As the door opened, Alex took a deep breath.

Here goes nothing.

He held the door open as he peeked around the hallway that followed the circular observation deck. The place had a few lights on, generating a stark contrast between light and shadow. Alex stepped out and let the door close, he walked around looking for cover when he saw a shadow moving. The shape of its owner was hard to discern but it made Alex's stomach churn and roll, sending chills down his spine.

Stupid vivid imagination.

It was a man, or at least the top half of a man, bald and covered by flexi tubes, cables and black metal implants all over the torso. Creepy, but nothing worse than he had seen before. Alex even found the implants oddly familiar. However, the thing that almost made him throw up was the lower half of the being. It was as if the man's torso had been sewn onto the body of a black, chitinous carcass of a spider, with what seemed to be vestigial mouths and atrophied eyes. The mouths emitted a constant unnerving clacking sound. It walked with stilted, mechanical movements that gave the creature a sensation of belonging to the uncanny valley. The stuff of nightmares.

"I know you are there," the creature said aloud. "I invited you here, after all, Alejandro León from the Straits."

Alex's breathing accelerated. He walked around, following the circular path until he reached the section where most of the machines and screens were plugged in. It was a chaotic web of cables and capacitors feeding and collecting the energy arriving through the towers' antennas that maintained the feedback loop to the seeds of the titans.

A cold, moist breath flooded the space behind his neck. An unnerving presence was standing behind him. Alex closed his eyes and clenched his fists, trying to control his fear or he would piss his pants.

"Like what I did with the place? The administration of the SkySpire was very accommodating." The way the creature pronounced the last word made Alex shiver even more.

"I can't say," Alex replied. By now the fear was so intense that it had circled around and had become madness. He at least had snark as a defensive mechanism. "I'm not the one interested in interior design. That's Fionn."

Alex jumped to a spot across the space, facing the creature's mockery of a human face, with seemingly endless rows of metallic, sharpened teeth. A part of him wished to be somewhere else, an ocean apart.

"Right. You are the one that collects toys," the creature said with politeness. It waved its hands around to emphasize its words, but it only made it look more unnatural. "Apologies. I have met so many aspiring heroes during these centuries that it's hard to keep track of what you mortals do with your petty lives."

"I think you are being unfair," Alex said.

"Unfair?" the creature seemed taken aback.

"You seem to know a lot about me." Alex replied. "But I don't even know your name. Your real one. If we are gonna chat, I would like to know how to address you. I don't want to be rude."

"You are right. I've been rude as you said," the creature said. "I've had many names, many avatars such as this one, across the millennia: Typhon the Necromancer, Asphut the Wizard, Lord Francis the Scientist, Marius the Provider of Miracles, Elher il Rohar the Traveler, Gilles the Artist, The Dark Father that rules over the deepest prisons of the Infinity Pits. You can choose any of those. In a few minutes it won't matter."

Goosebumps covered Alex's arms as the shivers increased. He recognized almost every single one of those names. They were the names that he had read in books about myths, horror stories, urban legends, or persons across history that had caused doom and death through their actions and machinations. All of those names belonged to one single being, an eldritch god from the Pits that in primeval times tried to destroy Theia: The Creeping Chaos. A primal fear flooded his mind, battling with the part of him that controlled the Gift, which was oddly defiant.

A part of me must be going insane, Alex thought. *There is no way I can stand against a god. Even if it's just an avatar. I guess I should just let loose the insanity.*

"Marius? That must be the stiffest, most boring name ever. No wonder you abbreviated it when you used the artist's persona," Alex said with sarcasm and a smile.

"I take it that you are not a fan of any of my creations," Marius sighed. "The artistic ones... nor the scientific ones. Although I applaud you. Not many mortals can comprehend what my inventions can do."

"I guess that's why you are talking with me instead of killing me." Alex hands twitched, trying to restrain himself from drawing his bow. It wouldn't be of any help.

"We both know that both of us are stalling for time," Marius replied. "You, until your friends do something, which will be futile. Me? I'm waiting till my latest creation is fully charged so I can finally take over this realm."

"The titans." Alex said, not taking his eyes from Marius, while trying to see the screens out of the corner of his eye. "You are not only sending energy to wake them. You are feeding from them as well, to increase your own powers once they are fully unleashed. Like a symbiont... or a parasite."

"As I said, you are one of the few that understands what is happening. I respect that," Marius replied. "It's a shame really. If you hadn't messed with my experiments, I might have left you to the last. But as it stands, you are not going to leave this place alive. I have enjoyed watching you solving all the challenges in the past few hours. But I'm not going to risk you stopping me now, as you killed my children last year."

"So those two freaks that attacked my university were your children. Are you mad that I killed them?" Alex smiled at the memory. That had been the one of the few times he had actually felt useful.

"No," Marius waved his left hand, dismissively. "They were failed experiments, like that tovainar that calls himself Joshua."

"You created the tovainar?" Alex asked, as his mind racing to put together all the facts. "Byron too?"

"Byron was more like an alliance of convenience. The only one of you mortals that understood my vision and wanted to be part of it. He wasn't part of the plan at first but the good thing about being the one behind a prophecy such as the rise of the tovainars, is that you get to fiddle around to make it fit your current circumstances. Prophecies are what you want them to be."

"You have been playing everyone, for centuries."

"And it has been fun. Except for that time a decade ago," Marius's tone of voice deepened, changing from polite and monotonous to penetrating, betraying the anger. "A true masterpiece put together by my supplicants, destroyed by a kid who didn't know what he was doing."

A decade ago? What is he talking about... Alex's eyes widened as it dawned on him. A decade ago is when he got the Gift, and fought the creatures summoned from the Infinity Pits by cultists through a hi-tech portal. Everything that had happened during those fateful days was Marius's fault.

"You murdered a lot of my friends and schoolmates," Alex said as his anger increased. Inside him, in his mind and heart, clouds formed, a storm was brewing. "You left my best friend paralyzed for life. And his injuries finally killed him."

"It wasn't just his injuries, if you catch my drift." Marius smiled, his eyes wide. Alex felt like he was looking into two black holes. "You on the other hand... you are so easy to play with. A nudge here, a whisper there, and your mind did the rest. You are insecure about being a loser, about not being useful. But the thing is: like the rest of your species, you *are* useless, a waste of matter, energy, oxygen, you name it. You are nothing but an insect who deludes himself by thinking that he is something that he is not. It would be hilarious if it wasn't so pathetic. I was expecting to have to spend time beating you to release my pent-up annoyance resulting from your meddling, but you did most of the job already by coming here in such a regrettable state. I might be losing my time with you here, actually. Because the truth is, you will never amount to nothing and no one will miss you when I kill you."

He is right, no one will miss you. They might even be better without you, hindering them with your pitiful cries.

Alex shook his head, trying to clear his thoughts. He tuned out the dark voice for a second and focused on the Gift. He lifted his head and stared at Marius.

"I'm gonna rip you apart limb by limb." The storm reached its peak as Alex's fists tightened. The fear was long gone, replaced by the thunderstorm of his anger. For the first time in his life, Alex didn't care about keeping his anger in check. This time, he was going all out. "And then I will use them to beat your head to a pulp."

"Ah! The fury of the righteous man, charming but useless," Marius said, clearly amused at Alex's reactions, which infuriated him even more. "Too many rules, too much order and honor. You can't beat me because you play by the rules."

"You are confusing me with someone else, perhaps Fionn," Alex replied. Deity or not, avatar or not, one of them was going down. And Alex wasn't planning to be that one. His anger wasn't hot as a fire, but cold as a winter storm. "For someone who's focused so much attention on me, you really don't understand me at all, do you? I don't play by the rules."

Alex's irises glowed once more. He had been saving enough energy for this. One shot, just one shot was all he had. And he was going to make it count. He drew all the energy from his surroundings. He drew almost all the energy he had inside. And focused on all of his anger. Sparks leaped all around as Alex took deep breaths. The coil around his cast glowed red hot. His arm became a beacon of light amidst the shadows in the room. Alex jumped towards Marius, his left fist aimed at his head.

"Really? I expected better," Marius easily dodged the attack.

Alex's punch hit the metal floor, his bones breaking again, sending waves of pain across his body as he let lose his storm. An explosion of light dispelled the darkness for a brief moment. Sparks jumped from all the consoles, the screens failed and the power went off. Marius's movements slowed, becoming clumsy. Marius looked at his biomechanical body and smiled.

"An EMP? That won't kill me."

"On its own, no." Alex smiled. "But I have killed your connection with the titans. For the next few minutes, you and I are on the same level." Alex's smile widened. "Mortals."

"You... you cheated?" Marius seemed confused.

"Cheated?" Alex laughed, trying to hide his pain. "That's funny coming from a god that thrives on chaos." His left arm hung at his side, numb from the pain.

"You are handicapped," Marius said matter-of-factly. "And unarmed."

Alex couldn't use the bow with only one arm and even if he had Yaha with him, the sword required both hands to be wielded effectively. But he had an ace up his sleeve. Or rather, under his vest.

He drew the sai from his back.

"I'm gonna show you how outmatched you are, right now," Alex said.

I only need to hold out for a few minutes. I can do it.

Marius, controlling the flexi tubes around him, threw a punch that Alex blocked with the sai. The impact of the hit sent Alex reeling back. He gritted his teeth. In the darkness, his eyes glowed gold.

Or maybe not.

† † †

You are not fighting Byron, Harland's words echoed in Fionn's head as he lifted the debris from the promotional statue off him. He counted his blessings that the statue was mostly a hollow shell of fiberglass. So instead of having been crushed into mush, he was only dealing with multiple cuts and lacerations. Harland was right. Fionn had been keeping his Gift in check. He'd grown so used to using the minimum power after the fight against Byron. But if he kept doing that, this fight would take more time, time that Alex didn't have. And he risked Xavier attacking the buildings out of malice, risking anybody hiding in them. For once, he would have to unleash the full power of the Gift to end the fight, now.

At that moment, the city's PA system crackled to life with a song by a voice that sounded familiar: it was one of Gaby's recordings. Hearing her voice, singing one of her songs made him smile. Fionn also felt an odd sensation, similar to goose bumps, running through his body, energizing him and clearing his mind.

Battle bard through PA systems and digital recordings, nice trick Har, Fionn thought.

Fionn focused on his breathing, using the song as his guide. His mind went to the inner core, where the Gift was created. There was the ball of green energy, growing, transforming itself into a maelstrom, a vortex of rapid streams of energy and wind. And in the center of the Tempest, there he was, his soul. He opened his eyes.

As he cleared the debris, he saw Xavier, floating on a piece of concrete.

"Bow before me, a titan of might, for I will show you how to respect a legend!"

Xavier gathered energy around his sword, as he prepared to unleash an attack. A signpost hit him in the face, breaking his concentration. Wind started to pick up in strength and speed.

"What?"

Fionn took deep breaths, as he gripped Black Fang with his left hand. His irises glowed with such intensity that his eyes resembled emeralds. Black Fang glowed with the same power. His blood boiled and each of his steps left a crack on the floor. He smiled. The smile of the wolf. He pointed Black Fang at Xavier.

"Legend? We will see about that. And for the record I bow before no one!" Fionn exclaimed. "I am Fionn Estel of the Greywolf clan! And you... you are dead meat!

"How?"

The glow from Black Fang increased as the blade grew,

shape shifting into a large, sharp crescent. Now, it did look like a dragon fang. The largest ever seen. Fionn smiled, flashing his own wolf fangs.

The wind became a gale. Beads of black sweat ran across Xavier's brow, as he gained altitude, trying to put distance between Fionn and himself.

"Weren't you saying that you were all powerful?" Fionn mocked him. "Why leave so soon?"

"Stay away, freak!"

Fionn didn't reply. Instead, he ran, looking for something to jump on. He spotted a canvas awning over a shop entrance. Fionn jumped on it, towards the highest level of a fire escape on the side of the building in front of him. With only the tip of his left foot, Fionn leaped back to the first building, bending the metal of the stairs in the process. He reached the building, where an automated high-rise window cleaner had stopped to clean a window. Xavier was still too high and Fionn was running out of places to jump from. Fionn saw a construction crane on top of a nearby building and jumped towards its jib, breaking the window cleaner in half.

He focused all his strength in the last jump, hoping that the counterweight would be enough to keep the crane from toppling. With a powerful leap he took to the sky, as the wind around him increased in force. Fionn reached Xavier, surprising him, leaving his opponent no time to react and use his sword as defense. Fionn slashed at Xavier with Black Fang, unleashing a gust of wind with a force that broke Xavier's sword and his armor, as well as the Titan core in his chest. A fine thread of black blood appeared on Xavier's neck as the force of the attack sent him crashing a large neon sign which exploded in a shower of sparks. Fionn was flung back against the side of a building. He pushed back with his legs and leaped towards Xavier. He landed on top of the sign, whose support beams squeaked under the weight.

With his eyes wide open, Xavier was in shock. He tried to speak, but his head was already separating from his neck.

Fionn looked down.

"Don't speak. You can't. So, in your final moments I will offer you some advice for your next life. First rule of becoming a legend: if you pick a fight, be sure to survive it."

Xavier's head fell ten floors, followed by his body, impacting the concrete below and leaving a pool of black ichor covering the remains of the ancient titan armor. Fionn looked down, as the support beams for the sign squeaked again.

I have survived falls from greater heights, Fionn thought, *but I'd rather not do it again.* He saw another window cleaner a few floors below and jumped down there, and from there, into the street below. Speckles of green light came out of his body and currents of air surrounded him. He landed in a graceful stance, as if he had been floating on the air.

And Alex once said I would never dare to attempt the superhero landing. Fionn looked at the SkySpire in the distance.

Fionn looked around as he considered if he could actually run from here to the SkySpire, but even at his maximum speed, it would take too long. He needed some kind of transportation. A trike would be perfect.

Gotcha!

Fionn saw a motorbike parked in a nearby alley and ran towards it. He looked for the keys, but there were none, forcing him to hotwire it.

It's a bike instead of a far superior trike, but it should do the trick. Fionn reeved the motorbike and dashed into the streets and towards the SkySpire. *Hold on Alex, I'm on my way.*

† † †

This is embarrassing, Gaby thought. She looked at the titan in front of her, and behind her, to the people taking cover inside the temple, praying and looking at the battle. She'd had several opportunities to hit the core of the titan, but every time she got close to landing a hit, the titan split into pieces, the core disappeared and reappeared on a different piece far from her reach. And to make matters worse, the golems were becoming a problem. Time was running out, for her, and for Alex. Harland was right, she didn't need to hold back. But the idea of that scared her. In the past, she had always kept herself under control because of the risk of losing herself once she entered the ice state. But she had left that behind during her duel against Madam Park, when she found a way around it. Now her best friend was in serious trouble. She would have to push it once more, even if she didn't know the full extent of the Gift's power.

A familiar song blasted through the city's PA. She recognized the tune and the voice. It was her own.

Now, that is super embarrassing. Where the Pits did he get that recording?

Hearing her own song had an interesting effect on her; she relaxed her shoulders, her breathing became deeper and slower, and a smile crossed her face. It felt right. Singing was what she was meant to do, regardless of what anyone else, even herself, thought. But if she wanted to keep singing, she needed to fight for it. And right now, the fight was against that stupid titan. The frustration of her fight until now had been a damp fog, muting the sound of her song, but now the Gift blazed strong, evaporating the feeling, letting her hear the song clearly.

Gaby recalled when she met Fionn for the first time, and his fight against that large monster at Carffadon. That, coupled with the memories from her match at the Games where she momentarily lost Heartguard gave her an idea.

Gaby ran towards the titan at blinding speed, leaving cracks in the ground with each step, extending her arms, holding her blades tight. The titan threw a punch that she evaded by jumping onto its left knee and from there onto its right shoulder. The core was in the chest, thus, with a swift move, Gaby sank Soulkeeper into the neck of the titan. It sliced through the stone, leaving her at the appropriate height to hit the core.

As the titan split once more, Gaby, pulled Soulkeeper free and jumped to attack the core again, trying to cleave it with Heartguard. The core disappeared, and she landed on top of the left leg. She closed her eyes for a second and with her left hand, summoning all her strength, threw Soulkeeper into the air, as if it were a spear. Soulkeeper shone blue with intensity as it cleaved itself into the core that was rematerializing a few meters behind Gaby. The core cracked and the titan cried in pain, its eyes releasing a blue light. Soulkeeper was doing its work. Gaby leaped from the leg and with a reverse somersault, grabbed Soulkeeper's hilt. Using the momentum, she stabbed the core with Heartguard, finally breaking it. The core glowed as Gaby pulled her blades out, closing her eyes in the process and covering her face with her arms and blades. The core exploded into millions of pieces and sent her crashing into a tree.

How I envy Fionn right now. Gaby thought, as her sight recovered from the light. All the floating stones and small golems that composed the titan fell to the ground with loud thuds.

She stood up, trying to catch her breath, and looked at the SkySpire. It wasn't that far on foot. If she pushed herself to the limit, she may reach it in time to help Alex. She began to run. A motorbike pulled up alongside her, ridden by a young man. He wore a jacket embroidered with the logo of the Curry house belonging to Kasumi's parents. He yelled at her, "I'm Shirô! Need a ride?"

"Yeah!"

Gaby jumped onto the motorbike.

Just hold on a little longer.

† † †

Burnt, tired and with only one canister left, with a nozzle had been melted, Joshua felt beaten. The only way to stop the titan was to hit its core and destroy it. But that would mean getting too close to the flames to survive. The heat was increasing, a wall of fire blazed in front of him, which meant he would have to find a better place to use the last canister. At that moment, the PA system changed from the evacuation alarm to a song by a voice that sounded familiar. One of Alex's friends. His mind became clearer, sharper. An idea came to mind. He took a deep breath, as a rush of adrenaline surged though his veins.

Joshua ran to the stairs to reach the upper deck. The song playing through the PA system somehow was the key needed to unlock long dormant memories. He saw himself standing over a grave, the grave of Aldai, his first true friend. He was making a promise to her, a promise to help others to honor her memory. And he had done that. First, protecting the people of the slums of Meteora, then moving to the Kuni Empire to seek help from the Shimizu family and help them in their work as demonhunters. Now rescuing people from threats, mortal and supernatural.

As he reached the upper deck and the light of the sunrise hit him, Joshua wondered if he had done enough, not just to avenge his friend, but to honor her belief that he was not a monster.

An anguished cry echoed through the streets. Joshua hurried to the edge. The moan came from the titan, who seemed to be examining its hands, as if it had dawned on him what he was.

"I'm a monster," the titan growled, as it stared at Joshua. "You are a monster too. You did this to me."

"I did nothing to you," Joshua replied. "It was your choice."

The titan growled once more and its flames increased. Time was running out.

If I'm gonna die, at least it will be while proving something, Joshua thought, biting his lip. He ran to the middle of the deck, grabbed the canister and took three calming breaths. The titan was climbing the building. He ran across the rooftop and jumped.

"I. Am. Not. A. Monster!" Joshua yelled as he leaped towards the creature, as it reached the upper deck. Joshua cracked opened the canister on the spot where the flames were coming from. The flames receded, leaving the pulsating core open to attack. Joshua punched his fist through it, while the Beast emerged from his spine and transformed into a dark cloud, a shadow that resembled a pair of leather wings. The last image in his mind was that of Aldai and Kasumi, juxtaposed on each other.

"I'm not a monster! I'm not a monster!" Joshua screamed as the flames engulfed him. From his back, the Beast broke free, protecting him and in turn, engulfing the titan and forcing him to fall backwards onto the streets. A gravelly voice echoed in the streets.

"We are not a monster! We are a hero!"

As the Beast, Joshua, and the titan fell, the flames left the body of the titan. Despite the relatively short fall, the amalgamation of the three beings hit the street with the force of a falling star. The street cracked around the crater left by the impact, which shook every building in a five-block radius.

Fire exploded from the crater, followed by tendrils of darkness that wriggled around the tongues of flame. A globe of pure darkness covered the crater and then exploded in tiny pieces, leaving nothing but dust and a dome of molten asphalt and concrete. Then the dome cracked and slid to the ground as massive slabs. A shape, a human form, made of flame stood in the center, immobile.

Joshua focused on the song still playing through the PA as he clenched his right fist to gain control. He wasn't sure what had happened exactly. He had a rough idea though.

Alex and Kasumi hadn't killed the Beast. But they had done something to it. Alex had mentioned something akin to 'restore it to factory settings so you could program it'. Apparently, that meant that the Beast had been in a dormant state, giving Joshua time to better control it. But the procedure had left the Beast almost dead from the lack of energy, so it couldn't finish the reboot, which in turn made it latch onto anything that could feed it. That's why he could rip the core from the wyvern without burning, and that would explain Alex's surprised, happy smile. When Joshua found himself facing the titan, the Beast had detected a potential source of energy that could finish the reboot. But in attempting to consume it, while protecting Joshua, the Beast had burned itself away, leaving behind flames.

This is weird. It feels weird, Joshua thought as he managed to finally breathe. His lungs didn't hurt when he did. Which was odd as by then they should have been burnt. The flames around his body subsided... correction, they wiggled around him, paired with small tendrils of darkness that receded into his body. As the flames went into his body, Joshua felt invigorated. He couldn't hear the voice of the Beast anymore, yet he knew it was there. However, the sensation was different. Before it had been as if he'd had this heavy thing inside his spine, tearing muscle and bone to get out. This time it felt as if it was part of him.

At last, Joshua opened his eyes. He stood atop the dead body of the titan, his clothes shredded and burnt. All that remained of the titan was compacted ash. It vaguely retained a humanoid shape, with a face that was composed of three empty slots in a rictus of pain.

Joshua remembered something Marius had told him: the symbionts of the tovainars were meant to serve as receptacles for the titans' powers.

"Well, I guess that there is a new Fire Titan," Joshua said, smiling. He snapped his fingers and flames danced on his fingertips. His smile turned into a grin. A few people had left their shelters to see what had happened and they started to whisper as they recognized him. They started to take pictures and clap.

Just then a bolt of lightning struck the SkySpire and seconds later, debris started to fall on their location, as the observation deck took heavy damage.

"Get out of here!" Joshua yelled at the people as a large slab of glass was about to fall on top of them. Moving his right arm in an arc, Joshua let a stream of fire hit the glass, evaporating it, as a tendril of darkness covered the people below.

"That was useful," Joshua mumbled, still astonished at his new powers. He wondered if this had been Alex's plan from the beginning.

"Alex," Joshua said, as he ran towards the collapsing structure of the SkySpire's observation deck.

† † †

"Listen to me titan of doom! I'm Shimizu Kasumi and with Breaker-sama, I will take your head!!" Kasumi yelled.

The titan opened its mouth, unleashing a scream as its reply, obliterating the asphalt where she was standing. Kasumi ran to the left side of the titan, each fiber in her muscles burning with pain, her tendons threatening to snap. All her training, all her efforts would be tested in a last-ditch attack. Not for her honor, not for the crown of the Games, but because it was what she had to do if she was to end this fight and help Alex and Joshua. She might not have the Gift, but she was a demonhunter, she had a Tempest Blade, and she had a purpose. And that's all she needed.

The titan aimed the scream at her once more.

Breaker's blade shone with its cold, white light. Kasumi slashed the air with the naginata, aiming at the cone of sound. Breaker, giving honor to its name, sliced the air, dispersing the shockwave. Kasumi then jumped to her right, landing on the titan's left knee and ran up, across its back and took to the air, raising Breaker. The titan tried to turn its head to attack her with a scream, but it almost broke its own neck in the attempt, making the sonic attack impossible.

Breaker's glow increased as Kasumi descended on the titan and put all of her strength and weight into the attack, splitting the titan in two. As she vivisected the creature, going down faster than she expected, courtesy of the always keen edge of Breaker, she hit the core, which exploded.

The shockwave sent Kasumi flying backward. Her grip on Breaker loosened and it hit the ground, leaving a large tear on the asphalt. Bev Johnson ran towards her and caught her, cushioning the fall with his own body. Both crashed into a statue of a cartoon robot, breaking it.

Dazed, Kasumi tried to stand up. Simon Beleforont offered his hand to help her and told her something.

"What? Let me turn on my aids."

Kasumi reached up and turned them on. Only the left one sounded the booting up chime. The right one only emitted a faint chirp. Sound returned to her left side, but the right had a muffled quality. It probably got damaged during the fight. The audio imbalance was bound to cause her quite an annoying headache.

She wondered if Harland would keep his promise to pay for the repair and the operation to affix it again. She looked at Simon.

"What did you say?" Kasumi asked, embarrassed.

"He asked if you were okay," Bev Johnson replied, breathing heavily as he stood up, helped by Simon. "And that as far as he is concerned, you are the new champion of the Games. And you know what, my lady? I don't think any of us will disagree. You are the best of us."

Kasumi turned around and saw the surviving titanfighters clapping and cheering at her. She blushed and struggled to keep the tears back.

A crashing boom broke the cheering. The sound came from an explosion near the base of the SkySpire. Seconds later, lightning crossed the sky, hitting the massive tower.

Joshua! Alex! Kasumi thought.

"Can someone lend me a motorbike?" Kasumi asked.

† † †

Through the external cameras, Sid saw that Yokoyawa had latched himself to the ship with cables wrapped around his waist and feet. His cousin took the obsidian knife and pricked his left thumb, letting out blood that glowed as the prayers were said. The blood floated from Yokoyawa's thumb as he kept pressing it to let it flow. The blood droplets formed the constellation, then quickly flew in different directions, tracing paths through the air. One glowed with a bright red hue leading toward Sid's five o'clock position, near the bottom of the hurricane. Normally that would be the path to avoid, but not this time. They were in a hurry.

Sid maneuvered the Figaro inside the eye of the storm. There, the winds were calm and there was a gentle mist that covered the windows of the cockpit. It was almost a relaxing flight, until the sensors bleeped and blared and Sid barely had time to dodge the attack. A water jet at least three meters in diameter crossed from one side of the storm's wall to the other at incredible speed. Sid had been able to dodge it by mere centimeters.

"Hey!" Yokoyawa yelled through the comms. "Watch it! I'm out here and that came close!"

Sid was about to say something, but a second jet almost hit the underside of the Figaro, forcing Sid to pull the yoke and gain altitude. Rotating the ship, he saw several random water jets crisscrossing the eye of the storm. As dumb as this titan might be, being a force of nature, it was clear that it was trying to defend itself.

"This is friggin crazy," Sid muttered. "Hold tight cousin! This will get wild."

"Just like surfing during a storm!" Yokoyawa replied.

After this, you better recognize me as the best pilot ever born, Sid thought.

He flew the Figaro near the inner eyewall, deftly dodging every jet that that tried to hit them. Sometimes he had to gain altitude, at other times he had to drop swiftly, hoping that his cousin would survive.

"I'm a feather floating in the wind. I'm a feather floating in the wind," Sid mumbled over and over, while all the proximity alarms blared non-stop. Sid was pushing the Figaro to its limits, making rapid, precise turns nearly every second, threading his way through the storm. As the ship shuddered and groaned under the stress, Sid said, "Come on, baby. Hold together." As long as the blood trail pointed to the right place, this was a race of precision rather than speed. As long as he kept close to the walls and paid attention, there would be little need for dramatic turns. Every time a water jet formed, the currents in the clouds on the eyewall changed, forming a vortex that was a telltale sign of the incoming attack.

"I'm a feather floating in the wind. I'm a feather floating in the wind," Sid kept mumbling as he surfed on the wall of the hurricane. As he kept dodging the increasing attacks, the Figaro closed in on the titan at the bottom of the eye of the storm. He was near enough that he could see where ocean water was being syphoned into the hurricane.

"Here we come!"

Sid maneuvered the Figaro closer to the titan.

"Get ready because I can only do one pass at the core, before it hits us!" Sid yelled through the comms.

"If you get me close, I will do the rest," Yokoyawa replied.

Easier said than done, Sid thought. He pushed the yoke and activated several inputs on the console as the Figaro plummeted towards the core of the titan. The blood trail was still clear, but the mist was turning into bona fide rain.

"Stand by... stand by... now!" Sid yelled and he pushed the engines, dodging another series of water jets in a hectic dance. Through the cameras he saw Yokoyawa keeping a low gravity center and profile, holding Stellar Ehecatl tight in his right hand. The core was close and when they reached it...

Yokoyawa stood up. Sid maneuvered to get him as close as possible. Stellar Ehecatl glowed... and with a swift cut that left a trail of stardust, the core was split in two, as well as the water wall and the surface of the ocean.

"You better get inside!" Sid yelled at Yokoyawa.

"What now?" Yokoyawa asked, dripping in water, as he jumped back into the ship. The sudden acceleration threw him against the wall, as the rooftop hatch closed.

"We hurry before this hurricane and its tons of water crash on us!" Sid pulled the yoke to raise the Figaro and flew it through the gap caused by Yokoyawa's attack, as the walls of the hurricane began to lose inertia and speed without the will that created it.

Sweat beaded across Sid's brow, as he rerouted the energy of any non-vital system to the engines to increase thrust. Yokoyawa crawled to the cockpit and into his seat.

"You could have warned me," Yokoyawa complained.

"Tell that to the ocean about to bury us under its weight," Sid replied without taking his eyes from the end of the tunnel.

"I'm an arrow in the air, see me fly," Sid mumbled.

"You keep changing that line, you know."

"Everybody is a critic."

The walls of turquoise water were crashing down on them, and for a second, the cockpit's windows were covered in sheets of water, making it almost impossible to see. The gap was becoming smaller and smaller.

"Just a little more," Sid muttered under his breath.

The hurricane collapsed, sending tons of water crashing into the ocean below with a loud roar.

But a second roar came from the hurricane's flank, as a small airship flew out like a garuda straight out from the Pits.

Sid gave a whoop of joy as he leveled the Figaro above the churning waves. "And we didn't crash this time!"

"You often crash?" Yokoyawa asked.

Sid ignored the comment, he was too happy. "The Figaro is the best ship there is. Proof of what samoharo, freefolk, and human collaboration can achieve." He patted the console affectionately.

Yokoyawa pointed to a display, "Your power output for your weapons is too low."

Sid set a course for the SkySpire and glared at Yokoyawa in the copilot's seat. "You are flooding my floor."

Yokoyawa looked at the large puddle of water. "I think I just took enough showers for the next dozen years," he said with a smile that showed all of his sharp teeth.

"You? Trying to make a joke?" Sid looked at his cousin, surprised.

"Was it bad?" Yokoyawa seemed to be confused.

"It needs work, but it is progress," Sid returned the smile.

"Where are we going now?" Yokoyawa asked.

"To help my friends," Sid replied. "There is an odd reading coming from the beach near the SkySpire. And I don't like that."

"Correction. Our friends," Yokoyawa added.

Sid smile grew wider. Maybe there was still hope. If not for all, at least for his cousin.

The Figaro roared as it breached the sound barrier. If dragons were reborn through technology, the Figaro was the first one of them. It had battled a storm and had come off victorious. Now it flew at full speed towards the SkySpire.

Sid saw lightning crossing the clouds above them, gaining strength.

"Did you see that?" Yokoyawa asked. "Lightning doesn't work that way. It's as if that streak has a mind of its own," Yokoyawa observed as matter-of-factly.

"I know," Sid replied, laughing. "It's magick."

It is about damn time, Sammy, he thought.

Chapter 18
A Sliver of Hope

Alex tasted the metallic flavor of blood in his mouth, felt water in his eyes, crying from pain and impotence. However, behind Marius, he managed to catch a glimpse of a familiar light, while he took hit after hit after hit. The sai only helped to block the strongest ones, the direct hits from the metallic arms. But with only one good arm he couldn't keep up his defense and the cumulative effect of Marius's attack was wearing him down. He took a hit to the face that sent him to the floor. Dazed, he tried to get up, but slipped. Alex blinked several times, trying to regain his focus.

Concussion. Great.

"I expected more of a challenge from you. I'm disappointed."

Alex eyes were full of tears. The glow in his irises was fading, as he ran out of energy.

You know what Yaha means? I know, Ywain found its meaning. Fionn had explained. *In an ancient language, Yaha means hope. In a way, that sword is a sliver of light, of hope that can be used to beat back darkness. Hope is something we hold in our own hands to tell ourselves that things will get better. But the tricky thing about hope, is that while others can inspire it, for it to work on oneself, it has to come from inside. That's why Yaha might be the most difficult Blade to wield. Because it asks from you to never give up and always believe in yourself.*

Alex propped himself up with his good arm. He breathed once more to clear his head.

I want you to be the best version of yourself, Fionn had told him. Alex didn't want to die here. And the only way to get through this was to keep standing up.

No matter how hard things got, Alex always got up.

No matter how injured he was, Alex always got up.

No matter how defeated he felt, Alex always got up.

It dawned on him then, what Fionn had been trying to teach him, to find the thing that made him the best version of himself. Because even when he was down, he was too stubborn to quit. The storm inside him, the one that threatened to blow up all the time, wasn't one of darkness, rather it was the source of energy that fueled his willpower to keep going even when he couldn't do more. That was why the voice in his head, the one that always put him down, never won. Because deeper down, there was a sliver of hope that he would always solve every problem. Because that's who he was.

And something inside him finally clicked. After a decade the Gift at last merged with Alex. He was still running low on energy. But he only needed to get up just one more time.

And he got up.

He grabbed the sai and spit the blood from his mouth onto the floor.

Clang!

There goes my wisdom tooth. Not like I was ever wise to begin with.

The glow in his irises returned. Subdued, but present. He could still see the energy running through Marius and from it to the flexi tubes. It helped him to block the next attack.

Exasperated, Marius said, "Why won't you stay down? You are worthless."

Alex smiled.

"You are useless!" Marius roared.

Alex spun the sai in his hand.

"You are meaningless!" Marius raged, spittle flying from his mouth.

"Nothing you say to me will ever be worse than what I say to myself every day. And I won't quit because I don't know how."

"Then I will put you out of your misery so I can restart my engine."

The emergency lights flickered to life as power returned to the tower.

"Seems that your luck ran out, mortal," Marius said with a broad grin that showed rows of teeth that better resembled a shark rather than a human. But Alex didn't flinch as he'd seen something as the power returned.

Marius closed the gap between them, the flexi tubes encircled Alex, entangling him. But Alex could see that the flows of energy through Marius were different now.

The connection between Marius and the titans was still gone.

Alex remained calm. This was it. The opening he was looking for.

Marius tried to attack him with a blow to the head. But Alex dodged the attack and stabbed him with the sai. Marius punched him in the abdomen. Alex staggered back and fell to one knee. He stood up again, looking at Marius straight in the eyes as the Dark Father closed the gap between them and put his hands around Alex's neck, attempting to strangle him.

Marius hands were pressed around his throat. And yet Alex was not worried. Maybe because of the certainty of death, maybe because this situation was exactly what Fionn had been training him for: keep calm in the face of adversity. He smiled. It had worked.

"Why are you smiling? I will send you to your grave."

Alex grabbed Marius's hands and pulled at his fingers to liberate his throat.

"And you will come with me," Alex smiled. Whether he died or not was of no consequence. This was the one opening to take down a god. "Sam, now!"

From the back of the room a light came closer. Sam jumped high into the air, Yaha in her hands, and impaled Marius with the sword.

Alex barely managed to dodge the blade that came close to his right temple. He saw Sam grimacing from the pain, as she held Yaha and the lightning ran through the sword and across Marius' body. Even if the sword was cooperating, the synchronicity between Blade and Wielder hadn't been achieved and its natural defenses were sending electric currents into Sam's hands. And yet she never let go.

The problem was that Marius could still move. The blade had pierced him below the core, cutting the wires feeding energy to his body. Electric sparks started to shoot off from his body as the blade descended, cutting him open. Marius fell to the ground, kneeling. Without the support Alex also fell to the floor, struggling to breathe. Marius clutched his abdomen, gripping the shinning blade of Yaha as it protruded from his body.

Marius twisted his head and arms to face Sam and slowly, reached for her neck. As long as Marius's core was intact, the avatar of the chaotic god wouldn't stop. Alex struggled to get to his feet. Clenching his teeth, he stood up, grabbed Yaha's glowing blade and pushed up. The keen edge of the blade cut into his hand while the rest of the blade, hot with energy, seared his flesh. Alex breathed slowly, as he focused his mind on the last trick Fionn had taught him: manipulating the Blade's edge.

Help me with this please, Alex thought, hoping that the spirit within Yaha understood what he wanted to do.

"Okay."

Alex heard another voice inside his head, this one coming from Yaha. It was female, and cheerful. He hadn't expected that. In another time, Alex would have made a quip about yet another voice in his head, but right now he had to focus. The edge of the blade that was in contact with his hand became dull and cold. It still hurt to push, but it wasn't cutting him. The hilt stopped sending electrical charges to Sam's hands. And the edge aiming upwards became as sharp as a laser beam.

"Sam, now!" Alex yelled, as Marius' hands were closing around Sam's neck.

"Ahhhh!" Sam yelled as well. Her irises glowed lilac with green specs.

As Alex pushed the blade up, reaching Marius' core, Sam yelled.

"Fasd'an!"

The room's ceiling crumbled as a lightning bolt struck Yaha with enough energy to evaporate everything... except for two Gifted, an avatar of an eldritch god, and the oldest of the Tempest Blades, light made matter.

The massive bolt tore the walls and crossed the room towards Sam's hands, and then into Yaha, which glowed with blinding intensity. Sparks flew everywhere, flooding the air with a burning scent. Sam let go the sword and fell backwards.

Alex felt the core melting away as his own body received the full brunt of the lightning's power. But the Gift, as weakened as it was, still pulsed inside Alex, absorbing the extra energy and keeping him alive.

The air filled with the smell of charred meat and molten metal as Marius' body twitched from the electrical currents and the destruction of his core. Alex kept pushing and the blade cleared the body, leaving a gap behind. Alex dropped Yaha to the floor.

Marius's body twitched as the gap in the body began to seal.

"If the head remains attached, he will heal!"

Sam kicked Yaha towards Alex, who grabbed it by the hilt. He put all of his strength and weight behind the stroke. Marius's head fell off, cleanly cut from the rest of the body.

"Is it over?" Sam asked, as she stood up and went to help Alex.

"I hope so," Alex replied. "I mean it would be crappy if..."

The floor shook beneath their feet and Alex and Sam struggled to stand. The room tilted with a sickening crash, then they were in free fall as the observation deck collapsed.

†††

"That was quick thinking. Thank you," Alex said, coughing to expel the dust from his throat. He and Sam were inside a Shield Bubble created by her True Spell she had cast at the last second. It had saved them from the fall, and from being hit by the debris that covered them now.

"Don't thank me. We are not out yet," Sam said. She was sporting the silver fox ears and tail that she grew when casting a spell. However, this time instead of appendages grown from her body, they looked as if they were made of energy the same color as the glow from her eyes. She moved her hands, pushing outward with her arms. The bubble exploded outwards, expelling the debris away and leaving them free, if covered by dust. Alex could now see that they were on the terrace of the ground level of the SkySpire, overlooking the beach.

As the dust settled, Alex examined his right hand. In hindsight, grabbing Yaha by the blade hadn't been a good idea. The gash was half open, half burnt from the energy running through the blade at that moment. It would heal. Like his severely damaged left arm, his knee, his back, the bloody nose, that swollen eye, the missing tooth that would have to be replaced... he really had put his body through the wringer.

If I manage to recover from this, Alex thought. *I will take better care of my body.*

Truth be told, he wasn't feeling well. He was having an odd sensation in his chest.

"Sam, I..." he started to say, but Sam wasn't listening. She ripped the hem of her shirt to improvise a bandage.

"Shhh. You need to rest. And I'm the one who needs to apologize..."

Alex barely had time to react, to push Sam away and roll to his right as a dart of rock hit the place where they had been.

Marius, or better said, the Creeping Chaos's avatar, had obtained a new body, made from the debris of the tower. The body barely resembled something humanoid... or anything natural at all. It was a three legged, three 'headed', four-armed swirling chaos of black ichor, rock, cables, metal, and crystal. The three 'heads' were more like overgrown tentacles, each one with a mouth full of row after row of sharp teeth, made from broken glass and metal. All three were mumbling something in different arcane languages and voices that didn't sound human, freefolk, or samoharo. The effect was confusing and migraine inducing.

"I thought we had destroyed him," Sam said. She was pretty relaxed for a situation like this.

"It seems he had a backup plan," Alex replied as he tried to stand up. He looked around but couldn't find Yaha. So, there went that idea.

"What now?" Sam asked, moving to stand next to Alex. She was already casting her True Spell, to protect them from the barrage of attacks from the monster. "This one doesn't seem to have a clear head and core to destroy."

"I also have a backup plan. I was just hoping I wouldn't have to use it," Alex said, through gritted teeth. Truth be told, he was not feeling well enough to pull it off. The only time he had tried what he was planning, it had left him knackered and with a severe warning from Fionn to not try that again. And he only had one shot to make it work.

Alex grabbed his collapsible bow with his right hand, but the gash hurt too much to hold it properly. He would have to pull the string with the right. Which meant holding the bow with his good hand... which was attached to his bad arm.

"I'm gonna need your help for this Sam," Alex said, trying to fight back the tears of pain. "I need you to keep your spell up and help me hold the bow steady. I can only do this one time and I need to keep it steady. And I'm too injured to do it alone."

Sam made a gesture and the bubble held firm, as if made from transparent metal. She stood next to him, grabbed the bow below Alex's hand and held it steady.

"You aim, I will keep it firm."

"You are not gonna ask me what I'm planning?"

"Probably something really stupid and dangerous," Sam replied with a smile. "But I trust you."

"Thanks."

Alex closed his eyes for a moment, as he pulled the string back. An arrow formed. But he didn't release. Pushing through the pain in both his arms and hands, he focused once more. The lightning had given him a temporary recharge, but it wouldn't be enough. Through the Gift, he extended his mind and pulled energy from the only two similar sources that were closing on their position: Fionn and Gaby.

Alex could have pulled energy from Sam, but she was

using all her strength to keep the bubble shield up. He could sense Fionn and Gaby close, a few blocks away. He saw the flows of energy coming from them, as they raced to reach where Alex and Sam were.

I'm sorry for this, Alex thought. He pulled the energy from them, knowing that it would weaken them for a second. Green and Blue-red rivers of energy flowed from their bodies and into the tip of the arrow. Alex then drew on the remaining energy he had inside himself and added it to the mix.

As the energy arrived, a tiny circle of light formed in front of the arrow tip. The circle grew into a ring of bright energy, taller than Alex. The ring rotated fast, creating a gap in the floor. Inside the ring, were four, smaller rings. One in the center, the size of a bike wheel. The remaining three rotated around the central ring, but inside of the larger one. It was a light mandala.

The monster, as if sensing what was happening, but unable to move because its roots were tied to the ground, redoubled its attacks, hitting the bubble shield with its arms, as the three mouths glowed, channeling energy.

"I'm gonna need for you to open the shield so the shot goes through," Alex said, almost out of breath.

"We need to be precise then," Sam replied. "On the count of three."

One of the heads descended on them. But it was cut clean off by a gust of wind. Breathing heavily, Fionn stood on a nearby terrace. Black Fang glowed bright green. He didn't look too happy. He was yelling something, but Alex couldn't hear under the constant barrage from the monster trying to break the bubble shield.

"One..."

The second head fell apart, cut in four pieces. A few meters beyond the monster, Gaby, trying to catch her breath, landed from her jump. Her face was one of concern.

"Two..."

The third head was knocked aside when a bike crashed into it. Kasumi leaped into the air and with a strike using Breaker, cut it down. She landed not far from where they were, her face covered in blood and her demonhunter armor sporting diverse fractures.

"It can't be... I'm a GOD!" The central head exclaimed as it fell and burst into flames. The rest of the body followed as Joshua, still bearing marks of burned flesh on his face and arms directed the Beast, now a combination of shadow and flames, to attack the monster at its base.

"Three!"

Alex released the arrow. As it flew, the rings collapsed into its tip and a single, thin ray of golden light crossed the sky towards the stars, splitting the clouds and the atmosphere. The Figaro avoided being hit by the beam by a few meters. A few seconds later, a sonic boom followed. In front of Alex and Sam, Marius, also known as Typhon, the Dark Father, the avatar of the Creeping Chaos, stood immobile, its arms hanging at its side, powerless, with a small perforation piercing his neck. The other side of the small perforation was a large crater that had obliterated his back, taking down the true head and core in a single shot.

"Did we kill him?" Sam asked, as the bubble shield disappeared.

"He was an avatar. So, I guess yes," Alex replied. The odd sensation in his chest was growing.

"That was an impressive feat."

"Not sure... I can do... it again," Alex gasped for air. The odd sensation became an oppressive weight on his chest. It was similar to the sensation he had during an anxiety attack but multiplied by ten. And it scared him.

"You don't look well," Sam said, her face betraying concern.

If she looks this worried, then this is bad, Alex thought. Then he said. "I'm not feeling well."

His eyelids felt heavy and the world around him was spinning out of control. He was tired. Really tired. He just wanted to close his eyes and sleep. In the distance, he saw the Figaro landing and wondered if there was a comfortable place to sleep there.

"Alex! Stay with me. Don't close your eyes."

"You know what's funny?" Alex mumbled as he collapsed into the floor. "I... I never had the chance... to visit KorbyWorld."

The last part came out as a whisper.

"Stay with me and I promise that I will take you there."

But Alex was too tired to keep his eyes open. So, he closed them.

†††

Alex lay face up on the ground, unresponsive. Sam was kneeling next to him and Kasumi ran towards him. She lost her balance on the slippery surface, sliding gracefully the last few meters. She immediately placed two fingers on his neck, to the side of his windpipe, to check for a pulse. It was the only accessible place given that Alex's wrists were a mess from several injuries and the badly damaged cast. She counted the beats. They were irregular and becoming fainter by the second. She ripped off his armor vest and placed her left hand on top of her right, over his chest, and started to compress. Kasumi began muttering a popular song whose rhythm was the same needed for the compression.

"What's going on?" Sam asked, her voice shaking.

"He is entering into cardiac arrest." Kasumi replied. Sweat from her brow mixed with the blood stains in her face. She was starting to feel exhausted; her arms were on fire as she kept compressing. "But it won't be enough, we need a defibrillator to reestablish his pulse."

"Does the Figaro have a defibrillator?" Sam asked Sid, who was running towards them, alongside Yokoyawa. By then, Fionn and Gaby were next to them as well.

"Yes. But it won't work on him," Sid said, looking down. "His body can withstand an electric discharge. He once used the defibrillator as a party shock box."

"Can you cast lightning on him?" Gaby asked.

"With his injuries and being unconscious, he is more likely to get burned," Kasumi interjected. "We would need a second body to absorb the excess."

Fionn knelt next to Alex, placed his left hand on Alex's left side and his right over Alex's chest, below the collarbone.

"Kasumi, move. Sam, do it," Fionn ordered.

"Dad?"

"Look, we are wasting time! I'm the only one that can survive being hit by lightning. So, do it! Everyone, get away from here and cover your eyes!"

As everyone ran to take cover, Sam closed her eyes and whispered. "Fasd'an."

Blinding light seared through Kasumi's eyelids, and the crash of thunder shook her body even with her hearing aids turned off. The air was instantly filled with the smell of burnt flesh. She opened her eyes to see Fionn's body covered with burns and blisters, half of his hair missing. Fionn didn't move as green sparkles flowed around him, his body already regenerating. Kasumi ran back and knelt to check for a pulse, and shook her head. "Do it again, Sam!"

"But, Dad..."

Fionn's look quelled any further discussion. Kasumi moved back again and turned away as a second bolt hit Fionn.

"Don't you dare die on me kid. Again!"

A third flash lit up the sky, filling the air with ozone and burned flesh.

Alex's body jerked, and he opened his eyes wide. He gasped for air.

"Third time's the charm," Fionn said, finally letting Alex go and sitting back. Kasumi turned on her aids and approached to check his pulse. It seemed to be returning to normal, but she didn't want to take any risk.

"We need to take him to a hospital!" Kasumi yelled. "And a freefolk healer would be useful too."

"Get him to the Figaro," Sid said. "We will call the Freefolk delegation on the way."

"You know?" Alex whispered to Kasumi, as Yokoyawa lifted him. "If this were one of those oldie movies, this is where the shot would open wide, credits would roll and a power ballad would blast, with us not knowing if the hero made it or not."

"Luckily for you, this is not a movie, so stop talking."

Alex smiled as Yokoyawa took him into the Figaro, with Sid leading the way.

Sam approached Kasumi as the Figaro took off.

"What did he say?" Sam asked.

"Something about oldie movies and power ballads. Does that make sense to you?" Kasumi was confused about the whole thing. She grew even more confused as Sam tried to contain a laugh that seemed more a release of stress than of amusement.

"He has this habit of narrating things as if he was in one of those schlocky action movies from when we were kids."

"Is that amusing?"

"Now it is," Sam replied. "Because it means that hopefully, he will recover."

Kasumi saw the Figaro speeding up into the air, as Fionn—still regenerating from his burns—Gaby, and Joshua examined what remained of the monster's body. It was turning to dust. Not far from there, stuck in a piece of concrete, she saw Yaha, shinning.

And Kasumi felt herself breathing again.

Chapter 19
Gatherings

The night sky was clear, allowing the stars, the Round and the Long Moons, and even the rings around Theia to be seen by the naked eye. The air was cold, so much so that Harland's breath formed small clouds every time he exhaled. He wondered how Fionn could walk around with relatively few warm clothes. At first, he thought it was due to the Gift, but Gaby was shivering as much as he was and she was wearing a thick winter jacket and cold weather clothes. Sid resembled a walking pile of clothes rather than a samoharo. In contrast, the freefolk walked around with comparatively nothing on.

I guess the freefolk have grown used to this place, Harland thought. This was the third time in his life he had been invited to a 'Gathering of Voices', the reunion of elders and notables of the Freefolk, where important matters were discussed. This was the second time in less than a year. For Gaby, it was the second one, while for Sid it would be the first time. Actually, probably it would be the first time ever that a samoharo had been invited to one. This Gathering would be a historical event, and Harland, as the student of history and lore that he was, felt honored to bear witness. All of them had arrived separately, to keep unwanted eyes off the final meeting point.

The place, called the Mistlands by the Freefolk, was well inside the forested region north of the Scar. This was where the freefolk had retreated centuries ago after the fall of their kingdom and where they had dwelled, hidden from the rest of the planet. The aurora borealis gave the night a charming feeling, as they trekked through the Grey Owl Forest. The ground was covered by snow, concealing any trace of a path. And yet Fionn and Sam were leading them with ease through the densely packed forest. The trees seemed to be surrounded by fireflies, though whenever Harland got too close to a pack of them, they simply vanished and reformed once he moved away. Through the dark, Harland saw lights in the distance, torches and lamps carried by other groups, surely freefolk traveling to the same place they were going.

"Why couldn't we fly to the meeting place?" Sid complained. Harland had to repress a laugh, as he had to admit that he found amusing how miserable Sid looked under the multiple layers of clothes.

"This forest is tightly packed with trees," Gaby said, breaking the silence. "More than it should be by nature. How did that happen? Magick?"

"Something simpler," Sam replied. "This is holy ground."

"Holy ground?" Sid said, and then his eyes opened wide in realization. "As in a graveyard?"

"Exactly," Fionn smiled. "Every tree grows where a freefolk is buried. When we die, we put a humbagoo tree seed inside the navel of the deceased. That way the tree feeds from the naturally decomposing body, while allowing contact with the final place of our souls. In this way we honor those that came before us and still commune with our ancestors and ask for their guidance, so our decisions as a community can feed from their experience. Each tree represents one of the freefolk that preceded us. It's also sustainable as it helps the forest to grow and recover from fires and logging. We need to keep the air clean."

"In a way, it's a form of immortality," Harland added. "I understand that the idea is related to the myth of the Life Tree, from where souls come from. I find interesting how many cultures in Theia have traditions for honoring their ancestors and mentions of the Life Tree myth. I wonder if there is a common source, even if the three species are different in origin."

"Are your parents buried here?" Gaby asked, changing topics.

"Yes, somewhere down that path," Fionn pointed towards a spot to the southwest. How he could pinpoint the place, was unknown, but Harland guessed that was due the spiritual connection he had just mentioned. "And before you ask, yes, Sam's too. All of them are together there, as a family."

"That's nice. I'm glad," Gaby replied. She seemed to be thinking on something else.

"What makes this meeting so special? And why does it have to be in a place so cold?" Sid asked beneath the mound of clothes covering him. "I might have warm blood, but still, this is too cold for a samoharo."

"It's the Gathering. A traditional meeting of the Free-folk elders and leaders beginning in the days of Asherah's Pilgrimage, to dicusss important matters that affect all. An essential part of our culture if you like. And it's usually in places like this because what we are gonna discuss is too important for others to hear, and no one, but the Freefolk, would be interested in attending and know how to move around this place," Fionn said with a smile.

"So, basically, you are hoping for any potential spy to be frozen to death," Sid replied, his voice dripping with sarcasm,

"Or eaten by any of the pets of the sentinels," Sam said with a grin.

"What kind of pet?" Sid asked, concerned.

"Dragonwolves," Sam replied, matter-of-factly.

"Ah! Those. How nice," Sid's voice dripped with more sarcasm.

"I'll be right back," Sam said while checking her phone. "It seems I need to go back and guide someone else to the Gathering."

† † †

The log Harland sat on was cold—no, frozen—and he tried to wrap his coat tighter. Fionn, on his left, seemed perfectly at ease, as if it was a mild summer day. Sid, under his mound of clothes, sat on Harland's right, while Gaby, shivered to the left of Fionn. Sam reappeared from the woods, guiding of all people, Yokoyawa, who looked not like a pile, but a mountain of clothes. Sam took a seat next to Gaby, while Yokoyawa slid in next to Sid. The log creaked under the weight of the massive samoharo.

"Alex?" Harland asked. He was still worried. Alex's condition, while improving by the day, was still not good. And having Yokoyawa here, who should be watching over him, gave him concern. If Alex was planning to come, the weather might affect his recovery. And if he was alone at the hospital, even if it was a small, inconspicuous one at Skarabear... there were other types of dangers lurking around.

"Doctor said that he is still too injured and weak to complete the trek here," Sam replied. "He is healing faster than a regular human, but it seems still too slow for a Gifted."

"The consequences of burning so much energy," Sid added. "Besides, with this cold, the screws and braces inserted into his arm would hurt as the Pits."

"But if Yokoyawa is here, who is keeping an eye on him?" Harland asked once more. "There are a few remaining cultists gunning for his head after you two killed their 'god'."

"Kasumi," Sam replied, her tone of voice sounding different. Harland was trying to decipher if she was concerned, relieved, or jealous. To this day, he was confused about what kind of relationship Sam and Alex had.

"I was half expecting for Joshua to be the one keeping an eye on Alex," Harland said.

"That was the plan," Sam replied. "And he was doing it. We were taking turns, but two days ago he said he had something to do and disappeared from the radar. Kasumi offered to stay while I came here, given that this is a freefolk event."

"Well," Harland said. "She is more inconspicuous than the big guy here or Joshua. And she would be the perfect bodyguard, with her own Tempest Blade and all that."

"Seems that you are considering offering her a job," Sid said.

"It's in the cards."

"Shhh! The Gathering is about to begin," Fionn said.

One by one the peripheral bonfires were put out, until only the central one remained, with the elders from each clan and the guests sitting around the massive bonfire. In turn, its flames became smaller in size, but not in brightness. Fireflies flew around, attracted by of the sweet smell from the borealis poinsettia—flowers that fed in part from the strong magick field of the Mistlands—that encircled the bonfire.

A small man, the eldest of all the leaders, stepped forward. He was slouched under the weight of probably more years than even Fionn had, and his long, braided white beard nearly touched the ground. He had large eyes, akin to the freefolk of old. His voice boomed with a force that contrasted with the seemingly frail body.

"People of the Freefolk, of the tribes that form our nation: Children of the Fireflies, Children of the Stars, Tide Riders, Cloud Dreamers, Forest Guardians, Stone Kokeshi, Snow Birds, Songmakers. We are gathered here once more in less than a year, to decide what to do next. As you know, we sent representatives to the Alliance diplomatic talks and events of great magnitude took place. The rebirth of the Titans of myth, the reappearance of the lost Iskandars, the winds of war, from humans and from the ancient enemy. So, I would ask the last son of the Wind Tribe, the Wind Chasers of the Greywolf and our staunch defender, to answer our questions," The elder looked at Fionn. "Greywolf, please rise."

Fionn stood up slowly. He left Black Fang in Harland's hands, to the surprise of many.

"I, Fionn the Greywolf, the Wind Chaser, humbly request to be allowed to answer your questions, oh great elders of my people!"

An older lady, with white and black hair and large lilac eyes spoke from her seat.

"Where is the Iskandar?" she asked. This took Harland by surprise, as he didn't expect that to be the first question.

"Still in the hospital," Fionn replied without a second thought. "We have someone keeping an eye on him while we are here."

"What's an Iskandar?" Sid whispered to Harland. "Sounds familiar."

"I believe it's the name the freefolk give to the humans descended from the first wielder of Yaha," Harland replied in hushed tones. "The one that fought alongside Asherah and your Prophet against the First Demon."

"That's why it sounded familiar," Sid said.

"Are you sure he is on our side?" The elder lady continued.

"Yes," Fionn replied. Harland had to concur. As much as Alex had these contrarian tendencies, his loyalty to Fionn and his friends would never be in question, especially after all he went through. But he could understand the reasoning behind the question. After all, having a Gifted with the oldest Tempest Blade of all on your side instead of against you was reassuring. And the freefolk seemed to be gearing up to fight a war while the rest of the three species were ignoring the signs. Harland was starting to understand why despite their current semi-nomadic status, at some point in the past, the Freefolk were the most powerful nation in the world. For they had something that humans often lacked: a strong sense of community. Harland wondered about how the samoharo would act. Millennia had passed and the rest of the world still knew little of that secretive species.

A third elder, a tall, bulky man with long, red and white strands of hair, clean shaven and wearing a modern jacket over his traditional freefolk clothes stood up. "While the representatives from Ravenstone already informed us about the events of the talks, we would like your impressions, as you have a peculiar insight that has helped our people before," he said. He had a firm voice and a demeanor that seemed to be friendly, despite his appearance of being tough as nails.

"Elders," Fionn said, looking across the bonfire to all the leaders of the Freefolk. "I would gladly share those insights, but I think there is someone here that is a keener observer of the human condition and politics, who can give us a better image of what's going on. I trust his wisdom as I trust him with my own life."

Fionn pointed to Harland.

"What? Me?" Harland replied, surprised. He felt a knot on his stomach, for it was rare that the freefolk allowed a guest into the Gatherings, rarer still for those guests to speak. If Fionn was requesting this in public, it was for one of two reasons: either he had already lobbied the issue with the elders before the actual reunion, or he had another surprise request in mind. And Harland speaking would feel less important after that.

"Yes," Fionn smiled at him. "You are far better at these things than me. That has been proven."

Harland stood tall in his meter and thirty-two centimeters. Next to Fionn, he seemed no taller than a child. And yet the words from the Goddess resonated in his head.

Your height or your physical attributes don't define your worth. It's the size of your heart and the strength of your will. What you decide to do with your life is what defines who you are.

Harland drew a deep breath.

"Ahem... well, yes," he began. "To put it simply. The old Free Alliance is no more. An Alliance does still exist, and it is stronger than before, as the Kuni and the Samoharo have agreed to join. But the region of the Straits has decided to remain neutral for the time being. And some of the southern city states of the Ionis continent might split during the upcoming months, to form their own power bloc below the Redstone Mountains. Portis may eventually join them, causing problems with sea trade."

"These are concerning developments, especially in light of recent events, the tovainar prophecies, the titans' rebirth, and the presence of the avatar of the Creeping Chaos..." the third elder said, as he stroked his chin.

"Yes, it is," Harland replied, raising his voice. "I won't sugarcoat my words. We have to prepare for a war. A different kind of war, less overt, more insidious. Ancient enemies seem to be behind the scenes. And if the Creeping Chaos was here, the Golden King won't be far behind. I'm confident that, based on recent events and the research that the Greywolf and the Goldenhart have carried out, that the Golden King's avatar is behind the actions of bigots such as the New Leadership party and the attacks on your settlements. Which proves that certain members of my own species have been corrupted."

"And where do you stand?" The first elder asked, looking straight into Harland's eyes. Harland held the gaze.

"With those that fight for the living, those of free will.

This is not a fight of political factions. This is a fight for the survival of all. So far only the first shots have been fired and we were lucky to have stopped them from becoming a growing menace. But we won't be so lucky every time, so we have to be prepared," Harland sighed, pinching the bridge of his nose. "Look, no one likes the idea of war less than me. I don't enjoy the idea of a large-scale conflict between nations, or against incursions after incursions, or a secret war. But this time we have an advantage: we know they are coming. And because of that, we took the liberty to set some plans of our own in motion, setting a base in Skarabear and its other, hidden half within your lands. Dawnstar of the Wind Tribe was nothing if not foresighted and left us with something to start with already. Of course, if you let us continue."

A heavy silence fell over the place. Harland looked around, and only saw long faces, concerned looks and perhaps, hints of fear. He couldn't blame them. These were dire suggestions.

"Thank you for your candor," the first elder said. "This is a topic that the elders of each tribe will have to discuss with their own and decide..."

"Regarding that," Fionn interrupted. "Two things: one, we will have to decide soon."

"We?" The second elder said. "Greywolf, you might be a hero for our people, you might even have managed in the recent talks to get most of our original territory south of the Scar, including the island where Ulmo's capital one stood, but you are not an elder."

"That's the second thing: I request the permission of the Gathering to restart the Wind Chasers. The Wind tribe has been dormant for ages. Aside from myself and my daughter, there are no more members to it. Thus, as the oldest surviving member of the tribe, I ask those that speak for our ancestors to allow me to recreate the tribe. To give it a new beginning."

"What if no other freefolk wants to join?" The third elder asked. "Not everyone will choose to leave their own tribe, and if what your friend said is right, each tribe will need the support of every member."

"I'm not asking for freefolk to leave their tribes of origin. They are welcome of course, but not required," Fionn said. He raised his voice, allowing his words to be heard around the whole forest. "No. I'm asking to be allowed to revive one of our oldest, almost forgotten traditions. Long in the past, the Freefolk were outcasts looking for a home. And we accepted other outcasts to join our ranks, including non-freefolk. Including my human father."

"And that spelled the doom for your tribe back then." The second elder replied.

"The Silverblade Tribe was a sad part on our history, they only sought an excuse to grab territory. Besides," Fionn flashed his wolf's smile. "I want to see who is brave enough to take on the persons I want to adopt into my tribe."

"Who are you proposing?" The first elder asked. The third elder, the one that seemed younger than the rest was smiling as well. Harland suspected that the old man already knew about the proposed new members.

"For starters, those who have fought in the recent past to defend our people," Fionn replied, pointing with his right open hand to Harland and the rest of their group. "My human friends, the Iskandar, samoharo outcast, the Kuni warrior and even the man called Joshua."

"The tovainar?" The first elder seemed taken aback. Not that Harland could blame him. If he was honest, even he was surprised at Fionn's change of heart.

"Ex-tovainar," Fionn said. "One that took down a Titan on his own."

"We could make an exception for the Little Great Man, the Goldenhart, and the Samoharo Outcast, as they have proven to be true friends of the freefolk. The Ravenstone academia can back their request. But who can vouch for the Iskandar, the Kuni and the ex-tovainar, as they are not here?" The first elder said. Harland wasn't fond of the nickname bestowed upon him, but he wasn't going to interrupt Fionn to change that. There would be time for that later.

"I will vouch for them," Fionn said, defiantly. He stood so tall that Harland thought the rest of the freefolk seemed a bit cowed before his friend. Then again, Fionn was a living legend for his own people and many in Ionis.

"No offense, Greywolf," The second elder said. "As we recognize your services and sacrifices for our people. But tradition dictates that only an elder can vouch for a person. And you are not an elder yet."

"Then make me an elder," Fionn replied.

"You can't ask for that, it is given, not requested. An elder..." the first elder explained.

"Yeah, I know, tradition," Fionn interrupted, not willing to take a no for an answer. Harland knew that Fionn's plans hinged in part of getting everyone status that would allow them to move freely if things became hostile within the Emerald Island. "But new challenges require new traditions. Asherah and Yahel, Kary and Goel, and Black Fang have taught us that."

"It could be argued that, yes," the first elder replied. "But you are requesting to recreate a tribe with a majority of non-freefolk. Who can assure us that you and they will uphold the traditions of our people, the very things that have allowed us to survive through the ages against all odds? You haven't even done the Pilgrimage. You might be a hero for many of our people, but you are not exactly the most observant of our ways."

"That's true," Fionn replied, hanging his head. Then he looked up once more. Harland noticed that there was a faint green glow in Fionn's irises. "But as I said, new circumstances require new ways. I'm not saying to eschew the tradition, I'm asking you to make adjustments and support my proposal."

Fionn paused. Then he said something Harland never expected to hear him say. Because while Fionn usually was confident but not to the point of ego, he rarely bragged about his deeds.

"I think I have more than earned the right after all the sacrifices and wars I've fought for our people. I won't leave this place until my request is fulfilled."

Fionn was dead serious as the glow in his irises became more intense. The air filled with a pungent, sharp smell, not unlike the one left by one of Alex's electrified arrows.

Voices and arguments broke out all over the place, some of surprise, some of menace. A part of the Freefolk agreed with Fionn, others didn't agree with the threat and the posturing by Fionn. A third group seemed too confused to take a position. Harland found himself clutching Black Fang for dear life, worried that this would end in a fight or worse, the breaking of the freefolk union. And that would be a bad thing. He wanted to support Fionn's claim, but there were also the practicalities of keeping the Freefolk united. The third elder seemed to be on Fionn's side, while the second yelled that she was dead set against it. The other elders were more or less split along those lines, while the first elder seemed to remain neutral.

If Harland recalled his—admittedly—limited knowledge of freefolk tradition, the only way Fionn would get the support of the Gathering would be if the Dragonking or Queen in turn took his side, as their vote counted more due to their prowess with magick. The role had been created for Asherah when she became the first leader of the Freefolk and had later evolved into the prime magus of Ravenstone. But there hadn't been a replacement since Byron killed Tharvol last year. That left only one person that might sway the tide. Harland prayed under his breath. While a follower of Kaan'a—the universal spirit—rather than gods of the freefolk, he knew that at least one of said gods was watching over them...

"He has my support!" A voice broke the impasse. "For who is more elder than I, Mekiri the Great!"

Thunder and lightning cracked in the background, an aurora of light crossed the sky, as the small magus with the body of a little girl, rabbit ears, green poncho, and a red and black mane of hair, walked towards the bonfire, helped by her staff.

"There is no rainstorm in sight." Sid whispered to Harland, while looking around for signs of clouds. "She just invoked the lightning out of the thin air."

"The perks of her being who she is," Harland replied in hushed tones, unsure that Sid had caught the double meaning of his comment. As Mekiri walked past them she winked at

Harland, who slightly shook his head, trying to stifle a smile. Mekiri emanated the same aura he had felt that day at the observation deck. He now knew it hadn't been a daydream.

"She sure likes to amp the dramatics of her entrance," Sid mumbled.

"Venerable one, we didn't expect your arrival," the first elder said.

"No one expects the Great Librarian!" Mekiri exclaimed, silencing the few remaining voices still whispering in the background.

"Does she need to yell every answer?" Sid whispered again.

"No, I don't need to, Sid of the samoharo. I choose to." Mekiri winked at Sid this time and replied in a low-pitched voice. "It's funnier that way."

Mekiri stood next to Fionn, hit him softly with her staff in the stomach and smiled at him.

"I vouch for Fionn to become an elder, to create his own tribe and I vouch for either the ex-tovainar or the Iskandar. Heh, I vouch for both of them if needed. My vote counts for as much."

"But... but... tradition," the second elder stuttered.

"Bah!" Mekiri exclaimed, looking at the elders with fire in her eyes. "If you lot were such sticklers to tradition as you said, there would be a Dragonqueen sitting here right now. But you have postponed the election for who knows what fears. And since there is no Dragonqueen, the Ravenhall librarian, which is me by the way, takes the role as the closest to the Trickster Goddess. And I have it on good authority that she once told Asherah that traditions can evolve, change, be created anew. The nature of the freefolk is mutable and adaptable. It's in our veins. I get that you are fearful to admit humans and samoharos into our fold. But we have been adding humans to our ranks for ages and the samoharo are not that different from us. Why not start with those that have proven themselves as friends of the freefolk? Who have shed blood defending us?"

"We can see that with the Iskandar. But the ex-tovainar? He was created to destroy us," the first elder replied.

"And yet he rebelled against that, forged his own path, and his actions through the years have kept others safe, even at the risk of his own life. Don't we owe him at least the consideration? If the Greywolf has showed us anything for more than a century, it is our actions and not our birth that define who has the right to be one of us. And whoever wants to deny him a hard earned right, will have to duel me with their best spells."

Mekiri hit the ground with her staff and sparks jumped around. She smiled and looked around. Her smile frightened Harland, for it was unsettling. Long gone was the friendly grin. This one was even more imposing than Fionn's wolf smile. Harland felt compelled to stand and walk next to Fionn and Mekiri. He handed Black Fang to Fionn and muttered to his friend.

"We are living in history."

"Take it from me," Fionn replied with a somber tone. "The tricky thing about living in history, is surviving it."

† † †

It was almost dawn when the debate was resolved, and the Gathering concluded. Fionn had obtained what he came for. And like that, Gaby found herself being a newly anointed member of the freefolk tribe, the unofficial matriarch of the Wind Chasers, who formed the Wind tribe. Someone had even murmured that her new position meant that the Greywolf was planning to ask her to become his heartmate, whatever that meant. The whole thought made her feel butterflies in her stomach. But in the back of her head, Gaby felt a pang of guilt.

As Fionn and Sam led the group back to the Figaro, Gaby slowed her pace. Her stomach was in a knot as she wondered how to tell Fionn what was on her mind. He was the first person she wanted to tell, for a myriad of reasons, that she was planning to leave and pursue a personal project. Since that argument with her father, she has been questioning herself about one thing: who she truly was. Gaby wasn't happy to admit that the man had a point, but since then she was wondering what she truly wanted to do with her life. Traveling around with Fionn has been amazing, with adventures full of fun, love, and discovery. But a part of her always returned to those afternoons, playing with Pamela, Freddie and Scud, after training with Sam. It was during those few days, composing and playing music in front of a live audience, even if it was just the few regulars at a small pub, that had made her feel as alive as having adventures alongside Fionn.

And damn, that track sounded epic on the Kyôkatô city's sound system, Gaby thought. And if she was lucky to have the means to afford this project and support this new band, then why not take the opportunity, at least before the imminent conflict that Fionn was expecting, came to happen? But Fionn was the reason she was still stopping herself from doing that. It would mean leaving him during an important time, when he would need her help. And her Gift was a responsibility. One that she had finally embraced.

Can I be that selfish? Gaby questioned herself. *Is it actually selfish to follow your heart's desires? Even when two of those desires seem to be opposing each other?*

Her heart and mind were torn in two.

"Penny for your thoughts?" Fionn said, breaking her reverie. He was smiling at her. Sometimes Gaby wondered if his smiles were only for her, as they were an uncommon sight. And yet they warmed her heart in the cold night.

Gaby remained silent for a minute. She took a deep breath. There wouldn't be a better moment to discuss this with Fionn. "Fionn, there is something I have to tell you," Gaby said.

"I kinda feel I know what it's about," Fionn replied. His smile was still present, but there was a hint of sadness in his voice.

"Look, you know I love travelling with you, helping people, having adventures," Gaby said. "But the past few days have given me time to reflect on some things, some issues I need to solve by myself. I want to help you with whatever you are planning to do at Skarabear. But I really need to do this. Otherwise I will regret it all my life, always wondering what it could have been."

Gaby waited for Fionn's reply. He also took a minute or

two to think, playing with a strand of hair that was falling over her face. "I understand," Fionn finally replied. "It's fine, don't worry. I'm still here for you. We will still be together, even if we are not in the same place."

"Do you?" Gaby was taken aback. She had expected him to argue with her—something that happened occasionally, but usually about where they would eat or sleep if they were on the road—but not this reply.

Am I disappointed that he is not fighting me on this? Gaby thought.

"Sure." Fionn said, calmly. "Take it from me. I know what it's like to have issues to solve on your own. And my only interest is for you to be happy, to not have any regrets of things left undone."

"Are you sure? You don't need me here to coordinate things and train people?" Gaby pressed on.

"Of course, I need you," Fionn replied with a laugh. "I always do. You're the best thing about me. I love you, and you know it. I never thought I could feel love again after losing Izia, but here we are. And I'm thankful that life has allowed me to be with you. But because I love you, I know you need to do this, otherwise you will always be second guessing yourself. And part of loving someone is giving them the space and support to grow into the person they want to be. So, go ahead and do what you always do: kick ass. We all heard that track. I know your musical project will be awesome and I want to see it come to pass and enjoy seeing you working for it. Life is more than just duty. Life is meant to be lived."

"You know this is neither a goodbye nor a break up, right?" Gaby asked, as her heartbeats accelerated.

"I know, this is just a 'see you soon.'" Fionn winked and then hugged her. "I'm gonna miss you every second though, so don't get annoyed if I call you every day."

"Thank you for understanding," Gaby said, inhaling slowly, enjoying the warmth of the embrace and his smell, combined with that from the trees.

"Hey, we are more than a team," Fionn replied, breaking the embrace and looking at her. Gaby blushed. "We are family. However, I need you to promise me one thing."

"Of course."

"I want a signed copy of your first recording," Fionn said. "I'm an old-fashioned guy, I don't like streaming music. I like my physical microdisk copies."

Gaby never wanted to kiss Fionn more than at that moment. Then, as her mind took her to the image of a microdisk cover, she realized something.

"You can have as many as you want. There is only one tiny problem," Gaby grimaced.

"Which is?" Fionn asked, confused.

"I still don't have a name for the band," Gaby shrugged, flashing her crooked smile.

"I'm sure it will come to mind soon. I admire the way you take charge of things," Fionn smiled as he hugged her once more and they looked at the stars above.

"By the way," Gaby asked. "What's a heartmate?"

Chapter 20
Here is to Us

Sam had been waiting for hours for Alex to finally be released from the hospital. Alex had been admitted to a private hospital with ties to the Foundation. It was the only place where his peculiar condition might have been treated without raising too many eyebrows. And after a few months, they finally allowed him to continue his recovery at home. That was why she was there, to pick him up and take him home.

Everybody had wanted to be there, but in light of the recent events and the eclectic collection of characters, they had decided against it, for it would attract far too much attention. Thus, Sam only visited from time to time, while Yokoyawa kept guard at the hospital, just in case. Besides, it would be better if the rest attended to more pressing matters, Sam had argued. In reality, she wanted to spend some time alone with Alex. No one had opposed her on the matter... well, perhaps her dad would have, but neither Gaby nor Harland gave him a chance to oppose it.

Impatient, Sam got out of the car, the vintage one that Gaby had lent her and was currently parked in the employee lot of the hospital. It was more practical for her to drive than use the warp trains: less people and her 'magick allergy' would not manifest on the road back to Mercia. She leaned against the passenger door. The wait wouldn't be so bad, if her hands didn't itch so much. The burns from holding Yaha healed nicely, leaving no scars. But they were in that annoying stage where the skin still itched. The green leaf balms she had been using had soothed the mild pain, and she was wearing a pair of leather driving gloves. But the need to scratch was getting on her nerves.

To the Pits with it, I'm gonna go in to see what's delaying him so much, she thought. But the door opened at that moment. A male nurse was holding the door open, as a female doctor and Alex came out. The doctor was saying something to Alex, but Sam couldn't hear them completely. Alex only nodded and looked at Sam, smiling. Alex and the doctor walked towards her.

Sam's heart broke looking at him. How come no one had noticed the level of punishment Alex had put himself through? Sam mentally kicked herself.

Alex was walking, with the help of a pair of crutches. He was thin. Really thin. Using the Gift to the extent he had must have burned not only fat but probably started to eat the muscle. No wonder he needed the crutches. He still had some band aids on his face and the right hand, the one that had held Yaha's blade, was still using the yellow bandage Sam had improvised for him from her t-shirt. Although it was clean and the edges had been stitched to keep it from unraveling.

Leave it to him, the king of nostalgia, to keep that thing around, Sam thought. As corny as it may have been, she found the detail endearing.

"I hope you are not expecting me to drive that thing," Alex joked. "I couldn't even kick a ball. I don't think I can push a pedal yet."

"Don't exaggerate," Sam replied, rolling her eyes. "You are not that weak or else the doctor wouldn't have signed your release. Although you are right, you won't drive this thing. You don't even know how to do it!"

"Foiled again by my lack of expertise driving a car!"

"Get in, we have a long road back," Sam said, while helping Alex to get into the car and closing the door.

"Three hours is not that long," Alex quipped.

"At some point we have to stop for food and a toilet break," Sam replied as she took her place behind the wheel, put her shades on and started the electric engine.

"Good point."

† † †

The ride through the red cedar and maple forests from Saint Lucy to Mercia had been uneventful for the most part. Aside from the occasional slow-moving lorry or the fae floating alongside the roads, while avoiding the Paidragh lamps, the road had been clear. The advantage of most people using the faster, and theoretically safer, warptrain.

"They don't know what they are missing though," Sam said aloud, forgetting for a second that she had a copilot. Alex had been quiet for most of the trip, falling into a light slumber from time to time.

"What was that?" Alex asked, opening his eyes. He took a deep breath, inhaling the clean air and smiling. "I love the smell of woods after a rain."

"I was thinking how people miss these views by taking the warptrain."

"For most people it's faster, and thus more convenient," Alex replied, trying to find a comfortable spot on the seat. "Besides, you never know what creature might be lurking on the open fields. And while most are animals in search of a meal or a place to rest, the ones that are mutated, or the clockwork golems, are dangerous. Not everyone can travel with someone as powerful as you."

"True. And while flattery won't get you anywhere with me," Sam turned to Alex for a brief moment, smiling. "You are right. Technology is that convenient."

"The thing is that I agree with you. We tend to miss the stuff that makes life worth living for. Or in our case, what give us a reason to fight. And to try to make it out alive," Alex said, moving his right hand in an arc, towards the landscape.

"Oh, my my, aren't you the philosopher now?" Sam laughed. It warmed her heart to see her friend back to his old quipping self. Maybe he only had lost the extra fat and muscle. But deep down, there was something worrying her. And she wanted to talk about it. She only needed an opening.

"Well, when you have not much to do between physiotherapy and being stuck in a bed with few visitors and a fewer TV channels, you get a lot of time to think about things. I even found a way to fix my Ph.D. dissertation, which will involve arcanotech, smart material, and proper magick to create portable armor that works with the residual energy we generate when we use the Gift. And if Andrea helps me to solve the power source issue, it could work for demonhunters as well... Sorry, I'm getting too technical. I was bored."

"You know all of us wanted to visit all the time. But the hospital didn't let us after the first week. Apparently, our presence was disturbing the recovery of the other patients. So they restricted the visits. Aside Yokoyawa, of course, who offered to be on guard duty at all times. It seems that killing the avatar of a god got some of its followers really mad at you."

"I know," Alex replied with a faint smile. "I'm not complaining, just explaining."

He shuffled again in the seat.

"What's wrong?" Sam asked him.

"The problem with shedding so much weight at an unnaturally fast pace is that you end up without buttocks. So, no matter how comfortable the seat, I can feel my bones touching it. And it's painful," Alex explained, shuffling a third time, until he found a spot that seemed to be less uncomfortable.

"I guess it will pass once you recover some weight and muscle," Sam said. "But we can buy one of those plush donuts in the next town. It's almost time to eat and I have a strict list of indications about keeping your calorie intake constant until you return to the lovable marshmallow you were before."

"Loveable marshmallow?" Alex raised an eyebrow. "Who are you and what did you do with my friend?"

"You are such an idiot," Sam replied, trying to stifle a laugh. "I'm gonna turn on the radio if you don't mind."

"Be my guest."

"Mr. Funktastic now recommends this classic song of a decade ago 'What the Voice Carried Away' by the synth pop group Late Thursday..."

"You can change stations if you want," Alex said.

"Nah, it's ok. The song ain't half bad. It actually reminds me a bit of what Gaby sings in the shower," Sam replied.

Alex gave Sam a quizzical look.

"Remember, I stayed at her house for months. I heard

things," Sam said, slowly shaking her head.

"Oh, I know, trust me, I know. But I thought you hated the kind of music I usually listen to."

"It doesn't matter. If that makes the trip more comfortable for you, then it's okay."

"Thank you."

"Maybe you need to take another nap. I will wake you up when we make the stop."

"Fine."

Sam would never admit it to Alex, but she actually enjoyed his kind of music. Just not all the songs.

†††

Sam came out of the small coffee shop with a tray, on which two sodas and three shellburgers were resting. Alex was seated at an outside table, on his brand-new plush donut. It barely covered his rear, but apparently made him feel less uncomfortable, judging from his relaxed posture. Sam placed the tray on the table and sat next to Alex.

"Three burgers?" Alex asked surprised.

"One is mine, the other two are yours. I can't say I don't envy you. You can eat almost anything."

"Not necessarily. I can't go crazy because my wild metabolism is not one hundred percent back. Right now, I'm not transforming everything I eat into energy. I don't want to kill myself by overeating."

"Says the guy that used to carry chocolate bars along with his arrow cartridges."

"Maybe I want to take better care of myself."

"Since when?"

"I already told you. Being in the hospital, going to therapy, makes you reflect upon a lot of things.

"About that, there is something I want to discuss with you."

"I was wondering how long it would take you to mention that."

"So..."

"No offense Sam, but that's something I don't want to talk about right now. I will. Trust me. We will talk about a lot of things. But I'm not ready yet."

"I don't want you to bottle things up again."

"I appreciate the concern, and I swear I'm not bottling things up. I'm just not ready. I... I need to put things in order inside my head first. That's why the doctor made appointments for me to see a therapist back at the university. I have mandatory sessions for the next few months. And I will have to talk a lot. Right now, I just want a friend to keep me company."

"Fine. But you won't escape that talk. You only get a reprieve."

"Deal. Now tell me what's going on with the others."

"Not much. Harland has a new bodyguard: Kasumi."

"That's great!"

"He is smart, between his actions at the conference, the increasing importance of the Foundation, and the secret project he has with my dad at Skarabear, Harland needs someone capable of protecting him from uncommon threats. I think he is planning to move the whole Foundation to Skarabear."

"Makes sense. What about Joshua?"

"I think only Kasumi truly knows. No one has seen him in a while."

"It doesn't matter, when we need a hand, I know he will be there."

"How do you know?"

"It takes one to know one."

"He has the same compulsion you have of getting into trouble?"

"Something like that." Alex avoided her gaze. Sam decided to not press. Just let him be for a while. She started to eat a burger. Alex looked at the table but didn't move.

Sam glared at him, tilting her head and pointing towards the burgers. She felt her annoyance releasing the familiar energy rush of the Gift. Her irises glowed lilac. It was an intimidating effect. Alex sighed and grabbed one. They ate in silence until Sam finished her meal.

"By the way, who is your therapist? Do I know them?" Sam asked, as she cleaned her lips with a napkin

"You won't believe it," Alex replied. "Yokoyawa."

"What? A samoharo therapist?"

While she wasn't as close to the samoharo as Alex or Gaby, Sam had spent a lot of time lately with him, at the hospital, and had found Yokoyawa's demeanor oddly calm. Meditative even. He acted more poet than warrior, which could work in favor for Alex's needs. A stark contrast with the always complaining Sid, who by the way, was going to blow a gasket when he heard who Alex's therapist was. That image made Sam laugh.

"Believe it or not, Sid was the one who suggested it."

"You are joking."

"No. And don't ask me why. I learned long ago that trying to understand the motives of a samoharo is pointless. But apparently, Yokoyawa is a certified therapist. And realistically speaking, there aren't many people that would understand my particular situation."

Alex was right. Understanding a samoharo's way of thinking was nigh impossible. Of the three species, they were the most alien of all. But if Sid had been the one to suggest his so much despised relative as the one to help Alex, it was because he was confident it was the best idea. After all, Sid was fiercely protective of his friends.

As long as it worked.

† † †

The temperature was dropping as the sun was setting upon the horizon. That didn't scare away the visitors to KorbyWells, the commercial area of KorbyWorld. It was packed with visitors, including several samoharos, which was something new. There was an endless stream of people coming in and out of the park. Sam could have sworn that she had seen a stall selling t-shirts with her family's crest, the running grey dragonwolf. And one copying the homemade logo Alex had designed for his hooded vest for the competition. She would have to make sure that notoriety didn't go to his head.

Sam was waiting for Alex to return with a cup of mocha coffee for her. That had been 20 minutes ago. She tried to be understanding. Although in four months Alex had recovered a lot of weight and muscle, he was still in recovery and weak enough that he wasn't able to string his bow yet or walk very fast without getting winded. It would take him another four months to regain his full strength.

Thank Heavens for the Gift's enhanced metabolism.

Sam rubbed her neck and stretched her legs. While she preferred traveling in the Figaro, for her "magick allergy issues", the fact was that the ship still wasn't as comfortable as Sid claimed. She would have to talk with Harland so he could make sure the Figaro Mark III had improved seats.

She was sitting on a bench in front of a small stage where a local band was playing that old song that had been on the radio after she picked up Alex from the hospital. She paid attention to the lyrics. It felt somehow appropriate to the current situation. If Sam didn't know better, she could swear Gaby had somehow composed the song and sent it back in time. That was the kind of divergent thoughts she had when waiting. Right now, it was time to enjoy, and perhaps, have that serious talk with Alex. Why was it that men were so complicated when it came to talking about their feelings?

She sighed. They had arrived not long ago at the park. Only Sam, Alex, and Sid had come. Harland and Kasumi would meet them here. But Fionn and Gaby had declined. "Too much attention." Fionn had said, "Let's allow Alex and you enjoy the park as it should be."

"I have a commitment with the band that day, but I will catch up," Gaby had said.

Sam really missed her best friend. But at least she would have the chance to spend more time with Kasumi, and get to know her better. After being voted the winner of the Chivalry Games by the rest of the contestants, Kasumi had used her influence to get them VIP passes for the park.

However, Harland and Kasumi hadn't arrived yet, Sid was nowhere to be seen and Alex appeared to have gone to grind up the coffee beans himself. Sam was about to get up when the security alarm blared. A masked man ran towards her, carrying a black bag that was probably full of stolen goods. She moved to the side, extended her leg, and tripped him.

The man got up, pissed at her. He took out a knife from

his jacket and pointed it towards her.

How quaint, she thought and smiled. Beating the guy would be a good way to deal with her frustrations. She didn't get the chance though. A soda can hit the man right in the side of the head, knocking him over a second time. Sam could have sworn that the can released tiny electric sparks. She rolled her eyes.

"I think Alex needs to change his definition of vacation," she muttered under her breath. The man, dazed by the hit, tried to stand up. But Sam kicked him hard in the ribs, clearly knocking the air out of him.

"Don't even think about it," Sam told the man. She allowed herself to release a bit of the Gift, just enough to make her irises glow. The effect was intimidating for regular people, and worked like a charm, as the man stood down till the security guards arrived to take him away.

"Miss, are you ok?" One of the guards asked her.

"Yes," Sam replied with a smile, as her eyes returned to normalcy. *Just bored,* she thought.

Alex arrived moments later. He offered her coffee which was still warm, but not piping hot as she liked. He kneeled to grab the soda can and when he got up, smiled at her.

"I wouldn't open the can if I were you," Sam said. "It's probably too agitated. Although being covered in sticky soda would serve you right as punishment."

"Why do you say that?" Alex feigned being hurt, but then smiled.

"Because you should be resting," a male voice said. Sam turned around and saw Harland and Kasumi. The height difference was quite pronounced. Kasumi was eating from a tub of ice cream. The cold apparently wasn't bothering her. No surprise there.

"This is a holiday, Alejandro. One we are giving to you by the way," Harland continued. "That means you need to rest. Not chase pretty criminals."

"I didn't chase anyone," Alex shrugged his shoulders. "I just threw a soda can. To be honest, I didn't expect I would hit him right in the head."

"So, the reason my coffee is warm instead of hot is because you chased a criminal... again... while recovering... again?" Sam sighed. The same qualities that made him endearing also made him very frustrating.

"No, the queue was way too long and... look as I said, I threw a can. I hardly call that a chase. A lucky throw perhaps..." Alex replied sheepishly.

"Lies! Lies!" Kasumi laughed. "I'm happy to see you are getting back into the saddle."

"Don't encourage him," Sam pleaded. "He hasn't fully recovered yet."

"At least he recovered his appetite," a fourth voice added. Sid had returned with his hands full of bistro sandwiches. "Thank you for ditching me at the bistro. You were meant to buy a coffee, not run after some thief!"

Alex elbowed Sid, but grimaced. He seemingly had forgotten the hard plates that covered part of the samoharo's chest.

"So, what are we gonna do now?" Kasumi asked, as she put a lid on the ice cream tub. "It's a bit late to go into the actual parks as they are gonna close in a couple of hours. Maybe hit the arcade and play some games?"

"This place closes well after midnight. Plenty of shops to visit for souvenirs you don't need..." Harland said.

"But you desire," Alex completed the sentence. "Ah! The true magick of the place: compulsive consumerism."

"Says the guy that collects toys," Sid interjected.

"Action figures," Alex noted. "Do you want me to explain the differences to you again?"

The argument seemed to increase, much to Sam's irritation. She looked around, wondering where the closest emergency exit was. Her eye caught a hot air balloon, tied to a stall. The only ride available at hand, where she would have some needed privacy. She grabbed Alex's hand and started dragging him towards the balloon.

"Let's go to that balloon ok? I heard that you can get a great view of the magick lightshow show from there.

Alex let himself be dragged by Sam. She walked fast, with the other three behind them. She could hear them muttering.

"Why do you want to ride that thing? I mean, when you have the Figaro to do that..." Sid shook his head.

Sam turned towards them and looked at Harland. She hoped that at least he would understand. The pressure she was feeling relented somewhat as she saw Harland stop and grab Sid and Kasumi by the arms.

"Let them be," Harland said. "They will be fine. We will visit that shop, alright?"

Sam mouthed a 'thank you' towards them. She felt her face turning red and turned back to continue dragging Alex. The clicks of her heels hitting the cobblestones echoed as she put space between her and Alex and the other three. She could still hear them but didn't pay any attention.

"I always worry with that kid," Sid muttered.

"He is not alone," Harland pointed. "She is with him."

† † †

As the balloon ascended, the sunset became night. Sam could see the vapor from her mouth condensing in front of her. Autumn nights could get really cold even this far south. Alex must have noticed as he stood closer to her. But always the gentleman, he kept a separation between them.

"Do you want my jacket?" he offered.

"It's okay, don't worry," Sam replied. "Besides, you are from the Straights and you're the one recovering the body fat. How come you are not shivering?"

"I guess I've been living this side of the world for so long I got used to the cold?"

Sam touched the tip of his nose. It was cold.

"You are a lousy liar. You can come closer. A hug would be welcome."

"Are you sure?"

Sam opened her eyes wide in frustration.

"Yes. I. Am."

Alex's cheeks turned bright red as he embraced her. And then she noticed that with heels, she was taller than him. It wasn't the image she had in mind. But it was comfortable. It would do. They stood there in silence. They had the hot air balloon all to themselves and the magick lightshow hadn't started yet. The view of the lights and the major landmarks of the park was breathtaking. More now that they could enjoy it without having to worry about a psychopathic cyborg. The air smelled of sea salt and fruits. She let out a long held breath of relief.

"So, you finally got us alone here, where I can't run away," Alex said, breaking the silence after a few minutes.

Sam was taken aback by that. Her mind scrambled to find a way to regain control of the situation.

"Did you know that Birm asked Andrea to marry him? A few hours ago, nonetheless!" Sam said in a hurry. In the history of heavy conversation deflection topics, she had failed miserably. Worst thing was that this had been her idea. Why was she so nervous? Was it because he had his arm around her shoulders? Right now, she would prefer to deal with the psychopathic cyborg.

"I know, I got the message about the same time you must have gotten Andrea's," Alex replied. "But that's not why you brought me here. So, spill it."

Sam gently broke the embrace and faced him. She focused on the amber coloring of his eyes. They stood there in silence again, then the sound of an explosion broke the spell. Alex's body suddenly tensed, or as much as he could considering he still had to build muscle mass back. But his eyes had the faint but unmistakable glow of the Gift.

"Relax. It was a warning shot to announce the magick lightshow."

The glow subsided. Sam wondered if it was a good idea to talk about the topic she had in mind, when it was clear that Alex was still, at least at a subconscious level, in combat ready mode. She saw him let out a depth breath and his body relaxed once more. Maybe the therapy was really working. He only needed more practice.

Sam felt her heart thumping fast inside her chest.

Here goes nothing, she thought. And then she saw him looking over the edge of the basket. He seemed more nervous than her. And then it hit her.

"After everything that happened, are you still afraid of heights?" Sam asked, incredulous. Maybe the best way to start her conversation was with another topic.

"I'm not afraid, I don't like them," Alex eyed the edge again.

"How the Pits will you enjoy a rollercoaster then?" Sam wondered.

"Because you are moving. Here we are static." Alex explained. Color left his face.

"I don't get you," Sam sighed. She shook her head.

"Don't worry. I don't get me either." Alex shrugged. He offered a half-hearted smile.

They stared at the lights of the skyline. A second warning explosion ensued. Alex barely reacted this time. Sam felt a hole in her stomach. She took a long breath and finally asked.

"How do you do it?"

"Do what?" Alex looked at her, confusion on his face.

"Keep pushing forward. I mean, you admitted to me that a part of you was trying to get yourself killed and yet at the last moment, you found a way to come back from the brink and you took down the bastard. How?" Sam asked, letting the question out in one go.

"I didn't do it alone, remember?" Alex sighed. "You helped me. It was team effort."

"That's the thing. You have said before that you are not good at teamwork," Sam explained, waiving her hand in front of her. "What changed at that moment? And how in the hell after all of that do you still keep putting yourself in risky situations? You don't have to fix every problem. You are allowed to take a break!"

Anger started to simmer inside Sam. She felt heat flushing through her body and the cold stopped bothering her.

"Okay, let's split that into parts," Alex offered, putting his hands in front of him in a defensive manner. "I keep doing what I do, because I enjoy helping others. It feels right. Yes, Big Y told me in therapy that I need to learn to not feel like I have to carry the weight of the world on my shoulders. That I can't help everyone, fix everything. But that doesn't mean that I can't try if I have the chance. Someone has too. And I have found that makes me feel better. Helping others is its own reward, I guess. As egotistical as it sounds."

Alex shrugged again as his cheeks got red. This time, there was an aura of innocence in his eyes. As far as Sam could tell, he was being honest. And that embarrassed him.

"I don't think it's necessarily egotistical, as long as you keep yourself in check instead of trying to go out in a blaze of glory," Sam replied. She closed the gap between them and looked at Alex, straight into his eyes. She felt as if she was scolding him. "Look, I'm not saying that you stop helping others. That's something I admire in you. The way you are willing to take on responsibilities that are not yours just to help. You did it when you helped with Byron, and you did it when Harland asked you to fight for him. But you are allowed to take a break, to let things go, to take care of yourself. To be taken care of. You are not alone y'know?"

"I know that. Now."

"Are you gonna answer my other question?" Sam asked, crossing her arms. She found herself tapping the floor, impatient. Her subconscious betrayed her.

Sam could feel Alex's intense gaze upon her. He smiled.

"I thought about something Fionn told me during his training from the Pits. When I asked him how he always managed to overcome the voice in your head that tells you that there is no way to keep going, he replied that the image of his family and friends being sad because he let himself get killed would spur him on. When I was facing Marius, I thought I could let go as you took him down. But the image of you being sad and pissed at me for doing that is what stirred me. Because that idea pained me."

Sam felt herself smiling at the last phrase. At last, she had confirmation of the suspicions she had had since they'd met at Ravenstone.

"Fionn told me that we are stronger than we think we are," Alex continued. "And even more if we ask for help. He had forgotten that after what had happened to Izia and Ywain but last year's adventure reminded him, and him being the teacher he reluctantly is, wanted me to avoid going that route. Big Y has explored that topic as well during our therapy sessions. Who would've thought that a samoharo warrior would be so good at therapy?"

"Maybe because he has gone through similar things? Freefolk, Human, Samoharo, we are not that different underneath," Sam replied in low voice.

"My depression bouts are something I will have to learn to deal with for the rest of my life," Alex said, turning around and focusing his gaze onto the lights of the park. He was hunched. Sam knew that was the posture he took when he felt embarrassed. "The monster inside my head is always lurking for a way to lead me to another breakdown. I'm not crazy..."

"I never said you were. Your ideas on the other hand..."

"I'm just unwell. And I'm getting help. I wish I could show you a better, different side of me. I wish I could be the person you deserve. But I'm not sure when I will be that person and I would hate myself if I dragged you down the rabbit hole when I have a bad day."

So, we are finally to be honest about that huh? Sam thought.

"Alex, I see your better side all the time. I willingly take the good days with the bad days, and you don't need to deal with the worst side alone. I can be there for you if you need help. I'm not a damsel in distress. I can take care of myself and you know it."

"Technically you are a walking WMD..."

"You are not helping yourself. As I was saying, I will be with you always. As a friend..."

"Only as a friend?

"Let me finish!" Sam punched Alex lightly on the arm. "As a friend... and as something more when you feel you are in the right place."

"Would you do that for me? Wait?"

"I'm not waiting. We are there already. You only need to realize that. Besides, how long have you waited for me to bring up the topic since you said what you said? And by the way, a deadly battle is the worst place to say what you feel."

"Fionn said it is sometimes the best place. Anyways. Around four months, one week and three days."

"And since you realized you were in love with me?" Sam said, her arms still crossed but she was smiling wide.

Alex looked up at the balloon, mumbling. He seemed to be doing calculations.

"Around a year, six months, one week, three days and sixteen hours?" Alex replied, looking at her.

"There you go. Well, you can be sure that I feel the same about you. So, you can tick that off the list of your worries." Sam replied, patting him on the arm.

"Since when did you take the leadership of this relationship?"

"I always had it. You are only catching up. Remember..."

"I'm not alone."

They remained silent for a few minutes. He was gazing at the sky while she was thinking over his words. He was right, as usual. Now she started to see why he was good at playing superhero. It was because despite the falls, all his flaws, he kept going, no matter the odds or the pain, because his heart was in the right place. Even if he was a little bit out of his mind. Maybe because he was out of his mind.

"So, to be perfectly clear, you let my coffee go cold to catch a robber?"

"And to protect others from him."

"You are unbelievable."

He replied with a smug smile. He placed his arm around her once more. "I know."

She gave him a small kiss on the cheek, leaving him stunned. He put his hand to his cheek, covering the kiss.

"What was that for? Not that I'm complaining." Alex asked.

"For being the hero of the day. "

"I need to save the day more often."

"You are still recovering, so don't get any ideas."

"What about this... she is a freefolk magi, he is a crazy archer. Together, they fight monsters..."

"Stop right there. Is this going to be another of your cheesy movie narrations?"

"Maybe..."

"Heavens!" Sam rolled her eyes.

A sharp noise, a feedback screech coming from the speakers interrupted Alex's narration. In the open-air stage below them, near the landing pad of the balloon, a band took their place in front of their instruments. A bespectacled girl took the bass, a samoharo sat at the drums, a thin guy with messy black hair stood in front of a keyboard, and then a familiar girl grabbed the other guitar. Gaby looked towards the balloon and waved. She was in full rocker regalia, with leather pants, a t-shirt, and a blue leather jacket. Her hair was styled in a 'messy' hairdo. Her left wrist was sporting a silver bracelet embossed with a dragonwolf holding an iridescent pearl in its mouth. Sam hadn't seen that bracelet before but was well aware of the meaning. She would have to talk with her dad soon. Gaby grabbed the mic in front of her and a second screech was heard. Gaby signaled something to a guy near the sound systems. Then she spoke.

"Hello!" Gaby yelled and people walking around stopped to see what was happening. A few, including Kasumi, Harland and Sid gathered around the stage.

"Some of you might know me already from the events that took place at the Chivalry Games a few months ago. Some of you, the lucky ones, don't. So, let me take this opportunity to introduce my band, 'Hildebrandtia.'"

Some of the audience yelled and clapped.

"Is that Gaby? And that's her band? The drummer is a samoharo?" Alex asked. His eyes were wide open and he was smiling.

"Yes, yes and yes. Oddly enough he is a fan of Sid. Can you believe that?" Sam replied, suppressing a laugh.

"No."

"I see some do remember me," Gaby continued. "Anyways, I want to open this show with a confession: I admit I was a bad friend because with all the events taking place at the Chivalry Games I forgot one of my best friend's birthday. And he was already going through a really bad patch. I think we can all relate because we all have been there at some point."

People said things to Gaby in jest. She laughed as she looked upwards, winking to Alex and Sam.

"I know, I know. But I'm here to fix that," Gaby continued, her voice booming through the speakers. "See, I have a surprise here, and with the help of my band mates..."

"Did you know about this?" Alex asked Sam, leaning closer to her.

"No, I'm as surprised as you are. She told me she had a gig with the band, I never suspected this was it," Sam replied, surprise in her voice. She couldn't stop smiling.

In the distance, the magick lightshow started, filling the sky with multicolored lights. Sam decided to enjoy the show and enjoy the moment. The wind gently rocked the balloon from one side to another as the show picked up intensity with the lights and explosions, illuminating the whole park. It was a great way to start a well-deserved vacation.

Gaby started to play the first few notes on her guitar, while she finished her speech.

"I wrote this song for him, for my friend, as a birthday present. To remind him that, while things change, that the past years have kicked our arses, and not everything lasts forever, at the end of the day all will be worth it, as long as we remember one important lesson..." Gaby looked up at Alex and Sam.

"You are not alone."

Epilogue
Deep into the Mistlands

After the Gathering, Mekiri walked alone into the forest. She walked for hours, deep into the Mistlands, but it wasn't as if time, or the cold, held any real meaning for her. The farther she walked, the more she would know that she was alone. She did this trek from time to time, her very own personal pilgrimage to the place where she had been born, so to speak. The trees receded, giving way to a snowy field with a frozen lake in the middle. As befitting of the region's name, the place was shrouded by a thick mist.

Mekiri walked into the mist, her body radiating a soft light. With each step she was transformed, becoming a tall, graceful woman with flowing red and black hair. Long gone were the poncho and bunny ears. Instead, she was clad in a black and silver armor that was made of small metallic feathers. The gleaming helm covering the front part of her head, resembled a raven's silhouette. Once the transformation ended, she kneeled in apparent prayer, but really to commune with the part of herself that existed outside this physical plane.

"You have been bloody busy these days, visiting dreams, using oracles from the minors, voting in an election. Impressive," said a male voice behind her. Masculine and seductive, with a hint of playfulness that hid poison, it was the kind of voice that would have melted the heart of even a goddess. Except for her. She only rolled her eyes in annoyance. "And I have to say that I prefer this shape than the silly one with the bunny ears."

"What are you doing here? You are well aware that this is my territory," Mekiri replied, standing up and turning around. She was not amused. Northern lights crossed the sky. "And what name are you using now?"

"You might call me Ben Erra. Much better than 'Mekiri'. Don't you like my snazzy new avatar? By your reaction, I would say no. Now, can't I visit the only sibling I actually care for?" the man asked. His hair was cut short and stylish. He was wearing a black pinstripe suit, a deep purple dress shirt and a ruby red tie. He fiddled with his cufflinks as he took a seat on a tree stump. As he sat, the suit glowed and transformed into a deep purple armor with red accents made of rubies. The shoulder pauldrons sported a single spike and a cape as dark as a starless night flowed like waves down his back. The air filled with a whiff of sulfur floating on the air.

"As if you ever cared for something other than yourself." Mekiri said. "Don't you have someone to tempt, judge, torture or guard in the Upper Pits?"

"My, my," Ben Erra, the Judge God of the Underworld and Jailer of the Pits replied. His dark eyes glowing red, his white teeth sparkling in a wide smile. He was affecting a posh accent. "Billions of years and you are still sore about what happened? You get to walk around mortals without issue. Me? I'm the one punished to keep an eye on the critters your protégés kill and send back to that... place."

At the mention of the Pits, his smile disappeared. Mekiri couldn't avoid feeling a degree of satisfaction at this.

"Critters that you woke up in the first place, thanks to your hubris." Mekiri said, crossing her arms. The irritation inside her grew by the second, like a nuclear furnace reaching critical mass. "You and your meddling. Now I have to fix your mess."

"No one asked you to," Ben Erra replied, seemingly amused. "And this attitude, all superior and judgmental. It seems familiar... ah right, just like me."

"You and I are nothing alike," Mekiri exclaimed. The Northern Lights roiled with frenetic cadence.

"Keep telling yourself that," Ben Erra said, waving his hand. "You meddle too. Helping your little *champions*."

"Someone has to. I wouldn't be a good patron of heroes if I didn't give them a hand from time to time," Mekiri replied, taking a seat on a rock.

"See? We are not any different, you and I," Ben Erra said. A lightning bolt hit the ground near his left foot. Mekiri's eyes were glowing with light. It had been a rough year, with the avatar of the Creeping Chaos almost managing to raise himself an army of titans. She was not in the mood to deal with this annoying 'sibling'.

"Careful, or you will break the world... again. I didn't come here to face the Holder of the Trumpet. Rather to give you fair warning and propose an alliance."

"An alliance with the Judge and Jailer of Sinners and Evil? Things that you unleashed the first time? And tempted others to commit?" Mekiri could feel the blood inside her avatar boil. Maybe a second lightning bolt, on top of his head, would help her get rid of this pest.

"Let's be clear on two things." Ben Erra said. "A penance I've been dutifully carrying out with no complaint. And I don't tempt anyone. I present them with tests of character, not unlike yours. Except that mine only bring forth what true desire lies in their heart."

He smiled again. For Kaan'a, Mekiri really hated that smile.

"So you can judge them."

"It's part of the job. I'm not one to deliver justice, that's the domain of our elder sibling. I just get to set and carry out the sentence." Ben Erra stroked his chin. "Makes me wonder if all of your little pets would pass one of my tests. You know, your favorite pet was in the middle of one at the upper levels of the Pits when his body was disintegrated in that explosion. It's a shame that *someone* pulled him out before the end."

"You know he didn't belong there. And I have no doubt they will pass. But you are not here for that. What's the warning?" Mekiri had decided that the only way to send her sibling away was to cut short the debate and force him to get to the point.

"You know the others won't see it kindly that you keep interfering with mortal affairs. You know they are sticklers for the rules, the whole free will thing and so on," Ben Erra wasn't smiling this time. If Mekiri didn't know him better, it would seem that his face was betraying real concern for her.

"I'm not interfering with free will. Just offering guidance," Mekiri defended herself.

"Same difference." Ben Erra said. "You need to be careful and think on how to convince them that your guidance is the right way to do it. Or at least trick them. I know you can."

"Why the sudden interest in getting our siblings to cooperate?"

"The Pits won't hold Him much longer," Ben Erra's body tensed, his voice got an octave deeper. There was real concern in his eyes now. It had been aeons since Mekiri had seen him worried. "And if he escapes, then the rest might follow. I won't be able to stop them alone. And then, not even our heroes will be able to do their part. You know that the battles to come will take place across several realities."

"I see. But what alliance?" Mekiri asked. Then noticed that very specific 'our' word and she got curious... and worried at the implication. "And our heroes?"

"You are not the only one who can pick your pieces," Ben Erra's mocking smile returned. As if he was a cat that ate the canary and then framed the dog.

"What did you do this time?" Mekiri's irritation grew once more.

"Nothing bad, I swear," Ben Erra raised his left hand, palm open, as if he was taking an oath. "And you know my word is my bond. I just adopted a champion from your flock and gave him a hint of what to do now."

Mekiri had a suspicion of who his sibling was referring to. The person that had disappeared a few days ago. Mekiri's heart hurt with a pierced pang of fear.

"Joshua. Why him?"

"You know monsters are mine," Ben Erra replied once more, matter-of-factly. "And he started as one. A tovainar of all things. A servant of the deepest of the Pits. And yet he found redemption. I like him, he passed several tests and I judged him innocent. And told him about The Despair... correction, now it's called The Fury. The previous owner's soul is raging with it."

"You did what?" Mekiri's voice sounded like a thunder-storm breaking the silent peace of the Mistlands. She wanted to kill her sibling, or at least his new avatar. "That's the only Tempest Blade no one managed to control fully. The one you convinced my children to forge at a great cost. The one whose owner died after it shattered because the owner faltered!"

"And one of the humans you like so much reforged it with a new, more willing and stronger soul. I took the liberty to hide it at the top of the Bedesala, in case it was needed again. No need to thank me."

"Who in the Pits gave you permission to do that? And you sent Joshua on a quest to the most dangerous peak in the world to get it? Unbelievable. I want to kill you!" The sky creaked as the thunderstorm grew closer.

"You and I know that's not possible. Not by your hand at least. Plus, the man needs a weapon at the level of the oth-ers," Ben Erra said, shrugging. "And if he passes this test too, then all the better. I will then gather my own set of pieces to help you with the upcoming battles."

"I want to punch you," Mekiri tightened her fists with such force that her knuckles turned white. She could feel the flow of magick energy flowing around her.

"Promises, promises," Ben Erra laughed. "You won't smite me, because you risk damaging your little retreat. Quaint place by the way. Now, are you interested in my pro-posal? We are on the same side, after all. We need to help each other."

On that, Mekiri conceded that he had a point. Even if she wasn't happy with the way he was doing it.

"As long as you respect his free will."

"I wouldn't have it another way." Ben Erra said, as his body dissolved into the air as if he had been a mirage, leaving only a faint white cloud behind.

I'm gonna regret this, Mekiri thought. Her multidimen-sional mind was already thinking on how to get Joshua out of this.

About the Author

Born in the frozen landscape of Toluca, Mexico, Ricardo dreamed of being a writer. But needing a job that could pay the rent while writing, he studied Industrial Design and later obtained a PhD in Sustainable Design, while living in the United Kingdom. There, he did a few things besides burning the midnight oil to get his degree:

-Trained in archery near Nottingham
-Worked in a comic book store to pay for his board game & toy addiction

He is back now in Toluca, living with his wife and his three dogs where he works as an academic at the local university. He has short stories featured in anthologies by Inklings Press and Rivenstone Press and he was nominated to a Sidewise Award for the short story "Twilight of the Mesozoic Moon", co-written with his arch-nemesis, Brent A. Harris. You can reach Ricardo on Twitter or Facebook or via email: scifantastique@gmail.com